YOU PROMISED ME PARIS

D. B. Burns Mysteries

THE COURTSHIP OF HARRY'S WIFE

THE LAST ROSES

YOU PROMISED ME PARIS

YOU PROMISED ME PARIS

By
Jeanette-Marie Mirich

You Promised Me Paris
Published by Mountain Brook Ink
White Salmon, WA U.S.A.

The website addresses shown in this book are not intended in any way to be or imply an endorsement on the part of Mountain Brook Ink, nor do we vouch for their content.

This story is a work of fiction. All characters and events are the product of the author's imagination. Any resemblance to any person, living or dead, is coincidental.

Scripture quotations are taken from the King James Version of the Bible. Public domain.
ISBN 978-1-943959-97-6
© 2021 Jeanette-Marie Mirich

The Team: Miralee Ferrell, Alyssa Roat, Nikki Wright, Kristen Johnson, Cindy Jackson
Cover Design: Lynnette Bonner

Mountain Brook Ink is an inspirational publisher offering fiction you can believe in.
Printed in the United States of America

Dedication

For those who impacted our lives for the Kingdom. You have loved us, mentored us and led us to His throne as we've prayed for one another and for couples who are challenged to love their spouse as Christ loved the church.

Dr. Charles and Marlys Casteel

Dr. Paul and Terri Looney

Dr. Chuck and Sandy Crown

Gary and Lisa Heim, who brought His light and truth when we walked in dark places.

Acknowledgments

Not everything in life is tied up in a lovely package and presented in a shaft of sunlight with Handel's Water Music in the background. Life is messy. The third book in the D. B. Burns series is about reconciliation and restitution. What does it take to restore a broken spirit?

My dad restored a 1915 model T Ford when I was little. There were bits of metal scattered throughout our garage and over the drive. Hunting for the right part, sanding, scraping, then fitting bits together before the priming, painting and final wax job took time and effort.

The Lord has planted many people who've tinkered with my life. They have been led by God to oil with prayer and align the gears that do not mesh, to grind down the sharp edges and polish to a shine what God wants revealed.

My beloved husband Rod is the one with the buffer that tells me to look into his eyes, not the mirror, when I'm being self-critical. What does love look like? It is dimpled and filled with grace.

I am grateful to Lydia Schweitzer, a word mechanic who challenges my thoughts, and to those who've come alongside to hand me spanners, wrenches, lug nuts, and tire gauges. Thank you, Sherry Bennett, Carolyn Spada, Heidi Wright, Linda Crabtree, Holly Lightvoet, Judy Spoelman and Sharon Pera for your prayers as words dent my manuscript and sometimes my heart.

Mountain Brook Ink handed me the road map for this part of my writing journey. Miralee Ferrell, Alyssa Roat, Lynnette Bonner, and Nikki Wright are the pit crew that filled my emotional tank with gas and helped with more than one flat tire when words eluded me.

Chapter One

SHAKESPEARE HAD IT RIGHT. TRUE LOVE never does run smooth. In fact, it has bumps that make the Alps look like molehills. We couldn't have a normal proposal like most folks. Oh, no! It had to have drama, a near melt down, and a trip to the courthouse.

So, after I asked Judge Lyle Henderson to marry me in the dining room of The Chicken Coop restaurant, with God, four local lawyers, half the bakery staff from down the street, friends, neighbors, and Carter MacDougal, the owner, in attendance, Lyle and I headed to the courthouse.

A chill autumn wind attacked my neck. I pulled up my coat collar. Lyle wrapped a warm arm around my shoulder and drew me close to his side. One does not snuggle in the middle of town for everyone to see but I almost did. Call it relief.

The banners resplendent with fall colors beat in the breeze like they were clapping. I smiled up at Lyle. He winked back. It was a long two blocks to the courthouse square because we kept getting stopped. While shaking hands and receiving hugs we ambled along as if we were leading a parade. Across the street the women in Maylene's Beauty Parlor got up from their chairs and peered out the window at us. One even waved with her fingertips. Waving at me was unheard of from one of the town's elite, but there she was breaking protocol. I looked at the woman, astonished.

I could have done without the stares. Especially since the gossip about the judge's and my relationship had out sizzled the curling irons. When a widow of a nationally acclaimed poet is courted, everyone thinks it's their business. And when the man doing the courting is debonair, handsome, and the town's heartthrob, well, we'd set on fire many a tongue from the college to Washington Street.

Lyle and I made it to the scarred wooden counter of the county office without a mishap. The county clerk rustled up the paperwork in record time. Lyle didn't let go of my hand until we had to fill out the forms, grins plastered across our faces.

The sheriff found us leaning over the clerk's oak counter like two star-struck kids. "Congratulations, you two." Bellows winked at me. "Word travels fast when the entire town is invited to your shotgun wedding."

The office staff and the line-up of locals getting license renewals laughed because every person in town knew I'd turned down Lyle's proposal the month before.

Bellows's dark eyebrows met in the middle above his nose. "I've a need to speak with both of you in private."

We followed him down a long hallway and into a cramped room that was more like a closet than office. "We'll chat here rather than make this look official down at the station. Lyle, we're getting pressure about keeping Clarisse in jail. Her lawyer is filing papers to get her out on bond. She's tried it before but been refused. I don't want her roaming the streets but looks like that's about to happen."

Was Bellows trying to put a kibosh on my exuberance?

Lyle frowned. "Who is her lawyer?"

"Some three-piece-suit from Chicago."

I looked from one to the other and wondered what was going on for they both seemed worried. Maybe I should be too, but I'd a wedding to plan. Well mostly participate in and that was enough on my plate.

"Delilah and I are about to depart these environs for a few weeks. Don't see Clarisse being a problem."

"Your ex-wife is a problem with a capital P." Sheriff Bellows pursed his lips. "Not only is she a flight risk, but where in tarnation is she supposed to stay?"

I smiled at them. "The Salvation Army has extra beds."

When we stopped laughing Lyle clapped the sheriff on the back. "Tom, this is one problem I can't solve."

As we mounted the back steps to Lyle's house, my best friend and housekeeper, Josephine, flung the kitchen door open and put her hands on her hips. "About time you got Miss Reluctant here to accept your offer." She stared at the judge. "Rumor is circulating though, that Miss Dee Dee did the proposing, but I reckon that can't be true, she is too shy."

Josephine waited for us to explain.

We didn't.

She raised her eyebrows. "As soon as the news reached my ears I trotted over to your house and got your dress ready, the one from the kids' recent wedding." She smiled at us both. "That was a nice affair, what with you getting your children married to one another and now you're going to up the ante." Josephine's eyes opened wide with wonder. "Ahem," she said, clearing her throat. "Your mama, daddy, and meemaw are on their way too." Her face broke into a smile. "Come on, Miss Dee Dee, I'm in need of a hug to get me motivated to tackle Mama and her yellow hat." Which would take some maneuvering, because her mama was afflicted with the Alzheimer's disease and could get everyone confused.

Josephine's hug nearly smothered me. With her work worn hands she moved me away from her and stared at Lyle. My lips curved upward. He couldn't avoid Josephine's scrutiny for long. "Reverend Daniel is in your office to give you both a talking to. Seems he thinks you need marriage counseling because it's all so sudden." That said, she marched in front of us from the shiny stainless-steel kitchen, through the mahogany furniture of the dining room toward the judge's home office.

When we got to Lyle's office, he shook Reverend Daniel's hand, then opened a locked drawer in his desk and produced his divorce decree. He presented it to me without a word. It seemed legitimate, but I'd only studied eighteenth-century deeds and legal papers for my historical novels.

I handed it back with a shrug. "I trust you, even though the legal jargon is Greek to me."

He smiled. "Mostly Latin."

Reverend Daniel cleared his throat. "I've been appointed by the wedding committee to have a chat with you."

I lifted my eyebrows. I didn't recall the church having a wedding committee.

My pastor shrugged. "Well, Josephine twisted my arm. Seems to me you're in your right minds. I have no objections." This former marine and serious man of God grinned like a mischievous schoolboy. "And when do you think I should propose to Josephine?"

Lyle stared at his friend. "Strike while the iron is hot." Without another word, the reverend deserted the room.

I walked to the chair by the fireplace and sunk into it. "Think I've been on a carnival ride." Lyle nodded. "Here's the good list. We've Savannah back." I raised one finger. "The mayor's being replaced." I lifted another finger. "I have water running through the pipes in my house and can have a cup of tea, alleluia!" Another finger went up. "But," a sigh escaped my lips, "my Harry's name is besmirched from McKeansville to Saint Petersburg."

Lyle reached for my hand. "We know he didn't write the poems. The entire town and discerning people know that it was beneath Harry to write such drivel." He rocked back on his heels. "My money is on Professor

Hamilton. A conniving man with little imagination or wit."

"But how do we prove it?"

"I'm working on it."

"I need to get organized with this wedding. I'm in such a tizz I don't know if I can get everything sorted out."

"Letting others put in their two cents could be useful," Lyle said, before kissing my forehead. "It doesn't really matter what goes on, because at the end of tomorrow we'll be married, and that is enough."

I grabbed his jacket front and planted a kiss straight on his lips. Our lips fit perfectly. I sighed. He'd put things in perspective because weddings seem to take on a life of their own. This one I only had to show up for. Sort of a mother of the groom role. As a detail person, not being allowed to lift a finger made me antsy. Josephine would snort with disgust if I checked to see whether we had enough fancy napkins. Maybe I should give up the organization business and let things fall into place like confetti at New Year's.

Chapter Two

Over the course of the evening all my Kentucky kin threw clothes into bags and headed to McKeansville. They filled my house with children, grandchildren, Meemaw, and my parents. Lyle's family and our kids in North Carolina planned to descend on us—when the wedding march trumpeted out the church doors. As things began to turn from bustle to soporific, I lay in my bed and snuggled against a pillow. Nodding off, the thought drifting through my mind was that tomorrow I'd be Mrs. Henderson not Mrs. Morgan.

With the early morning sun purpling the horizon, I walked into my rose garden. My phone said 6 a.m. A frost had obliterated the roses, freezing them in place like ice sculptures. Clipping a handful of stems with intact flowers I thrust them into a paper bag and went to talk to Harry. Lyle's car was parked where I usually parked mine. I walked through the black iron gate protecting the Morgan graves from interlopers and let it swing back to click into place.

"Morning, Di," he said when I reached his side. We stood at Harry's feet. The bluegrass covering Harry's grave like a fresh trimmed crewcut looked orderly.

"Morning, yourself, Judge Henderson."

"You going to call me that tomorrow?"

"Maybe. Depends on how things go tonight."

His eyebrows reached his hairline. "Had to ask Harry something."

"So do I."

"I'll leave you to it." He left without sharing a magical kiss.

My lips skewed sideways.

He turned back with a smile and leaned over the gate of the Morgan plot. "Kissing's not allowed until after the wedding vows, you know."

I wrinkled my nose then turned back to Harry's grassy mound. There had been enough rain to stir the scent of onion grass. "I still want you at the end of the aisle, Harry. Is that a disservice to Lyle? Still wanting you? How can I tell Lyle that I feel as if I'm betraying you, by loving him?"

I shook the roses over Harry and the twins' graves. Their haggard petals held only a hint of the colors of summer. I stood a while. The sun eased upward, brushing the tops of the trees with gold.

As the wind sang around the graveyard, a still, small voice spoke in my head. "I'm the one giving you away, Delilah." Feeling wrapped in the warmth of loving arms, I drove home in peace.

The chill wind that circled Harry's grave had penetrated my rain coat. I stepped into the kitchen and poured a cup of coffee. The bar stool beckoned my behind. As I plunked down and sipped the warm, familiar brew, the back door blasted open and Josephine bustled inside. She was encased in her warm, fleece coat and until she removed the hood, I couldn't really see her face. Josephine's eyes were red and her face blotchy.

Placing my coffee mug on the counter without making a sound, I rose and slipped an arm around her shoulders. "Want to tell me all about it?" She shook her head.

Can't be her relationship with the good reverend. It must be worry about Savannah.

I frowned. "What can I do to help?"

"You can't. My past is creeping up behind me."

Platitudes would go flat. I watched Josephine out of the corner of my eye for the rest of the time we had together. While Savannah wound and sprayed my hair, I kept turning my head to see Josephine's troubled face. She gave me a weak smile.

Last month, when Molly and Cam had gotten

married, I'd been a wreck. This time it was Josephine. Getting her through the day was my first priority. *Why had my wedding day become her disaster?*

At the church my grandson, Austin, wrapped his little arms around my legs and gave me a big squeeze. "I'm so happy," he declared, his three-year-old body wiggling with joy and excitement.

While we stood in the church foyer listening for the music that would send me down the aisle, Josephine's hands shook. Without a word, she handed me a bouquet of pale pink roses and picked up her smaller one. Standing at the back of the church, I watched as my grandson marched down the aisle, then Josephine glided away in her soft lavender dress. I spied her mama and my meemaw, head to head, yellow and purple hats bobbing to the music. It wasn't the usual wedding march. Someone had added an African beat that made you want to dance. Louisa Campbell was seated beside them, her hands beating a rhythm on her knees. Didn't think a sculptress had rhythm but she did.

Daddy offered me his arm. "About time somebody put spring into that tired old song." Daddy lost some of his Baptist ways as he danced me down the aisle. And I do mean danced. By the time Josephine had done her turnaround at the altar, the entire congregation was moving with us. The fussy white lawyers that lived on horse farms rocked along with Omer, the doorman at the country club.

Lyle's sideways smile was slashed across his face. George, on Lyle's left, grinned so wide I thought his eyes would merge with his lips. Lyle's sister, Cissy, winked at me as I passed her. Even though they had driven through the night from North Carolina, Conrad and Cissy looked fresh as new milk. They sat hip-to-hip close. I smiled.

Lyle took my hand from Daddy's and drew me nearer to him. Lyle's face above his light gray tux beamed. Pastor Daniel proceeded to give a mini-sermon on 1st Corinthians 13. Being a gospel loving congregation, Daniel took his time, knowing some of the attendees had never heard true love expounded on.

Lyle was saying, 'With this ring I thee wed,' when a man in uniform appeared at the back of the church and walked down the aisle. He whispered to Judge Patricia Hollister, sitting three pews from the front, on the groom's side. She scooched over. He sat down while nodding his head firmly at Lyle.

Best man George leaned toward the reverend then said in a voice that could be heard at the back of the building, "Better speed things up, Reverend. Looks like a legal emergency."

When all was said and done, Lyle kissed me for about a minute, waved to the congregation, and pulled me down the white carpet runner toward the front door.

"We'll be back!" he shouted above the laughter echoing down the aisle.

The whole shebang had the feel of a shotgun wedding. We ran down the church steps like escaping felons. I hiked up the long skirt of my blue mother-of-the-bride-dress-turned-wedding-ensemble,   climbed into the car, and waited for lift off. Lyle didn't disappoint. He burned rubber on the asphalt in front of our church. It took him three minutes to get through downtown and haul up to his designated parking place at the courthouse.

"Care to explain?"

"Wedding present." Lyle flashed a smile my way.

Security made us go through the scanner, then waved us in, trying to hide their surprise at seeing a formal dress and tux entering the courthouse at 11:32 a.m.

As we started up the stairs to the second floor a thunder of footsteps concussed behind us. I turned around. We were leading a parade. I caught a glimpse of Savannah and her grandmother's yellow hat before turning the corner of the landing.

"Courtroom three." Lyle spoke loud enough for our

entourage to hear.

Courtroom three turned out to be large and high ceilinged, with half the seats filled. The room had quarter-sawn oak floors, wainscoting, even the chairs for the lawyers and defendant were oak. Perry Mason could step in at any moment. No judge behind the bench. No one in the jury box, or in the defendant's chair. However, on the right side of the courtroom where the prosecution held sway, stood our local DA. Lyle and I walked forward then sat behind the DA's chair.

I opened my mouth to ask Lyle what was going on when the double doors leading to the hall banged against the wainscoting. I jumped at the sound.

At the entrance of the room stood Stephen Hamilton, his wife Lydia, and their lawyer, one Jeremy Thwaite. Thwaite was a man Harry claimed knew how to 'articulate the English language with the aplomb of Churchill and the deviousness of Machiavelli.' This had the potential of ruining a nice wedding.

Stephen Hamilton swept in with an imperial hand in the air. His mother and two sisters followed. They were dressed for a day at Keeneland race track—fancy, but without hats. A row of women behind us fidgeted. Across the aisle, Alice Mercer, Miss Vickie's usual attendant, waggled her fingers at me. I smiled with confusion. *What exactly was going on?* Hamilton looked closely at the women sitting quietly behind us. His face went from triumphant to pasty.

Josephine, her companions, and a gaggle of our wedding guests began to fill the room. They occupied the seats across from us and in their wake was our local reporter. Jim Bouchard flipped open a legal-sized notebook and waggled a pen in the air. He caught my eye. I nodded and shrugged. He wiggled his eyebrows several times, making his glasses move up and down on his nose.

Hamilton took his seat by his lawyer but not before narrowing his eyes and glaring at me. I let out a huff of breath. Lyle took my hand and kissed my fingers.

By the time Judge Patricia Hollister entered from a side door, it was standing room only. Judge Hollister whacked her gavel to call the proceedings to order. She was known as a don't-mess-with-me judge. I settled back for the show, but my neck was so tense my muscles were as tight as twisted rope.

Lyle leaned forward.

I wondered why I hadn't been questioned by Hamilton's lawyer since I'd been the one to find him with the mayor's teenage daughter in a compromising position. I tapped Lyle's shoulder. "Is this Hamilton's trial?"

"No. This determines if there is enough evidence for a trial."

Thwaite stood up and waved his hand dismissively at the DA. "I object to this proceeding. There is nothing but trumped up evidence that Professor Hamilton was involved in a relationship with an underaged girl."

The judge struck her gavel down hard. "In due time, Mr. Thwaite." She turned to the D.A. "You may present your evidence, Mrs. Fincastle."

"We have the signed statements of two security officers from the college, your honor. We have two other witnesses, a Mrs. Delilah Morgan and Mrs. Louisa Campbell. Their statements were taken on the night of Professor Hamilton's arrest. I have seven witnesses who attest that the accused displays a pattern of sexual activity with young women under the age of eighteen. Here is a list of names, addresses, and dates." The D.A. approached the bench and gave the papers to the bailiff. "By court order we also did DNA testing on three people, one of whom is Stephen Hamilton. The results of the tests are included in this lab report."

Directly behind her husband, Lydia Hamilton gasped. Her mother-in-law patted her hand and stoically lifted her chin as the sheaf of papers was handed over.

Hamilton's lawyer stood behind the ancient oak defense table. "We would like all copies of the spurious papers your local D.A. has presented, judge."

"They are at your office, counselor." Vivian Fincastle didn't glance his way. "We also have nine DVD's confiscated by the FBI in a human trafficking operation."

The stillness in the courtroom changed to a wave of sound that grew until the judge's gavel thumped yet again.

"In the DVDs, Stephen Hamilton is having nonconsensual sex with five girls. We can prove the girls were under the age of fifteen. Also, there are sexual encounters with four more girls. All less than seventeen. A copy of a 'little black book,' was found in a legal search of the office of Stephen Hamilton. The book includes dates, ages of the girls, and a log of his payments, whether by cash or credit card." The D.A.'s assistant plopped a box into the bailiff's hands.

"Finally"—the D.A.'s voice resonated like a renowned Shakespearean actress playing Lady Macbeth—"we will prove that Stephen Hamilton was the author of a series of pornographic poems he claimed were written by Professor Harry Morgan."

Hamilton's face reddened. He turned to whisper into his lawyer's ear. Thwaite shook his head with such force that Hamilton jerked back to avoid Thwaite's beak of a nose.

Lyle remained tense, his fingers tight on his knees.

I placed my hand on his and squeezed as lightly as a butterfly's touch.

He turned. "For you and Harry." Lyle's voice was barely audible.

His words made my heart thump so hard I thought he could hear it.

"May I call a witness, Your Honor?" The D.A.'s face was pinched.

"Yes."

"I call Miss Sophie Brixton to the stand."

Miss Sophie's cane thumped authoritatively down

the floor. The town's interim mayor took her vows to tell the truth and floated onto the seat in her wedding finery.

"Miss Brixton, please tell the court your association with the accused."

"He was a student in my advanced English class at McKeansville High School."

"You brought to the court poems you said he wrote while in your class."

"Yes, I did."

"Can you tell the court the nature of the papers you gave to me?"

"Three were poems he had written for an assignment. The fourth one, I confiscated from him. He was passing it to Jenny Leafers in my fourth period class. Miss Leafers, now Mrs. Johnson, is sitting in the fourth row, behind Mr. Hamilton."

"Would you enlighten us as to the contents of the poems, Miss Brixton?"

"One poem contains lines recently published in our local newspaper. They were attributed to Harry Morgan, but a poem I confiscated from Stephen Hamilton is identical to the one on the paper's third page, second column."

"You also gave me another poet's writings."

"Yes. Harry Morgan's poems from his senior year in high school and others from his grade school years."

"Why did you give me Professor Morgan's papers?"

"They revealed that Harry Morgan always dated his writings. He began the practice in fifth grade. By Harry Morgan's senior year, he was chronicling the time he'd finished."

"Thank you, Miss Brixton."

Jeremy Thwaite was on his feet and stomping over to the witness box.

The judge thumped her gavel on her desk. "Sit down, counselor. Save your theatrics for the trial."

Thwaite strolled back to his corner as if he had all morning.

Mrs. Fincastle hid a smile. "My next witness is Miss Josephine Hudson."

My mind hiccupped. *Oh, dear.*

After the preliminaries the D.A. turned to Josephine. "Miss Hudson, are you acquainted with the accused?"

"Yes, ma'am."

"Please tell the court your relationship with Professor Hamilton."

Josephine stared at her daughter. She let out a deep breath. "Stephen courted me. At least that's what I thought. He wrote me poems. I gave you the collection. I want the court to know that Mr. Harry could never have written those poems. Mr. Harry always wrote on special paper with his Mont Blanc pen. Had his paper delivered from someplace in the East. Made from linen with a watermark in the middle. Mr. Harry said he'd written on that paper since he'd returned from Vietnam and a friend had sent it to him."

When the judge nodded, Josephine took a steadying breath. "Professor Hamilton," she laid on the title like it was fresh manure, "promised he'd marry me. Gave me an antique opal ring. He said it was his great-grandmother's."

Hamilton's oldest sister, Deborah, stood up and yelled at her brother. "You rat! You're the one who stole it from my case and blamed the maid." She stomped out of the courtroom as if on fire. The judge gaveled us back into order.

"Stephen's courting took place before the Hamiltons refused to pay their bill to my daddy and sent us into bankruptcy." Josephine's eyes glinted hard as she looked first at Hamilton then at his mother.

Mrs. Hamilton the third, the chairwoman of the state's Miss Kentucky pageant, squirmed in her seat.

Josephine looked at her lap. Her fingers were busy twisting and untwisting. "I can't prove it, but I think it was all planned. Stephen was sent to court me, find out about my daddy's business, then get him ousted from the center of town like all the other black businesses."

"But not provable in court." The D.A. spoke toward the audience in the courtroom.

"No, ma'am. Stephen asked a lot of questions about the meat business, and I was happy to talk about it. He also wanted to know all about Mr. Harry, because I worked full time at the Morgans' and part time at the butchery. Later, I got suspicious about his interrogations, but it didn't matter. The damage had been done. When the poems were spread far and wide, I knew why he'd wanted to know about Mr. Harry. Man was jealous." Josephine looked up, glared at Hamilton and gave a firm head bob.

"I can imagine." Mrs. Fincastle's usual drawl turned flat as a board.

"When I told Stephen we were going to have a baby, he disappeared as quick as smoke."

The room grew silent.

I twisted the circlet of white gold Lyle had placed on my finger. Blinking back tears, I glanced up at Lyle. His brow was furrowed with care.

"Is Stephen Hamilton the father of your daughter, Miss Hudson?"

"Yes, he is."

"How can the court verify that statement?"

"You took a sample of my daughter's saliva, ran a DNA test and compared it with Stephen's DNA."

Lydia Hamilton jumped to her feet. "You fathered a black baby?" She swung her purse from its wooden handle and hit her husband over the head with its bulging side. Hamilton jumped to his feet and lifted his hands to protect himself from further assault. "How many women did you sleep with, Stephen?"

"All of us, ma'am," said a woman behind us.

Judge Hollister sat back and let her courtroom descend into chaos. Lydia and her mother-in-law dashed out of the room. Dignity was left shredded on the hard-oak floor planks.

The paper's crime reporter Jim Bouchard scribbled so fast he was bound to get writer's cramp. Miss Vickie rose with dignity from her seat and walked in front of the bench and reached for her daughter's hand. Savannah was a step behind her.

"You pay no never mind to all these people, Josephine. The most perfect gift you ever gave your daddy and me was this little 'un, Savannah." Miss Vickie put her arms around Savannah's shoulders and hugged her so tight I wondered if Savannah could take a breath. "You come on with me, girl, and let's go celebrate Miss Dee Dee's wedding. Their wedding celebration will turn this little town around. Mark my words. It's as much fun as Mr. Harry crossing the mayor with his chicken poems."

"You may step down, Miss Hudson," the D.A. said.

As soon as Josephine rose and took two steps, Savannah was in her arms. "Oh, Mama." Savannah cried.

"Baby girl. I hadn't planned for you to be here." With her forefinger, Josephine wiped the tears from Savannah's cheeks. As she looked at her daughter, Josephine's smile made the D.A. catch her breath. Josephine brushed a stray curl from her daughter's eyes. "It's all right, sweetheart. You are the best gift I've ever been given."

Pastor Daniel unwound his lanky frame from his seat and stood beside Josephine. "And I thought I was your greatest gift." Daniel, a modest man, blushed at his words then his strong arms encompassed the three Hudson women. They were gathered like Harry's imaginary chickens, protected and comforted. I wanted to fling my arms around Josephine, but my feet couldn't move. It wasn't my moment, it was Daniel's.

No order.

No gavel.

No one cared.

The bailiff took a parade rest posture in front of

Stephen Hamilton and waited.

When everyone had resumed their seats, Judge Patricia Hollister cleared her throat and stared directly at Hamilton. "I will look over these papers in my chambers. We will adjourn until after a wedding reception held at Ye Olde Inn. That will be 4 p.m., according to my watch."

Her gavel struck wood.

We stood side by side, my groom and I, watching Josephine lean into Daniel.

Bouchard took pictures of everyone he could, then flew out of the courtroom.

Josephine raised her head and gave me her bold, sassy look. The one that I imagined said, 'What you doing Miss Dee Dee, I need a hug and you do too.'

I almost trampled Lyle in my stampede to reach her. I flung my arms around Josephine and ruffled Savannah's curls.

Miss Vickie puffed out her chest and cocked her head. "What you gonna do with that fine man over there, Miss Dee Dee?" She pointed at Lyle.

"Go greet friends at our wedding reception."

"Oh. That's why I'm wearing my yellow hat."

Chapter Three

I SOBBED ON MY WEDDING NIGHT. NOT a tidy, dainty little cry, either. I flung myself at my groom like there was no tomorrow and hung on to his neck. My catapult into his arms made him a little unstable. I thought we'd fall onto the hotel room bed, but he stood up tall and supported my heaving body.

I hadn't done that the first time around—cried I mean. I'd been a little shy and hidden in the bathroom for a while. This time, well, my first husband was still warm in his grave when Judge Henderson had come courting, and with one thing and another, we were married when the grass started to look tidy on Harry's grave. That wasn't the reason I cried though. I cried because I felt guilty about my bubbling happiness. Being loved by two good men was something I didn't deserve. Lyle held me while I carried on. He looked a little bewildered.

"Too soon, dear?" he asked when I'd finally gotten some control.

"Oh, no!" I patted his hand in reassurance. "It's beautiful. The good Lord put us together and I'm overwhelmed."

I realize that claiming God engineered our nuptials stretched things a mite. It was Harry who put his two cents in and directed the whole courting thing. How a man could do that from the grave was another story, but he did, and I was glad. I dabbed at my eyes. It was a good thing I still used the special mascara that only comes off in a hurricane or Lyle's handkerchief would be black.

Lyle sat down on the bedcover and patted the place beside him. I sat down too, but a foot away. He waggled a finger at me. I inched closer.

"Better," he said. "Now, let's get some things

straight. This entire wedding has been unsettling for you and I will not rush you into anything you'll regret." I must have looked at him dumbfounded because he coughed into his hand and lifted his eyebrows. "What I mean is, we'll take our time getting to know one another."

"Shoot, Lyle," I said, turning toward him. "I didn't get married to you so we could hold hands." I know he got the picture because it was some time before I could talk again. We were fully clothed, mind, but his kisses were bold and made me think I'd better get a few things in order.

"Er," I began. "I think I need to explain something." He sat up with his eyes scrunched as if wary. "The Lord invented this thing called sex, and I don't have a problem enjoying the things He gives us, it's just...I don't want you to have a heart attack or something since you're only seven weeks out of the hospital."

"Ah." He grinned. "It'd be a great way to go."

"That's not funny!" I blubbered, the tears again deluging my cheeks. "You almost died."

Lyle got off the white duvet with gold hotel logo and opened his black leather briefcase. It was jam packed with handkerchiefs. There must be three dozen or so smashed in there. He winked at me as he unfurled one and handed it over.

"Doctor says I can enjoy my honeymoon," he announced.

I smiled at him.

He smiled back.

I took his hand and pulled him onto the bed. "Okay." I blew at a strand of golden-red hair that had invaded my right eye.

He lifted one sculpted eyebrow. "Not yet."

I must have looked surprised because he laughed, his nice rumbly laugh that made me grin.

"First things first, Di. Come here." He got up and

knelt beside the bed. I knelt next to him.

"Lord, we want this marriage to be blessed not only by our families and friends but by *You*. We made a covenant with You to honor and love one another. Keep me faithful to my promises. Teach me to walk in forgiveness because I'm human and will offend Delilah as she will offend me."

I wanted to say hold it right there, mister, but I knew he was right. I would get in a snit sometimes. Harry couldn't cajole me out of it until I'd had time to cool off. First thing Harry did that bugged me was flip the toilet paper roll upside down, so it came out backwards. I'd decided it wasn't worth firing the first shot for WWIII to mention it. I did it my way, he, his. He never complained.

Lyle continued in his conversation with the Lord as my mind gallivanted off. I made it shape up right quick.

"Lord, help me to treat this child of Yours with the grace I want for me. Amen."

"Do you want me to pray too?" I asked.

"It's up to you."

I chewed on my lip.

After an insane courtship where he proposed in front of our entire family and cadre of friends, here we were in private, and I was again overwhelmed.

"I want to pray." I blew my nose and bowed my head. "Lord, this is some surprise. A man like Lyle, loving me. You know me. He doesn't. I'm unworthy." I swallowed so the lump growing in my throat could get lubricated. "Oh, Lord, teach me to serve Lyle with Your hands, Your words, Your heart. You have given us a lifetime together. I'm honored by Your gift. Teach me to respect Lyle and love him as You love him." That was all I could say.

Lyle's arms wrapped around me and we clung together for a bit then did some old-fashioned necking, like you do when you're a little unsure about things.

Later, he woke up with a smile.

So, did I. "I've a question," I drowsily murmured. "I think I noticed something." I hesitated to pursue it, but it niggled at me. "On your left cheek I detected a shape. Do you have an old injury or mole?"

Lyle threw back his head and laughed. "You mean my tattoo? Allow me to explain. One wine-soaked night in Lyon, I and a few companions, became canvases to an itinerant tattoo artist. I wondered when you'd mention it."

"Ah," I said regally. "It wasn't my imagination then."

"No. The eagle has been with me since before law school."

He climbed out of bed. "You must be hungry, Di."

"Not for food."

When we woke up the second time, he shook his head. "Harry could have warned me."

"About what?"

"I'll explain on our first anniversary, if I should live so long," he laughed. "What was that?" he said at a series of popping noises from somewhere down the hall.

"Champagne corks." I smiled.

When my new husband stood beside the bed, I got a good look of the bullet wound that nearly killed him. My mouth went dry. I reached out to touch the puckered red circle on his chest.

"Oh, Lyle," I stammered. "Does it hurt?"

"I didn't notice it the last hour or so, but now I'm noticing. Think I'll take a shower before breakfast. I believe you must be hungry for some *food* now." He grinned.

Our hotel room was the honeymoon suite at a fancy resort in Lexington. The room's velvet drapes pooled on the floor like Scarlett O'Hara's dress. Antique furniture housed a small bar with coffee maker and mugs waiting to be filled. Harry and I had stayed in a few fancy places but nothing like this room. It stretched wide enough for an energetic exercise class to do aerobics.

Lyle cleared his throat. "Tomorrow, we will wake up at my cabin in North Carolina." He swept his hand through the air as if he were an actor exposing a stage setting. "As the land warms in the sun we'll ride over the hills. There's a sweet little valley tucked not far from the river. Maybe we can indulge in a picnic." There was such a little boy hope in his voice. I felt my tears coming again.

I shook my head to stop the flow. "What fun! Your house in the mountains will be perfect." I loved his cabin. Built with his own hands, it soared like a bird in flight as it perched on a hillside above a river.

"With the nefarious activities there recently I was worried that you'd think differently. Even the entertainment we got from McKeansville's former mayor being caught with a mistress can't compete with the river brimming with trout. Do you like fish for breakfast, Di?"

"It will remind me of my home place," I whispered up to Lyle.

He tilted my face toward his and massaged my lips with his pliant ones. "I love you more than words can say." He headed toward the bathroom but turned around at the door. "I'll order breakfast."

Hoped he didn't ask for eggs Benedict. The Chicken Coop restaurant in our town had everyone beat by a country mile when it came to Hollandaise sauce.

Chapter Four

BY NINE WE WERE RE-PACKED, DRESSED in jeans and shirts with turtlenecks to ward off the autumn chill—ready for Lyle's promised trip to North Carolina. A thump, as if a heavy object had been dropped sounded in the hall. Before Lyle could take three steps to cross the room someone yelled. The room was so large it took him several seconds to reach the door. Curiosity made me follow him. When he opened the flat paneled door, all we could see was a food cart with trays and silver plates with domed tops on it. No one in sight. Footsteps thumped down the stairwell at the end of the hall. Cutlery, jam jars, a little pitcher of spilled cream trailed by the rooms down the hall. The server must have flat out sprinted with the cart to our door, leaving detritus in his wake.

Lyle moved through the doorway and pushed the cart aside, then peered over it. He moved to the far side of the cart and knelt, disappearing behind the top. "Di, call 911," he said in a firm voice.

Dashing back into the room, I scooped up my cell phone from the bedside table, then dialed as I moved toward Lyle.

A pair of shiny black shoes with toes pointed up toward the ceiling greeted me as I stepped around the cart. Transfixed by an outstretched body with a knife handle sticking out of its chest, I jabbered on the phone to the 911 operator. The knife moved up and down jerkily as the victim fought for breath. He was young and looked like a student with a scuff of beard attempting to hide his chin. I gasped so loudly that the operator asked, "Are you all right?"

"Fine," I replied, "but the boy with the Bowie knife in his ribs will be deader than roadkill if an ambulance doesn't come soon."

"I'll have the police there in five minutes," she said in a voice that sounded scripted. There was a stain of blood on the man's white shirt. My gag reflex activated. Swallowing hard I stared at the slim figure.

The youth on the floor was turning the same color as the pale carpet. Which was the grayish-green hue Lyle had turned when his former wife plugged him with her revolver. I hovered beside the injured server, my eyes never leaving his young face. Sticky blood, the same hue as Lyle's, leaked around Lyle's hands as he put pressure on the chest wound. The kid had a yellow bow tie attached to his uniform's white collar. I removed it and unbuttoned two shirt buttons to make breathing easier. Closing my eyes, I squatted beside Lyle. It was better than fainting because it was too soon after Lyle tried to up and die on me. Still hanging onto the phone, I heard the injured boy say, "I saw him…take a briefcase and papers."

"What?" Lyle asked.

The lad's brown eyes blinked once as blood dribbled out of the left corner of his mouth. "Room 241," he mumbled before he slipped away. He was still breathing, mind, because his chest was still grabbing air.

The EMT's arrived with sirens, running feet, and metal tool chests. They took over pressing on the wound, then carted the boy away on a wheeled stretcher.

"You would think a calmer entry into nuptial bliss would be in order," Lyle muttered as he strode to our bathroom to wash his blood encrusted fingernails and hands. "We'll have police forms to fill out, press to deal with, and any number of phone calls to make. I'd rather be involved in something more interesting."

"A man going toes up on our doorstep is at least curious," I said.

"And a nuisance. We need to hit the road."

"Jack," I said automatically.

"What?"

"Hit the road, Jack. You know, the song." He was thinking up a reply when an authoritative knock reverberated on our door.

The police—a male and female—asked reporter-type questions: who, what, why, and how. We could only answer the knife instead of the lead pipe. Lyle offered to go along with them to room 241. They said they could handle it. Our food was congealed by the time the police got the hotel to open the door to room 241. We decided to head for breakfast downstairs and were hauling our suitcases out of our suite when the concierge backed out of room 241. His face was a mixture of alabaster and carnation. He bent over and proceeded to lose a substantial amount of stomach contents on his left shoe and the pristine carpet. He fingered a Kleenex from his pants pocket and patted his lips with the daintiness of a duchess.

The man shook his head as if it were on slow-motion mode. "Don't look inside," he cautioned. "A man's brains are plastered all over the walls and TV."

Not an appetizing comment on an empty stomach.

The woman officer backed out of the room, her eyes gazing at the floor, her brow sweaty.

"Don't move," she ordered us. "There might be footprints." She was right. Ours, the stabbing victim's, the EMT's, and assorted guests who'd wandered to the restaurant for breakfast.

With a flat voice she spit into her phone, "Looks like a murder at the Wilderness Inn, room 241. Along with a dead man, another person was stabbed and on the way to University Hospital. We'll need the coroner, crime reconstructionist, and photographer. Hale is in the room. I'll block off the corridor." The policewoman started to walk over the imaginary tracks in the tight carpet.

"My wife and I need breakfast and to leave," Lyle said, loudly.

"Oh." She turned to look at us. "Move along the edge of the wall, one foot in front of the other. Also, stick around for the chief. He'll have questions."

We dragged our rolling suitcases behind us. And on our way to the hotel dining room, we didn't leave a dent in the carpet, either from our shoes or plastic wheels because the fancy carpet's fibers were knotted so tight a flea couldn't hide.

Over a cup of yogurt and fruit I asked, "What do you think was so important about a bunch of papers that you'd kill for them?"

"I think," Lyle said with disgust, "that our leaving the country or even hiding out at my cabin will prove difficult." He nodded his head to someone behind me. Squirming in my seat I saw the police lady, a man in a business suit, and FBI special agent, Robert Madison. Madison was as pale as a ghost from being shot recently.

After she pointed us out, the policewoman and the squat man in the rumpled business suit vanished like apparitions. Madison caught my eye and nodded. The Special Agent usually had a smile for me. Not today. Today he cast a pall like the Grim Reaper. Maybe it's because he had the coloring of death and in my mind, I saw the young boy with the same coloring being wheeled out on a gurney.

As Madison aimed toward us, his reddish-brown hair shone like he'd oiled it recently. I'd never noticed he was a handsome man but he was. However, with the sour expression on his face no one wanted to smile at him as he skirted the tables toward ours. He was moving as slow as a snail covered a patio.

"What's Madison doing here?" Because it wasn't a question Lyle could answer, he shrugged and finished his coffee.

"Well, you two couldn't go quietly off on a honeymoon, now could you?" Madison said as he finally stood beside us.

"When opportunity knocks," Lyle said, "open the door."

I stabbed a strawberry with my fork and nibbled on a corner. Imported strawberries tend to be enormous and tasteless. This one confirmed my bias.

Madison studied Lyle, noted the smile slathered across my groom's face and tossed a smile back. "You considering leaving the country? France maybe?"

"I promised Delilah a trip to Paris. I believe you heard my invitation," Lyle answered.

More collapsing than sitting, Madison puddled into a chair between us. "Put it on hold. This might have something to do with sex trafficking. The murder victim was a well-known client. I've called your neighbor to stop the exodus of his retired sleuthing crew."

George Salas's spy friends had headed back to their usual Washington environs as soon as the job of ferreting out a trafficking ring and rescuing children was finished. Who was left to go on the hunt with George?

Without a by-your-leave, Madison ordered coffee. "The police chief would like to ask a few questions then I think we'll settle back for an interesting discussion."

There was nothing to discuss. I reached over for Lyle's hand. We were simply witnesses. Hadn't observed a thing except a body on the floor. I'd prayed while watching the thin young man attempt to breathe with the huge knife sticking in his ribs. I did again as Lyle and Madison talked of organizing the investigation.

"Delilah and I decline your invitation to join George's spies. We have other things more pressing," Lyle said as he rose from his seat.

"I considered getting a court order to keep you in the county."

Lyle looked at Madison like an irate judge looks at a nincompoop. "Robert," Lyle said clearly, "messing up my honeymoon isn't a wise idea."

"Thought not," said Madison. "How about I keep you tethered to your phone while you stay in Kentucky. I was counting on Miss Delilah's keen discernment. She sniffs out villains in ways that rival a pack of bloodhounds. She also puts two and two together that add up to four. Not like those silly math problems they're inflicting on our kids."

"I'll give you France's country code." Lyle's stare was a challenge. Madison had crossed Lyle's red line.

"I will politely appeal to you to stay in the country, Lyle. There is more to this than a dead real estate developer named Smothers, a missing briefcase, and papers scattered about the room. This has an international flavor to it, seeing that Smothers' company has offices in Europe and he was partners with a man named Jerry Lewis, alias, Danny Daugherty, or Daniel O'Neal, take your pick." Madison drank his coffee and let his words sink in. The O'Neal name rang a bell. The O'Neal cousins were mixed up in illegal activity eighteen years ago. Was this dead man part of the Irish mob involved with Lyle's ex-wife, Clarisse?

Or, maybe this *was* about trafficking because the men taking my goddaughter, Savannah Hudson, out of the country held Greek passports. Although they were sitting in the slammer in North Carolina, perhaps their slimy partners were involved. In spite of Lyle's protests, Madison's information intrigued me.

Lyle's thumb rubbed the back of my hand.

"Until next Monday." Lyle looked my way. "Oh," he said. "Di, forgive me. I'm not used to submitting my decisions to the court."

I smiled. He learned fast. Harry had taken more than a year to begin to ask my opinion on matters. "I've a little cottage on my farm. It's isolated and the horses need exercise." I looked at Lyle as I spoke.

"Do you have cell service at the cottage?" Madison asked.

"Yes. Harry would go out sometimes to ride. He

used to say it cleared his mind."

Lyle went to the Inn's office and made phone calls while Madison and I talked about his kids and horse racing. Living in Kentucky, horses were always on the mind.

As we drove away from the luxury hotel, I smiled at Lyle. "We'll need to buy food."

"There is a grocery store on the way home. We'll stop." Lyle spoke with an edge of disappointment.

We shopped as if we were a long-married couple. Lyle pushed the cart while I gathered supplies for our cottage interlude. A list of necessities romped through my head like ticker-tape in October 1929.

Lyle walked to the flower stand and stood in front of the refrigerated roses plopped into colored glass vases. I frowned. The flowers were expensive. Better to check on my roses from the garden. There might be a few that withstood the frost and they were free. He picked a vase of flowers. One that held two dozen blush pink roses and ferns all tidily wrapped in Hosta leaves. The vase required two hands to hold it steady. He wedged it in the cart next to the steaks, a bag of fancy lettuce greens, and milk.

"For mi'lady," he said with a bow.

"Lyle, they're expensive," I objected.

"Get used to it, Di. I'm going to shower you with flowers, presents, and any number of surprises. I like giving gifts."

"Harry always said it's better to buy a plant than let a bouquet get thrown away in a week."

"I realize I'm not Harry." The tip of Lyle's nose was pink and the words he spoke were stiff.

"*I'm* sorry. Thank you for thinking of me."

"You're welcome." But his voice still held an edge as we finished our shopping.

Who knew that grocery shopping might be a prelude to a skirmish?

Chapter Five

THERE IS NOTHING LIKE A TIFF to set the day at odds, let alone having a man squirting blood on your shoes. When we crossed from Jessamine county to our county, Lyle took a wrong turn.

"Lyle," I said. "The quickest way to the farm is on Remington Pike."

"Yes, it is. I prefer a more leisurely drive."

We reached the Morgans' farm cottage after a twenty-minute added wander. I don't know what he was thinking but it was time to get the steaks in the fridge. Resting under the winter sun, the land perched near a stream that spilled into the Kentucky River. My youngest son, Paul, and his family maintained the land and were 'trying experimental farming.' Which meant hydroponic. The old tobacco barn was now strung with pipes and green plants cascaded from the rafters. I grinned at the thought of seeing Paul and my adorable grandchildren.

The cottage was the first building along the dirt and gravel road dubbed Morgan Ave. The charming, two-story affair was built at the end of the nineteenth century for a hired man and his family. It had been occupied for most of the years that Harry's grandparents and parents had plowed the land. White paint had been slathered on a decade before and still looked presentable. A green shutter, however, was off-kilter and needed to be re-hung. I pushed at the back of the rocker near the door and listened to its familiar squeal. This had been Harry's and my first home. After our honeymoon, Harry had ushered me in with a grin and expectation.

I hadn't considered the awkwardness of duplication. I paused before plunging the key in the lock. We should rethink this, perhaps have dinner and talk about it. My hand automatically stuck the key into the lock. It turned with well-oiled smoothness. The stamped brass knob felt familiar in my grip and the door eased open. Before I could take a step, Lyle swept me into his arms and carried me over the threshold. His arms were wrapped tight and it was nice. The Victorian sofa was too low to park me, so he lowered me to an upholstered chair by the fireplace.

Kissing me on the top of my riot of strawberry-blonde curls, he disappeared to retrieve the luggage. I closed my eyes. Lyle, a tall, angular man, made my heart beat funny, almost like the hot syncopation of a jazz band. Opening them again, I saw cobwebs dancing in the breeze from the open door and went in search of a broom, rags, and dust spray. As I emerged from behind the cleaning closet's door Lyle wheeled our suitcases in a circle and headed back out the door.

"Not spending my honeymoon watching you chase dust bunnies."

"I don't get all tuckered out from a little dusting. It will take me only a little while to clean this place up." I would have begun slapping a broom at the cobwebs hanging from the ceiling, but Lyle tossed me his conniving smile. The one that told me I wouldn't win this argument which relieved me of my colliding emotions. Looking at the worn chair, I took a seat and watched as Lyle eased our luggage back into the car's trunk, then made a couple of calls while Lyle wandered off toward the barn. We met when he reentered the living room. He studied me briefly then lowered himself onto the permanent curve of the squishy sofa.

"This place doesn't need dusting, Delilah. It needs demolition. Paul could come over from the farm house to collect the perishable food. I've something else in mind than you cooking on our honeymoon."

I opened my mouth to say something about money down the drain but closed it as fast as a frog grabbing a fly when I heard my grandson's voice on the porch. "It appears you've already implemented that idea." I raised my eyebrows.

"I should have asked. I'm in the habit of ordering my days according to my desires." His eyes looked into mine. "I am sorry. Why don't we have a signal between us when I step over the boundaries."

Harry and I had signals. He got bored at gatherings lauding his talents and he'd give a signal by raising his right index finger in the air and making a whirling motion. It was his helicopter signal…meaning rescue me. I'd trot over and take his hand, whisper in his ear and he'd declare, "Sorry, family needs." Then we'd leave. I'd have to invent a signal for Lyle.

Austin's little feet hit the porch with a thud. "Hey, buddy," Lyle called as he wormed his way out of the dilapidated sofa and headed to the sound of Austin's voice.

Lyle and my grandson were pals. When Harry led the pack the three had enjoyed fishing, walking around the garden, and sneaking ice cream. Had Harry's inclusion of Lyle been prescient? The gift of Lyle always being part of Austin's life made me tear. Lyle could introduce Austin to Harry's oddities and instill in this little boy his own discerning taste. With his first grandchild on the way, Lyle might prove to be more sensible than Harry had been about grandchildren, but I doubted it. The respected judge I married had a gleam in his eye when it came to kids. A gleam that says, setting up an H.O. gauge train set and having dessert before dinner sound like good ideas.

Paul and Lyle wandered from the kitchen to the second floor. Their voices grew muted as they hit the landing, but they talked the whole time, as friends do.

I ruffled the hair of my blond grandson. He gave me a quick hug then dashed upstairs. Was he trailing behind the men, much like the judge's puppy, Bartles? His father had done the same when Harry and Lyle had gone fishing at the farm.

I whacked at cobwebs as footsteps clomped above my head going from one end of the upstairs to the other.

Doors were opened and shut. Someone used the bathroom while I tackled the kitchen window with a paper-towel roll and window cleaner. The trio reappeared as I eyed the smudged fingerprints on the white kitchen cupboards.

While my son cleared out the food that we'd picked up at the store, Lyle went to his car and returned with a notebook. "Paul mentioned that the house has a few problems. I told him I couldn't be bothered on my honeymoon." Lyle smiled then winked. "He said I should check a water stain on a bedroom ceiling and talk to you about it. It's family land, Di, and I don't want to interfere."

"But?"

"Looks like there is a leak in the ceiling. The roof should be checked."

"And?"

"Maybe we should get someone to climb up and take a look."

Lyle sat at the thrice painted kitchen table and scratched lines on his notepaper. On tiptoe so he could see what Lyle was up to, Austin scrutinized Lyle's drawings. "It didn't look like that," he said, plopping his finger on top of Lyle's paper. "It was like this." Austin made his right hand go at an angle, half-way between ceiling and floor.

Lyle handed the boy his pencil and ripped off paper from his pad. "Here you go. Show me what you mean."

Lines like chicken scratching were drawn all over the page.

"Ah, I see," said my new husband. "Good observation, Austin. The window *is* crooked. I'll come back and measure it if you will help me." They shook on it. "It will be a few days, though. Your grandmother has me tied up at the moment."

My son burst into laughter at his remark. With Austin in tow, Paul inched out of the kitchen and aimed for the front porch.

The wind was rising and rain gathering in the west.

As Austin and my son drove away in Harry's old truck, we waved beside the paint peeling rocker.

"I'll need one of your clipboards," Lyle said as he held up his handiwork.

"What are you up to?"

"I like to plan ahead. I think this house could do with a little maintenance."

Lyle taking control of things was startling. Harry let me call the shots in the organizing department.

Lyle had an opinion—about everything.

I knew my face was puckered with thought because he said, "Paul said he wouldn't breathe a word about our whereabouts. You and I are heading to a resort that serves three meals a day, no questions asked."

I held the vase of dancing flowers steady as we rocked down the farm road toward heaven knew where.

He looked at me out of the corner of his eyes. "And yes, Madison is aware of our change of venue, if you're worried."

Worry about Madison hadn't crossed my mind. With half-closed eyes I'd stepped on the scale before our wedding and had lost two pounds. Which was an amazing feat, considering all the food I'd ingested. Maybe my muscles were turning to jelly. Didn't fat weigh less than good solid muscle?

"Are you mad at me?" Lyle asked as he pulled into a Victorian farmhouse with a B&B sign out front.

"Not at all. Why do you ask?"

"Your face is scrunched up funny."

"Calories," I said with a toss of my curly hair. "I'm trying to lose the weight I gained vegetating while Harry was dying. Exercise seems a good idea."

"I can think of a few things that might help." He smiled, a big-bad-wolf kind of smile.

"Lyle Henderson. You are a rogue." I used my deep-south, flirtatious improvisation, and batted my eyelashes.

"Hmm. I was thinking of a brisk walk." I knew he was fibbing because his dimples flashed.

"The flowers are wonderful," I said, lifting them and smelling the roses. He nodded. "It's well...I'm not used to getting surprise gifts."

"I plan to amend that," Lyle said.

Did he mean that Harry had neglected me? As we mounted the front porch steps of the house, I thought of the little things Harry had done. Washing the dishes when we'd had a table full of guests, mopping the kitchen floor when I was too tired to lift my head. Harry was practical, solid. Lyle was an adventure. I took a deep breath, trying to get ready for the next surprise.

When we arrived at our assigned cottage, a white-painted building tucked above a thin stream, the owner of the bed and breakfast bowed before he opened the door. As I was reaching to stroll my luggage over the door frame, Lyle swooped me into his arms. The owner smirked and stepped into the front room as Lyle carried me across the threshold. I didn't wiggle, afraid it might be the last straw for a man fresh out of death's door. My new husband strode confidently toward the bedroom where the manager was standing.

"Thanks, Pete," Lyle said as the manager shoved open the bedroom door with his booted foot. "Place the bags in the living room and we'll see you for a late lunch. Plan for two o'clock."

Pete grinned and left. Which was a good thing because Lyle gently dropped me onto the bed and began to take off his shoes. He moved as slow as treacle. I was under the cold sheets and waiting before he had his shirt off.

For lunch I changed into my worn cowboy boots and jeans in case we went riding. After the best French dip sandwich I'd ever swallowed, we walked to the horse barn. Lyle's hand held mine like it was meant to be.

Harry's hand had been perfect. He'd hold mine as he helped me get out of a car and not relinquish it until he had to shake someone's hand or open a door. Harry's fingers were always warm, his hand surrounding mine a comfort.

Lyle's fingers were warm too, but long and thin. Holding his hand was like a gentle caress as we walked over the pebbled drive. Rain clouds building in the north-west were visible over the barn's roof.

"Don't think we'll outrun the weather," Lyle said, glancing skyward.

"Rainy days are nice," I said, putting my head on his shoulder. "We could start a fire in the fireplace, and 'er, maybe play a game?"

"Mrs. Henderson!" he said in a shocked voice. "Whatever are you suggesting?"

"Scrabble," I said straight-faced.

"I might be able to manage that."

We greeted four horses, picked our favorites for a ride, then dashed to the cottage as rain pelted on the barn's metal roof.

A stack of games resided on the living room bookshelf. While Lyle lit kindling in the already prepped fire, I hunted for a game we'd enjoy. I studied him as he knelt by the hearth. Lyle was beyond handsome. I'd seen women turn their heads to watch him pass. With his broad shoulders and his back tapered to a narrow waist, he looked like he should be in a tux.

My thoughts skittered to Harry. Harry had pursued me like my daddy's coon dog Geronimo hunted squirrels through the blackberry briars. Lyle had been diffident. Cautious. Perhaps because I'd been holding him at arm's length, afraid my emotions were running ahead of God's will.

"Where are you, Di?" Lyle asked as he turned around and studied my face. The fire was crackling in the grate.

"Thinking about Harry," I whispered to him, feeling disloyal. "I loved Harry with my whole soul." Lyle stood still, only his eyes moving. "I was devoted to him...but you could break my heart with a simple word or a frown. I've never quite felt this way before." My voice trailed off. I sounded like dialogue from a Broadway musical. Lyle's right hand reached for mine.

"You're vulnerable, Di. I know it must be awkward for you to see me on the pillow next to you. We'll let life unfold as it will."

"And I might call you Harry on occasion. And I'll be sorry." I smiled. "Please don't call me Clarisse, though. That would about beat all."

"Sweetheart, I'll keep a guard on my mouth." He kissed my forehead.

"And I'll try not to buy any clipboards."

An olive leaf offering not a branch. A branch wouldn't have me crossing my fingers behind my back because without clipboards I'd feel naked.

He laughed "I don't think you can help yourself in the clipboard department. I've a request, though. Leave my office alone when you're on an organizing binge."

"Okay." I'd need a clipboard for all the do's and don'ts that were emerging. "I'm wondering why you thought my home would be a better place for us to live?"

"Your home will be an easier transition. There is also more room for the kids and it's familiar to all of us."

My eyebrows puckered. "Your home is lovely. It reflects you with tidy rooms and the furniture you've made." I moved until my head was against his chest. "We could manage with a smaller place, less upkeep, and..." my throat clogged. "It's the gardens, Lyle. Giving up the gardens will be hard." My hands fidgeted like squirrels hunting for nuts.

"I'm not asking you to, dear. Keep the roses where they are. I like roses. They remind me of you."

Well, that did it.

I buried my face in his chest and cried.

He played with my hair.

"We can redesign the bedroom, sweetheart, so it

seems a new space." He studied my face. "Or," his voice sounded reflective, "we could reconfigure the boys' rooms at the back of the house. We'd make them into one large space, creating a new master with more closets. We could add on a bathroom with a jacuzzi tub."

"What a great idea!" I clasped my hands together. "We have a tidy shower but no tub, and I love a soak."

"Relieved at the thought, dear?"

"Yes," I almost shouted. "We need a bed for us since I gave the kids my four-poster. The three-quarters bed I moved into the master will be a little tight." With my eyes hunting for a pencil to make a list I was already imagining the new space.

"Your tiny bed could be a problem with our Olympic gymnastics practice." Lyle's eyes gleamed.

"A new sleek bed more in the lines of your furniture," I said trying to elevate the conversation.

"Well, I thought you wouldn't want...like my things."

"I love the things you made yourself."

I put his right hand against my cheek, closed my eyes, and saw golden spheres behind my lids. Lyle's hands were engaged in undoing my blouse when his phone chirruped.

"Drat!" he said, looking at the caller ID. "I'll have to take this, Di," he explained as he left the room.

Well, leaving the room to talk in private was odd. I followed him out the door. He stood on the verandah his face scrunched up with concentration.

"Yes. I've got it. About 3:10. Any witnesses? I see." He kept pausing to listen which didn't help my snooping. "Identify make and model of car? Madison involved?"

Mentioning the FBI man had my ears flapping. *Had Lyle's ex-wife escaped from jail?*

"I'll handle it," Lyle said before disconnecting.

"Sweetheart, I need to make a few phone calls. Why, don't you set up a game for us."

I had been dismissed. What in the world was going on?

"Are the kids all right?" I asked before leaving.

"What?" he said as he punched numbers into his cell.

"The kids? Everyone all right?"

"This wasn't about our children. Everyone is still in town celebrating our wedding without us."

His phone call better not be about my grandchildren or my best friend, Josephine, for that matter. Obviously, he wasn't going to elaborate so I went to fluff pillows and smooth out the bedcover. It took him fifteen minutes to meet me in the kitchen. Lyle folded me into his arms and put his chin on the top of my head.

"Something's, come up, Di. We need to head home."

"Lyle?"

"That was George. Madison's been quizzing him about your grandmother. Seems the police uncovered a paper at the hotel crime scene with Meemaw's name on it. George and Mamie are stalling him until we can get there, because Madison's going to talk to her."

"Afraid she might give him the what for?"

"Things don't go well when the women in your family deal with law enforcement."

All I could do was nod my head.

Chapter Six

LYLE DROVE TO MCKEANSVILLE WHILE I cogitated. "Didn't Madison mention that the dead man in the hotel room was a real estate agent?" I asked Lyle.

"Yes."

"Think he knows Neely Patrick? Could this character with the variety of names—including O'Neal—be another one of Neely's cousins?"

Lyle's face began to ease from the tension I'd seen. "That might be interesting."

"But why would Meemaw's name be found in his room? The only thing Meemaw has in her life is her vegetable garden sprouting zucchini enough to feed half her small town." I glanced at my groom. He needed to know a thing or two about his new family. "Er...Meemaw's green thumb turned the Burnses' farm into a productive and lucrative enterprise. According to my grandfather, not something his work-adverse Burns relations were familiar with. Perhaps it is now valuable, even though the county is one of the poorest in the country."

Lyle's gaze went sideways as if asking a question.

"Meemaw and Grandpa got married in 1940, a week after they had graduated from high school. She came from go-getters. The day after their wedding grandpa said she sat down with a pencil and paper and wrote columns of numbers. On another page she wrote a list of jobs a farm required."

"Does she have color-coded clipboards too?"

I nodded.

"So, I'm mixed up with an organization mob complete with clipboards, colored pens, and shotguns?"

"I prefer a revolver." We both laughed knowing Lyle had fixed a problem with my foyer wallpaper where I'd fired a round. I cleared my throat. "*Great*-Grandpa

Burns had the reputation of riding a horse to go fishing. Everybody else in the holler walked to the fishing hole, which was down at the foot of the farm and an eighth of a mile away from the house."

Once started I didn't need encouragement to tell the tale of Meemaw and the 'outlaws' as she called her younger brothers-in-law. "The story goes that her father-in-law was so flummoxed at her pronouncement that if you didn't work you didn't eat, he couldn't speak when she asked which chores he wanted."

I stopped talking when a drooling rain descended, the kind that looks like it has oil in it.

"Go on, dear. I need to unearth the family lore."

"After his service in World War II, Grandpa worked that bit of land until it produced so much, he started teaching about crop rotation, amending the soil, and land management in the grange hall."

"Think the cadaver in the hotel was interested in your grandparent's property?"

"I can't imagine why. After all the dividing up only two-hundred acres of land is left. However, it is a productive farm with a creek and woods. Rural Appalachia doesn't have a direct road to a major city. Not a good investment." I shrugged.

As Lyle grew still with thinking, his eyes became a softer blue. "Probably a good setting for a golf course or resort."

I shook my head. "No beach. Golfers like to swing their skinny clubs with ocean waves nearby."

We pulled into my drive. Trotting along the sidewalk toward George's was my next-door-neighbor Hank Abernathy. He waved at us like a crewman on an aircraft carrier bringing in a plane. Lyle stopped the car and rolled down the window. Hank leaned in and planted his forearms on Lyle's side of the car. "On my way to help George with the latest FBI activity." Hank's grin was as broad as the Mississippi. "Been more exciting around here lately than I recall in the thirty years I've lived in town."

Lyle nodded. "Any news?"

"Nothing yet. Candace," Hank tossed his chin upward to indicate his home, "is in hiding and isn't leaving the house until the furor over her brother's arrest subsides. I'm heading to George's to get something done rather than stare at the walls and listen to my sister-in-law whine about her husband's unlawful arrest." He shrugged. "Seems to me it was about time the mayor got his comeuppance, but I'm not offering that to a houseful of mourning women." He nodded his head at me. "Thank you for the personal invitation to your wedding Mrs. Morgan, er…Henderson. It was a joy-filled day and I was glad to be part of it."

I smiled at him. "You are welcome, Hank. We were pleased that you came."

"I must be off. George says he needs me and that's worth a lot." Hank vectored off along the wet sidewalk as we parked the car by the garage. I frowned. An unfamiliar car sat near the basketball hoop. The government license plate on a small beige car had an FBI shield on it. Madison had beaten us to the house.

We entered the foyer at a run to avoid the autumn drizzle. Trying to get the raindrops out, I shook my head like the judge's puppy. Meemaw, my parents, and Madison were conversing in the living room to our right.

Well, at least Madison's lips were moving. Meemaw was puddled on my loveseat as if someone had whopped her in the stomach. My mother, arms wrapped around Meemaw, huddled next to her. Obviously, Special Agent Madison had frightened my grandmother or Mama wouldn't be comforting her.

In front of the marble fireplace, Daddy stared at Madison like he'd seen a varmint that needed eradicating. Madison's eyes were narrow and his nostrils pinched. But he didn't look all that intimidating being the same putty color as his coat. *Wonder how much blood he'd lost when he'd gotten shot?*

Lyle clamped his hand around mine so I wouldn't fly across the room and give Madison a piece of my mind. Which wouldn't have helped, because my thoughts whipped around like a food processor on high.

"All I need to know is if you were acquainted with the deceased?" Madison brought his hands out of his raincoat pockets and crossed his arms to emphasize that he was in charge.

Daddy puffed out his chest. "Are you accusing my mother of something?" Now, my daddy is a big man, six-foot four, to be exact. And he intimidates most other men because his voice is deep and kind of echoey.

Madison lifted his chin. They locked eyes like duelers in the eighteenth-century. Lyle released my arm and stepped between the two men.

"Heard there was some interest about the Burns farm," Lyle drawled in a slathered on southern accent.

I stared at my groom. He was a wealth of surprises.

"Might be," Madison allowed. "The papers look like a copy of a land survey. One was dated five years ago and signed by Mrs. Elizabeth Grace Burns."

Meemaw looked up when her name was spoken. "I don't know anything about it. I know I went to the courthouse to file a renewal for the boat dock. I do it every year."

"But you don't recognize this paper?" Madison thrust a photocopy of a map and some words written by hand on the bottom right corner.

Meemaw leaned forward and scrunched up her eyes. "It's not familiar. It is a plat of the Burns farm, though." Her hand fluttered to her chest and she caught a ragged breath. "I feel hot," she said to my daddy. Meemaw had drops of sweat on her brow. The room wasn't over seventy-two.

As she began to rub her temple, Lyle reached for his phone.

"We're going to take a little trip to my doctor's office," Lyle announced. "Any other questions, Robert, will have to wait." Lyle looked at his phone, at Meemaw, then at me. He pursed his lips.

Madison's curt nod was his official response.

Lyle thrust his phone into my hands. "You speak to them, Di. I think I need to attend to something." Leaning over Meemaw he kissed her cheek. "My dear," he whispered, "we are going on a ride."

Meemaw wafted her hand in the air. "No use getting into a bother." She gazed at my new husband with a twinkle in her eye. "This is one of my little episodes."

"What?" sputtered my mother.

"Don't get into a tizz, Marybeth. These come and go like contrary barn cats. This one's moseying up the walk for a visit." Meemaw's voice faded to vowels, no consonants. She started to push herself upright, took a deep breath, made another attempt and rose to her feet. She tottered two steps before her ninety plus-year-old knees gave way. Lyle was at her side and scooped her up in his arms as if she were light as air. Her head of white hair brushed across Lyle's jacket, then sunk against his chest as if glued in place.

Madison streaked out of my living room entrance and into the foyer ahead of Lyle. He moved fast for a man who'd lost a significant amount of blood less than two weeks before. Lyle's long legs strode onto the wooden planked floor in my foyer. I walked a breath behind.

Mama and Daddy joined the parade to the verandah stairs. I didn't even lock the door, but jogged after Lyle and Madison.

Lyle made for the McKeansville's emergency room. No shillyshallying. They whisked Meemaw away in a wheelchair, moving so rapidly her hair looked windblown.

Mama followed.

I wrung my hands and plunked down in a hard, plastic chair. Daddy, Madison, and Lyle filled out papers. "Some honeymoon," I muttered as Lyle joined me in the chair line-up.

"Surely you didn't expect anything less than mayhem. We are destined for bigger things than a mere soporific vacation." His voice rose as he spoke and his pointer finger aimed toward the ceiling.

Madison glanced our way as did the nurse at reception and a mother corralling her three-year-old.

"You and I thrive on chaos, my dear."

"Should I expect Shakespeare next?"

"I did a little Hamlet in high school." Lyle picked up my hand and kissed my finger-tips one by one. "I love you, Mrs. Henderson."

And I knew the signal I needed to stop Lyle's independent thinking and include me as a partner in his dreams. My hand placed gently on his chest. "And I adore you. But we need some answers from your buddy Robert over there." Madison narrowed his eyes at the mention of his name. "Because whatever he asked Meemaw stressed her so much she's having a heart attack."

"Perhaps a stroke, dear."

Talking with his phone plastered to his ear, Madison aimed our direction. His lips looked like they were on fast forward. When he reached us, he said goodbye to the person on the other end then cleared his throat. "I'm simply doing my job."

"I know," I said.

Daddy moseyed over with him. "I'm not so sure. This was a little heavy handed. No need to question Meemaw." Daddy's voice sounded like he was dressing down teenage boys caught with a cigar. "Seems to me you're looking for answers about a dead fellow. Someone who got some paperwork on the Burns farm from a government office. Send the photo to our local law enforcement. They'll spread it around and find out if your dead man was in our county." Daddy's eyes didn't waver.

Madison shrugged then winced. "My daughter thinks Facebook is more effective." Special Agent Madison turned to me. "I'm truly sorry, Miss Delilah. I needed answers. Your grandmother said she didn't recall anyone with the name of Smothers asking questions." He pursed his lips together as if he doubted her.

"Meemaw's got a recall button that brings things up from seventy years ago. Nothing gets by her."

Madison shook his head with disbelief.

"My mama's as tough an old bird as they come," my father said. "She'll weather this."

I grabbed Lyle's hand and held it tight. I was not so sure Meemaw had the strength. She looked pasty white when they'd wheeled her through the gray double door. Why'd they have to be gray doors? A nice taupe would be more welcoming. I'd better not share my brain zingers or they'd be carting me into a cubical.

Madison cleared his throat. "That phone call was about the paperwork we found. There is a dispute about the ownership of the Burns land."

Daddy crossed his arms tight. "Burnses have been in our county since the late seventeen-hundreds. Provable. Ask the DAR."

"There were some shady land deals back after the revolution. Think about the trouble old Daniel Boone had testifying about land surveying. They say Boone left the Commonwealth because he was plain fatigued with lawyers and courts hauling him in to besmirch someone's name." Madison lifted his eyebrows waiting for a response. "Perhaps our real-estate developer was scouting around for old marker stones."

"Hoping to convince an old mountain woman to relinquish her land for a pittance, most likely." Daddy pursed his lips with distaste. "He hadn't reckoned on a woman with common sense and a mind for figures."

Meemaw wasn't allowed out of the hospital until they did more tests. Her face when informed by the doctor would cause a dairy cow to utterly dry up. Daddy left first, then Lyle. Not a pretty sight to watch my grandmother cross her arms so tight she made lines in the sheets.

"Wow," I said to my groom when I escaped her wrath. "Mama's going to have her hands full sorting this out."

Daddy raised his eyebrows. "Your mama's going to stay?"

"Looks like it. She asked for a roll-in bed."

"Think I'll go shoot some pool in your basement. I'll find my way to your house. It's only a few blocks." He looked at Lyle. "You coming?"

"I'm on my honeymoon." Lyle grabbed my hand and made for the stairway exit.

Standing in front of Lyle, Madison waylaid us. "Going back to your hide-a-way?"

"Maybe. You've my cell if you want me." The look Lyle gave Madison would make a dog grovel.

Madison smiled. "You need to know a thing or six, here, Lyle. For months we've had our eye on the corpus delecti in the hotel. He was one of the men involved with a money laundering scheme your friend Longworth uncovered. Money came from trafficking and drugs. No surprises there, but..." Madison held up a finger.

Before he continued in his speech I said, "You need to tell us about the boy who was stabbed. How is he doing?"

Special Agent Madison took a breath. "Holding his own." Which didn't tell us much. "Back to the case. There is one connection you will find interesting. Your ex-wife, Lyle, was a friend of our real estate cadaver. The FBI have been going through emails between the two. Some as recent as seven weeks ago. One of the reasons we've been on to Smothers was his connection with slippery Clarisse."

Last thing I wanted to think about was Clarisse Henderson and all she had done to the judge before the law caught up with her.

Lyle's brow was accordioned so tight it cast shadows. "And why is that pertinent?"

"Seems your Clarisse knew there were some shenanigans about a land deal back around the 1870's. Delilah's grandmother's land. You'd better look over the papers." Madison rummaged around in his fancy black leather briefcase. A plain vanilla file was produced and he thrust it toward Lyle.

If Clarisse knew about the land in Appalachia, she'd gotten the info from Neely, her lover and sneaky local realtor. Was she some sort of go-between so Neely looked squeaky clean on the deal? *What would Neely's wife know about all this? Was Olive Lorraine involved?*

"Don't go off on a tangent, Di," Lyle said after he gazed in my eyes. "First things first." He cleared his throat. "I'm on my honeymoon, Robert. I'll get back to you when I have time to peruse this."

The rain diminished as we aimed for our B&B. The only words Lyle said in the sixteen-mile journey were, "We need to find a hole to hide in." Concentrating on rearranging Meemaw's and my parents' lives, I didn't speak either. Silently we entered the cute cottage. Thumping the file onto the dining table, Lyle drummed his fingers on top of it.

"Come on, darlin'," he said, aiming toward the bedroom.

I followed.

We made it to dinner by 7:30.

Lyle leaned over the small dining table. "I'm going to postpone our Paris flight. We're needed here."

I nodded.

"Then, I'll see what can be done about rearranging our housing. I'm thinking of someplace quiet, where birds are singing, and no one knows where we are."

"Except Madison."

"Right." He grimaced with disgust.

A light supper of fruit, cheese, French bread with a nice crust, and a champagne flute of hazelnut mousse were placed before us by the smiling, dimpled daughter of our hosts. The meal was perfect after a tumultuous day.

Lyle reached for my hand over the tablecloth.

"I'm trying not to design a catastrophe clipboard," I said as the fruit plate was whisked away, and tiny cups of decaf coffee arrived.

"We can't organize life, sweetheart. It organizes us."

I slept only after I'd been assured by my mother that Meemaw was doing fine. Woke to find Lyle at the dining table studying the paperwork from Madison. A fire of orange/red flames danced in the grate. The sun was winking out of the east and Lyle had coffee brewing.

"Morning, sleepyhead." He rose and gave me a kiss that made me want to head back to the bedroom. "I would like your approval on today's schedule."

I backed up with surprise.

"Old dog learning new tricks," he laughed. "I keep reminding myself that making decisions on my own without consulting my other half is folly. Forgive me when I stumble, but today maybe a small victory lap is in order." He waltzed me around the table and closer to the warmth of the crackling fire.

"How about a ride before breakfast? Then off to explore the innards of the hospital, and a shopping trip. I've need of a new vehicle."

"Your BMW isn't that old."

"I've something else in mind than a small car." He lifted one eyebrow as if wanting me to play a guessing game.

"I'll bite. I'm guessing a new truck to replace the one nearly demolished when George was at the wheel."

"A tepid guess. I'll let you know when the temperature is more tropical. How about that ride."

"Wonderful."

"I'll change and saddle the horses."

The weather had cleared with the sun streaming warmth into the November chill. A perfect canter over rolling green hills made me laugh out loud. Heading across the rock walkway after stabling the horses, Lyle swept me off my feet and bent me backwards. He landed the kind of kiss you see in movies. The lingering kind that made your lips fizzy. He had to help me negotiate the front steps to the dining room because my feet were sort of floaty. Or maybe my brain. Who knew, the man merely touching my hand made my heart shiver.

Harry had too. I'd been hair-brained on my first honeymoon. Now, between my brain and my heart things weren't coordinating. How was I supposed to deal with Meemaw's health, the real estate mess, and a dead body in a hotel room with my thoughts focusing on Lyle's flashing eyes?

Over my egg casserole I said to my groom. "Since you brought up a new car, I'd like to request something."

His eyebrows aimed toward the ceiling.

"I'd like to see where you store this so-called sports car you race on tracks. It's probably some old heap, but if you've a mind we could kick the tires and maybe go for a spin."

"I'd have to drive because you're not qualified to sit in my 'hot' sports car and play with the steering wheel. You only get to be a passenger until driving classes with a professional."

"Is the car you drive made out of gold?"

"No, but the one who wants to drive it is. I want her safe."

His words made me blush. Lyle laughed, his nice carefree laugh, the one he used when no one was shooting at us. As soon as he took a sip from his coffee his phone rang. "Yes? Glad you got my text." A pause while he listened, then, "I'll send you the address and we could meet there after lunch. Say, three. That will give you time to drive in from Lexington.”

With Lyle filling up our day I put the kibosh on my plans for a late start to the hospital.

Lyle pushed his phone off and slipped it into his pocket. “We’d better head to McKeansville. You’ll want to see Meemaw and I need to speak with Josephine.”

Chapter Seven

It appeared that Lyle had something up his sleeve he wasn't willing to share. He dropped me off at the hospital entrance and I stewed as I walked down the third-floor corridor. Eyes at the nurse's station flitted up when they heard my shoes strike the hard tile. I pushed open the door to Meemaw's room.

Meemaw was *in absentia,* as was my mother. I turned back to the nurse's station and was informed by a thin-lipped nurse that they were having tests done. 'It will be hours,' she said with a wave of her hand. From the crook of her eyebrow, she intended that I feel dismissed. My nose quickly went out of joint.

I called Lyle's phone. It went to voicemail.

Hiking back to my house I contemplated *life.* Its twists and turns gave me emotional whiplash. Today was no exception. With Harry I could figure out what he was thinking. Thirty-odd years with a man gives a woman an advantage. My feet changed direction and I headed to the cemetery to chat with my late husband. Well, maybe that wasn't an accurate description now. If I thought of Harry as my first husband it sounded like I was a serial marrier.

But I'd only had two. And I figured that was enough. Who knew what living with Lyle would bring? With Harry, amid the laughter and poetry it brought six kids, four still living. So far with Lyle there had been laughter and a sweetness growing between us. No poetry.

Pushing open the iron gate to the Morgan cemetery plot, I decided not to tell Harry about how Lyle drew out the tenderness in me. I still trembled when remembering the grayness of Lyle's face as he was wheeled into the ambulance. "Hope all that drama is behind us, Lord," I whispered up to Him.

Except for the injured boy in the corridor. And the

dead man in the room down the hall. But nothing tied us to them.

Well, a piece of paper might. The one with Meemaw's name scrawled on it. But Lyle could straighten that out.

Harry's grave was within the shade of an enormous tree that was tossing its coat of many colors all over the grass. I stepped over a soggy pile of yellows and reds that the wind had formed and stopped at Harry's foot. The resident nut who kept depositing offerings had draped a wedding veil over Harry's grassy mound.

My eyes narrowed. "Harry already knows I'm married and pushed me to it," I said too loudly for politeness. My hands balled into fists. The sheriff had promised to discover the culprit and stop her visiting Harry. From Star Wars figures to lopsided flowers, she'd been busy. At least she hadn't put anything on the twins' graves.

"Harry. You know who this is. A student? Poetry aficionado? Give me a hint and I'll take care of it."

"Not a good idea, Di." I jumped at Lyle's voice. "Got your message and when you weren't marching through campus thought I'd find you here."

I went to my groom and reached for his hand. "I'm not about to give away our married secrets to Harry, Lyle. Thought Harry needed to know he was right about you, though. That you are the best gift he'd ever hidden from me." I drew my finger down Lyle's cheek and rested my head on his shoulder.

Lyle kissed my springy hair.

As we walked to his car Lyle said, "I've been speaking with Randall Longworth about the money he's missing from his office manager's thefts. He's going to be in town for weeks getting things squared away. He's bored staying at the local motel."

Last time Randall Longworth had stayed in the bypass hotel he'd been guarded by the police. Trying to keep a witness from absconding had been too difficult for our local constabulary. Slippery Longworth had taken off and nearly gotten himself killed. The man apparently was loath to enjoy the comforts of clean sheets, clean towels, and a hot breakfast.

"Your house is now occupied with your family, and mine houses Josephine and her family. Thought Longworth could use the little house at the Morgan farm."

Harry and I had spent our first three years of marriage in the little cottage. Having braggart Randall Longworth using the place didn't sit right. Knowing him, he'd also have any number of female visitors to keep him company. I wasn't about to offer that sweet place to Lyle's boyhood friend—the very idea galled me.

Lyle raised his eyebrows. "I'm guessing that Longworth occupying the house might be an offense to you." He pursed his lips before he continued, "But he is an old friend in need."

"He'll have to dust and vacuum. I can't see your friend lifting a finger."

"When his mama got sick with cancer, Rand cleaned their house every week. In fact, it was so thoroughly done and admired by the ladies in the neighborhood that he paid for college working as a house cleaner." Lyle looked at me with an expression I couldn't fathom. "Di, give the man some slack. There is more to Randall Longworth than a womanizing drinker."

I'd already judged the man and avoided him whenever possible. Randall Longworth made my hair stand on end. How can you reverse the way you think? My lips tightened, but I nodded in agreement with Lyle. The good Lord had given me more than one opportunity to change my thinking. It was the least I could offer the man whose life I'd saved.

Lyle drove us home. Well, to my home. We'd settled it would become ours. Harry's old truck was in the driveway, which meant my son Paul was there.

I grabbed Lyle's hand as we walked up the back steps. "Think he'll have Austin with him?" The excitement in my voice made Lyle grin.

"Best thing about being a parent is becoming a grandparent," he said. "Love to see the joy in your eyes."

"You'll be one soon."

"Already am, if you'll share."

"Harry gave them to you with both hands."

"I know." His voice held the quietness of still water.

We opened the kitchen door to the rich scents of bubbling marinara sauce and a squeal from a three-year-old boy. Austin and Lyle did their special handshake, a one-minute affair that included waves, palms slapping together, and wiggling eyebrows.

Josephine was at my enormous stove, a box of spaghetti noodles in one hand, a stirring spoon in the other. "I was expecting you," she said with a toss of her head. "Mr. Judge, there, didn't exactly beg for lunch, but when I mentioned heating up your homemade marinara sauce, he had to wipe drool off his chin."

I kissed her dark-hued cheek. "Thanks, Josephine. So, you and my new husband had a talk?"

Josephine winked at me. "Who's to tell about my having an assignation with your husband? My lips are sealed as tight as a pickle jar. And yes, I know the meaning of the word. I think Mr. Harry said it once or twice."

My cheeks heated up and I fanned my face with a green potholder.

"You should blush," she said. Josephine looked directly at Austin to make certain he wasn't listening. My grandson had Lyle by the hand and was dragging him toward the front parlor. Josephine put her hands on her hips. "As if I didn't know what was what around here. Now, I'm about to take the plunge and reacquaint myself with the birds and the bees." She lifted one eyebrow.

"If your mama isn't up to the conversation, I will be happy to substitute."

"Thank you, no. Think I'll let my groom be the teacher. We had this chat about his first marriage. Seems it was as shaky as the judge's to Clarisse. Turns out the first time Daniel was deployed to Iraq she was off with a staff sergeant making whoopie."

"Too much information, Josephine." I fake plugged my ears.

She slung the noodles into water boiling so hard it spit. "And don't you know it. Seems the good reverend's wife liked dating so much she made it a profession."

I rocked back on my heels. "Daniel didn't say a thing about his betrayal."

"Nor about her *not* wanting kids. Apparently, she also went to Planned Parenthood where she *planned* not to be a parent. Makes you wonder about the name of that organization because they get rid of the 'ev-ee-dence' of parenthood, so to speak."

"It's called an oxymoron, Josephine."

"Moron is right. If you're going to do "it" you might as well suck it up and choose to live with the consequences." She stirred the marinara sauce with such authority it spun.

I reached out and touched her arm.

"And that's not all." Her wooden spoon waggled in the air like a baton throwing red droplets around the stove top.

"My little girl cain't sleep nights because of what happened to her. Cain't let her go to school, 'cause of the gossip. Cain't let her go back to work because all she does is cry and hold her stomach. Talked to Mr. Judge about it. He said he's working on a solution."

Josephine stuck the big spoon back in the red

sauce and took a taste. "Best sauce you've ever made. When your new husband finds out you can cook like this, I might lose my job and you'll never eat out again."

I pushed both hands through the air as if removing the thought. "Last year's batch, before Harry got sick."

"You didn't do much cooking after Christmas."

"I cooked just for Harry." My voice trailed off as tears spurted from my eyes. I shook my head. On my honeymoon and weeping over the man who was playing with our children in heaven. Crying for myself wasn't pretty. The Judge's feet sounded in the hall. I wiped my eyes and forced a smile. "I guess I'll always miss my Harry," I said to Josephine. "But make no mistake, I'm in a dither about Lyle. Suspect it will stay that way for a few decades."

Josephine's big brown eyes had liquid moving out of the corners and down her cheeks. "We both loved that husband of yours. One of the best God ever placed on this earth, in spite of what a few people say about him."

"Who would say anything unkind about Harry?" I scrunched up my forehead not looking pleased.

"Charlene Higgenbottom blames him for her husband's arrest. Now seems that they've found a hidden bank account with town money in it, so she's spouting off that it was pressure from Harry that made Mayor Higgenbottom steal the funds for the roadwork on Man of War Boulevard."

"They charging him with that too?" Lyle asked as he walked into the kitchen. "All I heard about were charges for being an accessory to the attack on my sister."

"This evidence was uncovered here, not in your fancy cabin in North Carolina. More charges are pending, according to the new mayor. Miss Sylvia is up to her eyeballs in accountants and FBI people what with our former mayor being arrested in one state and doing illegal things in this one." Josephine waggled her head as if loosening her neck. "Say, how is agent Madison doing after getting shot? Heard he was the one who put your grandmother in the hospital."

I shrugged. "He pretends he's fine but he looks as pale as cotton balls and sits down when he can. I'm not blaming him for Meemaw's heart problems. He's following the scent of the case, sort of like a bloodhound trying to find a trail. It led him to her."

"Mr. Judge, best you set the dining table. Miss Dee Dee here is on her honeymoon."

Lyle had invited Paul to stay to lunch. 'They had business,' I was informed as I hunted up napkins in the dining room.

"What kind of business?"

"Monkey business," said Josephine from the kitchen. "They're in the middle of a negotiation. High finance." I must have looked confused because she patted the hand holding the paper napkins and said, "It's about the little house. When Mr. Judge gets his eyes on something, he rolls up his sleeves and sets to work. Look how he pursued you. Man didn't mess around. Now he's in a tizzy about setting things up for a recovery place for trafficked girls."

I wrapped an arm around Josephine's shoulder and gave it a squeeze. "I don't know what God has in mind, Josephine. Let's hear Lyle out. Maybe, just maybe this is for someone else."

Josephine shook her head. "Your new husband wants to talk with you about letting me stay with the girls. Mama could be the cook while I could see that things are run properly, and the girls stay out of trouble."

It was difficult enough to have Josephine getting married but leaving? I took a steadying breath. "And Daniel?"

"I'm talking to him tonight. Maybe we're moving too soon into this marriage business."

"Whoa, Josephine. You mean you don't want to marry Daniel?"

"No." Her voice creaked like a worn chair. "I don't know how to balance Daniel, a wedding, and protecting my mama and daughter."

"God has a way, Josephine. We just need to lean on Him. Now let's see what Lyle has in mind and where he thinks the money is coming from to revamp the cottage."

During lunch, Paul said that Longworth could stay at the caretaker's cottage and also agreed to have a roofer check out the water leak. Lyle winked at Paul so he wouldn't tell me anything more. Lyle was as sneaky about surprises as Harry had been.

After lunch, Lyle took the slow route to the farm. Two country roads, a jaunt toward the Shaker Village before turning back, had him whistling and smiling. A Lexus, Cadillac, and two pickups were waiting by the cottage's front porch. Not any old Cadillac either, but Olive Lorraine Patrick's fancy one with the special trim. She stood on the porch with the tall, angular friend of George's who worked for who knew what sneaky government agency. Olive and the man had become friends while working to find Savannah. However, from the sizzling look he gave her, the man wanted more than friendship.

"What is Olive and George's spy friend doing here?" I said to Lyle as we got out of the car.

"I invited Will as well as Olive. Think they can solve a problem I have."

I slid my arm through Lyle's and looked into his smiling face. "And what would that be, my closed-mouth friend?"

He tapped me on the side of my nose. "From roof leak to siding issues, this little house needs attention. I've had an idea percolating while I waited for a certain woman to say 'yes' to my proposal." He lifted an eyebrow waiting for me to respond.

"I'll bite."

"It is driving me to distraction...er not you at the moment...to find Savannah assaulted by her memories and friends. 'Can I make a difference?' I keep thinking. This place might be the answer, or it might not."

"A place of sanctuary? A place for healing?"

He nodded. "I had Paul make some phone calls."

As Lyle introduced me to an architect from Lexington, a contractor from Frankfort, and two county officials with a sheaf of papers, Paul drove up in Harry's old truck.

Olive Lorraine hugged me hard and long. I'd spent years being wary of Harry's high school sweetheart and her hug changed the atmosphere between us. "Hey," I said when I could back up. "Mind telling me what is up? Lyle is into secret keeping."

Olive's eyes began to sparkle. She turned to George's spy-friend and rested her hand on his arm. She smiled a genuine smile instead of the tight, business one she'd always displayed. Olive's whole body had a glow. Instead of the get-out-of-my-way-while-I-settle-things woman I had encountered over the years, there was a gentleness I hardly recognized. I smiled back, wondering if we could be friends. She sidled through the door. Her friend Will followed, and I stepped behind them.

Olive turned around in a circle staring at the fireplace. "I remember this place. Joe Lipski and his wife were here when Harry and I were dating. Sweet couple. Had five maybe six kids. He helped Harry's dad with the farm and was so good with animals that the Morgan's horses were the envy of the entire neighborhood with their shiny coats and style."

While her friend wandered into the kitchen, I stepped closer to Olive. "Do you mind an impertinent question?"

Olive's eyebrows went up into her hairline. "Er...I guess not."

"I wondered about the friend you brought. Are you,

well, serious?"

Olive blanched. "Don't think I can be right now. I'm still married to Neely. Although divorce is anathema to me, I need to make some decisions." She straightened her shoulders as a small tear trailed over a cheek. "I was too stupid to figure out he was using his vacations to meet with Clarisse." Her lips trembled. I put my arms around her.

"Not stupid, Olive Lorraine. Loyal, faithful, accepting."

Her sigh nearly broke my heart.

As measuring tapes emerged from pockets and clipboards appeared, I put my hand on her arm more to keep me rooted in place, because Olive's eyes had softened as did her tight lips. She looked like she wanted to talk. I wanted to follow the men upstairs and take notes while Lyle's cobbled-together team trooped around the cottage.

"I've had a couple of weeks to make some decisions. I'm not happy about them but they are the right things to do." Another sigh escaped her. "As we speak divorce papers are being served in his little jail cell. I must admit, it feels good to finally take a stand." Her voice held all the sadness of the world in it as she hid her face in her hands.

I looked over Olive's bent head and saw George's spy-friend in the kitchen doorway. He chewed on the side of his lip. Face puckered with worry, Will ambled up the staircase. Lyle's gang began to roam the upper floor from the sounds overhead. This empty old house being converted to something useful and filled again with love was a marvelous idea. My fingers itched to be with them.

Olive Lorraine's phone croaked. A full-throated bullfrog noise sounded twice before she picked up. She swiped out her tears before she spoke, then said automatically, "Patrick Real Estate Company." She waited a tick. "What do you mean he wasn't there? He's in jail!" She cast her startled eyes my way then stepped away from the fireplace and aimed for the front door.

Running footsteps told me that her companion was hurtling back down the stairs. He must have bat hearing, like Josephine. He was beside Olive as she slid out the door. "Bail? How'd he *make* bail?" was all I heard as the door quietly closed on the pair.

If Neely Patrick was out of the slammer what about Clarisse? Were they going to let her roam the countryside and look for ways to put us under the sod so there wouldn't be witnesses to her plugging Lyle?

I was about to hike up the stairs and inform my groom of the latest when I heard the door open. "Well, I never thought they'd let him out." Olive shook her head. Her phone croaked again. "Patrick Real Estate Company," she recited. Her mouth tightened into a straight line as she listened. "Of course, I changed the locks, Neely. I assume your cousins Frick and Frack bailed you out?" She paused, waiting. "Yes, I know I'm funny." She held the phone away from her ear and shook her head, then said into the mouthpiece, "I'm tied up at the moment but can be there in say, an hour. Can you wait?" She looked at the skinny man next to her and rolled her eyes. "Fine. See you then." She didn't hang up, but she punched a couple of buttons and spoke into the phone again. "He's at the house. Hand him the papers there. If I know Neely his squirrely cousins are with him. They're dangerous. Don't go alone."

"I need to see my lawyer about this." Olive held out her phone with disgust. "Lyle asked me about helping with this property, Delilah. I'm happy to do so."

"*We're* happy to do so," said the man beside her. He reached for her hand. "Olive and I need to be busy with something worthwhile while we wait for her divorce to be final."

Olive Lorraine's eyes almost fell out of her head they were so big. "I...er...we haven't spoken of...well." She swallowed and turned cardinal red.

"Time we did." The man slipped his arm around her

shoulders and kissed her cheek.

"Tell Lyle to call me." Olive Lorraine Patrick and her admirer closed the door as they left so quietly it didn't make its usual thunk sound.

I needed to sit down. Everything was moving in warp speed mode and I wanted to process at the pace of a slow-motion film. Olive Lorraine had a dilemma but so did I. Neely Patrick was dangerous. He'd be aiming for me since I'd aimed at him and shot him right in the buttocks. With his Irish mob cousins who knew what he might think up.

Then there was this much cherished little cottage where Harry and I had begun our marriage. Plopped down on the chintz couch I imagined Randall Longworth sitting before the fire with his feet on the coffee table, a glass of bubbly and a girl—probably at least twenty-years younger—snuggling at his side.

I blinked. Delilah, get a grip and rearrange your thinking. Envision Longworth cleaning toilets through college and maybe you'll be more charitable.

Chapter Eight

THE DESIGN AND PERMIT TEAM GATHERED in the kitchen. Lyle unrolled his dream on the scarred kitchen table where Harry and I had had coffee and held hands. Lyle imagined not only a half-way house, but a place where the girls could finish school. It was a big dream and needed many hands who could keep their mouths shut. Lyle's sketches covered the table, and the men hunched over them with red pens tracing lines and jotting notes.

After an hour, and with a back seat full of paperwork, we left the farm and headed toward town. "Hospital?" I asked, hoping to get an update on Meemaw.

"Shopping," he answered. He drove down the bypass and stopped at a storage unit. "Why don't you wait for me here?" Lyle said as he got out of the car. He stopped after taking three steps, came to my door and opened it. "I wanted this to be a solution to the problem you have with Rand but keeping mum about things until they're solved is a habit I'm trying to break. Come with me, my love."

He led me to a fancy RV that was tucked beside the line of blue-doored storage garages. The motorhome shone as if just washed. The college president stood beside the open door and nodded to Lyle. "You, buddy, might save my skin. Been trying to off load this since my brother-in-law died."

I'd never been in a motorhome. This one contained five slide-outs from living room to bedroom. The black leather seats and marbled dark wood were too masculine for my taste. I poked around while the men talked price, then I headed back to the car, grabbed my cell phone, and placed a call to the hospital. Daddy answered in Meemaw's room. "She's to stay another night," he growled into the phone. "Your poor mother is so tired she's falling asleep on her feet. I'm relieving her, no ifs, ands, or buts allowed. And tomorrow, if they try to keep Meemaw in the hospital I'm getting a court order. Your husband handy?"

"Not now. I'll let him know you want to speak with him, Daddy. You sound fit to be tied."

"This place is so noisy you couldn't hear a howitzer firing."

I laughed as I disconnected then speed dialed Special Agent Madison. When he said a brusque hello, I launched in. "Any more news about the boy stabbed in the hotel?"

"Recovering. He'll go home in a couple of days. The kid is a junior at the University of Kentucky studying veterinary medicine. I talked with the dean. Our young man is one of the top students. Tutoring has been arranged." Madison cleared his throat.

"That's kind, Robert."

"Er...least we could do. He lost a lot of blood and can't work while he recovers."

But not Robert Madison, who had almost bled out and was still on his feet chasing down villains and hunting up trouble. I wanted to slather some sympathy his direction, but he interrupted my thoughts. "We've set up a sort of scholarship fund for him. You might hit Lyle up for a dollar or two."

"I will."

"Your grandmother doing all right?"

"Raring to go home. Anything else you want to tell me?"

"I think I'll keep my investigation away from the amateurs. This way Lyle can't accuse me of interrupting his honeymoon." He laughed. We disconnected after his comment but it set me to thinking about papers and land deals. Was that what Lyle wanted to talk to Olive about? Not the farm house but Meemaw's land?

Lyle slid into the driver's seat—a grin plastered across his face. "You're looking at a happy man, Di. Think I've solved Rand's housing problem and eased the worry lines on your forehead. I need you, darlin', to think about clipboards."

Meemaw was easy. She kissed my cheek then winked at Lyle when he sat beside her. Never thought of her being a flirt until that moment. Papaw had been tagged and bagged before he was eighteen. Meemaw must have been something back in the day.

Lyle took a notecard from his pocket, then snapped his pen into write. "I've read over Madison's paperwork. What can you tell me about the Burns family land? Deeds go back to 1795. But there is a letter, notarized and signed by a Josiah Penworth Burns giving twenty acres of the property to Mr. Samuel Burns Ferris."

"I don't know those names."

Lyle nodded. "Dated 1866."

Meemaw stared at Lyle. "Maybe a relative?" She pursed her lips together and closed her eyes. "This makes my bones hurt," she added as she rubbed her hands. "Well, my family didn't have slaves except when they first came from North Carolina to Fort Boonesboro. In the early 1800s they grew poor trying to scratch out a living. Rumor has it, though, that the Burnses had slaves back before Emancipation."

Lyle kept his eyes on Meemaw's. "Not many folks in the mountains had slaves. Even in the Carolina mountains it was rare. If a man struggled to feed his family, he couldn't have slaves as well." Lyle moved his feet as he spoke. The Hendersons had owned plantations through North Carolina. The Morgans had slaves here in the Bluegrass. I hadn't thought about the Burnses being slave holders. In fact, I'd been a tinge proud of the fact that we hadn't been.

Meemaw rubbed a thin finger along her upper lip. "Do you suppose old Josiah gave his land away as a penance because this Samuel Burns Ferris was kin but from a misalliance?"

"That's my guess. Perhaps he was a son that couldn't be acknowledged."

Meemaw took a sip of water from the glass on her side table. "This whole conversation makes me uneasy, Lyle. Slavery is not much different than trafficking children for pleasure. Abusing some poor soul until they's all used up and then tossing them away like they was trash. Today's slavery isn't about picking cotton, it's about sex." Meemaw snorted. "It's what they did to that Weldon girl Delilah found. Dropped her off at the hospital when she was nearly dead. They would have done it to Savannah too if you hadn't caught them." Meemaw crossed her scrawny arms.

I didn't shush her. A woman in her nineties ought to speak her mind.

Meemaw nodded her head as if listening to someone. "I recall a conversation my father-in-law had with a man in town. Must have been back in the forties, because he died in '51. T'other man said, 'What you goin' to do about the promise?' Mr. Burns said, 'Nothin'. Ignoring it is the best thing. They won't win in court. Nobody going to force us off our land.' At that point they saw me peeking out of the kitchen and went onto the porch."

"Sounds like Di and I need a road trip."

Meemaw's eyes twinkled. "The house keys are in my purse. Marybeth will have it. Check on the garden, Delilah. I've some Brussel sprouts that need to be harvested. Getting mighty chilly in the mountains. You best get warm clothes."

"What you up to, scrambling around in the attic?" Josephine hollered up the attic stairs.

"Packing to go to the mountains. We need answers about Meemaw's property." My voice was so loud my ears rang.

Josephine huffed up the stairs and plopped down

on my sewing chair. "Well, if that don't beat all. You going on a sleuthing trip without me."

"I'm on my honeymoon." I pursed my lips at the thought of everything being upside down. "You need to keep your mama busy and comfort your daughter. So traipsing off with us is out of the question."

"Huh." Josephine's snort made me jump. "Sidney's doing the comforting. He's got Savannah putting mulch on your rose beds. She always liked to putter with Mr. Harry in the garden. Sidney knows that." She shook her head. "Never thought I'd say it, but Sidney's been a blessing. Doesn't talk to her much but when he does, he makes her smile." Josephine's face managed one as well. 'Course Mr. Judge has Sidney heading out to the farm tomorrow. Your new husband gave Sidney a clipboard with notes, lists, and all kinds of other things on it. Your man's already learning how to organize things and you've hardly begun on the training."

Lyle must have been up at the crack of dawn to get all his lists done. Was he an early riser? As in 4 a.m.? "Josephine, I think Lyle was a clipboard man long before I met him." *Not Harry, though. In thirty-three years of marriage Harry never picked up a clipboard or made lists. He wrote in his notebooks and created poems.*

"Hmm, Hmm." Josephine eased out of the chair. "Two clipboard fanatics in one house might not be a good idea." She clicked her tongue as she headed downstairs. "Maybe I'd better ask Daniel if he likes making lists. Best to be prepared for the battle."

Josephine's fiancé had been a Marine. He most certainly knew how to organize, dispense orders, and get people lined up like ducks on parade. Josephine was about to hit a brick wall.

It was almost dark when we tried to escape town, but as Lyle headed out of the driveway, Madison pulled in front of Lyle's car and turned off his engine.

Madison creaked out of his car as slow as Meemaw on a good day. His face was tight with pain. "Thought you might need a photo of our dead guy from the hotel to show to the locals." He handed Lyle another vanilla folder.

I wanted to ask Madison if it were a government regulation that all folders, envelops, and files be boring vanilla. From his pained expression when he moved, I kept it to myself. I got out of the car so Madison wouldn't have to bend over to talk. "Were the cousins who posted Neely's bail the same ones that are out of the pen?"

"Yes. A very interesting family tree. Not often you find the Irish up to their necks in drug running, prostitution, and shady real estate deals. There were the big city gangs, of course. Think of prohibition and the rum running some of them did. This particular gang has been at the art of intimidation since prior to the Civil War. They have it down to a fine science."

"Can the bell hop at the hotel recognize the person who stabbed him?"

"Apparently not. Baseball cap, bandana over his mouth, black shirt and pants. Boy thinks the assailant was Caucasian that's about it. I've other photos in the folder."

"How did you know we were heading east, Robert?" Lyle sounded more puzzled than upset.

"Mrs. Elizabeth Burns gave me a call. Said she asked you to water her houseplants." He coughed into his hand. "Said she forgave me for interrupting her tepid life and sending her to the hospital. She actually used the word tepid." Madison's pale face colored rose pink.

Lyle got out of the car and took Madison by the arm. "Robert and I need to talk, Di. Why, don't you wait for me here, in the car."

I eased into my seat and tried to read their lips. They put their heads together and talked in hushed voices. I heard a few words anyway. Lyle exclaimed, "So, they let her out? Bellows have anyone..." his voice trailed off, but I got the gist. Clarisse was wandering the streets of our fair city. The news didn't sit well with me. How easy would it be for her to procure a gun? I shivered at the thought then my stomach growled. Hustling up to the mountains in the dark wasn't the brightest idea. Maybe one more night, eating scrumptious food, sleeping in a cozy bed with my new husband was in order.

Lyle had the same idea.

As dawn broke, we aimed toward Berea then headed east on a squiggle of road that aimed for the bluish haze of mountains and pines. Lyle lifted his eyebrows when his GPS kept ordering us to turn around. I'd say it was because of the low cloud cover that obscured the satellite but it could be the trees as well. They hung over the road like distraught maidens at a wake.

I smiled as he tapped his phone to get it to quit squawking at him. "I'll be happy to drive."

"Why don't you play tour guide instead and acquaint me with flora and fauna."

I kept my face straight when I said, "A ranger at Fort Boonesboro was speaking about Eastern Kentucky to a bunch of tourists. He said, and I quote, 'don't use the local's directions. First, they'll have you driving on tarmac. Seems easy, right? But then, you'll find the roads turn to gravel, then dirt. Next, there will be a bridge or maybe not, and voila, you're fording a stream.' And always have a four-wheel drive vehicle when venturing into the hollers." Lyle was in for a surprise. Although Lyle and Harry had been up at my parent's farm, they hadn't hunted at Meemaw's. I didn't inform Lyle that Meemaw had a paved drive. Because teasing Lyle was fun.

I gave my new husband a college type geology tour, complete with professorial voice. "One must know," I concluded, "that the eastern mountain ranges were under water so limestone appears in the rock formations."

"Geology 101?"

"Daddy throughout my childhood. Mining engineers need to know bedrock information."

Lyle groaned. "No one told me you liked puns."

"Cut my incisors on them."

Following a flatbed truck hauling a beat-up Chevy, Lyle slowed to a crawl. He tried to pass on the two-lane highway, but the truck sped up at every straight-of-way. Muttering under his breath, Lyle quickly glanced my way. "Did you hear that?"

"No. But I can imagine I wouldn't like it. Harry said the good Lord used natural selection putting the slowpokes in front of the speeders. A buffoon will pass on a blind curve. You ever read about the Darwin Awards?"

Lyle cleared his throat. "Harry shared his collection of books."

"Well, then you get the gist. Like the thief who tries to climb down the chimney, gets stuck and is roasted like a Thanksgiving turkey. Harry thought they were funny. I hid them from the children."

Poking along behind the truck we sang silly songs all the way to Horsetail Falls. Lyle's baritone and my second soprano made nice harmony together. It kept Lyle from grinding his teeth.

My small hometown had seen better days. When the mines thrived, new trucks parked along the asphalt and the stores didn't have boards over the windows. Only one eating place remained open today, but there were signs of life along the main drag. The yellow stripe in the center of the street was crisp with fresh paint and a brand spanking new Kentucky blue awning spanned a window near the courthouse. The large truck stopped in the middle of the street, straddling the yellow line. His blinker flashed, but the flatbed was not moving. The only way around was to pass on the right.

I patted Lyle's hand. "Best place to meet the locals is a coffee shop. My cousin, Cheryl Lynn, runs the Coffee Maid Cafe." I pointed to a restaurant half-way up the block and across from the courthouse.

Lyle honked his horn. The truck driver got out and gave Lyle an impolite hand gesture. Lyle's knuckles turned white as he gripped his steering wheel.

"If you pull over into that parking place," I nodded to our right where an empty spot waited, "We'll let him decide where he is going and why. This being the south, it might take him a while."

Sitting at the counter on swivel stools, Lyle sipped his coffee and raised his eyebrows. "Is this True Kona Peaberry coffee?" he asked the girl behind the counter.

"Yes. But don't tell the locals. Miss Cheryl is a snob about her coffee. They think," she waved a thumb toward a table of overall-clad farmers, "that good coffee is the kind that is so thick your spoon stands upright in it. We may not roast our own but we grind it daily."

Lyle raised his cup. "My compliments to the chef."

"And don't you know it," said a voice behind us. "This Harry's replacement, Delilah?"

I spun around and eyed a man who farmed down the road a piece from Meemaw. "Lyle Henderson, meet Bruce Tweedy. Best cow roper this side of Clay county." I didn't add that he was a third cousin a couple of times removed. Most people were related up here and Lyle didn't need to sort out the connections.

The loiterers rose as one and tromped over for a meet and greet. They shook Lyle's hand like it was a pump they were priming. "Seeing you, Delilah, makes me as happy as a chicken with socks on." Tweedy grinned at me then cocked his head toward Lyle. "Better looking than Harry, Delilah. You always had good taste."

"Might soon after Harry's passing, don't you think?"

said one of the farmers.

I gulped down a lump that grew in my throat. All I could do was nod as the comments flew our direction.

"Heard tell Harry put his oar in and arranged the whole shebang. Courting, marriage, you name it." Jed McMurry, a grin plastered across his face clapped Lyle on the back, hard. Lyle didn't acknowledge the hit with even a wince. If Jed McMurry wanted insider information, he'd have to wait 'till he got to heaven and quiz Harry. "You look familiar," he said as he poked Lyle's shoulder. "You been up here before?"

"Hunting with Harry," Lyle said.

"The man who shot that ten-point buck a few years back, Jed." Tweedy nodded toward Lyle. "You remember. Harry brought him up and this city slicker out shot Delilah's daddy, brothers, and Harry."

I spun my seat toward Lyle. "You did?"

"Apparently." Lyle didn't look puffed up just amused.

Tweedy leaned forward and gave me a stare. "How's your meemaw? She went hightailing it off to the wedding without a bye-your-leave. Always asks me to check on her place. Guess it was a shotgun type of affair." Tweedy grinned so wide you'd think he'd won a turkey shoot.

I rose to my feet, cheeks blushing as red as a late July tomato. "Meemaw asked us to check on her plants. She'll be in McKeansville for a while. I'd appreciate it if you could water her house plants after we've gone. She had a question about some real estate man who was looking over land grants and paper work at city hall."

"A man with a tiny mustache above his lips was snooping around. City fella for sure with his fancy waxed car and shiny shoes."

My eyes glanced at Lyle's footwear. You could shave in their mirror shine but at least they were boots. "Do you know what he wanted?"

"Told Mrs. Peebles, the county clerk, he was looking at purchasing land for a golf course."

Bruce Tweedy put his thumbs through his overall straps. "Nobody around here is going to waste time chasing little balls through the pasture. I think he was scouting out land for a casino. With the new governor there's talk about one coming."

"No Indian land here, Bruce," interjected Driscoll. "Only a couple of places in Kentucky had settlements. Buffalo and deer hunting ground for many tribes, though. They spent most of the time hunting each other from the tales told."

A man in blue jeans removed his John Deere hat and put it back on. "What do the historians know? Those university fellas think we came from apes. Then they back-peddle on that and say they've found an ancestor that walked up right that wasn't an ape. Next thing you know we'll be descended from reptiles instead of chimpanzees."

I wanted to clap them on the back. Evolution is a theory. Not proven science and these men of the soil, who looked at the weather, calculated their days with wind shifts and sunlight, knew far more about life and love than academics focusing on minutia. People who controlled their world with automatic sprinklers and air conditioning would grab an umbrella when clouds scudded across the sky instead of enjoying the shape of the storm.

"That real estate man had Melvin Kennedy take him around." Bruce sniffed, then Tweedy's nose pinched with disapproval. "Best talk to Kennedy."

"I need to get to the Missus' shopping list," one man said as another slapped his change on the counter and headed fast toward the door.

Who was Kennedy and why did the mention of his name make everyone around us antsy?

Chapter Nine

WHEN WE WERE THE ONLY ONES in the Coffee Maid, Lyle leaned over the counter and said to the black-haired server, "Don't believe we know how to find Mr. Kennedy."

"He owns a real estate company. Two doors past the fire hydrant near the courthouse. This side of the tracks."

Lyle paid our bill and we headed right, eyes ranging along the street for a sign saying Kennedy or Real Estate. The office was in a squat brick building with black shutters by the windows and bronze colored chrysanthemums, in pots, by the door. A man I'd never laid eyes on jumped from his computer terminal when Lyle opened the door.

"What can I, er, may I do for you?" The middle-aged man wrung his hands while he talked.

"We're here about some property," Lyle said. "My little wife and I are looking for something near a stream where I can fish. We're thinking of building a cabin to use on weekends." Lyle spoke without his usual eloquence. His voice was rough around the edges.

The man didn't say his name but pushed his hands down the front of his neatly creased gray pants. A slick smile emerged on his lips. The smile didn't reach his close-set eyes. "Well, you've picked the right little town. Plenty of land with streams running through it. Fish almost jumpin' to get on your hook."

"Ah," said Lyle.

My groom telling an out and out lie didn't sit well with me. I gave him my skinny eye. He took my hand, lifted it up to his lips with the leisure of a sloth and kissed the back of it. I snagged a quick breath. Lyle would leave me half-brained if I didn't watch out.

He gave my hand a teensy squeeze, released my

fingers and stuck his hand out toward the gray pants man. "I don't believe I caught your name, sir."

"Kennedy, Melvin Kennedy," said the real estate man as he grabbed Lyle's hand and shook it. He reached over for mine next and gave me a sweaty shake. It was November. Day was chilly. Why was Kennedy sweating from his brow to his fingertips? "Got a sweet piece of property soon to be on the market. House already on it. A tad off Clay Pigeon road."

The Burns clan had renamed that road in the fifties to thumb their noses at city folks who wouldn't know an owl from a hawk. Only Burnses owned that land. Which of Papaw's brothers would be selling their farm?

My eyebrows shot up and no matter what I did, stayed there a while. I dropped my head to study my feet, grabbing time to control my face. Harry could tell a fib when he was reciting a tall tale. Being a lawyer by profession, Lyle had truth telling tied up in knots. Probably why most legislators were lawyers. Liked to pull one over on the public.

We followed Melvin Kennedy out to his Jeep Wrangler and hopped in, Lyle in the front. Not a spot of lint in the vehicle's back seat. Windows were clean, no mud on the sides of the Jeep. Melvin must be OCD judging from his pressed shirt and polished shoes. Lyle kept asking questions about the countryside and the real estate man chattered about the hidden gems of property tucked into the valleys. He didn't use the word hollers, and his accent said he wasn't a Kentuckian but from somewhere north. Kennedy pointed out Horsetail Falls Road where I'd grown up, Maple Sugar Lane, and Green's Mill Road before we headed down Clay Pigeon. Kennedy's head rotated around as if he were looking for something as he pulled into Meemaw's drive.

"Nice that it's paved," Lyle said as he aimed his eye my direction. I winked at him and he covered his grin with a hand.

"Prime piece of land. Good stand of trees too. They might be good to cut down and sell to one of the log cabin building companies." He lifted his right hand from the steering wheel and waved it in front of the windshield. "I've another customer interested in this property. Going to be on the market next week."

A coughing fit overtook me. Lyle handed me his handkerchief as I sputtered.

"You said there was a creek?" Lyle craned his neck around as if searching.

"At the bottom of the hill. More a stream though. Have anglers heading this way from Lexington and beyond to fly fish. You folks from Lexington?"

"We've acreage close to Harrodsburg Pike." Well, at least referencing the farm didn't take his lie to the naughty list. "When we stop, you can show my wife that cute little house while I ramble." Lyle pointed to Meemaw's two story log cabin re-sided with boards sometime in the Victorian era. The porch had been added in the twenties when the men had more gumption than Meemaw encountered when she married into the clan. I could give him the tour blindfolded.

"Er...well...papers not yet signed so can't go in." With his lips jerked sideways Melvin stumbled along. "Let me see if the owner is in." He stopped the jeep by Meemaw's vegetable garden and jumped out of the car. He cleared his throat. "Now, you two just wait here a bit."

Lyle nodded. I crossed my arms. I didn't want the man walking up Meemaw's white painted stairs, knocking on her blue door or doing anything but turning around and heading back to town. My eyes roved over to the trees shading the creek. Harry had a favorite rock he'd sit on and watch the water flow by. I blinked. Hard. Why I thought of Harry while Lyle was nearby, I couldn't fathom.

Lyle turned to face me. "I've a plan, Delilah."

"I'm certain you do, but being a party to a lie is galling."

"We need to know who is trying to sell this land."

As I opened my mouth to retort a rifle blast

shattered the drizzly air. The gun went off as Melvin Kennedy stepped onto the porch. The slug splintered wood from the porch facing onto his head.

He hit the deck. So did Lyle.

I looked around. The gun shot had come from the woods behind Meemaw's fenced in garden.

"Get down," Lyle hollered.

Before my eyes were lower than the car window a blur of green plaid merged with the pines. Not a small man, I reckoned as my face pressed into the vanilla scented carpet. Little lines from a vacuum attachment were etched across the flooring. At least Melvin was obsessive about cleaning even if he was loose with the truth.

We lay low for about three minutes. Then, Melvin scuttled back to the car and mumbled something about, 'nobody home,' before he hightailed it up the drive and back toward town.

"Odd way of greeting a neighbor," Lyle said as we rocketed past Green's Mill Road. Melvin hit the curve before Witham Hill too fast, and we careened toward the ravine. I grabbed the seat with both hands and prayed, "Lord, keep us from harm." I should have prayed 'keep us on the road' because without guardrails it was a long way down. Melvin wasn't the best driver. A scrawny pine tree stopped us as we aimed toward oblivion.

The air bags whacked out of their compartments and trapped Lyle and Melvin, then deflated like punctured souffles. My seatbelt strangled my chest. Vibrating with the thump of my heart, I climbed out of the jeep. Got my knife out of the sheath in my boot and sliced Lyle's seatbelt because he was handicapped by the bag remains.

"How is your chest?" I asked, thinking of his recent wound.

"Some honeymoon," he muttered as he rose and stood beside me.

Melvin wasn't hurt, simply spitting mad. After Lyle extricated him, Kennedy tugged at his pants crease to straighten them then marched to the front of his car and looked at the indent from the tree that went across the front to the windshield, and onto the roof. The jeep was a crumpled mess. Kennedy kicked the right front tire he was so mad, then reached for his cell phone.

He held it up above his head. Squinted. Chances of it being useful were nil.

Lyle rolled his eyes. "How far to town?"

I put my coat hood up as the mist turned to thick drops. "Three miles," I said.

Lyle nodded to Melvin. "We'll go get help."

Melvin Kennedy grabbed Lyle's coat sleeve. "You're not leaving me here with somebody shooting at me. We'd better run. Sheriff needs to know about all this." Melvin waved his hand at his car, then at the road.

I can walk fast when I want to. Lyle is a runner, but Kennedy outpaced us as he sprinted toward town. Halfway to Sugar Maple Lane an old Ford pickup stopped beside Lyle and I. "Need a ride, Miss Delilah?" asked Bruce Tweedy.

Lyle reached for the door handle. "We'd be obliged."

I slid in beside green shirt-clad Tweedy. "Nice plaid. Is that your tartan?"

"Nope. Christmas gift."

Lyle's eyes drifted to the rifle mounted behind our heads.

I smelled gunpowder. "Care to explain your hunting on Meemaw's property?" I laughed when I said Meemaw, so he'd not be offended.

"Thought I saw a skunk."

Lyle nodded. "Think you did."

"We need to know what's going on here. Meemaw's in the hospital with a heart condition. It would ease her mind if we had something concrete to tell her."

Bruce Tweedy shook his head of thick, white hair. "Kennedy has been here about five months. Made some bad deals, almost giving away the Calloway lands to a developer. Doesn't sit right, the Calloways getting a pittance while the property is selling for thirty-thousand an acre."

Lyle leaned forward. "Do you think Kennedy is working with this Mr. Smothers?"

"The guy with the beady eyes and tiny mustache?"

I nodded.

"Yep." Tweedy frowned. "That's what I suspect. And I'm not the only one. Thick as thieves when I saw them. Kennedy's hand was around the other guy's shoulders like they were comrades in arms. Kennedy's got a system. He hits up the old. Those with worn out land and worn out bodies. Flim-flams them into thinking they're helping their kids. He doesn't have a right to sell your Meemaw's land. Needs to go through the proper authorities."

Lyle's eyebrows knit together. "Who?"

"The Burns family. Land is theirs. Bought with sweat and blood." That said, Bruce Tweedy passed Melvin Kennedy without slowing down. "Suppose you want to talk to the sheriff."

Lyle shrugged. "Whatever for? If that shot was any closer, I would, though." Tweedy jerked his head into a nod. "Think we need to look at the courthouse records, however. Drop us off there."

Tweedy did, then disappeared in the direction of the Coffee Maid Café.

Chapter Ten

Before we climbed the courthouse steps, Lyle called the police to report a man walking into town that seemed to have car trouble. He nodded once, then hung up. "That should take care of our responsibility for Melvin Kennedy."

When we stood in front of the county clerk, Mrs. Peebles stared at us over her black framed readers. "You're not the only people looking at the land grants after the Revolution. Made several copies recently."

"Who were they for?"

"Man from Lexington said he was your Meemaw's real estate agent. Had a signed paper stating so."

My face went from smile to scowl. "I don't think so."

She shook her head and muttered, "So, they weren't for your Meemaw. I should have called your folks to check on it."

Lyle tapped his forefinger on the faded paperwork. "Could it have been a man named Smothers? Small mustache, little eyes?" She nodded. "Who else requested copies?"

"Kennedy of course, since they were working together." She looked at me over her glasses. "Or maybe they weren't. I assumed they were because the man said Kennedy had sent him my way." She took her glasses off and chewed on the earpiece. "And there was a dark-haired fellow who came in." She shook her head as if to rattle something loose. "Can't recall his name. I'll have it written down in the books. Give me a minute. Oh," she turned to look at us. "You want copies, too?"

"Yes, please." I sounded like a school girl.

Mrs. Peebles returned with a red ledger in her hands. She plopped her glasses back on her face and ran her finger over the month of September. "Ah, yes. You think I'd recall that name. Lewis, Gerald. He said,

"Just call me Jerry, like my friends do, then winked." Mrs. Peebles tossed us a half-smile. "You know, Jerry Lewis the comedian."

Lyle smiled with her. "Of course. Easy to remember. What did this comedian look like?"

"Very handsome. Blue-black hair with gray on the sides above his ears. He had big blue eyes and," she put her hands to her cheeks, "he…well…wondered if I was busy after work." Her cheeks behind her fingers were blazing fuchsia.

"He has good taste," Lyle said.

"I told him I had to get home to feed the chickens. Can you imagine! That just popped out of my mouth." She bit her lip.

"So you made him copies?"

"No. He wasn't authorized."

Lyle whipped out a picture of Smothers, the dead man. Mrs. Peebles turned as white as the printer papers she shuffled, even though it wasn't from the crime scene but from his passport photo.

"That's him." She tapped the picture. "I saw his photo in the Lexington paper. Said he was shot over at the fancy resort near the freeway."

I looked her square in the eye. "Did you call the police to tell them he'd been here?"

"Why should I? He'd simply come in to ask about some land."

Something didn't add up because after she knew Smothers was murdered, she should have called the police. Before I could say anything, Lyle took my hand in his. "Delilah's family needs some information about the land off Clay Pigeon road."

"You and about fifty others."

"Names," Lyle said.

"The Robinsons for one. And the Henrys. They came marching in here last week and said somebody was cutting pines in the forest. They asked if there was a permit given. I said it wasn't my department." She sniffed and looked at the big wall clock ticking away time. "Then, they said they needed to look over the land survey for the places off Clay Pigeon."

Doreen Peebles was tap dancing around. All she had to do was tell us straight out who'd been asking about the land. "Did they get copies too?"

She scowled over her glasses. "Of course not. They do have the right to look at the plats so I let them take a peek. Nothing wrong with that." Her voice rose as she crossed her arms.

Lyle nodded agreement as he spread out the fragile papers. "The land grant papers seem in order," he said as he folded them up. "Any letters, or court documents pertaining to this parcel?"

"Yes. A lawsuit was filed back in the fifties by the Ferris family. I wouldn't know about it except that man, Smothers, found the papers."

"We'd like to see them as well."

She huffed her way to the files. A blue folder was slapped down in front of Lyle like a dueling glove across a face. It beat me what had gotten her knickers in a knot.

Lyle flipped open the folder. It was empty. He lifted one curved eyebrow.

Mrs. Peebles leaned close to the file as if she'd missed something. "Well...the papers were there...I swear. I saw it not a month ago."

Lyle closed the baby blue file and put it into her hands. "Where can we find the Ferris family?"

She sniffed again, this time her eyes narrowed. "By the bunch of grain silos near the coal tracks."

The rain was misty and dampened our faces as we walked down the courthouse stairs. I glanced skyward. The sun would set in two hours. Being at the middle of the eastern time zone meant the days were shorter and sunlight scant in November.

Lyle spied Kennedy climbing out of the sheriff's car

and waved. Kennedy didn't see us. He was jabbing his finger in the sheriff's shirt front and talking so loudly we could hear him across the street. I only saw the sheriff's broad back, but the man had his hat pushed back and was scratching the top of his head.

We kept walking. A block from the Ferris place we knew why the county clerk had sniffed. The Ferrises raised pigs. According to the red sign painted on the silo beside their barn, giant hogs served up at the Bluegrass Barbecue competition were housed there.

The place was tidy. A vegetable garden gleaned, turned, and hidden under straw. The house bore fresh white paint. We walked up stairs recently swept from the look of them and knocked on a shiny red door.

A face peeked from behind a curtain beside us then slowly the door opened. I squealed as I recognized the woman in the pink exercise outfit.

"Missy Newland?" I reached out for a hug.

My classmate from high school hesitated then stepped onto the porch and flung her arms around my neck. "Haven't seen you since the reunion ten years ago." She backed up, keeping her mahogany hands on my shoulders. She looked me up and down as if I were a prized porker ready for market. "You're looking mighty fit considering your loss. I'm so sorry about your Harry."

"Me too." I gulped not knowing how to introduce Lyle. He did it for me by thrusting out his hand to shake hers.

"Lyle Henderson." His dimple flashed. "I'm helping Delilah with her Meemaw's farm. Her grandmother is in the hospital."

"This the one?" Missy crossed her arms and stared Lyle straight in the eyes.

"Yes. Lyle and I married a few days ago."

"Whole town's heard about it. Causing quite a flap. Rumor has it, Harry set it up."

Lyle and I synchronized our nods like the Olympic swimming team.

Missy grinned. "I should talk. Married Tyler Ferris

as soon as he asked, which was five years and six months ago. We had to off load a couple of spouses since high school before we were eligible, though." Missy had been married three or four times. I'd lost track over the years.

"Come in out of the mist." She opened the door wide and nearly shoved us through.

I turned to her in the tiny hallway. "Our class was small but I don't remember a Ferris."

"Ferrises have been here since early 1800's. Same as my ancestors. The family left in the seventies and were in Richmond for years then moved back."

I'd never thought of slavery in Missy's heritage. Her daddy had worked in the coal mines as had her grandfather. We'd become friends while in high school manning the labeling line at the creamery. We'd spoken of our dreams, boys, and sung a few songs together. She had a nice soprano.

Missy's kind smile was welcoming. "Don't stand there leaking rain water all over my floors, come sit. How about a cup of coffee to warm us up? You're a judge I hear. Friend of Harry's. Everyone I suppose was a friend of Harry's. He was that kind of man."

Missy waved us into the parlor. There was a fire shooting heat into the room. We backed up to it and steamed. This wasn't a parlor dressed for company but a work station with a wall for her computer desk, files, bookshelves, and electronic equipment lit up and charging.

I put my hand on Missy's arm to stop her disappearing into the kitchen. "Coffee would be too much of a bother, Missy. We've come to ask a couple of questions. There seems to be a dispute about the Burns land and there might be another owner claiming property along the river. Thought I'd ask your husband about it. Their family had been living on the property, I believe."

"Tyler's daddy would be the one to ask. That's my

husband's name too. He's named after his daddy, Tyler James Augustus Ferris." Her voice filled with pride when she spoke his name. Last time she'd talked about a husband it had been at the reunion. Her tone had been as dry as a desert wind. I smiled for her. Maybe this one was a keeper. The others had either disappeared with the hook in their mouths from another woman or Missy had landed them and after a year or two had thrown them back into the dating stream.

Lyle's eyes wandered to the wall of twenty-first century communication devices. Missy waved at the set up. "For our business. We ship our pork among other things."

Lyle nodded. "Where can we reach your husband?"

"He'll be home in a few minutes. Finishes at the shop about now. If you don't want coffee, I do. Will you excuse me while I get a cup?"

We stayed rooted by the fire. "We're not getting anywhere," I whispered.

"You have somewhere to go?"

"You know what I mean."

"Is there a hotel around here? Your Meemaw's farmhouse will be cold and we don't have food for supper."

"I'll make a phone call." I trotted to the porch and dialed my sister. "Do you have a B&B available for two wanderers?"

Suzanne laughed. "A daddy bird chirped and said you're headed my way. All set for you and your hunk of a husband."

When Tyler Ferris appeared, I thought he resembled a muscled GQ model even though he covered up in plain gray carpenter pants and a burgundy leather jacket.

After handshakes and what he called a proper

greeting for his wife—a kiss that could fuel moon rockets—he turned to face us. "What brings a Burns onto Ferris land?" His voice didn't hold bitterness, but it was tense.

"Some questions." My hands got active and began to rub together. Lyle took them in his to calm the agitation. "I've become aware that there was a promise given to your family."

"There was."

I frowned. "A notarized letter disappeared from the courthouse that may shed light on the promise. Would your family happen to have a copy?"
 He crossed his thick arms. "They would."

He was a man of short sentences. "May I have a copy?"

"Why?"

"I don't think my Meemaw wants to go to her grave knowing wrong has been done in her name." I stumbled over the word grave and Lyle's hand lightly pressed mine.

"A Burns with a conscience?"

"A Burns wanting to rectify a wrong, if one has been done."

"No ifs about it." Tyler Ferris's voice rumbled like a locomotive pulling a load. Missy Ferris placed a hand on her husband's arm. He cleared his throat. "I'll get the papers." He turned his back and went to the files under the computer desk. Thumbing through a drawer he unearthed a red folder and handed it to his wife.

Missy turned to her copy machine. "I'll make a copy."

As Tyler Ferris marched back to us, he thrust his hands into his pockets. "Don't mind my manners. Someone has stirred a hornet's nest of late. You're not the only one interested in broken promises."

The papers Missy handed me said it all. The land had been given to Samuel Burns Ferris. Not promised. After the Civil War someone at the courthouse mislaid the notarized papers, then the local sheriff evicted the

Ferris family from their home of twenty years. All the facts were written in a small tidy hand with schoolmarm cursive. I bit back the questions bubbling up. Now was not the time but my anger was rising at the injustice.

"Would you mind if I take these and speak with Meemaw?"

"Won't do any good. The powers that be around here have already decided we aren't fit to polish their boots."

Lyle handed me his handkerchief as the tears eased from the corners of my eyes. Missy wrapped her arms around me. "Not your fault, Delilah. You and your family haven't seen people's color, only their hearts."

I shook my head. "A wrong has been done. Would you pray with me about it?"

Both of their mouths flew open, but Missy kept her arms around me, and Lyle grabbed hold of Tyler's hand. We commenced to seek the face of the Lord about the season for building and not tearing down. A season of forgiveness.

Chapter Eleven

THERE WAS SO MUCH TO SAY to Lyle but I didn't have words. We'd soon be at Meemaw's to water the plants and all I could do was hold his hand and blow my nose as the road wound like a coiled snake through the trees. Lyle didn't speak either as night shadows hovered over the mountains, waiting.

He hadn't talked much since we finished praying. I think he was ruminating on what Tyler said as we headed toward the door. "All the reparations in the world won't make up for a whip across the back of my great-great-grandfather. No one from this generation is owed a dime. The generation who suffered are the one's owed and God is repaying them with His glory."

"Reconciliation is lasting. Reparations will be spent at the nearest casino," Missy added as we walked toward town. Our arms were around one another's waists like they had been when we were young.

No eyebrows were raised as we slow walked to the car even though the Holly brothers were loading their pickup at the feed store on the corner by the tracks. They'd lifted their baseball caps and nodded as we passed. Mama once said they'd been the orneriest pair she'd ever taught. Always fighting and swearing. Now, they smiled and nodded as if at peace with the world.

"In an ideal world," I heard Lyle say, "men would see beyond the façade and get to the truth of a matter."

"But this world is skewed, and we don't," Tyler said.

Pulling into the farm road leading to the house, I thought I spied lights on at Meemaw's. Did Daddy install a timer for her porch light? That would be odd. The house had knob and tube wiring, which Meemaw refused to update. "Too expensive, because you have to re-drywall to get to all the wires," she'd said one Thanksgiving. "And I'd have to hire someone to do it cause you," she looked at my father, "refuse to let me even climb a ladder."

A car was pulled up in front of the porch. Not any car but the Sheriff's judging from the blue printing on the side. A uniformed man stood on the porch and flashed a light into our eyes. A sleek dog stood beside him. The dog was brown-headed with a coat of liver and white. Its dark ears went skyward as Lyle screeched to a halt. Lyle got out of the car with his hands above his head, because a gun was leveled at him. The dog's eyes were glued our direction. "Easy, Browning," said the man with the badge.

"We're here to check on Mrs. Burns's plants," Lyle said as he took a step forward.

"You a real estate man from the city?" the Sheriff shot back. The dog lifted his nose and sniffed the air.

I gulped when I recognized the voice. "Derek?" I said as I opened the car door. I was not thrilled to see Derek Sullivan. In fact, I'd like to hightail it back to McKeansville and skip the introductions because I saw trouble on the horizon.

"That you, Delilah?" He didn't sound surprised. He sounded happy. The dog cocked his head and relaxed his posture.

"Here with my husband Lyle to check on the house." I hoped that would stop Derek from saying anything inappropriate.

Sheriff Derek Sullivan shuffled his feet on the porch floor. "Heard about that. Pretty soon to get remarried, don't you think?" Derek reached down and scratched behind his dog's ears.

I didn't comment because it would lead to questions and I didn't want any questions. Derek was the only boy I'd kissed before Harry and that had been on the stage in a school play. Derek had written a week after Harry died and asked to come for a visit. My mail arrived at nine-thirty-five. I'd sent a letter back before noon suggesting he wait until I visited my folks.

And here I was.

With a new husband in tow.

"Guess I waited too long, Delilah," Derek said as he stepped off the porch. He holstered his gun and stood straddle legged in front of Lyle. He didn't shake Lyle's hand. "You got the prettiest girl in the mountains and you'd better treat her good or I'll come calling." With that threat hanging in the air, he pointed to the house. "You the pair that was with Kennedy when he got shot at?"

Lyle leveled his eyes at the sheriff. Lyle's gaze had made grown men stutter.

Derek Sullivan sucked in his belly.

"Yes." Lyle's glowering eyebrows threatened to fly off his face.

"Kennedy seems to think you're looking for property around here."

I stepped between Derek and Lyle because their words were growing testy. "He thought that, yes. We came to help Meemaw settle something in her mind and care for her house plants. We've been in contact with the FBI about it. Special Agent Madison can be reached in Lexington if you care to contact him."

Derek stepped back a good foot. "No need for the Feds to get involved."

One of Lyle's eyebrows lowered from threatening to warning. "They already are. Perhaps you'd be willing to answer a few questions for us."

"Certainly." He removed his police cap and wiped his brow. "Whew. A federal case, you say? What are they looking for?"

Lyle smiled his lazy smile. The one that said, 'I've got your number and we're in for a merry ride.' "Tying a murder in Lexington to a shady land deal here in Owsley County."

Derek Sullivan rubbed his hands together like Fagan counting his riches. "Think Kennedy is involved? He hasn't been around here long. Bought the company from the Pervis family when the old man up and died. Paid cash. A lot of cash from what I hear. I can see Kennedy doing something shady. He's got no family around here and takes off for Lexington or who knows where most weekends." Derek rocked back on his heels with satisfaction.

Same thing he'd done at seventeen when the play director had left our 'private' rehearsal —apart from the cast—and Derek had grabbed me and kissed me like a starving man. He'd smiled like a jerk and rocked back on his heels. That was until I slapped him so hard, he fell on his behind and his ear rang for a couple of days. I'd never told Harry. Some things are best forgotten. I'm sorry that image was cavorting in my head.

"About the shooting this afternoon," I said, trying to erase the image of Derek having a stern talk from my daddy. "Seems the shot came from the woods. Probably someone aiming at a treed opossum. Shot was high. Think it hit several feet above Kennedy's head."

Derek nodded. "That's what I thought." He pointed toward the fascia board along the roof of the porch.

Lyle's gaze followed Derek's finger. "We need to check on Meemaw's house. Would you like to accompany us?" Lyle waited as Derek chewed on his lip.

Derek drew his gun. "I'll go first. There might be an intruder. Come, Browning." He tucked in his chin and looked me straight in the eye. "Stay behind me, Delilah, for protection." When he couldn't see me, I rolled my eyes at Lyle. Mounting the steps my hand gripped the familiar handrail. The one Papaw had replaced when I was small. It had been smoothed by the years and felt just right. Momentarily I closed my eyes and sensed his presence. I could almost hear his deep laugh.

The dog sniffed at the metal sculpture of a cat that sat by the door. It was fashioned out of garden trowels and salvage yard gleanings. It hadn't been there in the summer when I'd visited. With a whisk of its stubby tail, the dog led the way into Meemaw's dark house. Derek paused to study the nuts and bolts that kept the art piece together, then followed his dog. Never knew Meemaw to like statues but this one suited the place with its tail lifted high in a self-righteous pose.

We went top to bottom in Meemaw's small, two-story house. The wash cloth draped over the faucet in the kitchen made me pause. Meemaw had a blue cup and her matching teapot in the drainer, and her bottle of dish soap by the cold-water handle. She'd left in a hurry. My tidy grandmother always put things away. I smiled. Our wedding had been a hurry up affair, and she'd thrown things into a suitcase and booked it to McKeansville.

Nothing in the blue and white decorated house seemed amiss. The plants were depleted of H2O, however, which I applied. I locked the front door. "We need to head home soon to see to her." Derek nodded as solemnly as a funeral parlor director.

When we drove away, I looked at Lyle's chiseled jaw and smiled. "Sullivan is an Irish name. You think he's mixed up with the O'Neal real estate people?"

Lyle shook his head. "Let's not jump into the slough of suspicion until we've concrete facts. But he did try to point the finger at Kennedy. Also an Irish name, by the way." Twilight grayed the asphalt as we climbed higher into the mountains. Lyle's lips twisted up as if he was about to laugh. "Sullivan seems fond of you, which I consider a recommendation of the man. Has good taste."

I coughed into my hand and quickly looked out the window.

"You don't seem overly fond of him, though."

"I suppose I've an attitude about my former

classmate."

"And the reason is?" Lyle took Deadman's Corner too fast and I made a teeny squeak. He stepped on the brake to slow.

"Er. Experience."

"Ah." Lyle glanced at me then quickly focused back to the road as a hairpin turn emerged. "If I recall your parents' farm is nearby."

I nodded. "Yes. The road on the right of the next curve."

"Think I saw the falls once when I was up here with Harry. We were hunting on the other side of the river. Can we stop to look?"

"In my sister's driveway. It has the best view."

The lights from Suzanne's sleek house winked through the oaks and green pines as we went around the last bend before entering the falls area. The tiny community consisted of a road with a few scattered houses. When founded in 1815 the town had dreams. They evaporated like dew in July and the larger community had absconded with the name. We were an adjunct berg of five houses, no stores, closed gas station, no pizza delivery. The falls were a block from Main street, the only paved street.

Suzanne's modern home was perched across from the cataract and twenty feet below its top. She had a perfect view. Drawing nearer, the thunder of the water carving out the mountainside rumbled through a body. Horsetail Falls arched into a high curve and splashed on the rocky cliffs as it descended. We'd lived a mile from the cataract and as kids, on hot summer days, swam downstream in a pool of nearly still water.

My sister chose this quiet spot after her fiancé died in the Gulf War and built a one-story modern bungalow. 'It gives me breathing room,' was all she'd said when she'd purchased the property. Her international reputation impinged on her time now, but this was her sanctuary and where her paintings were birthed.

As we topped the hill, the sun splintered bronze fire on the top of the trees before sinking behind a western ridge. Lyle grabbed a breath. "Can you imagine seeing *that* every day?" Lyle parked the car in her drive then climbed out and stepped close to the fence Suzanne built to keep out interlopers. Peering over the side of the drop off he shook his head and said something the wind carried away.

The boiling water was so loud you couldn't hear birds chirrup. "What?" I shouted as I came to stand with him. The falls disappeared into the ink dark shadows of the cliff face.

"The bottom is hidden. How deep?"

I studied the foaming water. "Sixty-seven feet."

"I'll get a glimpse in the morning."

Turning to troop up the stairs to greet my sister, I caught an aura of light haloing the cliff edge. It had been Harry's favorite vista. I swallowed a lump and followed Lyle.

Lyle made the rounds of Suzanne's newest paintings before dinner. "Why the interest in landscapes? They seem fraught with difficulty. Lighting must be a challenge, for in a moment everything can change."

"My mountain paintings seem to draw people in. I've painted the falls dozens of times, but never from the same perspective, season, or time of day. It's as if creation is a living, breathing thing. The way the light bathes the water is always unique. Early morning, the sun hits the west face of the rocks and turns them white as ice in winter. In summer they are warm pink. The falls have a symphony of movements."

"I don't see any portraits."

"Only of horses. You need to see into someone's soul in a good portrait. For me they must be still for it to be exposed and I love capturing motion. If I could paint people's backs, muscles rippling from exertion, instead of their faces I'd be happy." She rubbed her thumb across her forehead. "Harry understood the poetry of landscapes. He used words to describe them. I use color value, placement of objects, and forcing the viewer to see light."

Suzanne's house was cozy with the kitchen and gathering space oddly in between the two bedrooms. With the bedrooms separated by several rooms, it made for privacy which Suzanne prized. However, because of her isolation cell phone connection was tricky. "Stand by the window near the fireplace. The one that faces the falls if you need to use your phone," she said as she shooed us toward the kitchen. "I prefer my landline." She did have internet but it was sometimes down when the winds tore the connecting cable from its nest.

Dinner was her usual mix of small salad, fruit, and cheese. We ate in the kitchen. It was a comfortable spot with a scattering of the old farm's bits hanging on the walls and holding court on the counter like Meemaw's bean pot that had been handed down since the nineteenth century.

Suzanne shrugged as she settled into her seat. "I hate to cook when my head is buzzing with ideas." She and Lyle enjoyed a glass of wine.

I peacefully sipped my ice tea until Lyle said, "Think I met a friend of the family this afternoon."

"Oh?" said my sister.

"Your local sheriff."

I spit the tea out of my mouth and had to wipe it up with Suzanne's damask napkin.

Suzanne began to laugh. "So, Delilah told you about Derek? She never would tell Harry. That was a funny story and it set a precedent. Daddy wouldn't let me try out for any plays after 'that Sullivan boy' as he was called by the men in the house, assaulted Delilah."

"Hmm," was Lyle's comment.

Suzanne looked at me from over her glass of Riesling. "You didn't tell him, did you?"

I refolded my napkin and sighed. "No."

"Allow me." Suzanne waved one arm in the air like a maestro cueing his orchestra. "You may correct me if needed but I rather like my version. It's *very* dramatic." My sister leaned close to Lyle. "Delilah was in a school play her senior year. She was the female lead, Derek the hero, although I'd say he was miscast. Derek was and still is a bit of a jerk. There was a kiss in the third act. Sort of like those Hallmark movies where the kiss happens about a minute before the end. Anyway, they had to practice. Derek talked his friend Iggie Jepson into getting the director out of the room so he could *really* kiss Delilah. I guess he did lay one on her. It was really something. He massaged her lips with his and next thing Derek knew he was on the floor. She'd whacked him so hard he fell down."

So far, she'd told the truth but a smidge embellished. Derek hadn't put his hands on any place that was taboo, just his lips.

"Then, Delilah stormed out of the room and called Daddy. It took only five minutes for Daddy to get to the school and corner Derek. If Mr. Foster the director hadn't intervened it's said Derek wouldn't have gotten only a lecture but a trip to the visiting nurse facility."

"I see," said Lyle sitting back and watching me fidget.

"That's not all. The principal got involved and found out there was a wager on who would kiss prissy Miss Burns first."

Lyle's eyebrows rose. "Ah. A bet about Delilah." He scratched his chin. "Someplace I've heard that before."

"Nice cheese, Suzanne." I held up a triangle of white. "What kind is it?"

"Havarti, but don't change the subject, Delilah. I'm getting to the good part." She stared into my eyes. I dropped my gaze and studied my plate. Suzanne's voice held laughter but I wasn't going to look at her for the life of me. I was too embarrassed. "I had to sit in on all the rest of the rehearsals because Daddy said, 'That pup Sullivan is going to try something else. Watch and see.' And he did."

Lyle shook his head, slowly. "You don't say."

"Last performance of the show on Saturday night he swings Delilah into his arms, dips her like a movie star and plants a kiss on her lips that you could hear. Daddy jumped up from his seat and if Mama hadn't restrained him Derek would have been flattened. And you should have heard the cat calls and cheering. It was like thunder."

"Very interesting," said my groom. "And the lesson learned was?"

"Daddy watched me like a hawk and Delilah didn't go to her senior prom because all the boys in the class were terrified of Daddy and my big brothers."

"A childhood fraught with conflict. Ah, Di. I had no idea." Lyle's dimples flashes as he grinned.

When we headed for bed, Lyle swept me into his arms and carried me into the bedroom. "Lyle, what are you doing?"

"I always liked the scene in *Gone with the Wind* with Scarlett in Rhett's arms. Get used to it, sweetheart."

It looked like there was a lot of 'getting used to it' with Lyle Henderson.

Chapter Twelve

MY FEET HIT A COLD SPOT on the sheets. I sat up. Light brightened the bottom edge of the window curtain. Lyle was already out of bed and gone. I threw on my jeans, shirt, and boots and went on a hunt for my groom. He was in the living room ogling the waterfall. The low, misty clouds had fled during the night and the sun shed light on the top of the falls. The descending water glittered like Christmas. Lyle's phone aimed toward the window creating a video of the cataract as it boiled into the thin stream of Draper's Creek. I put my arms around his waist and gave him a good morning squeeze.

"And good morning to you, Mrs. Henderson." His whole body vibrated every time he spoke. I didn't let go but held onto him with my head on his back, soaking in the warmth of him. His resonance was something I loved, because his words wrapped around me like his tender caress.

"How long have you been up?"

"A couple of hours. I've lists for what we need to do next. I believe you approve of lists?" Lyle disentangled himself from my clutch, took me in his arms and eased me back until my head looked at the ceiling. "Heard you liked action kissing." He planted one on my lips and stayed there massaging them until I got dizzy. "Ah," he muttered. "That's what *I* call a kiss." He stood me up, shook his head as if to clear it, and turned toward the kitchen. "Coming?" Lyle aimed for the coffee pot. "Suzanne mentioned this morning that your father and Tyler Ferris Senior were friends. Thought I'd make a phone call or two."

I trotted after him like a lap dog.

The day would have continued in its essence of harmony if Derek Sullivan hadn't driven his police car into view then hammered on the door. Lyle rose to answer. I exhaled a worried breath.

"I've plans," Derek announced as he and his furry companion entered.

Lyle stood before the sheriff with his mobile eyebrows lifted. "What sort of plans?"

"Why to protect this community from interlopers. I've been thinking, there must be a connection with Kennedy and the dead man in Lexington." Derek rubbed the back of his neck and looked up at Lyle's 6'3" frame. "I've been making lists." His canine guard leaned against Derek's leg.

Lyle smiled. Maybe because they had something in common. He went to the dining room table where we'd been sitting and pointed to his legal sized piece of paper with tight writing, bullet points, and numbers. He slid it toward Derek. "Why don't we compare?"

Derek shook his head. "No need. I've got it right up here." He tapped his forehead.

The kitchen door swung open and a cold wind skittered Lyle's paper to the floor. Suzanne wiped her paint splotched fingers on a paper towel "I thought I heard a car pull in. Want a cup of coffee, Derek?"

"Don't mind if I do." His eyes went from Suzanne to me then back to Suzanne. "I'd forgotten how much you two looked alike. Could be identical twins." He shook his head. "Good thing you resemble your mama." He picked up Lyle's paper and with it clutched in his hand, followed her into the kitchen. The tip tap of his dog's feet crossed the floor.

"Is this a German short-haired pointer?" Suzanne asked.

"Yep. Good hunting dog. Finds deer as well as other varmints." Derek laughed.

Lyle lifted his eyebrows and produced a second copy of his list from his jacket pocket. He waved it in front of me. "Always have a copy of your copy. Now, first things first. I need to call Mr. Ferris." Lyle headed toward the picture window overlooking the falls. Standing behind the leather lounge chair had the best reception for our cells.

With two conversations competing with one another I grabbed Lyle's list and stared at it. The bullet points had people's names listed and questions after them. In the center of the page was a large circle. The center said, 'Location, Horsetail Falls/Meemaw. Another circle surrounded it. The words, 'Who owns the land? Who has debts? What gained if sold?' were tightly written. The third circle said, 'Who wants it and why? Where is the paperwork? Was it stolen in Lexington?' The last circle was divided into pie shaped wedges. 'Who, What, When, Where, Why, and How' were placed in separate triangles.

The questions stopped me cold. Who? A family member? I flipped the paper over and wrote a list of relations who could claim the land. Second and third cousins, uncles, a couple of widowed aunts. How could we find out if they are desperate for money? I bit my lip. Most people in Appalachia were desperate for money. People had been vacating the place since before the First World War.

What? The land. But it was worthless, hard to get to, and although Meemaw saw that with horse manure it became fertile, even Draper's Creek didn't have enough brown trout to make a fish camp. There must be something, because somebody wanted the land. Or did they simply intend to harm the family? Take the land in revenge for long ago wrongs?

Before I got to when, Lyle arrived at the same time Derek emerged from the kitchen. "Great coffee, Suzanne. Tastes as good as the Coffee Maid's."

"It should. It's the same type." Suzanne used her dry voice that said Sheriff Derek bored her.

Derek crossed to the rough stone fireplace and gazed up at a painting of the falls. The dog's head craned upward, mimicking his master. "I've been studying your paintings. You capture the light and make us focus on it like a magician does. Then, ta-da. You do your trick of making us want to stay staring at it. The observer glances left and sees a bird in flight, or right and notices the colors of the dawn. Makes me think of that poem by Francis Scott Key. "By the Dawn's early light," he wrote. My favorite part of the whole poem."

I closed my mouth that had dropped open but Suzanne's remained agape and her eyes widened with astonishment. "I didn't know you liked paintings, Derek."

"Oh, yes. They speak to the heart. Urges me to climb up into the cliff face and see that eagle nest you've hidden there. I do that, you know. Climb." He pointed to the right of the falls. I squinted my eyes. I'd never noticed the nest before, but there it was, nestled in the lichen out of reach of the water.

Lyle smiled his lazy smile. The one that said his mind was on overdrive. "Where do you suggest we begin, Sheriff?"

"At the beginning. When did someone come here and start asking about the property? Next, trace that forward to the murder in Lexington. We'll need a time line. Might as well set things up here. My office is the size of a coat closet." He glanced at Suzanne. "Where can we spread out?"

"My studio. Delilah, don't you do a time line when you write?"

"Absolutely. It keeps things in order."

Suzanne laughed. "Which Delilah must have, because without order she begins to get hives." She raised her eyebrows as she swiveled her head to catch Lyle's expression. When he shrugged, she shook her head.

I crossed my arms and ignored them. "We'll get a string and hang it, clip note cards on with events, people, etc., and get started."

A bemused expression was on Lyle's face as he looked from Derek, to Suzanne, to me. "You three remind me of when I was a JAG lawyer. Nothing like a team to get things in order." He rubbed his hands together, seemingly eager to start.

Looking at Lyle I smiled. "Lyle what happened with your phone call?"

"It went as expected. Mr. Ferris said he'd given up hope about the land and because the property was going to be your daddy's he saw no reason to interfere. He and his son run a metal shop down by the tracks, as well as the hog farm. What do they do, repair cars?"

Derek shook his head. "Not that simple. They repair whatever comes in, tractors, trucks, appliances. On the side they make things. Lamps out of old telephones, garden art, stuff they collect and as they call it, 'repurpose.' Heard they sell their things through a catalog."

Suzanne tossed a warm wool jacket my way. "Follow me, y'all," she said. Lyle flung on his coat and Sullivan hitched up the collar on his uniform. Icy wind swirled between the house and Suzanne's studio, which was a small barn built in the early nineteen-hundreds. It still had weathered siding on the outside, but the inside was now insulated, heated, and air conditioned. She'd created an open space where large windows and skylights carried light to the far corners and track lighting hung from the ceilings as tidily as ropes and tackle had in the past.

Browning sniffed the air then wagged his docked tail, his behind doing a Latin American rhythm. There was a hint of snow in the air. It wouldn't snow here in early November, although it might threaten. Late November and December is when snow falls. I didn't want to be trapped up in the mountains when Meemaw might need us.

I frowned.

Our honeymoon had evaporated.

Suzanne turned toward us. "With Missy owning the old creamery and being computer savvy, she is turning her company and her husband's company into lucrative enterprises." The wind caught Suzanne's words and tossed them into the air. "She always was good with numbers and after her divorce from John Kettering Callaway, she bought the creamery, redesigned it and started creating specialty products. But you know about that, Delilah."

"Actually, I don't."

Suzanne slid open the weathered door she had for the entrance. The dog pushed in before her and circled the perimeter of the room as if scouting for enemies. Browning didn't look like he'd cotton to sitting by the fire with his springy step and alert dark eyes.

The vast room didn't have the scent of turpentine that she'd once used to clean her brushes. It simply smelled of the rich, spicy aroma of paint. I took a whiff. The scent reminded me of her at twelve, hunched over a table, face intense, creating a painting of our cat.

Suzanne glanced at her audience. "Why, I guess you haven't been caught up on our sleepy little burg. Missy put the town on the map. Been eight, nine years, maybe. She got the locals to make specialty foods. People clear to California buy Mountain Laurel Honey and cheeses made with spices. Has about thirty products listed in a catalog for food. Quilters make potholders and baby quilts, knitters make layettes. A whole industry erupted from Missy Newland's vision of local people finding work for their hands and minds."

"So things are turning around here financially." I chewed on my lip. "Do you get tourists?"

"More and more. Wouldn't you say, Derek? I've even sold paintings in the little gallery next to the Coffee Maid. Look, I need to get back to work. It's a commissioned piece I want out of here by Thanksgiving. Derek, you can work on that table." Suzanne pointed toward a picnic table near the north wall. Even though she teased me about being orderly, Suzanne's entire studio was neat as a pin. Paint brushes stood at attention in their assigned places. Like the dolls in her room lined up in order of height, Suzanne demanded a precise placement of her tools so she could create. Good thing she'd never had kids. Or maybe it wasn't.

My groom began to smile. I wanted to say, all the Burns women are tidy. Meemaw's vegetables are set out in lines the Marine Corps would envy, but I held my tongue as Derek Sullivan meandered through the room as if lost in a foreign market. He'd point to something in a painting then not say a word. Suzanne moved to her largest easel and ignored his slow walk through her studio.

Lyle reached for my hand and pulled me toward the door. "Tyler Ferris Sr. said something interesting. He said two men came to their shop in September claiming he owned land down by Draper's Creek. When Ferris said he didn't, they produced a legal looking document that said the land belonged to the Ferris family since 1869. They handed him a copy. He said we could come take a look. 'Even my son doesn't know about *that* visit. Wasn't important to dredge up lost promises.'"

Different paper than the one his son had given us?

Sullivan was still riveted to the paintings when we turned back. When he heard us moving, he turned his face our way and cleared his throat. "Need some string." He scouted around the room until Suzanne pointed with her brush to a peg board crammed with scissors, tape, circles of different size cord, string, and wire. Sullivan attached a brown braided cord to a hook on the peg board and the other end to a window latch. I went to the house to hunt through the laundry closet for clothes pins. Suzanne had a stack of computer paper sitting on her desk and I tore them into strips, and headed back.

Waiting by the studio door was Lyle, eyes flitting from the sun disappearing behind a cloud and changing the light, to the waterfall. "When the sun disappears the spray no longer gleams."

"You like this place," I said.

"I like *you* in this place. I'm trying to picture you as a child. Pigtails? Freckles? Long legs pumping as you ran into the woods? Am I close?"

"Spot on," I said in a phony British accent. "Now Mr.

Henderson, let's fill out a few slips of paper then hit the road."

Tyler Ferris Sr., 'call me T.J.,' was a sturdy, smiling man who shook our hands and waved us into his shop—a converted service station. Two car bays were crammed with metal bits, work benches, and welding tools. A hodge-podge of junk to my untrained eye, but when we passed into the old shop with ranks of refrigerator shelves still mounted on two walls, I craned my neck. The space was gift shop pristine. Yard art didn't quite describe the fountains, metal sculptures, and tools displayed like a department store window.

"Sorry you missed my son. He and our assistant are on their way to Richmond to deliver new products to one of our other stores. We like to keep things here moving and uncluttered."

"Amazing," Lyle said as he picked up a brass telephone lamp and lifted the black, bake-lite receiver and the light illumined. A phone from the thirties maybe. Something you'd see in a movie.

An hour later, we were half-way down the mountain, a copy of Mr. Ferris's paperwork in the back seat and a carefully wrapped old telephone lamp, when Lyle's cell phone rang. Looking surprised that it picked up in the mountains, he answered by speaking into a Bluetooth.

He waited, shrugged and disconnected. "Too much interference. If they want me badly enough, they will try again." We reached Berea at lunch time and drove straight to the Daniel Boone Inn. "Hiding out here might not be a bad idea," he muttered as he looked over the uninterested diners. I had taken two bites from my salad when Lyle's phone rang again. He glanced at it, raised his eyebrows and threw his napkin on the table top. 'Have to take this,' he mouthed before striding out of the room.

He returned with a sour look. I leaned close to him. "Well?"

"That was your father. Meemaw is at your house and has called a lawyer friend of mine George recommended. Seems someone visited her at the hospital. Someone named O'Neal."

"Neely Patrick?" My voice shook.

"A look-a-like cousin. He slid into the room when your father was hunting up some breakfast. Told Meemaw that she was about to be sued for breach of contract but didn't want her to worry because he had an idea." Lyle paused as our main course arrived, a platter of food that would serve a football team. I raised an eyebrow, waiting.

"*If* she would allow his company to represent her, he'd get the land deed re-registered in her name instead of a man named Ferris. Your Meemaw pushed the call button and a nurse came tearing in because Meemaw hadn't hit the button in the two days she'd been there." Lyle smiled and cut into his steak. "No one in their right mind has the temerity to take on a Burns woman."

"Well, your friend Randall Longworth might try it."

"And fail. Miserably. Eat, Di." He pointed a fork full of food my direction. "We've miles to go before we sleep and I'm a bit peckish about it."

In a shop near Berea College, Lyle's phone interrupted our looking at dulcimers. Shaking my head at another interruption, I listened to the woodworker play "Greensleeves" on an instrument. Watching the store owner's fingers move with balletic grace I jumped when Lyle grabbed my arm. "We have to go," he said with urgency.

My hands formed balls. *If that rogue O'Neal caused Meemaw stress he'll hear it from me.*

Lyle whisked me out the door, and before I could speak, he sprinted down the street to his car. I ran after him. He flung open my door. "I'll explain as we drive."

Lyle peeled out of the parking lot and spit out, "Weldons' daughter, Elise, was accosted after school. She took off running but was grabbed and tossed into a car." That sounded like what had happened to my goddaughter, Savannah. Had another part of the trafficking ring found Elise and taken her again? We had been told by the police that happened.

I cringed as Lyle spoke. "How long ago?"

"Not long, maybe twenty minutes. Sounds like kids from school. Group of them in a couple of cars."

"Remember what the doctor told us when she was found? Victims can become prey. Especially from their peers."

"Di, let's not borrow trouble."

"Oh, Lyle." I grabbed my purse to search for a Kleenex because moisture had invaded my eyes. He handed me a handkerchief. I cried and prayed out loud as we sped down the highway. They were simple prayers because Jesus taught us to pray for our daily bread, so I prayed for the protection, rescue, and the kids who took her to repent before they did any more harm. My tears had dried when Lyle pulled up at the Weldons' farm house. There was a congregation of jeans clad men at the Weldons' back stoop. They turned as one and stared our direction. My groom leaped out of the car and hustled around to open my door before I could bolt.

A uniformed police officer stepped out of the back door, spied Lyle, and waved us in. Lyle, being a renowned judge, must be recognized in more than our county.

Lyle held my hand all the way to the Weldons' entry.

Chapter Thirteen

THE WELDONS STOOD IN THEIR KITCHEN fused together like melted plastic. Everything looked the same as when I'd come with Josephine, tidy and polished to a shine. Even the toaster. But the space was elbow to elbow with the sheriff of Jessamine County, two policemen, and a man twisting his hat into a pretzel.

"Delilah?" Jim Weldon spoke in a voice so choked with tears I felt mine prickling by my eyelashes.

"We're here, Jim," Lyle said, putting his hand on Weldon's shoulder.

"Didn't think it could get worse." His voice shattered into little pieces of words. "Getting her home again, the comfort of it was really something." Jim Weldon rubbed one beefy hand along his jawline and with the other hung onto his petite wife.

My breaths came in tight knots. I stood by their small dining table like a frozen chicken, arms adhered to my sides, legs stuck to the floor. Not a squawk exited my mouth. Neither did words of comfort. I began to wring my hands.

"You came," Evalina Weldon said. All I could do was bob my head. She brushed past Lyle and flung her arms around my neck. "You came," she repeated in a whisper. And we sobbed. The men scurried out to the porch and left us alone in the white kitchen with the linoleum imitation brick floor and the drip of the kitchen faucet.

"God will rescue Elise," Evalina said into the quiet.

"Mmm-hmm," I managed.

"He loves that girl more than I."

I swiped at my wet cheeks and took a deep breath. "Then we'd better remind Him." I dropped to my knees. Holding hands so tight our knuckles turned red we bowed our heads.

"Lord, you know where Elise is right this minute," I started. "You love her so much you wrapped her up like a Christmas present and sent her home. Do it again, Lord and let no harm come to that sweet, little girl."

Evalina gulped. "You brought my lamb home, Lord," she sputtered, "like Josephine prayed. Now she's in trouble. Surround her by your army of angels and send in a David to bring her home. A David to slay the Goliath of fear and evil that surrounds her. A warrior to cause her enemies to flee. You know how she trembled to go to school. How her knees knocked together and sounded like they were made of wood. That's why we sent her to McKeansville for her last year where no one knew her. So, Lord, right now, let her be as brave as Joshua, as fearsome as Jael with the peg, slaying the general. Let her stand up, Lord, and look evil in the eye."

The door to the porch opened bringing in cool November air. Lyle and Jim Weldon looked at us kneeling on the floor and smiled. We could hear cell phones chirruping from the gathering on the porch.

"Sheriff got a call, Evie," Jim said. "Our girl's safe. We're going to meet her at the hospital in McKeansville." He didn't need to say more. We were on our feet and heading for the door before he'd finished.

"Coats," Lyle said as he whipped off two padded jackets from hooks by the door. Lyle thrust the coats into the Weldons' arms and moved aside to let them dash to their car.

A bitter wind swept around us as we left Lyle's car and rushed to the emergency room entrance at McKeansville's hospital. The sour taste of anger swirled in my mouth and lingered on my tongue. Must the innocent bear the scars of their pain? Which again brought me abruptly to the cross.

Innocence hung there.

For me.

I swallowed and tightened my hold on Lyle's hand.

I saw Josephine before she saw me. Her arms were wrapped around Evalina and she was murmuring in Evalina's ear. Jim Weldon was speaking to a lab-coat clad woman. When Weldon saw us, he waved us over, his troubled eyes on Lyle. I stopped by Evalina and kissed her cheek and Josephine's.

The fear in Josephine's dark eyes flickered into a flame. She blinked, took a hesitant breath, and said in a trembling voice, "This is what I thought might happen. People thinking our girls deserve to be treated like trash."

Evalina shook her head so hard Josephine's grip around her loosened. "No. That is not how this is going to be." Evalina's chin lifted and her voice rose until everyone in the E.R. waiting room stared at us. "What people think is no never mind. What we think is what will help our girls. And we think, Jesus can heal. We think Jesus can teach us all a thing or six about loving one another. It starts here." Someone put their hands together and made a sharp clap. Another joined until everyone stood and clapped including the over large nurse checking patients in.

"I need to see my daughter!" Evalina said so loudly I jumped. Evalina Weldon marched up to the woman in the white coat and said, "Are you a doctor?" When the woman nodded, Evaline said, "Now. I need to see my daughter *right this minute*."

The woman smiled. "Follow me, Mr. and Mrs. Weldon." I walked to Lyle and put my hand in his. The doctor turned toward us. "I give up. If it is all right with the Weldons you might as well come too, Lyle. Bellows is with the girl getting a statement."

Lyle followed the Weldons while I sat with Josephine. We held hands, because hers were shaking. "Savannah is fine, Josephine. Please, please don't look back. Today is today, and yesterday's fears are buried."

"They stay with us like a too tight suit that we can't give away."

"Only if we don't clean out the fear closet and let them go. There is enough evil today. Let's not look at the past."

Josephine shook her head and her warm tears spilled onto my hands.

In the doctor's lounge we encircled Elise as Bellows interviewed her. Elise was emotionally shattered, her voice a low trembling alto, her eyes darting from face to face. She pulled at the coat her father had placed on her shoulders and wadded a corner of it into her right hand.

"The girls grabbed my arm and I couldn't break free," she said with a shiver. "They were the ones who said they had a surprise for the new girl. I should have known. I should have waited in the office for my ride."

"Nothing that happened to you is your fault," Josephine whispered into her hair. "They were intent on evil. We can pray they repent, but their hearts were bent on doing you harm. God has a lot to say about people with wicked intent."

Elise wiped the tears flowing from her eyes and kissed Josephine's cheek.

"What can you tell us about the Anderson boy?" Bellows' voice was gentle, his eyes gazing at her like he would a skittish colt.

"His name is David. We are in honors English together. Is he going to be all right? They knocked him out with a fallen limb and they kept hitting him even when he was unconscious."

Bellows slowly turned his head, eyes scanning all of us. He licked his upper lip. "David Anderson saw the kids throw Elise into a red van and take off west. He dialed the police, then followed them to a patch of woods out Perryville Road. Brave kid. He's badly hurt. They're airlifting him to Lexington. He'll need surgery."

Elise grabbed Bellows' arm. "What kind?"

"He has head trauma." Bellows' voice trailed off. He

looked away from us toward the closed door. "Can you name the kids who attacked you?"

Elise listed seven boys' names, three girls'. "I don't know them well." One was a local doctor's daughter, another a school psychologist's son.

Bellows patted her hand. "We're holding them. Officer McEntire was near, so arrived first. Took them by surprise because she hadn't activated her siren. Has them on video. Would have been better if they hadn't attacked her." He nodded toward Sarah McEntire who had her arm bandaged and an abrasion on her left cheek. "I need you to tell Officer McEntire everything that happened. I'm going to make certain those kids can't communicate with one another before we tape their interviews. Lawyers present, yes. But no hysterical parents in the room. They will only confuse things." He headed out the door as Sarah McEntire sat beside Elise.

After shaking Jim Weldon's hand, Lyle took mine and led me out of the room. We headed onto the asphalt gray parking lot. Our destination was my home, a safe place. Josephine came with us. Her face held tension around her lips and her forehead lines were deep.

"That poor Anderson family. I know that boy. His mama worked at this hospital. From what Elise said they nearly killed him."

Lyle's jaw grew hard. I squeezed his hand. Lyle took a breath that came from deep within him. He didn't speak for a few seconds as if weighing his words. "Bellows told me David Anderson grabbed a boy who'd tossed Elise on the ground. That young man threw him off of her then tried to calm the situation and get Elise to his car. The police arrived as the Anderson boy was being savagely beaten." The skin around Lyle's eyes was tight with pain as we headed onto the sidewalk.

Rain fell like tears. Droplets splashed on the cement and stayed in rounded forms like beads of pain. "The sheriff said when they arrived, the girls were tearing off Elise's clothes while the boys attacked Anderson. One of his deputies has it on film from his body cam."

"What kind of kids are we raising around here?" Josephine was angry, her hands balled into fists. "Kids that attack one another like animals? Sneaky girls who lie, and set up another child to be raped?" Josephine's voice rose into a high-pitched first soprano. "I need to get Savannah away from here. She knows these kids. They'd do to her what they did to Elise."

Lyle reached for Josephine's hands. "I've a plan, Josephine. After I make a couple of phone calls, I'll talk about it." She leaned into him. Lyle held her in the parking lot, letting her tears wash him as the cold rain bathed us all.

Josephine slid into the backseat of Lyle's BMW. She sniffed loudly and blew her nose on one of Lyle's fancy, monogrammed handkerchiefs. "You're sure having a messed-up honeymoon." Josephine sighed. It was a tense sigh as if she held the weight of the world on her shoulders.

Lyle squeezed my hand as he helped me into my seat. "Honeymoons are a state of mind. We're going to go for ten maybe twelve years of honeymoon. Make certain, though, that you and the good reverend don't have sick relatives and dead bodies cluttering yours up."

Josephine snorted. "You know that Neely Patrick moved back into his house with his cousins? Olive Lorraine is hiding out in a motel. Talk of the town. And that's not all."

Lyle put the heater on tropical. I didn't need to think about the O'Neal hoodlums or Lyle's ex-wife. "Do I have a need to know, Josephine?"

"You both do." There was more bounce in Josephine's tone.

I turned to look at her. Her arms were crossed over her chest and her eyebrows said, 'Try me.'

"Shoot," I said.

"Only one shooting around here is when you shot Neely and Miss Clarisse, your new husband. And now, with Olive Lorraine getting her concealed carry permit, the whole town's filling up with Annie Oakleys. As I was saying, things are getting complicated for Mrs. Patrick. She's got her husband free of the slammer until he's convicted, and there's a man glued to her side who looks like he'd kill for the pleasure of it."

"I think he is an accountant," Lyle said, straight-faced.

Josephine nailed the back of his head with a look. "Can spies be accountants? He and Mr. George have been on 'trips' I heard him say. Trips! They've been slipping in and out of places like sneak thieves in the night. They were gathering information, is my bet, or they're assassins. Why, if Neely Patrick doesn't behave himself, he's toast."

I glanced at my new husband. "Lyle, where is Randall Longworth staying?"

"In that high-end motorhome at the playhouse campground. Remember my friend who needed to off-load a fancy R.V? I connected the two. Why?"

"With Longworth elsewhere, Olive could stay at my little house on the farm. Neely couldn't find her there."

"Be a bit noisy for her with the reconstruction I've in mind."

I patted his hand as we turned down our street. "We need to talk about that."

When we arrived, I shook my rain wet head and put our coats on the rack by the door before entering my parlor. Meemaw was in her favorite seat where she'd been when we rushed her to the hospital. And she wasn't alone. Miss Vickie, Josephine's mama, sat in the rocker humming and appliqueing a flower onto a quilt square. They were a pair. One raisin dark, the other pale as a magnolia blossom, but they'd bonded two months ago over the glory of hats and now talked like the oldest of friends.

Meemaw sat crocheting a baby sweater. She held up her turquoise ball of yarn. "I'm guessing Molly's going to have a boy but whether a boy or girl, think this will do?"

The yarn was the softest I'd ever felt. "This is lovely," I said as I sat beside her. "What is it made of?"

"Cotton and silk. Your mama thought I'd find it pleasurable." She winked at Lyle.

Miss Vickie beamed from her chair and held up her project. "This will get finished before Christmas and you'll have your wedding quilt by next summer. When are you two getting married?"

Meemaw looked at her companion. "Vickie dear, we went to that shindig a few days ago. You and your gorgeous yellow hat were the talk of the wedding."

"All I's remember is Josephine all dressed up and tripping down the church aisle in high heels."

"That was the day, Mama." Josephine kissed her mother's cheek. There was a glimmer of understanding in Miss Vickie's eyes that made Josephine's lips ease into a smile. What with one thing and another, Josephine's usually animated face had become solemn. Gazing at her mother, Josephine blinked back a tear. Watching a loved one battle Alzheimer's was a challenge for anyone, but Josephine was in grief recovery from her daughter's kidnapping. Life was piling on with all kinds of woes. How she was going to plan a wedding on top of everything was puzzling. Maybe I should stay and help.

Meemaw glanced at Lyle. "Y'all didn't come all the way here to ask about my projects. And yes, I think that oily man who visited me is up to no good and so does my lawyer."

"I concur," said Lyle as he reached for her hand. "We'll see that he doesn't bother you again." He looked me in the eye. "I need to speak to George and Olive's friend."

Meemaw put the ball of yarn I'd fingered back in her project bag so it wouldn't take off across the floor. "His name is William Hunter and he and George are 'on it' they said. You two need to go away together and not fuss about an old lady's problems." The crochet hook flew and the yarn ball shrank as we talked. "Now, scoot and go on that honeymoon you deserve." She waved us out of my parlor with her hook pointing to the door.

We crossed the hall to the library and settled in two chairs in front of the turret windows. "I think our help is not wanted," Lyle said with a laugh in his voice.

I blew a wet strand of hair from my eyes. "So it appears."

"I need to speak with George."

I put my hand out as he started to rise. "About the renovations for the manager's house. What do you have in mind?"

He reached in his pocket for his phone. "I'll show you. The architect sent sketches about an hour ago. The house needs a new roof. If we're going to use it as a house for rescued girls, we need to expand the back so there is a bigger kitchen-eating area. People open up around a table and food. That is one of the things I admired about you and Harry, Di. How you embraced the neighborhood kids around a tureen of soup and let the conversation flow. I learned a lot about my boys simply by listening."

His soft smile lit up his eyes. It was good to see the change in him. He seemed to carry the weight of the evil around us. How difficult it must be to sit on a bench and listen to heart-wrenching tales day in and day out.

He glanced at the window. The rain was softly pattering on my wrap-around porch. "What will really change things is another house being moved to the property, or perhaps two. Make it a community. Renovate the old barn so we keep animals." As his smile grew, a warmth rose up my face. Lyle was not a talker of dreams, his compassion had feet to it. "I believe the property should be able to house up to eight girls and several staff. We'll need to ask Dr. McLeod how many victims he recommends be in one place. From our conversation a few weeks ago, McLeod knew of places where up to a dozen girls were hidden and given time to heal."

Lyle handed me his phone and I flipped through the emailed pictures, marveling at how fast things were progressing and at the slight changes that would make the house into something where a family could live, a gathering place for their team, and a dining facility. I was catching Lyle's dream.

I shook my head. "We've a lot to learn." I rose, leaned over, and kissed Lyle. "And not only about how to care for these wounded girls."

"Ah...hem," said Josephine from the doorway. "Where you two goin' to sleep tonight? Our house, er, the judge's, is full up because we invited the Weldons to stay. Too much nonsense going on to go back to their farm. And not much privacy around here," she tilted her head and smiled, "for newlyweds." She raised one eyebrow. Her left. Very dangerous when Josephine raises that eyebrow. It means she's got an idea and I'd better not argue.

"So, I've been thinking you could sneak out of town and head back to that fancy B&B before Mr. George ropes you in to tackling those O'Neal felons."

Lyle rose to his feet. "Thank you for your input, Josephine. Think I'm going to mosey over to the Salases' and get a few things straightened out. And don't worry. I'll take care of our sleeping arrangements." He winked at me. "Care to join me, Delilah, in a little clandestine operation?"

I'd judged Will Hunter a quiet, limpet of a man when we were hunting Savannah's kidnappers. He'd worked alongside Olive Lorraine but hardly spoken to me, except in truncated sentences. But when he opened the Salases' door, Hunter shook Lyle's hand with such force that Lyle grinned as if he'd met a soul mate. I mentally took a step back and watched.

'Men judge other men', Daddy asserted one hot summer day. 'Best to find out what your daddy thinks about the boys you trot home for approval. Daddies know all.' Daddy hadn't been smiling as he'd tapped his temple and gave us his stern look. He'd had his eyes on my brothers, studying them like a scientist does a bug in a microscope, but his gaze wound around to Suzanne and finally to me. The way Lyle and Hunter looked at one another made my neck muscles relax.

"Come in out of the rain." Hunter waved us into the hall, relieved us of our soggy coats, and escorted us into George's office. "George and Hank Abernathy will be right in. Mamie is on a food run."

Hank Abernathy hanging out with George would not go over well in Abernathy's household. I tried to reign in my surprise but Hunter lifted his eyebrows.

"Exactly. The lady of the Abernathy's house, i.e., Candance, and her sister-in-law, your former mayor's wife, is quite perturbed that Hank is with us most of every day. Seems he enjoyed our last go-round with investigating and is set on participating in this one. I had the opportunity to meet the pair not long ago. Best I keep my opinion to myself." He chuckled but his nostrils were pinched with displeasure.

"Well," I stammered. "He was very helpful when we found Savannah."

"Precisely. I consider him an asset." Will crossed his lanky arms. "Olive tells me that you two should be on a honeymoon. Hear about the O'Neals' arrival?"

"That and a couple of other needs. Meemaw says she spoke to you about her little problem."

"That she did."

Lyle's thoughtful expression didn't change when he said, "Top-notch investigators are needed, and to keep you, George, and now Hank, from twiddling your thumbs I'd like to add a couple of other things that may be related."

"You have my attention."

"The man killed in Lexington is involved in a real estate franchise owned by an O'Neal associate. I don't have the resources to prove the O'Neals are interested in the property Delilah's Meemaw owns. Nor the ability to interfere in Madison's investigation, but perhaps you and George might be able to help. Too many connections with the land along Draper's Creek has me curious. There must be something valuable there that we are missing. Minerals come to mind. Isn't there gold in West Virginia and gem stones in North Carolina? People might think coal country has diamonds. South Africa does."

"Thought you'd never ask," George said as he entered the room, his arm around the shoulders of a beaming Hank Abernathy.

I'd never seen Hank with a grin. It was disconcerting to see all his teeth.

George ignored Lyle and gave me a big hug. "That rogue you married treating you right, Delilah?"

I kissed George's cheek. "Couldn't be better. But on to topics I can elaborate on..." I raised my eyebrows and George laughed. Like a clone, so did Hank.

"Olive had a visit from a woman named Clarisse." Will's lips turned down. "I was with her at the little Mexican restaurant when a woman came up and gave Olive a hug. Olive wasn't happy about it. This Clarisse settles into the seat next to Olive and says she needs her help. I think Olive would have pushed her onto the floor if a deputy hadn't come into the place and asked Clarisse to pick up her order and head back to the hotel." The lines around Will's mouth tightened. "Heard she was your ex-wife, Lyle."

Lyle nodded.

"Is this the woman who had Neely doing cartwheels

in the Caribbean?" Lyle nodded again. Will appeared as though he'd sucked on a lemon. "Olive has enough on her plate and doesn't need a visit from the past."

A sudden desire to wrap my arms around Olive made me take a deep breath. There must be a way to protect Olive from Clarisse's machinations. I swallowed, hard. "I would like Olive to move into the manager's house on the old farm. She would be safe there."

Will Hunter's serious expression softened and a smile flitted across his lips before he captured it and sent it back. "We would appreciate that."

I noted the we, but kept my face blank as a clean sheet of paper. "Good. There aren't any supplies or food in the house. A few cleaning things are in the kitchen."

"I'll take care of it," Hunter said as he turned back to Lyle. "George and I and er...Hank, have been searching for connections with Delilah's grandmother's farm and the dead man. We've simply scratched the surface."

Lyle recited our experiences in Horsetail Falls as if he were reading a teleprompter. No emotions, just the facts. "It might pay to see if the government has plans in the area for absorbing it into the national park. Perhaps somebody is investigating for mineral rights."

"On it," said George. "Now you two, scoot." Hank executed a firm nod for emphasis or he was stretching his neck. "Your Meemaw is in good hands."

Lyle held up a finger. "One more thing. You'll hear it on the news. Several kids assaulted the Weldon girl. The Weldons need protection. They are currently in my home. I'm assuming you two, er, three can set something up until we establish a security unit?"

"*We?*" George raised his robust eyebrows. "*We* are on a honeymoon. Neglecting your bride is a criminal offense, Lyle." George shooed us toward the door. "And, don't forget your coats." He grabbed them and thrust them into Lyle's arms.

Chapter Fourteen

THE RAIN HAD BECOME A DELUGE complete with thunder. As we dashed through pelting rain to Lyle's car, my thoughts were wrapped up in the sorrow on Josephine's face, worry for the Anderson boy, and fretting about Meemaw. The rain was colder. The day held a gray, dismal pall.

I gazed up at Lyle as he eased me into my seat. "George is a romantic."

"He's not the only one," Lyle whispered as he kissed the top of my head.

Lyle settled into his seat, puddling rain water onto the carpet and his leather upholstery. "Honeymoon Part Deux coming up." He turned to me with a smile that faded when he saw my face. "You look sad. What is the problem?"

"I'm worried about everyone. What a mess we're leaving."

"Then we need to pray." He drove the car toward the college. "Well, Lord, here we are. Our hearts are filled with grief and worry about Meemaw, Savannah, Elise, and David. We expect you to watch over them, protect them, heal them from their physical wounds and those that linger in their minds. Lord, you are a healer, provider, and protector. Bathe all of them in your peace." Lyle took a deep breath. "And Father, minister to the hearts of their parents who are suffering as they watch their wounded children." He finished as we waited at the stop light on Secretariat Way.

Harry had been a quiet man about prayer. He'd sit in his rocking chair in our bedroom and study scripture then pray with only an occasional lip movement, no sound. For a lifelong Presbyterian, Lyle had a robust way of addressing the Lord. He must have had practice living alone, raising his boys, and having to make life and death decisions as a judge.

He turned to look at me as the light changed. His eyes softened, and as a horn blared behind him, he shrugged. "Unusual impatience for a Kentucky driver. Wonder what's up his britches?"

Lyle had been known to honk a horn or two. I raised my eyebrows. He stepped on the gas. "I'm learning to slow down. Patience is a virtue that cannot be hurried." He smirked when he noticed my lips tightly closed so I wouldn't comment.

After campus the street widened to four lanes and the car behind us sped past on the right. I glanced at the impatient driver, gasped, and scooted down in my seat in case he looked our direction. "You know who that is?"

Lyle squinted at the car as it passed. "No, who?"

"Melvin Kennedy from Horsetail Falls."

"The real estate agent?"

"Yes. What in the world is he doing in Central Kentucky?"

Lyle waggled his eyebrows. "Maybe we should follow him and see what he's up to." When two cars separated ours from Kennedy's Lexus, Lyle eased into the right lane. Kennedy turned onto Main street which ran north-south and aimed toward the bypass. Then, he parked in front of Patrick and Patrick Real Estate Company. Their office was from the early twentieth century. The rest of the strip mall, consisting of the Jiffy Lube, Sandwich shop, and Western Wear Emporium, was designed with the same brick but of a newer vintage. Lyle drove into the movie theater lot across the street and parked so we faced the office.

I dialed Olive Lorraine Patrick on my cell phone. She picked up after the first ring. "Hi, Olive. Are you at the office?" I waited. "Oh, you're heading to the cottage? Have a nice time settling in." I waited for her to finish thanking me for the use of the cottage then hung up.

"I got the gist of the phone call." Lyle nodded toward the door of the Real Estate office. "Look at what we have here." Neely Patrick and two dark-haired men stood in the covered porch waiting for Melvin Kennedy to get out of his white Lexus.

I opened the glove box. "Do you have any binoculars in here?"

"No. I'm not a cheap private eye snooping on an errant husband. What do you expect to see?"

"I was a mother of four. I can read lips if I can see better." Cell phone in hand, I shot a picture of the family group, then began to use video when Kennedy left his car, trotted up the seven wide steps to the porch and shook hands with them all. They stood for a few moments chatting, then stepped into the Arts and Crafts style house the Patricks used for their office. Lyle's phone rang.

"Hello, Robert," Lyle said after glancing at his screen. "All right." He pushed the speaker button and held his cell between us. "Go ahead."

"Thought it would be easier to say this once to the two love birds. Might I suggest that you two cruise to a little hide-a-way while we do our job?"

I craned my neck to see if he was within sight.

"Miss Delilah," he said with a laugh. "Don't think you'll see me, but I'm in the white van parked two spaces from you. It may appear empty but we've some monitoring equipment snooping on a meeting across the street." He cleared his throat. "I'm certain you understand the need for hitting the road."

I mouthed the word, 'Jack' to finish the lyric and Lyle grinned. "We'll scuttle away, Robert." Lyle laughed as he disconnected. "We've been busted, my love."

I settled back in my seat and snapped on my seat belt. "At least they're on to Kennedy."

Lyle's forehead was scrunched like an accordion. "Apparently," he said in a voice that sounded like he didn't quite believe it. "Why is it that everyone wants us out of their hair?"

I shrugged. "Maybe we should interfere with one another instead of with Meemaw, the FBI, and the doings in Horsetail Falls."

"Not a bad suggestion. I kept the cottage, in case we returned." Lyle hummed as he drove back to the familiar B&B, where privacy and gourmet food awaited.

"I married a very smart man." He didn't argue the point.

A phone call jarred us awake before dawn. It was my cell. "Delilah!" Olive Lorraine's voice vibrated with panic. "I saw someone following me here last night. Now there's a person snooping around the barn. I've called your son. He called the police. Thought it might be you, but er...you're on your honeymoon so I couldn't imagine...well that you'd be here."

"No. Not us." Worry lines etched across my forehead. The only person who would be following Olive would be Neely or his cousins. "You're out a-ways. It will take the police a while to get there. Do you have a gun?"

"Yes. Well..."

I started to say, 'get it loaded, lock yourself up tight, and wait for the police' but Lyle grabbed the phone.

"Are you on the second floor or the first?" he asked. "The first floor has a bath attached to the kitchen. Go in there. Whoever is snooping around will look in the closet first, then under the bed." He listened for a moment. "Do it now!" Lyle almost spit out the words. "Keep the phone with you, but don't talk. I'll keep on the line as we head your way. We're closer to you than McKeansville."

Lyle covered the phone with his hand. "Get dressed, Di. The intruder is on the porch." I jumped into my jeans and threw on my shirt, and pushed on my boots as Lyle flew into his clothes. We were on the road in three minutes. We could see our breath in the frigid air. I shivered and wrapped my arms around my chest as the heater blasted warmth onto my cheeks.

"Do you think Neely's having Olive watched?"

"It's a possibility. Could be a vagrant."

"The farm is a quarter mile from the highway."

I saw him nod in the lights of an oncoming car. "Bellows will have an eye on Neely and on Clarisse. Doesn't have enough man power to keep an eye on the rest of his family. What they really want is the diamonds Clarisse's lover hid and Harry found—plus no witnesses. And they may plan to use Olive as leverage or get her to stop pursuing the divorce. Lots of money at stake in the split up of Patrick and Patrick Real Estate Company."

"So Olive is a liability and you also mean us?"

"Absolutely." Lyle's voice sounded strangled. "I want us to stay clear of them. Josephine too, because she spied Neely sneaking into your yard after Clarisse shot me. Eliminate witnesses and they think the case will be tossed. Problem is we've already been questioned by the police. There are records."

What I was thinking was troublesome. "I suppose we'll have to let Will Hunter be Olive's gunslinger until Neely is back in jail and his cousins out of town."

"Could be."

In the dark Lyle's face was hidden. Lyle couldn't see my face either but it was tense. I wasn't worried because Neely Patrick was gunning for us—something else conjured up unwelcome images in my head. I grabbed my hands so I wouldn't wring them. "I've a problem, Mr. Henderson."

"Yes?"

"I don't want Olive and her new boyfriend to play hanky-panky in my little cottage."

"I see. Only married folk get to play, what did you call it?" I heard the laughter in Lyle's voice. "Oh, yes, something Shakespearian." I opened my mouth and shut it quick. 'Let him talk,' a little voice said.

"Olive doesn't need more complications and I believe Hunter sees that. I promise I will speak with him about your concern."

A peachy-pink glow in the east fingered the sky as we turned off the main road. A perfect dawn. Lyle doused the car lights. We drove down Morgan Lane and crunched to a stop. Lyle parked beside an old shed across the road and about two hundred feet shy of the house. No interior lights shone from the cottage.

Lyle grabbed his gun from the glove box, secured the clip, and turned off the dome light so when he opened the door it wouldn't shine. "Stay here." He held out his hand like a traffic cop halting a semi. I'd already opened the door. Easing it shut I scooched into the seat and waited. The porch was shadowed but looked empty. Lyle made a circle with his fingers, signaling okay, then disappeared on the right side of the porch to circle the house. I waited with hands wrapped so tight together that they hurt. It was light enough to see the outline of a car's hood at the side of the barn. Olive was right. Someone had followed her and was now in the house or skulking in the dark waiting for an opportunity. But for what? Murder? Threat?

Olive's Cadillac was parked by the stairs and aimed toward the porch like an exclamation point. I chewed on my lip. A sharp noise, like metal hitting rock disturbed the air. It came from behind the house. I sprung out of the car and, crouching like I'd seen in the movies, then ran to the Cadillac for shelter and a better view. I peered inside the car. Nothing but a Kleenex box on the passenger seat and an empty water bottle standing between the seats as upright as a Puritan minister. Olive was tidy.

A grunt emerged from the back. I held my breath. If the O'Neals were there, Lyle was outnumbered and likely out foxed. He could get hurt, or worse. Wish I had my gun.

Moving away from the car's protection I skittered

toward a scraggly rose bush near the porch. A man's voice, guttural, threatening, broke the silence. Sneaking toward the sounds, I went left of the porch, then sheltered in the flower bed beside a scrawny hydrangea in want of leaves. November sucked the life out of a garden.

Accidentally rubbing my backside against the house shingles made a scraping sound like sandpaper on hard wood. I stepped toward the footsteps on the gravel separating the back from the yard. Craning my head to peek I watched two men grapple with one another by the kitchen door. First, they were upright, next on the ground, then rolling over the dirt and wet grass. Lyle suddenly jumped to his feet and jerked the slighter man upright. It was too dark to see faces but Lyle had his arms around the other man like an octopus. It subdued him. Odd way to do it but it worked, for the man now stood stock still with his arms flat to his sides.

"What in the world are you doing here?" Lyle's voice was puzzled as he thrust the man away from him and peered into his face. "And I'm not addressing you, Delilah, because I know exactly why you're prowling around in the dark."

The man sputtered, rubbed his jaw and said, "Reconnoitering. I've been assigned to guard duty." Lyle had wrapped an arm around the shoulders of the slight figure of my neighbor, Hank Abernathy.

A blaze of light shot through the kitchen curtains and hit the back stoop like a thunder bolt. Olive Lorraine flung open the door, a fierce look on her face. Armed with a broom, handle pointed like a sword, she looked ready to spring to action in a fluffy hot pink bathrobe with matching slippers. She shook her head of brown curls and started to laugh. An all-out, deep throated whoop. Olive wasn't known for her laughter. In fact, she rarely chuckled.

I straightened my shoulders, lifted my chin, and stepped into the light.

Olive shook her head. "What a relief. You really had me scared."

Hank tested his jaw with his fingertips. "I thought George let you know I'd be around."

"I didn't check my emails before I went to bed."

Lyle patted Hank's back. "Sorry I clobbered you."

"If you'd given me warning I'd have ducked." Hank Abernathy's voice was trembling. "Will said to expect trouble. I didn't think I'd have to face my neighbor using his pugilistic skills."

Olive unearthed her phone from her robe pocket and dialed. "Wish I would have checked my messages. I've gotten the county sheriff in a tizzy and I'm having palpitations."

"Best sit down, Olive." Hank grabbed her arm and helped her back into the house. He steered her through the kitchen and toward the sofa. Lyle retrieved his gun from where it had fallen in the rocks. He swiped off the dew-damp barrel and removed the magazine before he placed both in his pocket. I tiptoed after Lyle as he trooped behind them. Hank set Olive down as if she were easily bruised. I closed the door and locked it before grabbing the broom to store it in the closet.

Olive fluffed a faded blue pillow and pushed it behind her back. She listened for a moment to her phone. "Please call off the deputy. It was a neighbor checking to see if I was all right." That was a little white lie. The entire world seemed to think spreading them around was acceptable. "Oh." Her voice faded. She waited another moment for the dispatcher to comment. "Of course. Well, I'll put on the coffee then." Olive slipped her phone into her bathrobe pocket. "A county deputy is on his way." She tapped the toes of her slippers together in thought. "Sweet of Will to have you on protection detail but unnecessary." Olive waved her hand dismissively.

Lyle stared down at her. "Actually, it is a reasonable precaution. A professional is a better choice, however. Poor Hank." Lyle went to the kitchen, soaked a paper towel in cold water and slapped it into Hank's hand. "For your jaw. It'll be sore and bruised from the wallop I gave you."

Lyle walked to Olive and crossed his arms. "And Olive, you need 24/7 protection. Neely is up to something and it's best to be prepared. And you, Mrs. Henderson, may join the party." He grinned at me then turned toward the fireplace. His voice was funny. I walked over and put my hand on his arm. His shoulders were moving up and down as he tried to hold in his laughing. "Why did I think you'd stay put? Hmm? And why did I think our honeymoon would be normal?"

I went to fix coffee.

Chapter Fifteen

DAWN WHISPERED ACROSS THE FIELDS AS we headed toward the county road. "As long as we're awake we might as well check on something at my house." Lyle had already had two cups of coffee and was talking fast. "Glad Deputy Raines thought the mix up with Hank was amusing." Lyle patted my hand. "What say we go for a ride in the country, Mrs. Henderson. You, me, a couple of horses?"

The sun glinted the asphalt golden gray. The sky was a deep cobalt, and the day held warmth. "Sounds promising."

Lyle turned onto our street from the four-lane road of the by-pass. Driving toward our homes, Lyle screeched to a halt and turned into George's drive across the street from his abode.

"What!" I said reflexively. Lyle liked surprises but I needed a little prep so I could grab something for support.

"There's a man walking up my steps. A little early for visitors, wouldn't you say?" Lyle leaped out of the car. "No use my asking you to stay put. Come on." I was out before he could open the door.

Glancing toward Lyle's home, I caught sight of a trench coated man, briefcase in hand peering in the small windows on either side of the front door. He was about the size of the men at the real estate company that had a meeting with Melvin Kennedy. Were the O'Neals scouting our neighborhood?

Instead of heading for Lyle's we aimed toward George's stoop. A smart rap on the door brought George. "I've a stranger lurking on my front step," Lyle said when the door cracked open. "Bring your gun." Lyle revealed his weapon as he slapped the magazine into place.

The mention of a gun sent shiver bumps up my arms. I waited until George slipped past me, gun in hand, then entered the Salases' house. Mamie Salas found me by the front window, peering out like a voyeur.

She lifted a steaming mug of hot coffee and cocked her eyebrow. "Coffee?"

I nodded. A ceramic mug was slipped into my fingers and we huddled together watching our husbands cross the street and stride toward Lyle's perfectly appointed Federal style house. Mamie put her hand on my arm. "Why is Lyle so upset?"

"Traffickers often search out their victims and rekidnap them." I wish I didn't know how vulnerable Savannah was. I hadn't told Josephine all the doctor in Blowing Rock told me about the danger for those reentering their lives after being trafficked. Drugs were an issue as was humiliation and the feeling of helplessness. For Elise Weldon that had been multiplied in the past twenty-four hours. Who could they trust?

We watched Lyle's front door slowly open. Lyle and George were on the sidewalk.

Running.

Miss Vickie stood in the doorway, dressed in her Cincinnati Reds baseball cap and floral housecoat. She leaned forward, then her head tilted left as she listened. She opened the door wide to allow the man entry.

Lyle and George dashed up the steps. George had his gun out. Each grabbed the man under the armpits and hoisted him into the house. The stranger's legs were flailing the air as his fedora flew off his head and rolled on its brim along the stoop and out into the soggy grass. The front door slammed shut.

I un-balled my fingers and shook them to ease the tension. Turning toward Mamie I started to say, *"Well, that was a surprise,"* but stopped myself. Mamie had her hands clasped to her chest and focus riveted across the street.

"Wasn't that exciting? I've never seen George in action before." Mamie's brown eyes glimmered like a teenage girl with a crush.

"You should have seen him shooting at the Hummer that attacked us in Paducah." I shivered. Not a good memory overall, but we'd survived and would someday laugh about it. Maybe when Lyle's ex-wife and Neely Patrick were locked up in the state pen.

My phone chirruped. "Come on over, Di, and bring Mamie. You need to meet our new guest." *Was this Lyle's surprise?*

We hot footed it to Lyle's like sprinters in a race. Mamie didn't even pant. I thrust open the door and then stopped as if hit by a cannonball. Lyle and George towered over the stranger. Unearthing papers from his briefcase the man said words that had Miss Vickie plugging her ears.

"Mr. Judge," Josephine said as she entered the hall, "you best remove him from my mama or he's going to get a piece of her mind." Savannah stood behind her mother and when she caught a glimpse of the short man, she turned around and dashed back to the kitchen. Josephine shook her head. Savannah couldn't handle strangers after her kidnapping.

Lyle leaned toward the shorter man and glowered. "He's going to get it from me, for saying those words in the presence of ladies." At the sound of his master's voice, Bartles made a dash down the stairs and pawed Lyle's pant leg. Lyle squatted to pick up his puppy.

"Girl," said the stranger, looking at Josephine. "Fetch my hat. It fell off as I was assaulted. And you," he pointed a finger at Miss Vickie, "show me to the office so I can present my papers."

No one moved. We simply stared at the man as if he were an alien. George was first to react. "First," he said, shaking a finger in the face of the man, "you will address Miss Hudson with respect. Second, the only one being ordered around here is you. If you have a complaint as to your treatment, call the sheriff. I have his number on speed dial." George thrust his phone under the man's nose.

"No need to get huffy," the man held up his hands. Three large gold rings glittered in the overhead light. "I'm Clarisse Henderson's attorney and I'm here to present papers to her husband, Lyle Henderson. You should be aware that your local sheriff has taken her back into custody for merely chatting to an old friend. She is presently at your inadequate jail waiting for you to speak with her."

"I am her *former* husband." Lyle's voice became a bass rather than a baritone. Bartles licked him on the nose. "Clarisse is no longer my concern."

The attorney waved his hand in the air dismissing Lyle's comment. "According to *Mrs.* Henderson, she never signed divorce papers. Hence the divorce is not finalized."

Lyle bent so he could look the man in the eyes. As he did, Jim Weldon came down the stairs to take in the drama.

"A small legal matter, Jim. Perhaps it is best you and your family wait until things are more settled." Lyle refocused on his unwanted guest. His steely look made Josephine take a deep breath.

The little man backed up a step.

"Where is your law practice? License legal in what states?" Lyle's voice cracked the air like a whip.

"I am licensed in Illinois but am currently working with the firm of Baxter and Bayer in Louisville."

"Perhaps you are unaware that in this state, desertion after three years qualifies legally for divorce action."

"Your wife protests."

Lyle placed Bartles on the floor. "I'm certain she does, however it is not germane. My divorce decree is legal."

"Your wife said you would claim that the divorce was legal because you bribed the judge. She would like to speak to you on the issue. You are aware of the case in Texas, correct?"

Looking at me over the head of Clarisse's diminutive lawyer, Lyle winked.

I chewed on my lip. The town's hoi polloi already thought of me as a man trapper. When I'd come to town as Harry's bride, I'd received the cold shoulder that had lasted until this past summer. Not Harry's family, of course. They had welcomed me with open arms and hearts, but the movers and shakers in McKeansville had said more than unkind words.

Stubbornness grabbed my heart. I came by it honestly because my Appalachian roots were deeply entrenched. It would not be a problem living with Lyle until this sorted itself out. Let the tongues wag until they were tied in knots. I picked up Bartles and tickled his chin, then winked back at Lyle. Placing Bartles on the hall carpet, I put my hands behind my back so Lyle couldn't see me wringing them.

Lyle's forehead rumpled as he went through the lawyer's sheaf of fancy papers. The lines didn't ease when he'd finished. Mamie grabbed my hands from behind my back and began to pat them like I would pat a dog hearing Fourth of July fireworks. Sweat formed on my brow, not the polite dewy look New York models had in makeup ads but a cold, nervous sweat.

Josephine tromped over to my new husband and put her hands on her ample hips. "Miss Dee Dee is a little worried, Mr. Judge. Think you'd better get this straightened out right quick or she's going to give that felon Clarisse the what for. And it won't be pretty."

Lyle's face broke into a grin. "Nothing to be concerned about, sweetheart." His eyes softened as he looked at me. "I need to show our undistinguished guest a few papers. Perhaps a cup of coffee all around is in order."

The three men walked into Lyle's library and surrounded Lyle's desk. Bartles took up residence by the fire and Miss Vickie straightened her baseball cap and tilted her head before following them. George placed his Glock on Lyle's desk and looked at Clarisse's lawyer, at the gun, and back at the small man in the nondescript raincoat.

I knew that Lyle had a few choice words on his lips that I'd rather not hear so I directed the women to the kitchen. Miss Vickie, however, had settled in Lyle's love seat by the fireplace and shook her head when asked to come. "No, thank you. I've had enough coffee to float a battleship. I'm not leaving until this funny looking man gives me the money from the magazine sweepstakes. Where are the balloons and cameras?" She craned her neck around and squinted her eyes.

After shaking her head, Josephine disappeared in the direction of the kitchen. Mamie and I trooped after her. Josephine's mama could handle the man. She'd been a nurse at the hospital and had listened to a few words that would curl my toes.

Opting for water instead of more coffee, I almost dropped my glass when Miss Vickie dashed into the kitchen and yelled, "Wooee. That man said something to the judge that made his honor's face turn red as a ladybug. I thought there was going to be a fight, but that Mr. George took the stranger by the armpits and shoved him in the wing chair. The words that tiny man said sounded like a bad movie where everyone can't say two words without swearing." That was the longest trail of words I'd heard from Miss Vickie in ages. Maybe the new Alzheimer's medicine was helping.

Loud voices disturbed our kaffeeklatsch. Mamie raised her eyebrows. "I think George is not happy." Mamie sidled out of the room and squirted back through the dining room toward the front hall. I followed. "In fact," she tossed the words over her shoulder, "from the sound of things he's probably fingering his Glock."

The three men were clustered in the hall, Lyle calmly staring at Clarisse's lawyer, George slipping his gun into his pants pocket. Mamie knew her man.

"As soon as I speak with Delilah, I'll accompany you," Lyle said as we stopped at the hall entrance.

A wan smile crossed my face. "Not without me, Judge Henderson. We're in this together, thick or thin."

Lyle lifted an eyebrow. "I thought it was for better or worse."

"Same thing."

Lyle bobbed his head. "Clarisse is in custody because she made contact with Sidney. Can't intimidate a witness."

I blew out a breath of hot air. Sidney was flighty enough. After Clarisse and Neely's attack, he still jumped at sudden noises.

Lyle made a courtly bow. "After you, counselor."

"You needn't be sarcastic," the man said in a nasally whine.

When Sheriff Bellows spied Clarisse's lawyer standing by the reception desk, he licked his lips. "Ah, Mr. Delaney, back so soon?"

I squeezed Lyle's hand which I'd been hanging onto. Bellows glanced our way, his eyes skinny as a snake's. "She's expecting you, Lyle."

Lyle nodded. I tossed Bellows a smile. With all the nonsense going on in our little town we were beginning to be friends.

"I don't see any objection to *all* of you," his gaze roved over Mamie, George, Josephine, her mama, and the squirrely lawyer, "observing Clarisse and Lyle's interaction. Unless Mr. Delaney wishes to be present in the interrogation room."

"Of course I do. I'm not allowing my client to be intimidated by her former...er... husband."

Marching past the reception desk and down a softly lit hallway, Tom Bellows beckoned. "Follow me."

My tongue itched to ask about the kids' interviews and if their parents interfered with the police investigation, but I trooped after Lyle and kept my questions imprisoned.

Miss Vickie walked up to the mirrored window and tapped on the glass. "Why, this is just like that police show on TV."

Bellows opened a door beside the window. Lyle and the diminutive lawyer entered a small, square room with vanilla walls that weren't inviting. They pulled chairs back from a long metal table and sat opposite each other.

A deputy opened a door on the back wall. Clarisse sashayed into the room with her long-legged stride as if she hadn't a care in the world. Even in a flat-gray jail uniform she looked attractive. Maybe it was the hip action she exhibited as she walked toward Lyle that made George suck in his breath. Mamie crossed her arms.

Clarisse slid her right hand along Lyle's neck, then with her hand still there, bowed toward the mirror on the wall as if seeing us behind it. "Hello, Delilah. Hope you don't mind if Lyle and I get reacquainted." Clarisse's lips were hard at the edges.

"It will be interesting to see how Lyle deals with her," Mamie muttered.

"What is that woman doing here?" Miss Vickie asked. "She's the one who plugged the hole in the judge on Miss Delilah's fancy rug." Miss Vickie let out a snort of disgust.

If I could simply let Miss Vickie echo my thoughts I wouldn't have to speak.

Bellows tugged at his bottom lip with his fingers but barely suppressed a smile.

Clarisse bent over to whisper in Lyle's ear.

"Huh!" Miss Vickie erupted. "That woman came into our butcher shop once and ordered up the most expensive steaks we had. 'Your husband is going to love these,' I said. She lifted an eyebrow and said, 'I never said they were for my husband.'" Miss Vickie shook her head. "I asked her how she was going to prepare them and she said, 'I'm not. I've a friend who handles a barbecue grill like a symphony conductor…just like he handles a woman.'"

Josephine stepped beside her mama and took her by the arm. "Mama, I think I need to sit down. Why don't we sit in the sheriff's office while Miss Dee Dee waits for her husband."

Clarisse began to swing her leg. Her baggy, dull jail clothes didn't make the move attractive. "You know, Lyle. We were quite the pair. Made heads turn at the officer's club."

"Look at that hussy," Miss Vickie said, not budging from her front row stand. "Why, isn't Mr. Judge a married man? And that woman is giving him the eye." Clarisse was giving him more than the eye. She had unbuttoned the top two buttons on her gray shapeless shirt and leaned over toward Lyle so he had a good look at her cleavage.

Lyle pushed his chair back, hard. It scraped across the gray flecked tiles, making a metallic noise that made me squint. Lyle rose so abruptly that Clarisse jerked back.

"If that is all you have to offer, Clarisse," Lyle said coldly, "I've other things on my schedule."

"Oh, there's more, Lyle." Clarisse's voice was low and sultry like a blues singer selling a love song. "There is, what is the word, Delany?" Clarisse snapped her fingers at her lawyer.

His face looked blank.

"You can't divorce me without my signing the papers."

"I can and did. It was over fourteen years ago, Clarisse. You have no legal standing on the issue."

Clarisse snapped her fingers again.

Her lawyer sat up straight.

Miss Vickie leaned so far toward the window her

nose almost touched it. "That man acts like a dog learning a trick."

Mamie snorted through her nose. George didn't even hold in his laugh, while the sheriff put his hand in front of his lips and tried to hide his smirk.

Mr. Delany cleared his throat. "Well, actually, Mrs. Henderson, he is correct. Your desertion and lack of communication for over eighteen years is reason to dissolve a marriage."

Clarisse jumped to her feet, turned, and stared at the little man. "You're as incompetent as I feared you'd be. Well, if that is the case, I have one simple request, Lyle." She crossed her arms and smiled her brittle smile. "Get me out of here. The sheriff made a mistake. I was speaking to the Morgans' hired man about the weather. I'm no threat to you or your hillbilly fiancée. In fact, I'd welcome a visit from your soon-to-be spouse. She needs to know a thing or two about you."

Josephine squinted at me. "Don't you dare darken that hussy's door, Miss Dee Dee. That woman hasn't a lick of sense. Going near her might cause a brain infection. Will you look at that man?" She pointed a finger at Delany. "He should grab his briefcase and dignity and get out of that room. She must be paying him a lot of money for him to sit there and take her insults."

"My *wife* will not accept your invitation, Clarisse. Now, if you will excuse me, I'm leaving. Ask your lawyer if I have authority to get you out of jail. The judge said you violated your bail by speaking to a witness. Breaking international laws and money laundering are also some of your charges. Let your lawyer explain it all, Clarisse."

"It was a simple mistake to speak to what's his name at the Morgans'." She glowered at her lawyer. "I'm not finished with you, Lyle." Clarisse strode over to my new husband and poked him in the chest with her fingernail. "You don't want me to tell them certain things I know about your family. Embarrassing things, Lyle. Your brother's DUI's and Cissy's quick removal from college when she had that little 'accident' ought to make headlines. A drunk girl, sports car, and speed are a bad combination, Lyle."

Delany rushed toward Clarisse like a lynx on the hunt. "Mustn't say anything about family matters, Clarisse. People could misconstrue your comments."

Lyle looked at his former wife with his eyebrows almost crossed. "Intimidation and threatening a witness are not good ideas, Clarisse."

"Pooh, Lyle. I'm only repeating family stories. Remember how we'd sit around the table with your parents and they'd laugh and tell things on one another. Those times were such fun." The sneer in her voice said otherwise.

Lyle shook his head. "And I recall you used to best me at target practice on the range at the farm. Must not have had any practice lately, since you missed Delilah both times you aimed." Lyle turned toward the door.

Clarisse narrowed her eyes. "You got in the way the second time, Lyle. Shooting from a moving car is more difficult."

Delany grabbed her hand to keep her from continuing. Clarisse shook him off.

"You did manage to plug the Hummer but that's about it."

"I thought Josephine went to the hospital. If I couldn't get Delilah, next best thing was Josephine."

"They are taping this interview!" Delany sputtered.

"So?" Clarisse looked disgusted.

"You are not up for charges on the shooting in Paducah."

"Oh," said Lyle's ex-wife as the deputy opened the door and Lyle exited the room.

Chapter Sixteen

Bellows wrote in a notebook so fast I thought the paper would shred under his assault. George looked uncommonly pleased. As Lyle joined us, he clapped George on the back. Lyle smiled as if his team had won the Super Bowl.

"Why didn't you stop me!" squawked over the speaker. Clarisse lifted her fist to whack her lawyer and Delany backed up so fast he hit the table with his hip and crumpled onto the floor. The deputy twitched as if to move but let Clarisse vent with words that made Miss Vickie plug her ears. The deputy looked into the mirrored glass window, shook his head, then with sloth like energy moved toward his prisoner. Only when Clarisse kicked Delany hard in the leg did the deputy act.

Bellows dipped his head Lyle's direction. "I need to answer a couple of phone calls then I'll have another little chat with Neely about his trip to Paducah last summer. Seems some loose ends need tying."

"Is she in a heap of trouble?" I asked Lyle as we drove to his home.

"More than she realizes."

Miss Vickie poked me on the shoulder. "That woman has a temper like old man Fogerty down at the Fleece and Farm store."

"Mama, that is the Farm and Garden store." Josephine sounded amused.

Miss Vickie began to chuckle. "From the prices on their skinny tomato plants, fleece fits." Miss Vickie sniffed. "You could get Mr. Fogerty mad as all get out giving correct change for the item. I figure he short changed people and wanted to make a dime or two on each transaction."

I leaned close to Lyle. "I need to remember that you are very adept at riling people up. All you had to do was wave the red cape and Clarisse charged."

"She always had a temper. When Clarisse didn't get her way, life went sideways. My poor boys had to listen to many an argument complete with flying china and words that scorched the wallpaper."

"Hmm-hmm," Miss Vickie said. "She uses her tongue as a flame thrower. Not a pretty sight."

I turned around to see Josephine patting her mother's hand. "I think she'll be in need of another lawyer after she kicked Mr. Delany. Maybe they will add that to her charges. Assaulting her lawyer."

"I guess she won't be getting no more bail," Miss Vickie said.

Lyle looked into the mirror at the pair in the backseat. "No. She has settled that matter quite handily." There was a touch of sadness to his voice. I winced for him. Difficult to see someone you once loved destroying their life.

Lyle's surprise at his house was in his library. He opened his safe, in a place one would expect, behind a picture above the fireplace. Lyle smiled as he withdrew a set of keys. One was fancy, the other old-fashioned, that could open an old trunk or the front door of a Victorian house. They were attached to a ring emblazoned with the name Porsche.

I raised my eyebrows. Maybe, just maybe I'd get a ride in the car he drove on the track. And, perhaps he'd let me take a turn at the wheel. I grinned. He grinned, then grabbed my hand. "Time we left this overcrowded venue and spent some hours discussing life's simple pleasures."

Josephine stood in the doorway of the library

shaking her head. She took her mama's hand. "Mama, we've people to feed and comfort. And let's find the judge's little rat of a dog and take him for a walk in the backyard."

"No siree." Miss Vickie aimed for the front door. "Savannah and I need to visit my friend across the street. Savannah is learning to knit. It's going to be a washcloth for Miss Dee Dee, but don't tell her. It's a surprise."

"I'll find her, Mama." Josephine took off toward the back of the house.

As we grabbed our coats to head out, we heard a shout from the kitchen. Lyle wrapped his hand around mine and pulled me that direction. Josephine, Savannah, and Deputy McEntire were crowded around a group of rumpled papers.

"I called the sheriff's office when I recognized the man in the hall." Savannah's forefinger pointed to the top paper. "Do you see the likeness, Mama?"

"I surely do. The police have copies of these, right, Deputy?"

"Yes, ma'am. Think I'll have a chat with my boss and see what we can do." Officer McEntire turned toward Savannah. "Did you show these to the Weldon girl?"

"Not yet."

"Hold off on it until I get Bellows over here. Looks like we might have an opportunity to arrest another perp."

Lyle and I ambled to the counter and looked at the drawings Savannah had made while a trafficking victim. Lyle scratched his chin. "What was the name he used during the er…encounter?"

Savannah chewed on the inside of her lip. She pulled down the sleeves of her sweater as if hoping it would swallow her. "He wasn't my client. I think he was called Mr. D, though. He liked one of the little girls."

Vomit rose in my throat. I made a bee-line for the bathroom in the guest bedroom off the kitchen. Bartless trotted after me. It had been our hide-a-way while Lyle searched for Savannah. I managed to keep my breakfast down, but it wouldn't take much to stir things up again. I rose from kneeling by the toilet to see Lyle standing in the doorway.

"I'm sorry, my dear. This is not what I had in mind for our afternoon." I wrapped my arms around my groom as he brushed a curl away from my eyes.

"I love you, Lyle Henderson," I whispered into his shirt pocket.

By the time Bellows had interviewed both girls and spoken to Josephine and Lyle in the library, lunch time had segued into four o'clock tea. We waited for the D.A. to take their statements. Both girls recognized Clarisse's lawyer. Elise remembered Delany being at Lyle's North Carolina cabin.

When she saw Bellows the first words out of Elise Weldon's mouth were, "How is David?"

The tight lines around Bellow's eyes softened. "He's one tough kid. And the prayers being sent up on his behalf are making the difference. Twenty members of his church showed up in the tiny hospital chapel and began a worship service that echoed down the halls."

Elise gave a tentative smile at the news. "We'll find a way to get Delany's fingerprints and DNA for comparison with the ones from your house, Lyle," Bellows said as he hurried down the steps to his car. "Oh," Bellows turned around as fast as a first baseman throwing to second. "Keep this quiet. Don't want him lawyering up before we have all the facts." Bellows lips canted sideways when he said lawyering. "And, your dear, sweet ex has been fired by her lawyer. Delany hobbled into the emergency room thinking she'd broken his leg with her swift kick."

He shook his head so slowly you'd think he was on tranquilizers. "I forgot. The kids that attacked Elise are out on bail except one. Didn't have a lick of trouble with the D.A. pressing charges after she saw the video, but I am having an issue with two of the parents. One being Charlene Higgenbottom. According to three of the kids her daughter Kaylene is the instigator and we're up against a rock and a hard place with the town's political elite and Kaylene's mama leading the pack."

Our grand day for a horseback ride was swallowed by emotion. After arriving at the B&B we noticed dark clouds scudding in. They spit rain all over our heads as we ran to the barn to greet the horses and feed them apples. "Guess we'll have to build a fire and stare at one another," Lyle said with a fake sigh.

"There is always Scrabble."

He took my hand and we made a run for the little cottage we called home. The door was unlocked. Lyle pushed me back and put his finger to his lips. We tiptoed into the rain and dashed down the walkway. When we reached the car, Lyle removed his Smith and Wesson as well as the magazine from the glove box then headed back toward the cottage.

I put a restraining hand on his arm. "It may be the girl who cleans the place."

Lyle shook his head. "There is a large muddy footprint on the stoop. The owner's daughter is five foot one or so." The rain beat down on our heads like sharp bits of glass. "Stay behind me, Di."

"The last thing we need is for you to get shot. Call 911."

Lyle shook his head then eased the door open, both hands on the gun in front of him. Like a detective in a TV series, he swept the room. When he aimed at the fireplace, his arm eased down.

"Fine way to greet an old friend, Lyle," said the hard-edged voice of Special Agent Madison.

"One can't be too careful. We're both liabilities for

Neely Patrick."

"We won't let him get near you."

"Think I've heard that before." Sarcasm dripped from Lyle's words. "You have an interesting way of intruding on my honeymoon." I inched around Lyle and shook hands with Madison. "And don't try to charm my bride. That's my department."

"I'm here to enlist help from both of you."

This might be interesting. I tossed Madison a smile. "Okay."

Lyle crossed his arms. "Not okay."

"Hear me out, Lyle. Something has come up. Difficult to send a man in to get information in a town as small as Horsetail Falls. We need someone who they won't suspect. If not a local then a couple trying to escape being the front page of every newspaper in the country. You fit the bill."

"We won't be on the news." I wrinkled my brow.

"You already are. A little bird named Longworth had an interview on a cable news show. Longworth not only told about his narrow escape from being burned alive in the tobacco barn by Buck Mays but told one and all how Delilah saved his skin, saved a troubled girl at a truck accident, and was the mysterious author of a series of best-selling books."

"Sheesh." Longworth complicated my life by simply opening his mouth.

"We gave him the go ahead with the interview. Thought it would help our investigation if we got you two heading back to Horsetail Falls as if on the lam." Madison's eyes danced with humor.

Mine did not. I scrunched them up until they narrowed to a slit. "Madison, you're not helping Meemaw a whit." *Did he think we could get any more information from my family's tight-lipped neighbors?*

"I can assure you, Miss Delilah, your meemaw is in my thoughts every day. By the by, why is she called meemaw instead of mamaw like most other grandmothers?"

"Blame my oldest brother. He was two when he climbed into her lap, put his hands on her cheeks and said, 'Meemaw all mine.' Daddy said, Mamaw, and Billy put his hands on his hips and said, Me,' he pointed to his chest with his thumb, 'have a Meemaw.' No one could dissuade him so Meemaw she became."

"There is a gift of persistence cemented into the Burns DNA," Lyle kept a straight face.

"That brother the surgeon, pastor, or lawyer?"

Madison knew too much about me. "Guess," I challenged.

"Lawyer. I've watched a few in action. Take your husband for instance. Nothing moves him if he thinks he's on the right track."

Scrutinizing Lyle, I nodded. "Ever heard of the word sisu?" They both shook their heads. "Finnish word for stubborn. But sisu is beyond stubborn. Harry found that word and swore I must have a drop or two of Finnish blood because I was uber-stubborn. According to Harry's research, the Finns fought forty-seven wars with the Russians and lost every one of them."

Madison laughed. "You're in for a rough ride, Your Honor."

"Think we're evenly matched in that department." Lyle gestured for Madison to sit down. The special agent shook his head. "Too tiring to get back up. I'll mosey along after I've had my say. Horsetail Falls is the distribution center for opiates."

I took a breath. *The town was beginning to turn around. Were illegal drugs the reason?*

Madison lowered his gaze from Lyle's face and turned his head my direction. "They come in from the east, are dispersed to Lexington then west and north. We're keeping an eye on an auto repair shop that also does garden sculptures. Family are recent arrivals in the area. They've got trucks coming and going every day and deliver to Cincinnati, Louisville, and Lexington. Easy to hide merchandise in those cobbled together shapes."

If Missy Newland Ferris's husband was up to his neck in drug running would she know about it? Was she involved too? Fancy electronics, a few trucks, and money would roll in faster than you could blink. And Missy had always liked money. She'd married well several times and come away richer from the experience. Turning toward the fire I closed my eyes and remembered the skinny girl from high school who'd pinched every penny so she could have a prom dress like Miss America's.

Madison held up his hands as if to say, this is not my fault. "One more thing that will cause you to leave town. Clarisse got a new lawyer and he convinced a new judge to set bail for her. This time it is astronomical, but she came up with the cash, gave it to the court and is out on the town as we speak." Madison's feet shuffled past the love seat.

Alarm bells jangled in my head. I reached for Lyle's hand and hung on tight.

"You've got my number, Lyle. You two think about heading for the hills. Bellows says he's now short manned and can't keep an eye on her and Neely both." Madison moved with aching slowness toward the door. "Let me know if you want to help shut this thing down in Horsetail Falls. Too many opiate deaths in West Virginia, Eastern Kentucky, and Tennessee to not put up some kind of fight."

Lyle gazed at the agent "Robert, you should be on leave until you recover."

"Just following an example of a local judge. Man gets shot, bleeds like a stuck hog, and a couple of weeks later sashays around at his son's wedding as if he were immortal."

"Take care, Robert."

"I will. You do the same."

As the door closed behind him my stomach growled.

"I'm famished too, sweetheart. Let's get something to eat and then discuss Robert's proposal."

"If the Ferrises are dealing drugs how can we, in

good conscience, talk Meemaw into giving them the land?"

Lyle pulled on the lobe of his left ear. "And I thought things were twisted into knots with Clarisse, her lawyer, and the toes-up realtor in Lexington."

"And Neely, his felon cousins, and Kennedy showing up from Horsetail Falls and conniving with them. Hey, maybe he's the one involved with drugs and not the Ferrises."

"At the moment I'm more interested in a steak than if Mrs. Ferris is the mastermind behind a drug ring." With that he directed me out the door and toward sustenance. Plotting would have to wait until after dessert.

Chapter Seventeen

We found things to occupy our minds other than working on Madison's challenge. After a bag of microwaved popcorn for a late snack, Lyle suggested we get our brains in gear.

I'd conveniently tucked a notebook in my smallest bag. I unearthed a highlighter, three pens and two pencils from my purse and slid one of each toward Lyle.

"Where have you hidden the clipboard?" he asked with a smirk.

"In my suitcase. One must always be prepared."

He tapped the end of my nose with his forefinger. "I knew what I was getting into after all the kids' wedding arrangements on color-coded clipboards."

"Headings," I said, waving a pen his direction.

"Let's start with people. Then we'll go to Madison's suspicions." He picked up the highlighter and waved it like a magician's wand. "All the town locals who showed an interest in the land, from Kennedy, the Sheriff, the Ferris family, to Meemaw's neighbors."

I scribbled as he talked, putting all the names of the people at the Coffee Maid on the list. Although the Ferris family was new to me, if T.J. Ferris was a friend of my father's most likely he was above suspicion. Daddy had a good nose for people. He saw into their hearts—he called it discernment. "Any man that treats a woman without courtesy is a scoundrel," he'd said to my brothers. "If you don't respect and serve your mother, you'll be a miserable catch for some poor woman. Best throw you back into the stream to let the rocks bash some sense into you. A smart woman watches how a man treats his mother."

On my second wedding day, when Lyle stood at the end of the church aisle waiting with his eyes brimming with delight, Daddy had whispered, "I think I'll enjoy getting better acquainted with your husband. He's a good, kind man, Delilah. See that you treat him with respect." I'd kissed Daddy's cheek and would have marched to the front of the church in quick step I was so excited, but the music had us dancing.

I chewed on the end of my pen then wiped it dry and scribbled a note. "I think Kennedy was sent by some sort of mob to check out the land and perhaps get it under market value. But why? We're missing something. Eastern Kentucky has been lived on for hundreds of years. The land's been plowed, tunneled into, and mined since the Revolution. If there are minerals someone would have already discovered them."

Lyle snapped his fingers. "I've been distracted." He wiggled his eyebrows at me. "Let me get back to my internet search." After several minutes making ticking noises on his laptop, Lyle looked up. "Bingo!"

I dropped my pen onto the floor. "What?"

"Last year, a mining engineer from the Colorado School of Mines brought a group of students to the county. They mapped streams, searched through old mining records and shafts, then headed back home. A month later someone arrived to buy land near your Meemaw's. Name of Jackman. Same last name as the engineer in charge of the students."

"So they must have found something. George thought as much."

"Seems likely."

I printed Jackman onto my list. "Meemaw would know if she had new neighbors. We need to speak with her."

"How about tomorrow, Di. After today, I need a little break from mayhem."

In the morning, when we arrived at my house, Meemaw and Savannah were crocheting flowers— pink, turquoise, and lime ones spread out on the coffee table. Curled up by Savannah's feet, Bartles snored softly. The small dog stirred, then jumped up and dashed at us. If he had been a larger dog Lyle would have been tackled.

"Spoiling my dog, ladies?" Lyle smiled as he picked up his Shih Tzu.

"From the looks of it, only one around here being spoiled is you," Miss Vickie piped up from her chair by the fireplace.

Lyle saluted her.

I fingered one of the flowers and tossed it in the air. "These are wonderful. What are they for?"

Miss Vickie pointed a bony finger at the daisy-like petals. "Why for baby caps and little girl headbands." She held up a half-done burgundy headband attached to her crochet hook. "The Christmas bazaar at the church will sell these out in nothing flat."

"Meemaw, have you any new neighbors? Maybe in the last couple of years?"

"Well, the Jones family sold their place two maybe three years ago. Owners tore down their house and put up a fancy cottage. When old Joe Hatfield inherited some land, they up and headed back to Breathitt County. Why are you askin'?"

"Did Joe and Myrtle sell the property?"

"Yep. To a man that comes only to fish. He isn't there much. Was during the summer a bit. Said our little town was recommended by his brother. When he mentioned his brother's name it all came together. A summer ago, we had a bunch of youngin's from a mining school tromping around the hills. One of them told Bruce Tweedy that their professor dragged them to the Blue Ridge to check out the coal country and rock formations. A couple of months later my neighbors up and sell to this western character. He hangs out at the Coffee Maid when he's around. Not a Kentuckian, that's for sure. Accent like you see on TV. All smooth and ripe with round vowels."

Lyle rolled Bartles onto his back and scratched his tummy. "So, he just comes to fish?"

"I think so. He built a kind of dock and seems to spend a fair amount of time by the water. Cain't see him clear, though. There's a bend at the end of the corn field. His land is beyond that and surrounded by trees. Ol' Joe liked things private. Thought he might be running his still. Rumor has it, he made the best moonshine in three counties." Meemaw shivered. She was a teetotaler.

Lyle's eyes glanced at mine as he bit his lip. He didn't need to speak. I could guess what he was thinking. Lyle may have grown up in the south, but he had been the upper crust. The rich didn't need to skirt the law. Eastern Kentuckians, half-starved for opportunity and education, pushed their limits.

After kissing the ladies goodbye, Lyle opened the front door letting icy air swirl around our legs. We'd barely taken two steps when Olive Lorraine Patrick and her escort Will opened the gate between the Salases' house and ours. "Good, we caught you before you could escape." Olive laughed as she spoke.

"Could you look over some paperwork at the office, Delilah? We're going to push for another sewer and electric line for your property. Shouldn't take long, I've the file all prepared."

Lyle lifted his eyebrows. No quick exit from McKeansville. "We'll follow you."

At Patrick and Patrick's brick office a fleet of cars were parked near the stairs. Four cars. A Mercedes, Olive's Cadillac, one plain beige car with a rental sticker on it, and an Illinois licensed Lexus. Lyle pulled in beside the Caddy.

Olive and Will got out of her car. She lifted her chin as if for battle. Will tilted his head and looked left then right as if calculating his next move. As I pushed Olive's telephone number, Lyle said, "I'm calling Bellows." We were eyewitnesses to Neely's attempted murder of Lyle.

I did not want a confrontation.

"Olive," I began as Lyle said, "Bellows," into his phone. We looked at one another. Lyle lifted his gaze to the car ceiling.

"Don't go in. Lyle's calling the sheriff. We don't want to face Neely since we've got to testify against him."

Olive dropped her shoulders and slid back into her car. Peering at them, I watched Will climb in beside her, lean over and take her hand. I swallowed, hard.

It took Bellows and Officer McEntire three minutes to reach us. Bellows strode over to Olive's car and spoke to her as McEntire trotted up the stairs. After a couple of minutes, Neely's gang swaggered down the steps. The entire entourage scowled. When Delany limped out yelling at Bellows, I scrunched down in my seat and began to laugh.

"This circus has four rings instead of the usual three," Lyle muttered.

My laughter stopped when Clarisse emerged on Neely Patrick's arm. Clarisse tossed her head and stared at us, her lips curving into a smirk the size of a hippo's. The car was getting hot in the sun. I rolled my window down. Olive put her hands to her face. "If Clarisse fired Delany why would he still be around?"

Lyle shrugged. "Good question."

If a Mercedes and a Lexus can peel out of a parking spot and race down the street like 60s Mustangs, they did. Nose to tailpipe, the fancy cars screeched past us. The rental car Delany drove limped along resembling its driver.

Lyle lifted his eyebrows. "Impressive. Median age of those characters is five."

I crossed my arms. "Legally can Neely and Clarisse be together?"

"In this state, yes. They were not arrested for the same crime. Neely will be tried for his attempt to shoot me. Clarisse for actually shooting me and for fleecing the locals with her missionary fund scheme. The Feds don't like money laundering and mail fraud."

"What about shooting Josephine in Paducah?"

"Clarisse just confessed, but there is no evidence pointing to Neely. At present it doesn't look like we can get them to testify against each other."

My eyebrows almost locked with tension. Lyle rubbed a thumb over the lines forming on my forehead. "I want you to know that I made a decision seventeen years ago that my covenant with God was more important than my marriage covenant with Clarisse." His blue eyes grayed. "I'd let my emotions and pride cloud my thinking. When Clarisse left, I struggled but finally released her and embraced my relationship with the Lord."

I squeezed his hand.

His eyes lightened. "Maybe Robert is right, and we should saddle our horses and head for the hills."

Patrick and Patrick's reception area looked like a boy's locker room, with a sweater flung over the back of chair, the smell of cigarette smoke and stale food. Olive Lorraine's nose wrinkled with disgust when she sniffed the fetid air.

"Think I'll just stick around for a bit," Bellows said when we joined him in. "Don't trust Neely. He might turn back and intimidate a witness or two." He looked directly at us and dipped his head. "I'll park on the front porch while McEntire wanders around the back."

"Think I'll keep my gun visible." McEntire winked.

Olive wafted her hand in the air to move a curl of cigarette smoke away. "It will take me days to get the stink out of this place. Neely is sabotaging the business."

Will took her hand. "I think not. From my brief acquaintance with your soon to be ex-husband, he never cared about anything but his comfort. I'm here to see that he doesn't pull any shenanigans."

Olive blushed as red as a cranberry. "Well. . ." She stretched out the word like an exercise band. "I've never had a man want to spend extra time with me. I mean, Harry was the exception." She opened her eyes wide as if she had misspoken. "But then we were just kids, Delilah," she spoke rapidly. "You know how high school sweethearts are, they can't even breathe unless they're staring at one another." Olive fidgeted, her feet moving in place.

I shrugged at her. How could I explain that Harry had been more than attentive to me? Harry studied my heart like a biologist did a new species. He'd always found ways to act kindly, open doors, help with the little things. The only time he'd been absent was when a poem was bubbling up like an artisan well and splashing him with words.

Towering behind Olive, Will stood like a colossus. All she had to do was turn around and let him be her fortress.

Olive's face softened. "Well, there was this one time, oh, years ago when we were first married when Neely came home from a business trip and said he'd caught a bad bacterial infection and needed to take antibiotics." Olive smiled. "He stated the doctor had prescribed them for me as well as a preventative measure. Sweet of him to worry about me."

Will looked over her head directly into Lyle's eyes. The look they exchanged was worrisome.

I'd quiz Lyle when we were alone. This wasn't the time. At present all I wanted to do was grab the paperwork and head out of town.

Olive disappeared into her office. Emerging from the office environs and into the hall with a plain vanilla file, her teeth were clenched, and her eyes shot out lightning bolts.

"Olive?" Will stuttered when he saw the look on her face.

"He's been through my files. Papers are strewn over my desk. My copy machine is out of ink so he's been copying things. Probably taking pictures as well. I'll need a week to undo the damage and I've only been in *my* office." When her mouth closed, she sunk down into a heap on a straight-back chair.

Will stood with his hands at his sides, then he thrust them into his pants pockets and pulled them out again. He awkwardly patted her on the shoulder. "Know anyone who can help you sort this out?"

"No," she said in a lost voice.

Lyle raised his hand. "My secretary, Janice. With my sabbatical she's most likely twiddling her thumbs. I'll give her a call."

Phone in hand, Lyle speed dialed Janice.

I studied the paperwork in Olive's folder.

Harry's family farm was large enough to have several houses on the property. It was the county amenities that were going to be difficult. Water, sewer, power all needed authorization. Could we use a well and a drain field? Fortunately, the land was in an adjacent county and they were more amenable to the Morgan name. Unfortunately, we had to keep things from becoming public knowledge. Building permits, wells to be dug, power lines strewn across the landscape would bring questions.

Slapping the folder closed, I tapped my finger on it.

"Puzzled?" Lyle asked.

"How can we keep what we're up to a secret?"

"I've a plan and you won't have to lie about it, either."

"Good. Because I won't."

"I know, sweetheart."

"Well, what?" Olive said sitting up straight.

"Paul is going to apply for the building permits. It will be for a Bed and Breakfast business. He wants several cottages built and to renovate the barn for group activities."

"That might work," I said, kissing him on the cheek.

"It better. I've already put it in motion."

Lyle had a way of conquering the giants before I

knew there were any on the horizon. He studied the matter and took action. Harry liked to contemplate life and come up with a pithy remark. Maybe that is why they were fast friends.

I headed to Olive's office. "Do I need to sign any papers before we head for the hills?"

Olive sighed. "You'll have to stick around for a day or so while I get things in order."

Chapter Eighteen

LYLE'S SECRETARY, JANICE HAD MADE A few phone calls before she hotfooted it our way. As we moved to vacate Olive's office, Mamie, George, Savannah, Elise Weldon, and Josephine arrived overloaded with shopping bags.

"Shoo," Janice said when she spied Lyle. "This is my party. I called in the troops so we can take the bridgehead." She grinned at her witticism. "Boss, I'll see you at the office when you get back from your *honeymoon*." She looked over her glasses at me. "And you, my friend, need to keep him out of our hair. I imagine you've an idea or two."

At that, George lost his composure and punched Will in the arm as he laughed. "And I'm here to relieve Bellows of Olive's protection, right, Will?"

Will winked at Olive. Blushing, she looked quickly away.

Janice's mouth made a serious straight line. "Out of chaos comes order, then creativity. We need to find a method of filing that will confuse Neely or else lock up the files." She handed out brown hued clipboards to anyone within reach. "What is upstairs, Olive?"

"Old files, another office for an additional realtor, cleaning supplies."

Janice wrote something on a slip of paper. "We'll do that last." The women gathered around getting their marching orders.

With a twinkle in his eyes, Lyle drove through the countryside toward our bed & breakfast abode. "Do you have the keys I gave you handy?"

I pulled up my purse that rested on my right foot, unearthed the keys and waggled them at him.

"We're going to see if you can start my car."

The day was sunshiny, winds calm, my heart however was beating an unfamiliar syncopated rhythm. "You trust me?" My voice quavered.

"With everything." Lyle's soft words were a blessing.

He turned off the four-lane highway onto a country road, then a mile south pulled into a tidy farm. At the end of a lane on a swath of bluegrass, horses grazed in a white fenced pasture. A red metal barn stood beside the fence. Using a small key, Lyle opened the padlock on the barn door. The building held rows of canvas covered cars. The flooring wasn't dirt but pristine cement, nary an oil splatter. In the back was a shop with tires, rims, and tools waiting for use.

Six cars were lined up on the left, five on the right of the open space. Lyle strode down the right side with the confidence of a horseman striding through his stables. A smile creased his eyes, and the word joy rocketed through my mind. It was the same smile I'd seen from the back of the church as he first caught sight of me.

Stopping at the third veiled car he squatted and began removing the beige canvas that hid his prize. One left fender became exposed, then the door and back fender, until I tugged at the top of the canvas from the other side of the car. I stood back star struck when the platinum beauty was revealed. I had no words. Waxed like a new model, the 1985, 928 Porsche gleamed. My mouth made the shape of an 'Oh,' but nothing emerged.

Lyle studied me over the top of the car. "And?"

"It's magnificent. May I just sit in it?"

He laughed. "I believe that is allowed."

I could smell the new leather as I lowered into the tan passenger seat. The entire dashboard was clothed in leather as soft as expensive Italian gloves. It was the most luxurious car I'd ever placed my backside in. I shook my head. Driving Harry's vintage pickup hadn't prepared me for a hot sports car, although I'd dreamed of one.

Lyle settled into the driver's seat. "I'd love to watch you drive." My voice held little girl awe and fear.

He chose backroads, the kind that were pale gray on maps but you could explore on lazy Sunday afternoons. The engine purred a soft thrumming sound that could put you to sleep. Harry and I owned practical cars, our van was for hauling soccer equipment and piles of kids, a truck for hauling hay and a horse trailer. I'd dreamed of a convertible. I allowed a contented sigh to escape.

Lyle glanced my way. A smile curved his mouth, replacing his serious straight-lined expression with the smile of a mischievous boy seeking adventure. His foot pressed on the accelerator. The car no longer thrummed but sounded like a day at Daytona. We whizzed on a straight-of-way, then just before a curve, he braked and cornered so smoothly that it took my breath away. It must be how he cornered on a track.

He kept his eyes on the road, one hand relaxed on the steering wheel, his right on top of the gear shift. "Smoothness is everything in managing a curvy road, Di. Control and keeping the car hugging the road like a young man hugs his sweetheart. As much body contact as allowed."

"Is that a quote?"

"From a female driving instructor." Lyle's hand rested on the leather knob as if it were an old friend.

"Do you double clutch when you down shift?"

"Occasionally. Do you want to give it a try?"

"Not yet. I want to watch you." And I did. His face lit up as he cornered and his eyes studied the road like I'd studied the kids to see what their mood was when they came home from school. Fields scrubbed bare of foliage and plowed under were a brown blur as we aimed toward the rolling hills of horse country. We'd missed lunch and were heading to a place Lyle knew of in Lexington when we spotted a truck emblazoned with the Ferris Ironworks logo. Tyler Ferris Jr. was at the wheel. A skinny young man with his ear glued to his phone was next to him.

Lyle pointed at the truck. "What do you say we scout out their haul and see if they've anything we could use in your garden?"

"A wedding present to ourselves," I said. I didn't want to tell Lyle that country fashion wasn't what I had in mind for my European style garden.

We followed as they pulled into a large garden center on Nicholasville Pike. Trees shedding their curled golden leaves stood at the entrance and marched with their crimson hued brothers up the hillside to the garden shop and nursery. Parking in a lot below the loading dock we hiked up the steep drive and reached Tyler as he exited his truck.

Lyle stuck out his hand. The handshake was friendly as were their smiles. "I've decided to buy a little something for Delilah. Liked what I saw in your store and when we saw you, we decided to follow and see what wonders you might have."

Tyler Ferris looked from Lyle to me, his smile radiating to his eyes. The young man in the passenger seat shuffled around the back of the truck as if his feet were half-glued to the asphalt. He pulled his baseball cap low and wouldn't look me in the eyes.

"Joseph, open the back and let the Henderson's see what we've brought."

The anorexic Joseph grunted as if displeased. The twenty-something-young man opened the back of the paneled truck and hoisted himself onto it. Everything was secured with tie-downs and surrounded by moving van blankets. From the cushioned look of things, no dents could damage the metal creations.

"I've in mind something resembling a bicycle," Lyle mused aloud. "My bride likes to ride hers to stay fit."

It also saves gas for town errands, but I'll keep that to myself. Lyle will find out soon enough that I still pinched pennies.

"Take out the things we're going to leave here," Tyler advised his assistant. Joseph turned away and kept his back to us while lowering the shrouded items one by one onto the garden center's tarmac. Was he an introvert?

Slowly the company's assistant and a man from the business unwrapped a cute hedgehog I could envision peeking from behind the tree by the Hosta area, an enormous turtle, one angular unicycle, a monkey with a happy smile, and a wagon stuffed with wrapping to keep it from rattling. Each was cobbled together with odd bits that could be found in car graveyards or a dump.

Lyle circled the pieces. Joseph handed the garden man the bale of papers still stuffed in the wagon. "Y'all can get rid of the paper," he mumbled.

"I'll take the hedgehog if it's available," Lyle said. "And commission a figure on a bicycle. Must have a basket on the back so groceries can be stuffed in. I'll give you a rough sketch."

Lyle glanced back at the sports car then at the animal figure. It was two feet wide by two feet tall and pointy, which would puncture the leather seats. "Maybe you should deliver? I don't believe squeezing it into the hatchback is going to work. Could you add a few miles to your journey?"

"For the right price." Ferris's lips curved upward while an eyebrow sought his hairline.

"Considering the mileage, your inconvenience and the wear and tear on your sensibilities, an even hundred extra and a meal at the best restaurant McKeansville has to offer." They shook on it.

"We'll follow your snazzy sports car," Tyler said.

"What was that all about?" I said as Lyle started his

engine.

"Making friends." He patted my hand. "I'm simply doing Madison's bidding. Only way to discover the culprit is to build relationships."

"Then we should offer them tea and crumpets when they get to my house."

"Great idea. Call your mother and have her get the supplies ready. Would you like your new object d'art behind the garage where no one can see it?" His dimples flashed when he laughed.

"The little critter is really cute, Lyle."

"But?"

"It's like mounting a gargoyle at Monet's Giverny."

"We'll take it out to your farm after we're through. I can't see it in your pristine rose garden. Although Sidney's comments might be interesting."

We put it in the Hosta bed. The hedgehog sat ten feet from where the grass from the trench dug for the new sewer line still was sparse. I hid my wince from the men, took a deep breath and headed up the backsteps to plate cookies Daddy had found at the bakery.

Tyler's helper, Joseph Peebles fidgeted as he swallowed coffee and wolfed down four cookies in short order.

Accepting a mug of coffee, Tyler lifted it and took a sip. His brow indicated he approved. "How is Mrs. Burns?" His voice said, 'I'm really interested.'

I smiled. "Let me see if she's up."

Meemaw was holding court in the parlor. Miss Vickie was crocheting a pile of granny squares. Red, white, and blue filled a basket at her side. I nodded at Tyler and his feet skidded to a halt when he saw Miss Vickie. Eyes opened in surprise, he looked first at Meemaw then and her guest.

"Tyler, land sakes. What a surprise." Meemaw started to rise but Ferris waved her back and strode over to her. "You've come during my social hour." Meemaw grinned. "I don't believe you've met my friend

Mrs. Vickie Hudson."

Tyler crossed the Turkish rug and shook Miss Vickie's hand, then turned to face Meemaw. "I've just come to see how you are faring. Need to report to your fans back in Horsetail Falls that the reports of your demise are erroneous." A man who could alter a Twain quote had my admiration.

Meemaw started to laugh. It built to a crescendo as Miss Vickie joined her. Miss Vickie wiped a tear from her eye. "Don't that beat all, Elizabeth? This kind young man coming to check on you. I'm thinking I need to have one on my doorstep. A man come to court an old woman is a sight to be seen."

Missy's husband didn't miss a beat. "If I weren't a married man, you'd see me with flowers in one hand and candy in the other." A grin shot across his face. "You're missed, Mrs. Burns."

"Pshaw." Meemaw waved her hand as if to bat away a fly. "Only thing missing me is my garden. Cain't leave this dern town until they cut me loose. From the look of things, I'm tethered here as firm as a contrary bull in a stockyard." She lifted an eyebrow. "But I'm about to bust out of town. I've business to do." She crossed her arms, eyebrows fused on her forehead.

"You take care of yourself, ma'am." Tyler dipped his head.

"You tell your father I've a legal matter to settle with him. Time to set things in order. Like King Solomon said there's a time for everything under heaven, and this is a time to heal, to build, and to laugh." Meemaw slapped her right leg.

Ferris took a step back, his eyes big as a whiffle ball. "Yes, ma'am." Tyler walked away as if in a trance.

I kissed Meemaw's cheek then Miss Vickie's and followed him out of the room. Lyle, who'd been standing in the doorway, clasped my hand as I moved past. He lifted it up and brushed his lips across the back of my hand.

As we wandered into the kitchen, Ferris grabbed his companion and headed for the door. "I've a lot to think about. First, the romantic landscape with rose garden and European design isn't suited for my creations. You brought me here under false pretenses." His face softened as he looked at Lyle.

Lyle nodded. "Yes. But I've another place that *is* perfect. I'll have you deliver the pieces I order there. I've a proposition for you." Lyle looked at his watch. "Without ice cream there would be darkness and chaos. Let's celebrate your creativity with a cone or two before you head back to Horsetail Falls. Dessert first, then I'll pay for you to indulge in Carter MacDougal's amazing cuisine."

Tyler's assistant shuffled his feet as if ill at ease. Maybe he was a vegan and walking into a restaurant rife with meat smells, plates bulging with chicken or steak and a menu crowded with offerings including cheese sauces offended him. Even ice cream might prove an issue if he was dairy free. The young man had a two-scoop cone so maybe he was a partial vegetarian. We left the pair staring at Carter's menu like men who'd been eating raw fish on a deserted island.

"One last stop," Lyle said as we eased away from The Chicken Coop.

He drove into the place where the soldiers clothed in blue or gray are lined up across the grass from one another. Here lay the men who had perished in battle of Perryville or lingered in the houses turned into hospitals until pneumonia or gangrene snuffed out their lives. In that generation my family had fought in blue uniforms. One had been captured by Morgan's raiders and freed to return to his Appalachian home. Lyle's ancestors had ventured north in gray cloth.

We drove past the march of graves and settled near the Morgan plot. Lyle held up a finger. "I need a moment with Harry." He smiled his soft smile and I smiled back. I had only spoken with Harry once while on my honeymoon with Lyle. It seemed disloyal to Lyle.

Chapter Nineteen

LOOKING TOWARD THE IRON FENCE HUGGING the Morgan graves I spied a woman hunched over the newest addition. She was dressed in widow's black, a veiled hat perched on her head, a spray of dark roses draped in her arms. I narrowed my eyes and grabbed the door handle.

"Oh, no you don't," Lyle said. "My turn. If the sheriff can't dislodge Harry's mourner, I'll see to it."

Lyle eased the Porsche door open like a new mother peeks in on her sleeping child. He shut it as quietly then walked toward the center of the section as if he were going to visit another site. Circling back, he hid behind the large tree that sheltered Harry's grave and watched. I blinked. The bench I'd ordered months ago sat beneath the tree waiting for me to sit a spell. *Was that why Lyle wanted to stop? He knew the bench had arrived?*

The potato-shaped woman was quite a sight. She drooped over the headstone as if her bones were made of jelly. With a large handkerchief she wiped her eyes, blew her nose, then rose with difficulty, using the headstone for leverage. She took three steps and flopped down on the bench, *my* bench, and took up residence. If she'd simply scuttled out of the Morgan site and headed for home I would have stayed put. But she put her ample derriere on *my* bench and didn't look as if she'd move.

I opened the door and strode toward her. Lyle lifted his head, shook it slowly, eased around the tree and stepped over the Morgans' wrought iron fence. Arms crossed and eyes breathing fire, I guarded the exit gate while Lyle took position on her right flank.

I stared at the woman then gasped, took a step forward and shook my head. "Candace?" I asked in a faint voice.

Lyle leaned forward and looked at his across-the-street neighbor. The one with the binoculars that stared at all of us and I'm sure kept a record of our comings and goings.

"Well, er, I liked Harry," she said, with a sob in her voice. "He always smiled and waved and talked to me while he gardened."

Liking Harry had nothing to do with the odd bits strewn around his grave from time to time. Candance was a nut case in my opinion, but I put my tongue between my teeth and tried to smile.

"Hank said that I'd been all wrong about you both." She looked at her hands and sighed. "Charlene and I were classmates in school and when she married my brother, well, we became friends. I know Charlene is distraught and her raving about you has nothing to do with my brother's arrest. But after Harry died, I've begun to see things differently." Candance's shoulders were slumped. She couldn't look me in the eyes. "Hank confiscated my binoculars and said it was time for me to face the music. I came to apologize to Harry and ask his forgiveness about the things I've said and done."

Why Harry's grave was the place for the women in McKeansville to repent beat me. First Olive Lorraine. Now Candace Abernathy carrying on like it was judgment day and she had to set things right. I stood rooted to the ground as if encased in cement. My face probably was stuck in a Pharisee expression as well. I moved my feet one step at a time until I stood near her.

I took a deep breath. "Candace, I'm thankful you've come. I'm certain Harry is too." I dragged my hand out of my pocket and placed it on her shoulder. She quivered at my touch.

"I know what Hank is doing to help Olive." Candace licked her upper lip. "I've always liked Olive. She's been a friend." Candace stumbled over her words as if she wasn't used to speaking.

I opened my mouth and words poured out too fast to suck them back in. "And Hank has been a great help. We are all thankful that you share him with the community. It was Hank that helped find Savannah, you know."

She nodded. "And he got clobbered guarding Olive the other night."

Lyle coughed into his hand. I glanced up at him. His eyes danced the jitterbug.

Candace sniffed soggily. "With Neely Patrick out of jail it's very dangerous for Olive, you know."

I patted her shoulder.

"I've offered for her to stay with us but she refused, saying she didn't want us in harm's way. Kind of her, don't you think?"

"Yes, very," Lyle said. "It's a little damp and chilly out here, Candace. Why don't we escort you to your car."

"Oh, that is the sweetest thing." She almost cooed. I helped her to her feet, for she was a little unsteady in her black pumps on squishy ground.

Lyle offered his arm. "I'll see to the lady, Di. Why don't you chat with Harry for a moment?"

As Lyle directed Candace toward her blue Prius, I scoured the ground around Harry's grave, kicking away the leaves to see, aside from the flowers, what new offerings Candace had bequeathed on Harry. There was nothing. No Star Wars figures, no faded plastic flowers, not a syrupy note or lacy handkerchief. Unusual for the cemetery sob sister to forget to slather Harry's grave with objects d'art. I turned my head to watch Candace swing her hefty purse into the front seat of her car. "I think we interrupted her," I said to Harry. "You must be having a good laugh about all this fuss. From the weird gifts to discovering our snoopy neighbor was the culprit, must give you joy. It would have been nice if you'd given a hint." I chewed on my lip. "Is she the nut, Harry, or is it someone else?"

Two rocks were stacked on the corner of Harry's headstone. Had someone left a memorial noting their visit to Harry? I picked up the smallest one and rolled it around in my fingers. It was smooth and round, like a stone used for skipping across water, the second stone was lava, pocked with air holes and dark. Lifting it to remove and slip it in my pocket, I exposed a smooshed bit of paper. Uncurling the note, my lips twitched into a smile. "Harry, I so miss your visits with my troop of girls with your sweet bunnies. I'm sorry I flung myself at Delilah in my grief and carried on at the grocery a while back. How I wish I could see your smiling eyes again. Yours forever, Maureen."

I laughed with relief. Maureen Thackery, of all people! She didn't strike me as a woman creative enough to deposit Star Wars figures let alone a bare-naked mannequin draped over Harry's grave. Could it have been the death of her husband and son in the car accident that loosened a mental screw? Hadn't they always dressed as Star Wars figures at Halloween? That would explain the plastic figures littering the twins' graves.

Candace drove off in her usual snail's pace, inching around the outer drive of the cemetery as if afraid of dislodging the leaves.

I sat on the bench. It was still warm which made me smile. If a thaw was occurring with the mayor's sister, pigs would be flying by dusk.

"Signed, sealed, delivered," I sang to Lyle as we exited the courthouse eighteen hours later. I wafted the building permits in his face. "Now on to the property to see how the addition is coming."

"You knew we'd already started?" Lyle's eyebrows lifted toward the gray clouds that promised more rain.

"Elementary, my dear fellow. Too many phone calls and Olive Lorraine had sawdust on her raincoat this morning."

"Remind me not to try to pull one over on you."

"Mothers have to be observant or their kids will tell you they've taken a shower when their hair isn't wet and there is dirt on their chin."

"How did Harry keep a secret?"

"As I recall he hid my birthday presents at your house."

Lyle shook his head as we drove toward The Chicken Coop. "Guilty." He let out a pent-up breath. "I hoped we'd arrive at The Coop after a proper honeymoon. Are you ready for the town's scrutiny?"

"Not much choice since my stomach is growling and I've fried chicken on my mind. Say, you never did explain to me the look you and Will exchanged when Olive talked about Neely."

Lyle cleared his throat. "Mmm. Difficult subject. Perhaps another time." He parked his swank car and we aimed toward the diner.

I put my hand on his chest, halting him in the middle of the sidewalk, right in front of the Bridal Shop with its red and green window display of Christmasy bridesmaid's dresses. "You're as closed mouthed as a spinster sucking alum."

Nodding, Lyle said, "Well, when men are deployed in the military or for long periods of time in clandestine operations there is opportunity for...er...entertainment." Lyle stared at me, hoping I'd get the picture. I scrunched up my forehead.

"I see I need to clarify." Lyle scratched the back of his head. "Well, it's like this. I'm not talking about seeing a movie or playing golf. Women and men of a certain occupation are available for a few hours."

Blinking to get water into my eyes from my bug-eyed gaze I nodded. "I think I'm getting the picture."

"I thought you might. Needless to say, if said Romeo or Juliet is sent home unexpectedly, they might carry a little present to their companion. Hence a convenient lie. Sometimes they claim malaria or something tropical. There are any number of diseases a person thinks up so their partner takes antibiotics."

"An STD isn't the only disease they bring home. Lies corrode a relationship." I didn't want to speak about our topic d'jour at The Coop. "Did you, um, have any problems in that department since Clarisse was behaving like an alley cat?"

"Once." His eyes left my face and gazed across the street. "After she left, I went to the doctor and had a complete physical. After a course of antibiotics and another check-up I'm told I'm a fit specimen for a middle-aged man."

I drew my hand up his arm. "I'll say. The word hunk comes to mind."

Carter MacDougal was at the cash register when we entered. He lowered his chin and gave Lyle a look that would have stopped a charging lion. "Little soon, don't you think, Your Honor?"

Lyle shrugged. "Dead bodies, thievery, family crisis all put a stop to my festivities."

Carter slid out from behind the register desk and took my hand. "He treating you like a princess?"

I kissed Carter's cheek. "Better than that. He is treating me as the daughter of the High King."

"Delilah, Judge." Miss Sophie Brixton waved from a corner booth. Our interim mayor then turned back to two city councilmen, and a secretary whose fingers were flying over a notebook as if they were wings.

Lyle raised a brow. "You violating the open meetings act, Mayor?"

Miss Brixton laughed. "Only if a potluck planning committee needs to be on the local agenda."

We followed BethAnn Tate past the plaques of Harry's poems and the chicken renditions mounted on the walls. When seated at a booth in the back of the diner, she gently placed two black menus on the table. BethAnn's efficient blonde ponytail had been replaced with loose curls streaming over her shoulders.

I smiled at her transformation. "I like your hairdo."

"Thank you. I decided the time had come for a new look." As soon as the words exited her mouth the cell phone in her pocket rang. "I must get this." She hauled it out and looked at it. "Yes, Olive?" she said as she stepped away. BethAnn bent over an empty table and scribbled notes on her order pad as she listened.

Our waitress and Olive being friends didn't compute. What was going on? When BethAnn took our order, I opened my mouth to ask a question when Lyle's reprobate friend, Randall Longworth sauntered into The Coop and hailed Lyle.

I winced. If our honeymoon hadn't already been scuttled, Longworth would stab it to death with a verbal harpoon or two. He didn't disappoint as he slid into the booth beside Lyle without an invitation.

"Well, well, well. So nice to catch up with you two. Word is, you've had a very exciting honeymoon."

"Yes," Lyle said.

"I'm actually here to thank you for my home away from home. I've decided to use the RV as a second residence so I don't have to haul luggage in and out of hotels when I travel. As long as I've WiFi I can function." He glanced up at BethAnn who remained by our booth to finish our order. "I'll have a cup of coffee, sweetheart. No cream, no sugar." He gave her a double take then shook his head.

"I believe I can remember that," BethAnn said tartly. "Miss Delilah, what would *you* like to drink?"

"Coffee will be fine, thank you."

She eyed Longworth as if waiting for his order. "Okay then."

"Hmm." Longworth held up a finger. "I'm going to be at the counter...unless...?"

"No," Lyle said firmly.

"Make mine the usual."

"Of course, *Mr.* Longworth." BethAnn rolled her eyes as she went past me and I grinned.

"As I was saying," Lyle's loquacious friend continued. "You're up to your elbows in adventure and

I'm stuck with spreadsheets and undoing my *former* office manager's larceny."

He sat and drank his coffee with us until our meal arrived, then Randall wandered off to the counter stools, casting a sad look our way as he left.

"Don't say it," Lyle said, holding up his hand. "I should be shot thinking I could waltz in here and have a peaceful meal with my bride."

The chatter in the restaurant stopped suddenly as if a chill wind had blown through. Lyle, who was facing the door, looked up from cutting into his chicken breast. "Oh, hello. This is looking more awkward than a junior high dance."

I laughed at him until I turned around. Clarisse, Neely Patrick and his look-alike cousins stood at the register waiting to be ushered to their seats. BethAnn flipped her hair back with a toss of her head and grabbed four menus. "This way, please," she said in a voice that carried to the back corners. She seated them by the front window and close to the door. The table Harry said made you as cold as a popsicle on a ninety-degree day.

"Ah, BethAnn has seated them in the Arctic Circle," said Lyle with satisfaction.

"That way she can keep an eye on them," I muttered. I turned back toward my groom. "After we check on the building crew let's plan to head for the hills and ask a few questions of the natives."

As Lyle paid our lunch bill, a chirp came from his phone. He fished it out of his pocket. "Of course, that will be fine. We certainly can accompany you." He winked at me. Lyle paid BethAnn a healthy tip and brought me to the door circuitously, so we didn't cross paths with Neely and company or Randall Longworth, but they saw us from the skinny eyed look Neely tossed our way. However, nearly every person stopped us to shake Lyle's hand and make a comment. By the time we were outside the rain had begun in earnest and puddles were forming along the sidewalk cracks.

I looked at my groom. "Care to inform the curious?" I lifted an eyebrow.

"That was your father. Meemaw insists that she return home. The doctor, who your father says is in cahoots with her, actually agreed. Apparently tomorrow we are heading back with them. I think your dad wants a parade to escort her home."

I slid into the luscious seat in Lyle's hot car. "Good. That gives us an excuse to be there." I gazed at Lyle with love-sick eyes and saw a figure behind him that made me frown. One of Neely Patrick's ne'er-do-well cousins had followed us out of The Coop.

Lyle whipped around to face him. "Yes?" he said in a loud voice.

"Admiring your car." The man tossed a half-smile our direction and took a step closer to Lyle.

I turned on my phone, and aiming it around Lyle, began to record the scene.

Lyle, well over six-foot, looked down at the man and stared at the top of his head. The man lifted his eyes and winced at the stern gaze burrowing into him. "And?"

"Be a shame to see it wrecked, a classic car like this." The man put his hand on the roof.

"Be a shame to threaten me."

"Not a threat. A promise." Putting his hands in his pockets Neely's cousin whistled his way back to the diner.

Chapter Twenty

AS SOON AS HE SAT IN the car, Lyle dialed Bellows. "Tom, we were just threatened by one of the O'Neal felons. Delilah has it on her cell phone."

"Which one?" Bellows growled out of Lyle's speaker.

"Curly, not Moe."

"Ah, that would be Liam. He has a ring of hair around his head and in his ears."

I snorted a tense laugh.

"More muscle than brains, is Mr. O'Neal." Bellows' voice didn't have a whit of amusement in it.

"Thought you'd like to know." Lyle looked at me and winked.

"Turn around, Your Honor. Behind you is one of McKeansville's finest. We're keeping an eye on things."

Through the rain splattered back window of Lyle's car, it was hard to spot the plainclothes policeman sitting in a Volvo of 1990's vintage. White paint had peeled to rusty metal. The derelict car looked abandoned. However, a lanky young man sat sipping coffee in a Styrofoam cup in the driver's seat. I waved at Deputy Fergus. He waved back.

"Thought you two needed to know that the Anderson boy sat up in the hospital this morning and wrote he wanted a hamburger. Boy can't chew a thing because of a broken jaw but he wants a burger. Probably going to have to pulverize it." Bellows' voice trailed off. "Take care, Lyle."

Rain descended like Noah's flood as Lyle maneuvered over the sloppy gravel drive of the Morgan's old farm. Parking near the barn, the wheels kicked muddy goo onto Lyle's race car. As we walked up the porch steps,

Lyle's nostrils tightened when he studied the combination of bronze and brown mud that had licked up his pants legs like flames. At least he didn't speak since an irritated Lyle could wither a fresh-plucked rose.

Whistling outside on the porch, Sidney seemed in his element, quietly helping without fanfare or a thank you. Lyle's face perked up at the sound. When he spied Sidney hauling a 2X4 up the staircase he was back to smiling.

In the kitchen a sheaf of architect drawings curled on the table. He unrolled the top one and hunched over it, using both hands to rest on the corners so they wouldn't retract. "Come, love," he said. I moved next to him. He placed an empty coffee mug on one corner and wrapped an arm around my wet shoulder. "This is the landscape with the buildings surrounding a central garden. What do you think?"

The cottage we stood in was the southern side of a quadrangle. Smaller houses formed the remainder that would create a center garden. "So, three cottages are to be built?"

"Not exactly." Lyle had a cat-like smile that turned up on the corners of his lips. I crossed my arms, waiting. "We are moving some one-story houses out here. I've been informed it is faster to either have pre-formed houses or move a couple I've found. Foundations are being poured tomorrow. With this cold it will take a bit of time to cure, but the temperature is not too cold yet so should be fine."

I backed up a step and cocked my head left. "One sketch," I tapped my finger on the paper, "looks decidedly like Josephine's house."

"We thought it a good idea for Miss Vickie to have the same place to avoid confusion. And, she and Miss Vickie can love on the girls. Grandmothers are non - threatening for the most part."

"We, meaning?"

"Josephine, the good reverend, and I. Their present

property will become a neighborhood garden and play place for children.

"How wonderful. That part of town is cramped together as tight as a packrat's suitcase. They need a park. But who is footing the bill?"

Lyle glanced away and cleared his throat. "It is the least I can do. I sit in my robes and swing a gavel. Few lives are changed except for a moment the victims of a crime breathe easier. I want to make a difference."

I crossed my arms. "When did you think about consulting me?"

"Er...I guess I forged ahead without sharing my ideas."

"I guess you did."

"Forgive me, Di. I tend to think things up and do them."

I took his hand in mine. "We're partners, Lyle. We both have to adjust."

Sidney thumped down the staircase, nodded to us as he passed through the kitchen, and opened the back door. The wind blew rain straight in where it scattered droplets on the wood floor like tears. Every time I thought about Savannah and the other child victims of trafficking my stomach roiled as if on a storm-tossed ship. Water on the floor would dry, maybe leave a spot until the floor was cleaned but they would disappear. The girls' tears were shed in hidden places, where only God collected them.

The new day greeted us with low hanging clouds and drizzle. Lyle washed the car in the rain—I don't think he could help himself. He squelched into the house an hour later, ice-cold but content. Close to midmorning we loaded Meemaw and my parents into Dad's sedan and followed them back to the mountains.

Lyle hadn't taken time to reclaim his BMW at the sports car barn so we careened around sharp corners like we were on a race track. However, the pace was in slow motion because my father drove slower than a slug. Not his usual pace, but as he explained to Lyle before heading out, "I don't want to jar my mother into another hospital visit. If you follow us, you'll be gnashing your teeth."

Lyle chewed his lip once on a hairpin turn that he took at thirty miles an hour. He kept glancing in the mirror and frowning as we crawled along the road.

I patted his hand. "I imagine we're holding up a line of traffic that goes back to Berea."

"Good guess. I noticed one car following us as we left McKeansville. Madison must have someone tailing us."

"Or someone else." Who knew Lyle had this over-priced sports car? He didn't drive it in town and had only escorted me around in it for two days. I frowned. *The O'Neals.* The thought made me crane my neck around to spot the car, but the road was so curvy I only saw a cement truck with its rotating cylinder and a pair of motorcycles taking the curves in slow motion.

We arrived in Horsetail Falls as meager sunlight fought through the cloud cover. Dad pulled over at the Coffee Maid, and we parked at the curb behind him.

The usual assortment of well-used trucks sat along the street. I recognized a couple— they'd been around for decades. Bruce Tweedy's Ford pickup straddled a line. Cozying up to his worn truck was Jed McMurry's dented Chevy 4x4. The usual crowd when the autumn winds howled and the crops were in.

I straightened my shoulders. One never knew what might happen in a country diner with Meemaw and Daddy. Mama wasn't a problem in social gatherings. She had the manners of an aristocrat and had taught most of the people here how to diagram a sentence.

When he saw my face, Lyle looked serious. "Need to tell me something?"

"Meemaw can be an interesting lunch guest." My new husband was in for a wild ride if I knew the locals and the way Meemaw could tease.

We had barely taken our seats when McMurry sauntered over and kissed Meemaw's cheek. "Nice to see you on this side of the sod, Miss Elizabeth."

"Glad to be on top of it, too," she returned. "Although, cain't say I'm not looking forward to a better place."

"This son of yours taking good care of you?"

"Cain't complain. He has my daughter-in-law bringing me breakfast in bed while he runs around trying to find yarn at the knitting store. I've still got things to do. I suppose you know all about the sitting around part, eh, Jed? You still making those wreaths of straw and Christmas fir cones?"

"Yes, ma'am. A farmer whose hands are idle in the winter months ain't much."

McMurry doffed his cap at Mama then at me and returned to his table. Tweedy took his place beside Meemaw.

"Ma'am," he said, as he removed his John Deere cap and held it between his fingers. "Right happy to see you."

"And I you. Thank you for caring for my property."

"My pleasure, ma'am."

Meemaw looked him square in the eye. The kind of look that said,' I know what you're up to.' "Still collecting   on   that   bet?" Tweedy turned fuchsia. "I'm not a betting man. What bet would that be, ma'am?"

Meemaw's eyes glimmered. "Have to say that in front of my son the lay-preacher but I've a notion you know what I'm speaking about. I just want to say thank you on behalf of my neighbors the Calloways. They needed to get back to Clay County and you provided the way. Mighty kind of you to get their property sold if you ask me."

Tweedy scuttled off as if he'd been rebuked.

While nodding to her neighbors, Meemaw buttered her cornbread then sipped her vegetable soup. A smile invaded her lined face as young friends kindly fussed over her.

Daddy and Mama kept an eagle eye on her and hardly ate.

Lyle was moving Meemaw's chair back so she could rise when a man dressed in a leather jacket with a sheared wool lining sauntered into the Coffee Maid. He moved like the Marlboro man out on the range. His cowboy boots were worn, his jeans cuffs frayed, and his expression condescending.

All the locals concentrated on the newcomer. Coffee cups halted in mid-air and conversations stalled as silence crawled through the room.

Behind the counter, my cousin cracked a smile. "Afternoon, Mr. Jackman."

"My new neighbor," Meemaw whispered as she struggled to her feet. Lyle helped her on with her coat before she toddled over to the stranger by the counter.

As Meemaw drew near he moved his shoulders back as if he wanted to escape. She stopped and smiled. It was her friendly smile, but the man's eyebrows pulled together. "Never did catch your name when you came a wandering by the river."

"Jackman," he muttered. "Amory Jackman. Didn't mean to trespass. I was looking for a fishing spot." Jackman stood head and shoulders above most men in the diner. Early fifties maybe, but his eyes had the sad look of a man who'd seen too much.

Meemaw's face said she didn't believe a word he uttered. "Not a problem. Just give me a call before you set out. Less likely to get buckshot in your behind that way."

"You missed," he countered.

"On purpose. Don't want to mess with the law around here. Derek can be contrary." That said, Meemaw nodded at Daddy and slipped her hand into the crook of his arm.

"Meet you at Meemaw's," I said to Mama as I lifted my unfinished coffee cup.

Lyle joined me as the locals went back to talking and Amory Jackman settled onto a stool at the counter.

Lyle's eyes crinkled up with amusement. "That was interesting."

I made swirls with my spoon around the dots on the tabletop. "Around here it's a mistake to wander. People like their privacy."

"Your grandmother, I suppose, is a crack shot."

"If she wanted to shoot a varmint at fifty yards, she'd nail it between the eyes."

"She certainly would," piped up Tweedy. "That man from out west been snooping around lots of folks' land when he's in town."

One of the men at the table behind me began to snicker. "Going to get hisself in trouble, if he don't watch it."

"Yep," said a voice filled with laughter. "Maybe you should warn him, Miss Delilah."

Taking my final sip before speaking, I waited a half minute then said, "I'll think about it."

"Something's up," I said to Lyle as we pulled our jacket collars around our necks and headed into the rain.

"What do you mean?"

"Fishing is limited around here. Maybe someone is stocking the river to attract tourists."

"It's beautiful country. You think you have to break the law to get people to appreciate it?"

"This was land scraped clean by ice, rain, and wind. Weather ground the mountains down to hills. Hard scrabble land where people eke out a living and work a job on the side to pay taxes on the farms. If that's the man from Colorado, there's better fishing in the Rockies or on the Holsten River than here."

"What could his reason be for buying property here and occasionally occupying it?" Lyle's voice was thoughtful as he drove toward Meemaw's.

"Think he might be part of the drug gang that's using this area?"

"Colorado does have marijuana drifting across its borders. Experience says that once that takes hold other things come in on pot's coattails. Maybe we should pay the professor's brother a visit."

I laughed. "I'll get out my chart and add him to the suspect list. By the time we're through most of the county will be on it except the toddlers."

With Meemaw's house the temperature of an iceberg, Daddy settled her in his guest bedroom, and we headed to my sister's. A golden glow shone through the evergreens as we rose higher and higher toward Horsetail Falls. Light won its battle with the rain clouds, as Lyle braked for a curve. A car sped up as if to pass us.

"Looks like the car following us from McKeansville is back on our tail." Lyle didn't look pleased.

We'd been to this dance before, a Hummer trying to drown us near Paducah had been enough excitement for a lifetime. I glanced at my cell phone. No bars. Lyle stepped on the accelerator and took the curved posted for 35 at 70. Throat dry with fright, nothing came out of my mouth as I grabbed the edges of the seat with my hands.

"Hang on," said my groom.

His words were a little late in my opinion. He took the next squiggle of curves at sixty-five, keeping all four tires barely on the tarmac. The white car was lost somewhere behind us.

Eyes intently on the road, Lyle said, "Where can we pull off and wait?"

"Next rise is a dirt track leading to the Flannery place. It's on the left not more than a half-mile ahead. I'll tell you when you need to slow down." The sky darkened as the road aimed skyward. "Now, Lyle. See the giant pine on your left. Turn just past it."

A weathered signpost and a broken fence rail indicated their drive. Lyle hit the brakes and slid onto the dirt road heading toward the holler where the Flannery's had their home place.

He drove down the road until he could inch the car away from view. I turned around and counted the seconds out loud as we waited for the Ford Fiesta. Twenty-five seconds passed before it stormed up the hill in front of us.

"We'll let them come back down, then find a spot and turn around. Did you get their license?"

I stared at him as if he'd grown another head. His steeply sloped back window didn't leave room for seeing lower than a car roof.

"I think I just asked you for the impossible. My apologies. I should have used my side mirror." Lyle climbed out of the car with his cell phone, slunk up to the road and hid beside a thin birch trunk.

I sat fogging the windows with my breath until the white car appeared, headed north, and Lyle snapped a picture. "Did you see their faces?" I asked when he slid into the driver's seat.

"No. But I'll have your friend Derek check the plate." Turning around in the Flannery's gravel drive we headed south again. I'd scribbled a couple of things in my notepad while waiting and looked at them again.

"FBI on duty, could be McEntire or Fergus or maybe...just maybe the O'Neal duo."

My voice had the otherworldly tone of an announcer of a 50s horror movie. I thought it was funny. Lyle merely shook his head.

"There are other possibilities. A client picking up a painting from your sister. A lost tourist, a local who was in McKeansville and returning home."

"And wandering the obscure hills in search of what? Shangri-La?"

"It's pretty close to that mystical place with the foggy hidden passages and cliffs."

I wrinkled my nose. My home place was a simple country environment, filled with farmers, miners and working folk. Nothing much romantic about it, although Lyle seemed to speak as if it were.

When we drew up, I spied Suzanne near the falls. Waving over her head she didn't turn around as she sketched. Mist swirled along the bottom of the falls and danced upward until light caught it and made the water droplets sparkle like diamonds.

Lyle grabbed his phone. "I need cell service and the number of the Sheriff's office." Opening my door, he stared at his no service message and held the phone above his head. "I'll go to the window in the living room," he muttered as we walked toward my sister.

"House is open, just put your suitcases in the same room." Suzanne pointed her pencil toward the house without looking at us. I trod over the water-smoothed rocks to her. She sat on a little folding stool before an easel. The lines on her canvas were the shade of the rocks, a light grayish-yellow.

I kissed her cheek then squatted beside her. "Did anyone pull in here a few minutes ago?"

"A couple of women in a white car stopped. They claimed they were lost and trying to find the town. Funny, they didn't even look at the Falls. Just glanced around and took off. Not a Kentucky accent, though. Midwest, I'd guess."

Lyle had disappeared into the house, so I trucked the luggage into the bedroom. Not a problem with wheels and small bags. He heard me as I brought in the second bag and raced over from his hotspot by the window. I waved him away with a shrug. My mind was puzzling on the two women in the car. To think, I needed to be active. Unpacking the bag contents into the dresser I decided to take a hike.

Lyle was still on the phone when I reappeared. I kissed his cheek then left him with his phone glued to his ear. I took the muddy trail toward the falls. Misty air curled my hair into ringlets as I headed along the rock-strewn path. As children, Suzanne and I had raced through the woods from our house to the falls, chasing our brothers and one another like mountain swallows. A guard rail of sorts—a rope tied to metal poles, followed the trail down to the landing where the mist beaded the viewer until water ran like rain. The falls—tumbling and concussing the rocks and water below—made me pause on a ledge and feel the rumble of the thundering water.

This place was the mountain's heartbeat, where water pulsed to nourish the land and sustain its people. I leaned against the fissured rocks and saw the water fall like spasms. My brothers and dad had jumped into the pool from a ledge ten feet up the falls. 'Go feet first, straight down,' Daddy said, 'the limestone has been carved out from the water and the pool is deep.' They'd loved it and climbed the rocks over and over for a repeat plunge. I'd never jumped. Give me terra firma, thank you.

The trail bisected. I took the left-hand route, a deer trail that wandered over slippery gravel to the bottom, then followed the river downstream. The trail on the right led upward to the top, where a viewing platform overhung the falls. It cantilevered from the shore to soar above the falls with giant logs supporting its railed frame.

A shingle of beach edged Horsetail Falls' pool. Pulling my raincoat down to cover a large rock, I settled on it, squirming to make the hard surface more palatable. On a hot summer day when I was little, the water spray cooled me. Today, I shivered. Who would follow us from McKeansville? Did Neely's Irish mob include women? A hand touched my shoulder and I jumped to my feet and whipped around with fingers balled into a fist.

Lyle took a step back. "Whoa! Next time I'll whistle to announce my presence."

"Sorry. Thinking about gangs and the car following us."

"Your old boyfriend is searching the internet as we speak."

He wrapped his arms around me and we watched the water plunge into the pool. Swooping above the torrent in search of prey, a falcon's feathers caught the sunlight on its dark wings, sending a flash of color into the sky. Lyle's warm breath tickled my neck. Wiggling around until I faced him, I planted a kiss on his lips. "Race you up the hill."

He put his hands on my shoulders. "One step at a time, sweetheart." We walked hand in hand up the hill, Lyle in front when the path narrowed.

Glancing to my right I saw the small line of houses that made up the original township of Horsetail Falls. Usually one of the McMillans were perched on their back porch and spying on all visitors. The place seemed desolate, no lights on or snoopy old folks.

Chapter Twenty-One

Parked beside Lyle's sports car was the white car. I stiffened when I saw it. No sign of the occupants or of my sister. Lyle unlocked his Porsche door and retrieved a gun from the glove box. It was the baby one with a metal grip. Maybe I'd shoot straight if I had a teeny-weenie pistol.

Odd that every car he owned came equipped with deterrents. Perhaps being a judge was dangerous. Lyle's eyes swept the area. No one in sight. He waved me behind him. He didn't have to wave twice. I crouched and followed, step by step onto the porch. Lyle's hand turned the carved brass knob. Without a sound, the door swung open. He held his weapon in front of him, left hand supporting his right and both straight out like you see on T.V. Metal clanked in the kitchen.

Closing the front door so quietly you didn't hear the air move, Lyle slunk toward the kitchen doorway. He put his shoulders against the wall, eased his finger onto the trigger and peered into the room, gun in front. He slid into the kitchen staying adhered to the doorjamb.

A woman's voice screeched out, "Mylanta!"

My sister said in a disgusted tone, "Oh, for heaven's sakes, Lyle. Put your pea shooter up and meet some of Delilah's fans."

Lyle laughed, lowered his Smith and Wesson, and stuffed the gun into his jacket pocket. I crept up behind him.

Sitting on wicker chairs at Suzanne's small kitchen table were two women dressed in pants, turtlenecks, and vests. Not any old vests either. One had a turkey emblazoned across the front and the words, 'Be thankful you're not on the menu.', and the other was in a black vest with colorful fabric leaves trailing down a shoulder onto a pile on the bottom. Spying me, the two women jumped up. One clasped her hands in front of her and let out a sigh. The other stood with her mouth open.

"We don't mean to bother you," one said. Which certainly wasn't an honest statement because they'd tailed us from the bluegrass to the mountains. I wanted to say, 'you scared us to death since felons are on the loose and aiming our direction,' but I looked at Lyle, who smiled so broadly his eye lids squinted.

"Ladies," he said with a bow. "Allow me to introduce my wife, Delilah Belle Burns Morgan Henderson. I assume you are here with a book or two in hand." He pointed to a bulging briefcase.

"How did you *know*?" The woman with the turkey basted on her front looked intently at him. Her eyes got soft and gooey, mirroring the women in our town when Lyle walked by. After grabbing the case and dropping it on the table, she unearthed from its depths three of my novels. The red binding told me they were the ones from the French and Indian War series, 'The Mohican Elegy.'

My sister grinned. "About time you learned how to handle your admirers, Delilah." Suzanne put three tea bags into a china pot and opened her cookie jar.

With a hesitant step I moved past Lyle to shake their hands. He gave me a pat on the back for encouragement. It wouldn't bother him a whit to glad hand strangers and make small talk. Maybe he should be a politician. Don't most lawyers end up in the legislature sometime in their life?

My hand was clasped firmly by the turkey clad woman. As she hefted it up and down, the kitchen door banged open. Frigid air brought with it a revolver aimed inward. The woman wrestling with my hand, thrust me in front of her like a shield.

"Well, now," said Derek as he stepped into the room, his ever-present dog by his side. "Having a spot of trouble, Lyle?"

"Not at the moment." My new husband wandered

over to the counter and began to set out tea mugs. Browning took one sniff in the air and seemed to smile with contentment.

"Sheesh Louise," the woman hissed in my ear. "You should announce yourself before you break down the door even if you are the law."

With eyes the size of an ostrich, her friend stared at Derek. "Isn't this exciting, Roslyn? Twice in one day we've had guns pointed our direction. You do live an exciting life, Miss Burns."

Derek holstered his gun. His scraggly eyebrows reached for his hairline. "Which one of you is the owner of the Fiesta?"

The woman using me as her protection said, "I am."

"Well, Mrs. Pruitt, our little town is honored to have the Cincinnati head librarian visit us. Are you here to see Miss Burns's paintings?"

She shook her head of gray curls. "No. To get D.B. Burns to sign our books for a library fundraiser." She turned her gaze back to me. "Do you paint as well?"

"My sister is the nationally acclaimed artist, Suzanne Burns." I smiled at Suzanne over the head of the woman.

The librarian brought her hands to her cheeks like a stunned emoji. "Oh. We weren't told that. This is exciting, isn't it, Anna?"

"Who informed you that Mrs. Morgan, er Henderson would be in McKeansville?"

"My sister, of course, who lives in McKeansville. She showed me a picture of D.B. Burns from the newspaper. When it was announced that Miss Burns resided in that little college town I set right out to find her. My sister gave me her address. Just as this man's Porsche headed out the driveway, we spotted her in the passenger seat. I had the day off, you see, so we followed."

Which I suppose makes as much sense as anything.

"You must be hungry." Suzanne motioned toward the plate of cookies. "Write down your names so Delilah can autograph your books and I'll serve tea."

Tea kettle whistling, Derek standing flat-footed in Suzanne's kitchen, and the two women looking unapologetic didn't strike me as funny but as a bother. *Oh, dear, Lord. Let me accept the interruptions with grace.* Browning circled the room and snarfed a dog biscuit from my sister, which was a surprise, because Suzanne didn't have a dog. "Who is your sister?" I thought I'd have a word or two with the woman.

"Maureen Thackery," she said as she eyed the cookies. "You are good friends, I believe."

"She was a friend of my husband, Harry."

"Glad to meet you, Harry." Roslyn walked to Lyle and shook his hand.

"I'm Lyle. Mrs. Henderson's second husband. She collects them."

I gave Lyle my scrunched up, don't-mess-with-me look. He waggled his eyebrows.

"It's no wonder, her being a pretty thing. Some women have men circling like a shark circles a swimmer."

I signed their books. They gobbled up all the cookies, drank two cups of tea each, and would have followed Derek down the mountain if Suzanne hadn't invited him to dinner.

"I like this better than those little bacon wrapped weenies you served the other night," Derek said as he filled his plate with antipasto salad and eyed the prosciutto wrapped pile of cheese sticks.

I glanced at my sister.

She shrugged.

Suzanne did not entertain male friends. Suzanne painted. She lifted a blonde eyebrow. "Derek was here checking the security latches on my studio. He thought they were wobbly when he was here last."

I lifted a brow in return. "Huh."

"Suzanne has thousands of dollars' worth of work laying around. All it would take is a van to clean her out." Derek popped a Castelvetrano olive in his mouth. A man who shot his own meat and dressed it liking high end Italian foods seemed a bit odd. "Nice ladies you had for tea. All your fans probably are." Derek waited for me to answer.

"I don't know. I've kept a low profile."

"From what I've heard, you've been as hard to find as a moonshiner in Breathitt County."

Lyle looked up from his seat at the kitchen table. "She likes her privacy."

Derek reached down to pet his dog. "Always was shy and bookish."

"Still is bookish," Lyle said. He sipped from his water glass, put it down and added, "Introverts like to pick and choose their company."

Derek laughed. Not an uptight laugh but a warm, amused one that made you want to smile. "If you get too close, introverts will likely whack you with whatever is handy." He rubbed his jaw. "I've had some experience in the matter."

He had that right. I slid my glance toward my sister. Her cheeks were cherry colored. "I've cannoli for dessert."

Derek took the only chair with arms. Suzanne sat opposite him. "Would you care to join us in blessing the food?" he asked as if he were the master of the house.

I opened my mouth to say something and felt Lyle's foot press on mine. His eyes were twinkling so I bowed my head and waited for things to play out.

"Blessed Lord," Derek said in his low bass voice, "we are grateful for the abundance you have provided. The abundance of family, love, and this food. Thank you for giving us this time and one another. In Jesus's name, amen."

This was not the gawky kid I remembered. Derek had never darkened the door of a church when we were kids. Derek's grandfather had been a Pentecostal evangelist that stormed through the mountains and left his family to manage the farm. Made quite a reputation for himself, what with his wife having to clean houses and work plucking chickens at the butchery. Turned his kids against the church. Don't know if it did against the Lord.

I let out a sigh. The problem with small places is we park people in spots and never let them drive out and explore the countryside. Derek being a Christian would certainly make him acceptable to Daddy, *if* Derek was courting Suzanne.

I leaned forward and grabbed a pair of olives. "Do the McMillans travel to Florida this early in the fall? The house seemed empty when I saw it."

Suzanne looked at me sideways. "They went early because their Navy son has a new baby in Pensacola. They do rent it out sometimes. Don't know if Kennedy will find a willing victim for high rent and the winter isolation."

"Kind of lonely up here with the house shuttered. Where are the Talberts?"

Derek waggled a celery stick at me. "Off on a cruise. Then they spend time in their condo on a beach in Florida. I keep an eye on things." His eyes roved to my sister's face and stayed there.

When Suzanne and Derek headed for the studio after dinner, Lyle patted the couch seat near the fireplace. "People change. He seems a good ol' boy."

"Since when did my erudite husband start speaking like a country song?"

"I'm a man who was raised on the soil, Di. Mine just happened to be many acres and have people who worked the land. As long as Derek's eyes are cast a different direction than toward you, I'm fine with him sitting at the table in the cat-bird seat."

The first day of snooping didn't get us any closer to the

drug pipeline. While Tyler Ferris and Lyle sketched a rude drawing of a bicycle, I caught lunch with Missy Ferris at the Coffee Maid. She seemed preoccupied, her gaze wandering from coffee machine to the old cash register standing behind the counter.

"You seem a mile away," I murmured.

"I've a feeling that something weird is going on, or you wouldn't be back in town again. What's up?"

"Meemaw. I need to get her comfortably settled. She's worried about living all alone on the farm. I'd like her to come live near me."

"Your mama wouldn't put up with that. She's been in charge of the comings and goings in your family since she married into the Burns clan. Takes after her mother-in-law, I reckon." Missy shrugged.

I lifted the cup in salute. "Your husband's operation has a rather strange young man working with them. What's his story?"

Missy snorted. "Joseph is the county clerk's nephew, and not worth much more than the clothes he stands up in. He had a vacation at the juvenile hall when he was seventeen. Then he wandered around town and stirred up trouble. My sweet husband listened to Mrs. Peebles begging for him to get a job. Tyler offered one. Joseph does what he's told, but little else. I like an employee that has some gumption. Wants to get ahead."

Gushingly in love, not a negative word leaked from Missy during our conversation. Her admiration for her husband and her dream of a thriving town, with businesses that encouraged and provided for people, shone through our time. An exciting vision.

Later that evening when comparing notes, Lyle reported that Tyler Ferris was juggling three balls at once with two companies, an entrepreneur for a wife, and was enjoying the entire adventure.

Day two found us tromping over Meemaw's property at

dawn, fishing poles over our shoulders, bait and tackle box in hand. In Autumn the river became a torrent, water racing past without its summer chuckle. Ice was on the puddles and my gloves didn't keep my fingers from feeling like fish sticks in a supermarket freezer. We weren't casting for fish but for Meemaw's neighbor.

Harry's fishing rock was moss covered and seemed lonely without his rear end occupying it. I shook my head to let the thoughts of Harry flee, but they had lodged in a brain crevice. His uninhibited laugh filled the air as we sauntered along the creek bank. I hesitated to reach for Lyle's hand with my thoughts on Harry.

Sighing, I studied the old poles I'd unearthed in Meemaw's barn. They had rust on the guides. At least the fishing line wasn't a rat's nest and the bail moved. Time to start clearing out her barn and get things ready for her move. She'd been in the process for years, giving this and that tool to the grandchildren for their gardens, but a farm's accumulation was a mountain of work. I'd need to write that on our schedule. Between hunting up villains and dodging Clarisse, we should have time to cart tools to the Ferris establishment for repurposing.

My long johns didn't keep the cold from settling on my calves and feet. Lyle promised we would only be here long enough to make contact with the Marlboro man, and see what he was up to. Dusting the pole on my jeans leg, I watched Lyle's breath merge with the low-lying fog. He huffed a visible puff of air onto his hands to warm them. The trees dripped dew down my neck as I stepped along the riverbank. Removing my gloves, I started to bait my hook, when Lyle took the pole from me.

"On her honeymoon a wife is served by her adoring spouse. Allow me." He put the nightcrawler on the hook and handed me the pole.

I cast into the greeny-blue water and began to reel in the line when I felt a tug. "Lyle, think I've caught a twig or something."

"Reel it in and I'll unsnarl you."

It wasn't a twig but a ten-inch rainbow trout. I waggled it in front of Lyle, my pride bursting out with a laugh. "We can eat this one. If it was a Brookie we'd have to release it. It's the law." Being a judge, I figured Lyle would be a stickler on the matter. Lyle cast in his line. I unhooked my fish and dropped it in a bucket.

I baited my own hook as Lyle reeled in and recast. Another fish hit my line as soon as the worm entered the water. Five fish later, Lyle threw his pole down. "I give up. Think I'll sit and watch while you get us dinner as well. Harry never said you could out fish him. Another thing I'll have to chat with him about."

Lyle hadn't been skunked. He'd caught a tangle of moss, a Brownie he had to toss back, and a twig. I had out fished Harry a time or two but why brag about it. We'd been a team. Sometimes he'd land the fish, sometimes I would. I smiled at Lyle. "Seven should do. Let's take these to the man next door." I held up the largest two.

Lyle grinned. "Should have known a mountain woman was resourceful."

"But I'm not so handy with a gun."

"I noticed. Something else to add to your repertoire."

We hiked along the bank, pushing aside the frozen brambles and avoiding the poison ivy that snaked up the trees. Mr. Amory Jackman strode down the hillside when he saw us. No gun in sight, but he didn't look pleased because his nostrils were distended and his mouth tight as a tick.

"My wife caught some fish this morning," Lyle said with a nod toward me, "we thought you might like a couple."

Marlboro man's face changed from tense to a hesitant smile. "That would be very nice," he said in a western drawl. I handed him the line I'd tied the fish to. They gleamed blue and silver with a scale or two of rusty red. "Looks like a nice breakfast for one." He smiled. "If you have any more, I could fry some up for all of us."

Lyle looked at me. I shook Jackman's hand. "That would be lovely." My polished voice sounded foreign in the setting. "May I help?"

"No, ma'am. I'm an old bachelor and can rustle up a breakfast without aid. Come in for some coffee to warm up. From the blue look on your lips, you'll be a popsicle in a moment." He thrust open a door that squealed in protest at being disturbed and nodded toward the interior. "The house is in the middle of a remodel but I've a clean seat or two. I'll clear off the table."

Meemaw's former neighbors had grown old like the gnarled oak heaving up the ground by the back door. Their eyesight and energy had disappeared with their youth. Last time I'd seen the pair, they'd been toddling down their drive for the mail. Nice that they could now live closer to their kin.

The house canted north and if jarred, might slide down the backyard and end up in the river. However, Jackman's abode was habitable and had a sort of order. Tool boxes inhabited corners and it appeared that the new owner had a renovation in progress. There wasn't any sign of sawdust or fresh lumber about, though. Or cement, which was needed for the foundation.

On the dining table rested a pile of papers with topics on minerals in the Appalachian range, gold mining in Alaska, and a wildlife field guide from the Kentucky government.

Jackman heaped them onto the floor. "I've coffee ready. Grab a mug, Mrs. Henderson, and sit by the fire while I take care of the fish. Have any objections if I add fried potatoes and orange juice?"

Lyle gave Jackman his judicial, stern gaze. "I believe I can fillet a fish or two. Why don't we work together while the fisherwoman gets a moment to put her feet up?"

"Would it be all right with you if I visited your lady's room?"

Jackman shot a grin my direction. "Be my guest.

Down the hall, first door on the left." He pointed past a stack of paint cans.

I didn't need his facilities. What I wanted to do was snoop. Was he growing a stash of marijuana for his personal use or for selling? Was he part of the drug problem here or into something else? Nothing in the bathroom or the two small bedrooms further down the hall. After my quiet-as-a-cat search, I plopped down on a cushy man-sized couch that was so deep my feet were off the floor. Sitting back, I studied the living room. It was spare as a New England farm house but above the fireplace was a painting. I recognized the distinctive color choices. Pushing out of the couch and stepping to the mantle, I studied the brush strokes. The right-hand corner had Suzanne's scrawled S. Burns. The man had good taste even if his house was sliding down hill.

"It's a Burns," said a voice behind me. "Local artist with national acclaim. One of the reasons I settled here. I like the feel of the country and that particular waterfall."

"You've moved next to the Burns matriarch. Have you met the artist?"

"No. Don't expect to. She's been around a long time judging from the amount of work she's produced. Probably my neighbor's sister-in-law and in her eighties I'd guess."

He turned on his boot clad heels and aimed back to the kitchen. Apparently, he wasn't much of a conversationalist or he'd have heard an earful about Suzanne from the locals, who adored her.

Chapter Twenty-Two

THE DAY TURNED COLDER. RAIN HAD a hint of ice in it as we walked past Meemaw's garden fence. I was not ready for winter to set in. Cold weather meant huddling in coats and searching for gloves in pockets. "The man can certainly fry a fish," I said as we climbed Meemaw's porch steps.

"And seems friendly enough."

"What did he mean about finding hidden treasure in the hollers?"

"Not certain. Perhaps he has dreams of settling down. Perhaps he thinks there's gold in them thar hills." Lyle laughed and shook his head. "He's an engineer, like his brother, who buys a house with a bad foundation, plumbing that's seen a better day, and no internet. Something doesn't add up, my sweet."

"Something else is bothering me about Meemaw's new neighbor. Did you hear how he pronounced Versailles? Like a Kentuckian...Versales instead of Versigh. I should have gotten him to say Yosemite, Kentucky. If he'd said, Yosomight like we do instead of the western pronunciation we'd know he was originally from the Blue Ridge area."

"Hmm," was Lyle's comment.

The cold was settling in and my face and ears burned from it. "Our new neighbor is from Colorado where dope has afflicted the population." I chased on with my thoughts, letting Lyle sort as I went. "I didn't find any pot growing in the back rooms."

"Hold it!" Lyle stopped me in my tracks. "You checked out his house?"

"Of course. The bathroom stop was a ruse. I needed to see if he was up to no good. He and Kennedy are new to the area and both take off for who knows where. I mean, has anybody checked out Jackman's teaching credentials? And then there's Kennedy. He disappears on weekends. Your friend, Jackman, also takes off for weeks on end. Are they working together on moving drugs from here to there? I doubt if locals are involved. After all, this is still the Bible Belt."

"Di. I've handled many a case of nefarious behavior in the 'Bible Belt'. There is nothing new under the sun and that includes deception and lies."

I knocked on Meemaw's door. She'd taken up residence as soon as the heat was at 75 degrees. "Some old people," she said once, "don't have any blubber to keep them warm."

My mother's blue eyes stared at me through the side window. She flung the door open and ushered us in. "Saw your car. What have you been up to?"

Lyle smiled. "On a fishing expedition."

My mother lifted her eyebrows. "Care to enlighten the locals?"

Lyle shook his head. "We're here on unofficial government business."

"Monkey business, if you ask me." Meemaw came into the hall. "You two need to skedaddle off on your honeymoon and ignore the government initial folk, whether DEA, FBI, or any of that lot. Including my new friend, Madison." She wiped her hands on her apron. "You find out anything regarding my property?"

Lyle nodded. "Yes, ma'am. From the paperwork I've seen, the Ferris family has a good case. I think getting a second opinion is advisable."

Mom put her hands on her hips. "Humph. Losing the land is the least of our worries. Meemaw needs to come live with us and let us care for her."

"Pooh!" Meemaw waved her hand. "Last thing I need is a caretaker. Divesting myself of this old heap"—she patted the casing of the living room doorway—"won't be a problem. What will be, is making certain that Mr. Ferris isn't tricked by some city slicker into giving the land away for a pittance." Meemaw's face grew pale.

I took her arm and guided her toward the Victorian

rocking chair. The one by the fireplace that had hushed many a fussy child.

She settled slowly. "I wouldn't trust Kennedy either. Man is in cahoots with some unsavory characters."

My mother eased onto the high-backed settee. "I might have seen them when we were grocery shopping yesterday."

"Oh?" Lyle's eyebrows went upward.

Shrugging, mom looked at her feet. "A fancy Mercedes was hitched up in front of Kennedy's office. Had an Illinois license plate."

Lyle slowly raised his head, looking first at my mother then at me. "That is very interesting. Ladies, I fear my wife and I must excuse ourselves." With a nod of his head, he grabbed my hand and led me toward the door.

"Odd," muttered my mother.

"Not for them," I heard Meemaw say.

The way Lyle drove toward town you'd think a posse was after him. The roads were getting slick with ice so I grabbed the seat, one hand on each side. We swerved around curves and flat out ignored the white dividing line. I didn't let my piggy squeal noise erupt but it was a close call.

Lyle let out a whistle as we swept past Horsetail Falls Road. "Good thing there isn't much traffic here."

I was breathing so fast words couldn't get past my vocal cords. Lyle hit the dirt side of the road and a plume of mud and leaves formed a cyclone behind his sports car. It enveloped a black truck following us. I noticed Lyle smiling to himself as I heard a screech of brakes.

"Enjoying yourself?" My words more tart than amused.

"So are you or I would have heard your chicken

squawk."

"I stifled it."

Lyle eased on the brakes when he saw the white steeple of the first Free Will Baptist Church of the three Free Will Baptist churches scattered around Horsetail Falls. "But not your schoolmarm disapproving face."

I squinted at the speedometer. We were now going fifty-five in a posted thirty-five zone. It was better than eighty but not by much. "If you're planning to keep an eye on Kennedy's visitors, I suggest you sneak into town rather than getting an escort with a siren from Derek."

Lyle smiled his easy smile that made his dimples flash and began to slow his speed. The Mercedes was nestled up to the curb in front of Kennedy's office when we drove past. Lyle parked near the courthouse where we could keep an eye on things. A wisp of cloud fingered through the trees, then congregated with others until they came together like couples on a dance floor. Inclement weather had crept through the countryside and settled on the town.

We eased down in the seats and got comfortable. A long minute slid by. I gazed at Lyle and smiled. "I suppose on a stake out we have to lay low."

"Been my experience."

"When?"

"Oh, I've done a couple of ride-along trips with the local police. Educational."

"Do they let civilians do that?"

Lyle raised his eyebrows. "Interested, are we?"

I nodded. "If I ever write mysteries, I'd need to know police procedures."

"You've had enough experiences with lowlifes from Neely to Buck Mays. You need to be an observer, my sweet." Lyle drew his finger down my nose and bent to kiss me. It was the kind of kiss that said, "I like you very much."

It was cozy being together, alone. We steamed up the car windows with our breathing which didn't help with visibility. I glanced up, breaking our little tête a tete. Someone was walking out of the courthouse. Swiveling my head to see more clearly, I caught a glimpse of a trench-coated O'Neal taking the alley behind the courthouse and then walking toward the center of town. I pointed him out to Lyle. We didn't speak. He'd recognize Lyle's car if he saw us, but keeping his eyes on his footing in the rock-strewn alley, he didn't turn our direction.

A few minutes later, skipping down the courthouse steps was Joseph of Ferris and Co. He held a thick white envelope in his hand, and eyes stretched wide, stared at it. When he reached the sidewalk, he had a grin plastered across his face. He began to whistle and displayed a stylish dance move with each step. The skinny young man walked our direction.

Lyle scrunched down until only his eyeballs and forehead were visible. I copied him but kept my eyes on the figure in jeans, overcoat, and fancy leather boots. We were close enough to see they were the type of footwear worn by Hollywood stars pretending to be cowboys. Nary a scuff mark. Once a shoe salesgirl, always an observer of what covered other's toes. Inadvertently I looked at Lyle's feet. His boots had enjoyed many a year, judging from the wear on the heels.

Joseph looked over his shoulder. Thinking he was the only person around he opened the envelope. A smirk flitted across his face as he drew out a wad of cash. Stuffing the money into his coat pocket, Joseph headed toward my cousin's establishment. There was a bounce in his step that hadn't been there when he'd hoisted garden art from the back of the van.

Lyle raised himself from his bi-folded position. "Didn't know the courthouse had a bank inside it." Before I could comment, he started the engine. "Movement at the real estate office. Two over-dressed Chicagoans are heading out. What say, we follow them?"

"I'll call Derek while we have cell service." Derek

answered on the first ring. "Hey."

"Hey yourself."

"There's a couple of visitors to your city that need looking into. The O'Neals are ex-felons and have been at Kennedy's office. They're just heading out."

"Heard of 'em from the FBI. On it." He disconnected.

Lyle let a truck touting a red and a blue feed-and-seed store logo slip past us. Then, before we could turn onto the street, a rusty Jeep with a Colorado plate left the coffee shop. The jeep hung close to the bumper of the feed truck. It gave our clandestine maneuvers coverage.

Derek's tires squealed in protest as his official car spun out of its parking spot. With his foot stomping on the accelerator, he entered the cavalcade. Keeping two car lengths' distance, the sheriff followed Neely Patrick's cousins. Subtle wasn't a word in Derek's vocabulary.

Joseph whipped his head around at the sound of the sheriff's departure and sped up his leisurely amble to a sprint. He changed his direction and aimed toward the train tracks where the sculpture creating took place.

An icy rain began to hit the windshield. Our higher elevation usually meant drier air, but mountain areas had persnickety weather. Lyle switched on the wipers. The ice on the windshield made cracked patterns on the edges, obscuring our view.

We followed four pairs of tail lights. Fog swirled among the trees and snuck over the tarmac like an apparition. It grew dense and the cars were swallowed in its soup. Fog meant ice on the roads and that meant conditions were ripe for sliding. I prayed Lyle would slow to a crawl. He didn't have a chance to speed up with the slow vehicles ahead. When the feed truck turned up Clay Pidgeon Road, we had opportunity to see a few feet in front of it. The first pair of lights disappeared.

Lyle's voice broke the silence. "They're either headed toward the Burns turn off or the state highway that will take them toward Berea."

I hoped it wasn't toward the family properties sprawling along the road. Burns Road connected the large tracts of the Burns land. The three parcels as well as the old farm Meemaw inhabited, had to be protected. Well, Meemaw, my uncle, and widowed aunts had to be protected. Land can take care of itself. I wriggled in my seat, suspecting the pair were going to strong-arm Meemaw into giving away her land for a pittance.

The four-wheel-drive jeep gathered speed and disappeared around Fellers Bend. It was a tricky spot and many a stranger had ended up in the ditch. Derek's police car slid sideways as it hit a patch of slick road then straightened. Lyle slowed.

Reaching the top of the ridge the fog thickened, reminding me of a horror movie in a secluded area. We heard a squeal of brakes then a loud crunch of metal. It was at the Burns Road turn off. A series of metallic groans echoed in the soggy air before we saw the Mercedes' rear imbedded into the trunk of a giant yellow pine, the jeep pulled in behind it. Derek was next, then we stopped. The driver of the jeep leaned over and grabbed something from his passenger's seat. A jeans clad Amory Jackman levered himself out of his Jeep's seat. Opening his jacket, Jackman slid his retrieved object into an inner pocket. It was shaped like a gun. Derek switched on his emergency lights.

We all had parked haphazardly at the top of the hill. Not a safe location with the roads treacherous. The pair of hoodlums in the Mercedes exploded from each side of the car. The passenger, the plumper of the two, was holding his head. Blood dripped between his fingers. He got in the driver's face, balled his fist, and punched the other man in the nose.

With a brief shove to the plumper O'Neal, the thin driver, whose nose was canted sideways and bloody, got ready to fight. Jackman separated the pair.

Lyle's lips straightened into a line. "Better stay here. Their choice of prehistoric language will not be fit for your ears."

My view of flaying arms and flapping lips was amusing. Jackman tried to wipe off a bemused smile. When he arrived, Lyle smiled at Meemaw's new neighbor, then removed the man with the bleeding head to a spot down the road and a safe distance from his irate cousin. Because his legs wobbled as he walked across the rut crusted dirt, Lyle kept a hand on the O'Neal thug.

Derek tapped on my window, gave me a thumbs up sign, then sauntered into the scene, his energetic dog running circles around his master's legs. Derek didn't aim toward the gathering of men but wandered around the smashed car, squatted by the passenger side to examine something, then rose. With a slight smile, he scratched the back of his neck. After picking up an armload of red cones from his car trunk, the sheriff headed toward the road. Minutes later he led the pair of cousins to his car. Derek didn't go back to town but down the farm road toward Meemaw's.

Jackman jumped into his jeep, giving a slight wave as he backed past me. Lyle mumbled as he slid into the car that we'd better protect Meemaw from marauders. At the top of the rise he gazed down at the farmstead. The sight of my mother hustling out of the front door with a shotgun aimed at Derek's windshield made Lyle shake his head. "Guess I'm not needed," he mumbled as she lowered her weapon when the sheriff climbed from his car.

Can't recall my mother being familiar with guns so I didn't want to miss this encounter. Before Lyle stopped the car, my hand was on the door handle and my feet aimed toward the grass.

Lyle slid his gaze my direction. "If I don't do my gentlemanly duty, I'll hear about it from at least two Burns women and an ex-boyfriend."

"Derek's not an ..." before I could finish Lyle winked.

The men in the backseat of the sheriff's car emerged looking miserable. Blood dripped from one's cut eyebrow while the other exited with hunched shoulders and a nose that had been flattened.

Jumping out of the car, Derek's brown spotted dog investigated his backseat companions. With his nose inches from one O'Neal's pants zipper, the man hit him with the back of his hand. The dog yelped. Derek whipped his head around to see Browning flying away from the car. In mid-air the dog spun around, landed on his feet, and attached his teeth to his attacker's arm. Derek made a dive to collar his K9 companion, but Browning hung on with the tenacity of a crocodile to a warthog. Browning wasn't moving and neither was the O'Neal until Derek whistled two notes. The pointer released his grip then backed away, but not without a snarl aimed at the offending hand.

When he spied Meemaw creeping around the side of the house, aiming her shotgun at the backside of the two miserable looking O'Neals, Lyle shook his head. "Let me handle this." He squeezed my hand and moving as fast as a lizard swallowing a fly, he went to placate my grandmother.

I grabbed a breath. I should have concluded my mother wouldn't be the only one with a shotgun since Meemaw had fired buckshot at her trespassing neighbor. Afraid she was going to cock her gun before I could convince her to lower the barrel, I opened the car door. Meemaw took offense at mistreating any of God's creatures. And my grandmother was a dog lover.

The wind blew the frigid rain sideways. Pulling up my collar, I hustled toward her as the men headed for the porch. Derek glanced toward my grandmother and chewed on his lip. She stood with her legs spread apart to get strength to fire and didn't lower her gun when their eyes met.

Lyle reached her before I did. After relieving her of the gun, Lyle offered Meemaw his elbow. They joined the group on the porch. Following, I shook the rain from my wet hair and sidled to the side of the front door. A better position for watching the action.

Chapter Twenty-Three

MEEMAW CLEARED HER THROAT. "HARRUMPH. DON'T think much of your manners, but mine would be derelict if I let you stand out here looking pathetic and freezing. We'll venture inside and let the fire steam our damp clothes and drink a cup of coffee." She bent down slowly and petted the dog. "I've a bakery made coffee cake begging to be consumed. And you two"—she pointed a bony finger at the O'Neals—"need some attending too. After you, gentlemen. And you"—she pointed at Browning—"wipe your paws." Her laugh made everyone join her, except the two surely men named O'Neal.

Lyle leaned over to me and whispered into my ear, "Shall we find out what the O'Neals are up to, my dear? Their little mishap was no accident."

The first thing Derek did when he came in was head for Meemaw's landline phone. "Always have trouble connecting to civilization up here," he said. "Only way for good service is to stick to the old things." He placed a call to the local car repair shop, Ferris and Ferris, then took up residence by the kitchen doorway.

Meemaw's hospitality didn't loosen the injured men's lips. After examination of their injuries and Meemaw cleaning the man's forehead and giving a baggie with ice in it to his injured companion, the pair sat side by side on Meemaw's Victorian settee with their lips fused. Easing down into a blue floral side chair, I studied the pair. The one who'd threatened us outside of The Coop had a thesaurus of words to share and the other one was probably as loquacious. What had driven them to silence?

Finally, with his blue chintz mug of coffee, the

plumper one pointed at Browning. "Get your mutt to sit down."

Meemaw gave him the look of death. She'd used it a time or two on me when I'd shown up for a piano lesson without practicing for a week.

Derek shook his head. "Cain't. Browning's doing his job. He is on patrol duty." Derek fingered his lip. 'Course, if you hadn't attacked a K9 officer maybe he would settle down." He smiled. The smile, I recall, that he attempted just before his lips hit mine. "No telling about a dog, though. He always knows when something smells fishy, being a good hunting dog."

The talkative O'Neal spit out, "We're injured." His voice held a Midwestern whiny tone that made Meemaw narrow her eyes. "If we must wait for a tow truck to take my car in for repairs, I don't want to be around a mutt that is an attack dog."

Derek shrugged with one shoulder and sipped his coffee.

Standing by the fireplace, Lyle glanced down at the pair. "Thought you'd be sticking with Neely, not snooping through the mountains."

"We're not snooping." The plump one rose to his feet in anger. His companion waved him back. He looked at his fingernails as if interested in their shape. "Er...actually, we're fishermen. We came up here looking for a piece of land along a river. Heard there's good fishing and lots of quiet."

"Wrong time of year for the salmon." Lyle's sideways smile almost gave him away. "Perhaps you're hoping for the tuna that is found in the rivers when the snow flies."

The one Lyle named Frick licked his lips. "Yeah. We love to fish for tuna."

The other man jabbed him in the ribs with his elbow.

Coughing into his hand the talker continued, "Well, what I mean is, your real estate man in town suggested some land around here is on the market."

My mother stomped over to the pair and stared them in the eyes. "You see a for-sale sign on the road?"

"No, lady, we didn't. If we hadn't hydroplaned, we'd be in Berea 'cause we were heading out before the storm hit."

With her soft tread, Meemaw crossed the room and eased into her rocker. She began to work it gently back and forth like she was soothing a small child. "Well, the subject of selling the land is of interest to me, Marybeth. If family doesn't want it, why not sell at a profit? I could use the money now that I'm heading for the old folks' home."

My mother turned away to hide the surprised look on her face. Meemaw was up to something by the glimmer in her eyes.

Oblivious to their hostess's emotions, the pair by the fireplace fixed their vulture like gaze on her.

Meemaw picked up her crocheting and began to form a chain. "It would have to be a cash deal." She gave one firm head bob. "I'm not young enough to wait for a bank to cough up mortgage money for some youngin's." Meemaw put her hook down and wrung her hands, then heaved out a wrenching sigh. "Marybeth, I've some paperwork around here that may be appropriate. Have a look see on my kitchen desk." She put her hand to her head. "Where are my manners. I apologize." Meemaw clapped her hands, which made me sit up tall. "Delilah, I promised coffee cake. Can't have a good cup of coffee without the trimmings. You need to get us some. Use the nice blue china. The ones I got from the grocery store special. No use standing around like funeral parlor visitors. Take a seat, Derek, Lyle. And...er...what are your names? I like to know the names of my gentlemen callers."

Meemaw had taken a lesson from Miss Vickie. Scurrying to the kitchen so they couldn't hear me laugh, I hunted for the cake. Glancing back, I saw the larger man thump a finger on his chest. "Liam O'Neal and my cousin here is called Danny."

Lyle followed me, chewing on his cheek to keep his emotions locked. Lyle cut the cake and I toted it into the living room. I leaned into Lyle. "Large or small piece, Mr. Henderson?"

"Make it large." He looked from Derek to Frick and Frack who were now lounging on the floral upholstery of the settee. "Gentlemen?"

"Large if you will," said the talkative O'Neal.

"Ditto," uttered Derek. The dog didn't speak. He was too busy pacing along the edge of Meemaw's braided rug.

The cake was finished and plates cleared when Meemaw yawned. "My, oh my. I'm a little tired, Marybeth. Gentlemen. Why don't you speak with my lawyer," she pointed at Lyle, "while I take a tiny snooze. Won't be long. Usually I sleep only an hour or so."

Meemaw creaked out of the old rocker and taking my mother's arm, toddled off to her bedroom near the kitchen.

Lyle took a handful of plates to the kitchen and returned with sheaf of papers and pen. "I hear a sound of a diesel engine. Must be your tow truck. Gentlemen, before you head back to town, I've a few questions regarding your ability to afford this property. Have you obtained steady jobs since you were released from prison?"

Danny O'Neal looked Lyle straight in the eye. "We're buying the land for a fishing lodge. We're part of a con...sort um."

Lyle raised an eyebrow. "A consortium?"

"Yeah. That's what Neely calls it."

Lyle looked down his nose at the pair. "Irwin Smothers also like fishing?"

As soon as the dead man's name from the hotel met the air, Liam O'Neal's right hand clenched. Danny O'Neal rose and stood with his feet ready to pounce.

Standing stiff by the fireplace, Browning made a low snort and cocked his ears. "We don't know who that man is. Looks like we're in need of the real estate agent, Kennedy, to get the papers in order."

There was a knock on the door.

"We'll see ourselves out," Danny O'Neal said. "Our ride has come."

Browning accompanied them to the door, his nose inches from the pant leg of Liam O'Neal. When the truck driver had piled them into his vehicle and headed up hill Meemaw said from the kitchen, "How'd I do with my acting debut?"

"Keep your shotgun handy, Miss Elizabeth," Derek said as he opened the door for his dog.

"I intend to, Sheriff."

Chapter Twenty-Four

"I NEED TO CHECK SOMETHING OUT before we settle in at Suzanne's," Lyle said as he drove past the road heading to the falls. The birch trees—all white with bark peeling as if scraped by a giant—flashed by as he negotiated the curves.

"What?"

"We need to call on the local real estate office. Find out if Kennedy and the O'Neals are in cahoots or if Neely's relatives are conning Kennedy into selling them property."

Between the First Church of Free Will Baptists and the Courthouse was the real estate office where we saw Kennedy loading a suitcase into the trunk of his car. It wasn't a weekend but a work day. What was he up to?

Lyle stepped away from his car and waved. "Hello." Lyle sang out with a happy smile.

Kennedy jumped up from bending to place his suitcase and whacked his head on the trunk lid. I winced.

"Hoped to catch you. The wife and I," Lyle jerked a thumb my way, "remain interested in that small parcel of land by the river."

Kennedy massaged his forehead and looked sour.

I exited the car and smiled. A broad, non-threatening smile. Kennedy turtled his neck into his shirt collar and squirted his glance left then right as if looking for a savior. Derek pulled his official car in beside us. I don't think the sheriff was the rescuer Kennedy had in mind.

Derek stepped out of his car and closed the door shutting in his dog. "Going somewhere, Melvin?"

"I've a business meeting in Cincinnati." His voice was flat and unwelcoming.

Lyle shrugged. "We won't take up much of your

time."

"You won't take up any of my time. I can't be late." He pointed at his watch. One of the fancy ones that cost a year's salary.

"Traffic's light this time of day," Derek said. "You should make it to Cincy in record time."

"Make it quick, then. And don't give me this nonsense about you being interested in land around here. I know who you are." Melvin Kennedy slammed his trunk shut. Glaring at us, he led the way back toward his office.

Lyle clapped Kennedy on the back of his shoulder. "Yes, my wife grew up around here, but land is not what we are here to speak about."

Kennedy stopped and spun around. "Your word is as reliable as the two clowns that came in here this morning."

Derek scratched a spot behind his ear. "How so?"

He pointed to me. "The pair wanted to know about her Grandmother's land. I only took *you* there because I'd heard she was selling." Kennedy's voice was defensive. He unlocked the door to his office and sarcastically bowed.

When we were off the street Lyle stepped up to Kennedy. "Who mentioned that Mrs. Burns wanted to sell?"

"Her neighbor, Tweedy. Said it to me in the local coffee shop."

In slow motion Lyle shook his head. "A slight elongation of the truth. Mrs. Burns is *not* selling her property."

"I gathered that." The phone on Kennedy's hip jangled. I was closest to the door and Kennedy moved toward me to gain privacy. "Yes," he snarled into the receiver. "I see." His face grimaced as he listened. "Fine, Robert. I'll add it to my list." Another two second pause. "I quite understand. It will be my pleasure to finish the assign...deal." He hung up, typed something into his cell phone, and turned to face Lyle. "Excuse the interruption, that was my boss. Why are you here then?"

"Your two visitors interest me."

Browning's muffled bark sounded displeased. Derek turned toward the door. "Me too. Hold your answer while I see to my dog."

Kennedy's eyebrows raised with pique. After Browning joined the party Kennedy pushed back his desk chair and sat on it not inviting us to sit on the chairs scattered around the room. The dog sniffed the area at the entrance. His stub of tail grew excited. "Let's lay our cards on the table, shall we? I'm in this town to make a living. I sell houses. You're here to take care of Mrs. Burns's property. Tell me if I've gotten anything wrong." When he didn't get an answer, he nodded. "That's what I thought." He leaned back in his chair and put his hands behind his head. "You strung me along for your amusement and wasted my time." His head turned to each of our faces then settled on mine. Kennedy's lips softened. "However, as I recall, your wife never did tell a little white lie." He tipped an imaginary hat my direction. "For that I applaud you." He clapped his hands once.

Lyle held up his hand to stop the snide barrage. "Just answer one question."

"Shoot."

"Why did Liam O'Neal go to the courthouse?"

Kennedy didn't look surprised by the question. "He *said* he wanted to look over deeds to land in this part of the county. I don't know if that is what he did. When he returned, he mentioned that the county clerk was most helpful. You can check with her. That all?"

Lyle's head went up and down.

I cleared my throat. "Well, I've a question."

Kennedy tilted his head to look at me.

"Why is Robert Madison calling you?"

Kennedy's dark eyes widened with surprise. "Who did you say?"

"I've good hearing, Mr. Kennedy. I recognized Madison's voice. Care to explain?"

"Blew my cover, did I?" Kennedy began to laugh.

I didn't. Neither did Derek, who looked stunned.

"That was a good deduction, Mrs. Morgan, or I believe it's Henderson now." He lifted his eyebrows. I bobbed my head. "I'm undercover. Special Agent Madison assigned me to Horsetail Falls on a sting operation. We hoped we'd corner the people infesting the countryside with drugs."

Derek strode over to Kennedy and poked him in the chest. Browning growled. "You should have checked in with me before you Feds set up anything in my jurisdiction."

"Not if you're the primary suspect."

That took the umbrage out of Derek and his face purpled. "Last thing I'd do is cause more harm to this place. Just look at it. Town's turning around and I'm not about to bring shame to my kinfolk."

Kennedy's entire posture changed. His chin went up, chest out, and he no longer resembled a subservient man scrabbling for his paycheck. He was a man in charge. "If you've any questions, I'll give you the number of the field office. As I said, I've a meeting."

"Not so fast." At five foot ten Derek towered over Kennedy and seemed to grow bigger by the second. "You've a lot of things I need answers to. Think I'll accept a cup of coffee." Derek pointed to the machine with an empty coffee pot. "And settle in for a while. Sit, Browning," he ordered in a stern voice. The dog thumped its rump on the small entry carpet and lowered his head to his paws. "Delilah, I'll take this from here. You and Lyle aren't needed."

"We're on our way out," Lyle said with a laugh in his voice.

A glimmer of sunshine peeked out from a cloud. Standing on the sidewalk in front of Kennedy's office I studied Lyle's bemused face. "Well, that's a surprise."

"I'm still going to call Madison and check him out. We've one more stop before planning our afternoon fun." We began walking past his car toward the Coffee Maid.

Across the street was the Bide a Wee hotel. Rumor had circulated for years that it had been a house of ill repute since it had opened in the 1890s and became a speakeasy during prohibition. A familiar figure pushed open the lobby door. "Is that Liam or Danny?" I asked my groom.

"Danny. He's thinner."

"Good to know where they're staying. Think Derek knows?"

"This is a small village, Di. Everyone in the entire county knows where the Chicago boys are staying." Lyle crossed the street and aimed toward the railroad tracks. He stopped at the Ferris auto and sculpture company. "I want to know how long the repair job will take and Neely's cousins will be about." The O'Neals' Mercedes was in the parking lot next to the Ferris sculpture truck.

With a cigarette hanging out of his mouth, Joseph's arms were draped across a furniture dolly's handle. On it rested an odd figure. Six-foot high with a rounded top tapering to a rectangular bottom, the linen shrouded shape resembled a mummy's casket.

Joseph looked up, recognized us, and scowled. Stuffing something in his pocket, he returned to lounging. Tyler Ferris the Second appeared from the shop's interior and scowled. Joseph dropped his half-smoked cigarette on the asphalt, ground it into unrecognizable dust, then began to push the dolly up the truck ramp.

"Joseph!" Tyler's voice was harsh.

His assistant whirled around. "Yeah!"

"I asked you to have the truck loaded and ready to go an hour ago."

Joseph shrugged. "I'm getting there."

"I think you're done."

"What?"

"You're fired. Get your things. I'll pay your week's wages before you leave."

Joseph glanced Lyle's way. "Whatever." He dropped the dolly's handle. It fell to the ground leaving the mummy figure rattling on the asphalt. Tyler dashed to the sculpture. Lyle also moved to steady it. Joseph flinched, as if afraid of Lyle. If looks could kill my husband would be toes up. The kid put up his hands to fight. Lyle shook his head, turned his back, and helped Tyler put the sculpture back on the dolly.

Deciding to let the men handle it, I stifled a laugh. The skinny kid resembled a comic–all he needed to do was thumb his nose.

Then Joseph reached into his jeans pocket and drew out a concealed knife. I sucked in a breath. Before Peebles could open the blade, Lyle caught the flicker of movement. He turned as the erstwhile helper opened the blade and made a slow-motion stabbing gesture.

I put my hand to my lips, keeping the scream bottled up.

My spouse balled his fist and, with one punch to the jaw, flattened Joseph. Tyler's assistant hit the wet asphalt, rolled over and lay still as a wet noodle. My husband kicked the weapon out of Joseph's hand, then grabbing Peebles by the scruff of his neck, Lyle pulled him to a half sitting position. He shook the kid like a dog would shake a chew toy. Joseph's head wobbled back and forth as if his neck were a spring.

Tyler straddled the cloth encased statue and yelled to his father. Dressed in dungarees and a helmet, T. J. Ferris marched out of his workshop. The elder Ferris held a small welding torch as if it were a saber. Looking like a knight in his helmet of plastic and metal, T.J. pushed up his protective face shield. His brow crunched with confusion. Father and son spoke quietly. The older man nodded with the solemnity of a pallbearer.

When Lyle jerked Joseph to his feet, the young man seemed weak kneed as a drunk. Lyle didn't offer to assist him but grabbed the knife from the tarmac and walked away to speak with Tyler, Missy Newland's husband.

Lyle surprised me with his quick reflexes. No wonder he was a threat on the Presbyterian's softball team. With things calming down I headed toward my husband. A soft smile played across his lips as he bent over the still vibrating casket shape on the dolly. "Let me help load."

T.J. signaled with his head toward his former employee. "I'll settle your account." Shoulders slumped in defeat, Joseph Peebles schlepped behind him, one hand on his jaw, the other staunching the blood leaking from his nose.

A plastic baggie lay on the ground where Joseph had fallen. Bending to pick it up I noticed white powder on the inside. Taking a step back I glanced around for something to cover it with—this might be drugs. Dropping a cardboard box from the dumpster on top, I watched Lyle and Tyler push the metal shape up the truck ramp. I backed out of their way then headed through the door to the sculpture studio.

Before I was out of earshot, Lyle leaned toward Tyler. "Kid has constricted pupils."

Loud voices drew me to the back of the shop where the sculptures were welded together. As I skirted a pile of hub caps and a cow made from bits of metal including a plow, my feet stuttered to a halt. Joseph stood by the high wooden counter arguing with the senior Ferris. He waved a check in the older man's face then ripped it into several bits and threw the pieces in the air. They floated down like pale confetti. When the fired assistant began to wave his arms and scream words I couldn't repeat, his former boss merely shook his head and turned away.

The younger man grabbed Ferris's arm and spun him around. I glanced behind me to see if Lyle was nearby, but the store was filled with inanimate objects— no humans. Squatting low behind the cow shape, I grabbed the nearest weapon I could find, a heavy metal hub cap.

Joseph latched on to something as well, an acetylene torch Mr. Ferris had placed on a metal table to cool. Before Peebles could flick on the flame, Ferris turned off the flow of oxygen from the tank. Next, T.J. twisted the acetylene's knob, then took a step toward his assailant. Joseph's hand found a smaller torch and pulled the trigger.

Ferris's eyes narrowed. "Put it down, son. This will get you nowhere."

T. J. backed up until trapped by an immovable work bench. "You're going to become toast," screamed Joseph. "That will serve you right for trying to cheat me out of my money."

"Son, I paid you extra for hours you didn't work. A little firing bonus you might say."

Pebbles put the tool in front of him like a handgun. With a turn of the knob the flame grew until it was a foot long and hot. Red hot from the color of its yellow flicker.

Hoping the sputtering and hiss of his weapon would keep him from hearing me, I slipped to the counter. A stapler was within reach. Snagging it left-handed I whipped it toward Joseph's head. Crashing into the metal tools on the bench, the stapler sent them flying all over the floor. Joseph jerked around. He grinned when he saw me.

"Really?" he yelled. "You?" His one word was an impolite sneer. "Where is your husband? Afraid to tackle me again?"

Holding the hubcap like a discus as if ready to throw, I gave T. J. Ferris time to escape.

I inched closer. Peebles laughed at me. Moving the torch back and forth, he made the flame dance. He had no fear in his eyes as he stared at me.

Ferris bumped a piece of metal. The reverberation of the metal made Pebbles turn. T. J. reached behind his back, grabbed something on top of the wooden slab and, one handed, released a heavy hardy tool, one of a set used on an anvil. It struck Peebles in the arm, bounced against his chest and spun away from him. Peebles' hand holding the flaming torch angled sideways and the fire seared his chest. His screams brought Lyle and Tyler running.

By the time the torch trigger released, Peebles shirt was fried, and where the broiling tip of the gun hit, his jeans smoldered. Flame had burned through his clothing. His former boss flung the red-hot tool away. Writhing in pain, Peebles collapsed into the metal shavings and bits of solder on the cement floor.

Lyle called Derek while someone else called 911.

The weapon Joseph Peebles threatened us with would cause permanent damage judging from the look of his blackened flesh. Peebles was in for a rough time because he smelled like smoked barbecue.

Before Derek allowed the EMT's to escort Peebles to the medical clinic he studied the baggie I'd found littering the tarmac. "Yep," Derek said. "Looks like we've found our source. I'll call a forensics squad from Lexington. They need to search this place. My guess is the Ferris operation will be shut down permanently."

Chapter Twenty-Five

T.J. FERRIS SUCKED IN A BREATH. His son's eyes narrowed. "Taking us in, Sheriff?" Missy's husband's voice was close to boiling over with anger.

"I'm suspecting drugs are in this bag. Think I'll find more in your establishment and perhaps that truck. Convenient way to distribute, having things hidden away in your so called 'art' works."

Father and son exchanged glances.

Derek was plain wrong about the Ferrises. They looked a man in the eye, seemed straight shooters, and Daddy trusted them. Which was as good as the gold in Fort Knox. If I were a bettor, I'd place my money on Joseph.

Lyle stepped closer to Tyler and put his hand on Tyler's shoulder. His move said, 'I'll stand with you.'

A cold wind buffeted the buildings and settled on my neck. I drifted toward the town's only patrol car and opened the passenger door. Browning bounded from the interior and gave my hand a sniff of gratitude. Then, nose to the ground, he pranced toward Derek. Fishing gloves out of his back pocket, Derek was startled when his dog stopped and began to growl at the bag on the ground. Browning backed up a step and pointed an accusatory nose at the white powder.

Derek patted his dog then slapped on thin medical gloves. "I know, boy. My suspicions exactly." Before Derek scooped up the baggie, Browning pranced toward the ambulance. The dog pushed his nose at Joseph's tormented figure on the gurney. The dog again began to growl.

"Better call your dog, Sheriff," one of the men said.

Derek finished stuffing the baggie into a thicker bag before he moved.

My feet were turning into ice as I crossed my arms

and looked at Derek. "Browning been trained to sniff out drugs?"

Browning paced back and forth by the gurney then circled it like prey. Derek narrowed his eyes and finally marched toward the EMT's. The crowd gathering from the ambulance's wail edged closer.

"Something smells fishy," I said to Derek's back. Not that I thought Derek would pay attention to anything I said, but placing the blame on the Ferris men was wrong. Derek didn't turn around or even wave his hand over his head to acknowledge he heard me.

I shouted at his retreating back, "Joseph put something in his pocket before attacking Lyle."

Good thing Derek kept on his gloves. After wrestling with Joseph's flailing hands, he had the EMT's force them flat before retrieving another bag of white powder from Joseph's pocket.

Jumping around his master's legs, Browning would have knocked the suspicious bag out of his hand if Derek hadn't had it in a firm grip. A smile moved over Derek's lips. "Good dog. Now, find the rest." The dog's ears went up and he dashed off to check out Lyle's legs, then the Ferris men.

"Hey, Derek," shouted one of the onlookers. "Your mutt ain't exactly trained for this is he?"

Browning circled from Lyle's sports car to the ambulance.

Derek waggled the bag in front of Peebles. "Doesn't look like that plastic cream you put in coffee. We'll see what forensics lab says about this." The sheriff stepped to the EMT and said in a voice that made me blink. "Get him to Lexington where I can have the FBI question him. We're working on the same case." I think Derek would have ridden off in his car like a western lawman who won the shoot-out, if his dog hadn't trotted over to a small maple tree to relieve himself. The liver spotted hound lowered his nose. He sniffed the weeds growing by a bourbon barrel of rust colored mums. He backed away and vectored toward a green Camry. The dog sat down by the left rear tire and began to bark. Not an annoying bark but one that said, 'Over here.'

Derek strode toward the entrance and jerked his head toward the car. "Who's car?"

Tyler spat out, "Guess."

"Maybe I was a bit hasty in my conclusions." Derek waved the baggies in the air. "It seemed natural, you being new in town. The state police should check out his car and the Peebles place."

The Peebles clan were old school Church of Christ folks. Not likely into drugs.

Derek forgot to grab Joseph's car keys, so amid cat calls from the sidewalk audience, he retrieved them from Tyler's ex-employee's pocket and opened the door lock, then unlatched the trunk. Neatly stacked in four large boxes was a treasure trove of baggies with white powder. The German Short-Hair K9 officer went berserk. Missy had stuck her nose out of the front door when the sirens blared, but now Browning's yapping and barking made her dash from the house and nearly smother her husband by flinging her arms around his neck.

When she disentangled herself from Tyler, Missy didn't look happy. "What is going on, Derek?" she asked, as she crossed her arms and marched over to him.

"We've got a situation here."

"Right. Define." Her stare was icy.

"Now, Missy. You need to stand with your husband and be a gawker like all the other yahoos." Derek drew a laugh from the locals. He shook his head and took out his phone to take pictures of the jam-packed boxes in the trunk.

Lyle wandered over to Derek. "Think we're done here. Let me know when we need to give a statement." He took my hand, waved at the crowd spilling over the sidewalk onto the parking area, and headed to the car.

At Suzanne's, Lyle spent an hour scribbling notes on his legal-size pad. I made my own list. Things didn't add up. Jackman drove around armed. Being a westerner from a drug zone he might need to, but he seemed experienced when he slid his revolver nonchalantly into his pocket. Then there was Joseph with his baggies, wads of cash, and suspicious car. And with the FBI's man, Kennedy on the case, perhaps law enforcement could lock down this drug business. I drank a sip from my cooling tea and thought.

What had Frack of the O'Neals been doing in the courthouse? The O'Neals obviously were in cahoots with Smothers, which brought me to the family land. Why was it of interest to people as far away as Colorado? My head ached from the questions pummeling my little gray matter.

Derek didn't join us for dinner. In fact, no dinner. We nibbled on apples and cheese while Suzanne stayed glued to a canvas.

Morning sparkled through the windows when I finally stirred. Flinging back the linen curtains, I squinted my eyes. A bright blue day greeted me. However, there was a glare of sunlight off a puddle large enough to drown an elephant. We weren't going anywhere until it dried up a little.

The smell of coffee lured me to the kitchen.

"Hey." My sister raised her coffee cup. "Don't recall you being a sleepy head."

I held up one finger as I aimed for the coffee machine.

"Right. Don't speak unless spoken to." My sister laughed. "Your adorable spouse has absconded with my truck. After he grazed through my empty refrigerator, he announced sustenance was in order."

"November seems odd for this amount of rain. Usually it afflicts the mountains in the spring and summer. And I stuck my nose out the door and it's very cold."

"It's unusual. Maybe twenty years ago we had a series of storms and hurricanes that can bring things in from the east. But weather has been odd for the last three years. Hot, hot, hot summers and winter coming as the leaves fall."

"They having school today?"

"No. Creeks running full. And it may get icy. Usually only in January and February do we get ice." Suzanne pointed to a stack of breakfast bars on the counter. "Help yourself. I'm out of eggs and bacon." When Suzanne was in a painting frenzy food was the last thing on her mind.

A clear, cold winter day in Horsetail Falls was a rare thing. I plopped on my sunglasses and headed out the door to help Lyle finish unloading the groceries. When the eggs and bacon were tucked away, Lyle wrinkled his nose at driving Suzanne's Ford truck, and we bi-folded into his sports car to head toward Meemaw's.

The sky was blue with nary a cloud. That could change in a millisecond, but there was hope of a dry day and mud turning into hard dirt. With scattered power outages throughout the county, we wanted to check on the farm.

I tapped on the back of Lyle's hand resting on the gear shift knob. "If the creeks rise enough to cover the roads, we'll need to shelter at Meemaw's."

"That will prove interesting."

Rain drops clinging to branches made little fairy lights that disappeared when the water hit asphalt. Lyle babied his car over the icy road. When we reached the highway, a car moving like an octogenarian with a walker crept past us. Lyle chewed on the inside of his cheek. I was content to keep my hands in my lap and not have a death grip on the seat.

I pulled down my rhinestone sunglasses and stared at the blue Mazda some distance in front of us. "That car looks familiar."

"What?"

"I've seen it before. Not here though. Most folks in the mountains drive trucks or well-used SUV's." I closed my eyes and tried to recall the memory. My mind flashed through a camera roll of pictures. One popped up. My eyebrows collided with each other. "Uh, oh. That's Neely Patrick's run-around car. He's probably here to rescue his cousins." There were three heads upright and visible in the car.

"Maybe, maybe not."

"Is one allowed to leave the county while on bail?"

"Not usually."

"Hmm."

A shadow moved across the road and suddenly our sunny day became shrouded in a thick cloud. When the blue car turned onto Burns Road I chewed on the corner of my lip. 'No service' showed on my phone.

I couldn't call Derek.

My hands became fists.

Lyle drove beyond the scarred oak tree and the sprinkle of red taillight plastic. He parked in the shadows of the pines. The Mazda driver topped the hill, then slid into the mud on the edge of the drive. In that position he could see the house, barn, and garden. I prayed that my mother's Toyota Camry was parked in front and they wouldn't find Meemaw alone.

The dark cloud grew and shared its bounty of rain, splatting on our car, the road, and further obscuring the view. Lyle reached over me and opened the glove box. "Excuse me, my dear." He drew out his small gun. "I believe I've business with these gentlemen. Do me a favor. Get in the driver's seat and turn the car around. We may need to have a quick get-away."

I frowned. That made no sense. I didn't know how to drive Lyle's very expensive toy, and as for him confronting two felons and Neely, *alone*, the idea was absurd. I tromped around the car as Lyle headed for the woods to remain out of sight.

As I crept into the driver's seat, my shoes tracked mud onto Lyle's clean carpet. I studied the leather dashboard and line of gadgets in front of me. My right hand fondled the gear shift knob. It was a fancy type of wood and smooth to the touch. I started the car with a jerk. It died as soon as I took my foot off the brake to put it on the accelerator. I tried again. The Porsche rumbled to life. The engine's strength made the car vibrate like a massage chair at a nail salon. A smile crept over my lips. "Nice car, Judge Henderson," I said as I eased the car into first gear. The engine stalled. "Oh, bother." I revved the engine. The car jerked backwards. Doing a four point turn on the narrow drive I drove up the hillside and off onto a side road that Papaw had carved for a logging road.

Lyle wasn't one to stay safe. Neither was Meemaw. I turned off the car, pocketed the keys, and headed in the direction Lyle had taken. Snaking between the trees I rounded a large hemlock. Meemaw's farm house came into view. Relieved to see my mother's car in front of the house, I let out a pent-up sigh then squinted my eyes. Meemaw stood on the porch wiping her hands on a towel, while Mother was on the porch steps. She aimed Papaw's gun squarely at three men halted in front of the mud-splattered blue car. Their hands were lifted above their heads. It was comical. Two women, one in her late seventies and the other in her mid-nineties had out-foxed the thugs.

Swiping at my rain damp hair, I scouted for Lyle as I snuck along the tree line. With hair across my eyes, I stumbled over a half-hidden stump. As I descended toward the ground an arm wrapped around my waist, keeping me upright. Starting to turn to smile at my alert husband, I gasped when a hand clapped over my mouth.

"Not a word, Mrs. Henderson," said the Marlboro

man. I wriggled. He must have had experience nobbling people because I couldn't move. My arms were snagged in one of his and his gloved hand didn't move from my lips. He pulled me to his chest. "I didn't want you crying out as you fell. Might draw attention to me." The man had slathered on a southern accent as neatly as an actor. I felt a hard object at the side of his chest. My guess—a gun holster.

"Mufflwuffle," I mumbled. His leather glove was dirt encrusted and tasted like wood smoke. Snooping on Meemaw made my blood boil. If he was into a land grab like the men in Meemaw's drive, I'd find a way to stop the snake.

"All is not as it seems, Mrs. Henderson." He spoke into my riot of curls. I shook my head, hoping my curls would choke him. His chest against my back moved and a laugh erupt from his lips. "The locals said the Burns women were a feisty lot. At least you don't have a shotgun." At this range, the only thing I could do was whack him with it.

"We're going to creep back up the road, then you need to get back into that fancy car of yours." Making hardly a sound, we inched up the hillside. When we were well out of earshot of the party at Meemaw's, he removed his hands and turned me around to face him. His eyes twinkled with amusement and his lips were smiling. "I realize it is not a proper thank you for your gift of breakfast yesterday, but," he shrugged, "you became an inconvenience. I'd appreciate it if you didn't mention our little encounter."

Balling my fists, I thumped them onto my waist and leaned toward him. "You, sir, are a scoundrel." I slapped a hand over my lips. "Good grief, I sound like an eighteenth-century heroine."

"A rather dreadful interpretation, I'm afraid. I prefer the dialogue you wrote in *The Dutchman From Troy*. If you will excuse me, I need to make a phone call." Amory

Jackman left me standing in the rain and wondering where his sudden southern accent came from. Wasn't he a westerner?

241

Chapter Twenty-Six

CLIMBING INTO THE SCOOPED SEAT OF Lyle's car, I shook my wet head. I should lay low, but I began to worry. Who knew what Neely Patrick, et al were up to?

The engine kept going. I put it in gear and drove down the hillside into the Burns family farm. The O'Neals and Neely were on the porch. Meemaw had a kitchen towel resting on one arm and she leaned on her cane with the other. Mom and Lyle stood facing the trio as I pulled up. The shotgun in Mom's arms was pointed at the floor but would take a millisecond for her to raise it and fire.

The Porsche jerked to a halt, shuddered, and revved before it died. I stayed put until Lyle lifted his head and waved at me. Lyle's gun was in his hand. When I reached the porch, Lyle kissed my cheek. "Well, Mrs. Henderson, we've an interesting turn of events." I waited for him to continue or say something about my driving skills. He said nothing.

Danny O'Neal's right hand was in the pocket of his duck yellow jacket. That wasn't the only thing in his pocket judging from the bulge. Lugar? Glock? What did the gangs use in Chicago?

Lyle turned toward Danny. "I'd like to see both your hands at your sides." It wasn't a request. Right hand came out. But there remained a telltale cylindrical lump in his pocket. Mom's gun barrel lifted a few inches.

Neely licked his lips. "I've come with some real estate papers." He lifted a black briefcase he'd brought from the car.

"Bellows say you could leave the county?" Lyle's voice was tight as a piano wire.

"Family emergency," muttered Neely.

Lyle glanced toward Meemaw, noted her smile, and swept his hand low letting her take the stage.

Meemaw took her time. Her eyes wandered toward the woods by the road. A half-smile crossed her lips. There was a flash of color beside a large southern red oak. Probably Jackman—he'd worn a turquoise jacket and the hue I spied wasn't a Blue Jay. "Why don't you leave them with me." Meemaw stretched out her hand for the papers.

Mom kept her finger on the trigger of the shotgun.

Ignoring the movements around her, Meemaw gave a swift nod. Her white hair flopped across her forehead and stopped in a straight line. "And do these papers refer to these gentlemen's offer yesterday?"

Neely put on an oily smile. "Not exactly. We've a few questions before our conglomerate makes an offer on the land. No hurry. We can wait." Neely eyes looked at the front door.

Meemaw glared at Neely. "If you're looking for an invitation, I must be un-neighborly. My power went kaput." Meemaw shrugged. "I'll meet you at Kennedy's office. Say, at four this afternoon."

Neely and his cohorts did a sideways shuffle down the staircase, keeping their eyes on the shotgun. After they all climbed in, Neely's muddy car threw rocks and dirt in the air as it sped up the drive.

Meemaw laughed. "Think we're reeling them in."

Lyle's eyebrows had scrunched together. He didn't look happy. "For what?"

"Their comeuppance."

Lyle shook his head. "Meemaw, those men are part of the underworld. They shoot before they think, and have long memories and connections that span the globe. Your game plan is dangerous. Revenge is part of their playbook."

My mother shivered. Taking Meemaw by the arm she hustled her inside but left the door open for us.

I grabbed Lyle's hand "My thoughts exactly. Maybe we should have Derek put Meemaw's house on his rounds or hire neighbors to keep a look out." I sighed. Keeping everyone safe until Neely's trial and figuring out why they were interested in her land was a pain. "I've got something else on my mind." I pulled him aside—out of earshot of the pair in the house.

His face tilted toward mine, lips ready for a kiss. "So do I."

"Marlboro man was spying in the woods."

Lyle leaned closer. "I saw him."

"Well what do you suppose he's up to?"

"Looking for Montezuma's treasure in the wrong state."

"Not funny, Lyle. He grabbed me and said not to tell anyone he was here."

"I know."

I lowered my eyebrows. "Why didn't you do something?"

"I wanted to prevent your mom from blasting a hole in the visitors and ending up spending the night in lockup. If Derek needed to take Neely in because he left the county without permission, who knows? They might be jail companions. Have a feeling she'd have empathy for Neely, which I'd rather she'd treat as a ne'er do well."

I began to laugh, recalling my puncturing Neely Patrick's ego as well as rear end. "That does conjure up an interesting picture. My mom sharing a cell with Neely."

'This left us with a whole lot of nothing,' as Daddy would say. Peebles being head of a drug ring was unimaginable. He hadn't the drive to organize anything beyond his next meal. With no information about the interest in Meemaw's land we were left spinning our mental wheels. Another problem was Meemaw. Neely and family knew where she lived. She needed to go into hiding. With her house only having a fire for light and heat, she would have to move for a night or two anyway.

I was plotting how to broach the subject when Meemaw and Mom hustled out of the house with a small suitcase and determination. "We're heading to lunch, then my home," Mom announced. "Your father will provide protection. Just talked to Derek. He's going to swear in a couple of men as deputies to keep an eye on those scoundrels. Your father can't meet us for lunch. Something about checking on the McMillans' land down the road. He thought he saw some activity there."

Bundled up, they headed to town in Mom's car, and we followed. The Coffee Maid served soup and sandwiches as well as hot drinks. I needed to wrap my fingers around a mug of coffee. Lights winked in the coffee shop's window. Relieved to find power after five miles of darkened farms, we chose a table by the heater blasting air mostly toward the ceiling.

Cheryl Lynn was at the counter chatting with the locals. The usual gang were diving into sandwiches thick with meat. She waved, then lifted one red eyebrow at us when she saw Meemaw. Her quizzical look made me smile. My cousin had been away when Meemaw had made her last appearance. Cheryl Lynn gave Meemaw a tender hug.

"Meemaw," she said, after kissing her check, "you had us scared silly. Don't go off and do that again. Best you stay in the mountains where we can keep an eye on you."

"Shaw, honey. When my times up, it's up. The good Lord knows the day and hour. I'm simply fiddling around here until He calls my name." Cheryl Lynn patted Meemaw's frail arm and hustled back to her patrons.

Before she took off her coat, Meemaw flopped the sheaf of real estate papers on the table with a thump so loud heads craned our direction. She squinted at the papers. "I need my glasses." She sounded disgusted. She'd had perfect eyesight until cataracts attacked. After surgery she had weathered aging with little glasses on chains around her neck. Foraging in her oversized purse, she let my mother order lunch. After ten minutes of scrutinizing the papers, she sat back in her chair.

"Cain't make head nor tail of this mess. Delilah, you think your friend Olive will be able to decipher it?"

I looked at the top sheet. The print was minute. "We can have a copy sent to her. Let me speak with Cheryl Lynn."

Hearing her name my cousin came to the table. She swung her long auburn ponytail over her shoulder. "At your service, Delilah. What may I do?" Our food arrived as the message was sent to Olive Lorraine.

Lyle's pen flew over his paper napkin. Lyle could be so like Harry, who created poetry on whatever paper proved handy. Lyle's tidy lines of names all aimed at a rough sketch of Meemaw's property.

Taking a bite of my Rueben, I tapped on the name Ferris.

Lyle held up a finger to stall and kept writing, his bowl of soup chilling. When he finally looked up, I'd finished my sandwich and collected Meemaw's papers when my phone rang. Ambling over to the counter I mouthed 'thank you', to Cheryl, and said hello to Olive Lorraine. Settling on a stool I began a conversation with my new friend.

"I'm going to talk to you as I read through this," Olive said as fast as a washer on spin. "First two pages are the usual legal jargon, but the third page is a surprise. They're asking for mineral rights to the center of the river and want to expand the property lines to include all the land from the original land granted. There were three kinds of rights to the land. War veterans have one, that included the French and Indian War as well as the Revolutionary War. Then there were settlements and warrants from the treasury. Four hundred acres, if a man had planted corn during a year of occupation and a pre-emption of one thousand acres where a cabin had been built. That was when Kentucky was still Virginia, of course. After 1780 things changed. It was called land patenting."

Finished with our conversation, I walked slowly back to the table. Her info dump had familiar bits to it because I'd written about that time period in my historical novels. How it applied to my family was a mystery. Fourteen hundred acres covered a lot of land. Around two miles give or take a yard. What was around the old farm? Two abandoned coal mines, several farms, but nothing else of value. Even the holler a mile down the road didn't have promise, though the land had good soil.

I put my elbows on the table and leaned toward Meemaw. "When was the first time someone began asking about the land?"

"Just after Bo Feeney's funeral. He had some relatives who'd come down from Ohio and spoke about it."

Bo Feeney had been the county land assessor and collected geodes. I had a couple he'd given out instead of Halloween candy. My lips went sideways as I chewed on the thought.

Lyle's eyes strayed to mine. "You look like a mathematician solving an equation."

"Too many people with interest in rocks. A group from Colorado, Mr. Jackman with info about minerals scattered about and no work done on his 'fixer upper', and our Mr. Feeney who always had a metal detector in his trunk."

My mother met our eyes and nodded her head. "Gold?" she whispered.

"Diamonds," Meemaw said. "Coal. Pressure means diamonds. We just dreamed that geodes held diamonds among their crystals."

"Er," Lyle interrupted. "Diamonds, I believe are made from Granite, not coal. There is a possibility some are made from coal, but this is not a volcanic area where the earth's mantle is forced upward." He shrugged. "Term paper."

Meemaw put down her coffee mug. "But people around here believe diamonds come from coal. And coal we've got by the ton."

Mother slapped the table with her hand. "If people

believe that diamonds come from coal, then this would be a logical place to search for them. Look at the road cuts when you drive. Wavy lines of black gold."

Meemaw scratched her head. "I wonder." Her voice trailed off and she waved her hand at Cheryl Lynn. "I think I may have an answer, but how would the real estate people know about a little shell and pea game?"

Lyle looked as confused as I felt.

Cheryl Lynn arrived with a pot of coffee. The large clock on the wall said it was time for the lunch crowd to head out the door to their chores. She poured coffee refills, returned the pot and settled beside Mom, a cup of tea in her hand. "You wanted to talk with me?"

Meemaw stirred sugar into her coffee then slowly trickled a stream of half and half into her pottery mug. "You'll have to tell them about the Eldorado mine gang and Jackman."

Cheryl Lynn cleared her throat. "Er...I don't think I can break a confidence."

"I've scoundrels knocking at my door to steal my land, and I've a feeling threats of bodily harm are next on the menu. So spill the beans, girl." She reached across Mom and patted Cheryl Lynn's hand.

The Coffee Maid's owner looked around. Only the staff and her family were close enough to overhear. "Well, it makes me laugh, that's all. Those snooty students would come in here and demand coffee with all kinds of things in it, from fancy creams to flavorings the locals can't afford. I didn't accommodate them. Told their professor they could jolly well buy their own coffee and cream or live like the hard-working locals. Then those kids started arguments about the use of our land. Talked to Bruce Tweedy as if he were imbecilic. Got on the stump about the environment being damaged by the farming. What farming? People here raise their own food crops and tobacco is not the cash crop it used to be. This rocky land has been amended by cow manure for the last two hundred years and still a crop is hard to produce. Trees? They loved the trees. Went on and on about the forests. We've got plenty of oaks and hickory. It's mixed hardwood that woodworkers come here to harvest. 'Course the woods needed to regrow after too much harvesting but we're on the incline in that department."

Meemaw shifted her old bones in the seat. From the pinched look on her face she was uncomfortable. "Hurry it up, girl. I've got to meet these people and want some answers when I do."

Cheryl Lynn smiled. "Well, their attitudes made Jed and the boys so mad they decided to do a little something about their arrogance and disrespect of their elders. They formed a corporation. Titled it fancy. The Eldorado Mining Company, Inc. The board meets here first Monday of every month."

"Get to the point, dear." Meemaw was more than impatient.

"One lazy Saturday, when the students were sipping their coffee, Jed McMurry paid his bill with gold dust. I got out some scales and weighed it and put the little bag in the register. Made is seem normal."

Lyle began to laugh.

My cousin grinned at him and continued. "Those students sat and stared. They quizzed me about it. I shrugged and said it was usual. Added that this was the poorest county in the whole U.S. except for Puerto Rico. Said, lots of folks began to pay their bills with gold dust when in 2013 the government cut back on food stamps." Cheryl Lynn began to laugh until moisture leaked from her eyes. "They bought the whole shebang."

Cheryl Lynn had the kind of laugh that took off, rolled around, and began to shake up your prissiness. I laughed with her. She shook her head to gain control. "Next time Jed was here those students sidled up to him and bought him a coffee. They peppered him with questions, and old Jed led them down a path as wandering as most of the roads around here."

My mother put her hands to her cheeks she was so shocked. Cheryl Lynn patted her hand and rushed on, her words colliding because she talked so fast. "They out and out asked Jed where he'd found the gold and ol' Jed put both hands up in the air and said, 'Every creek around here is laden with it. Why'd you think we stay here summers instead of in our air-conditioned Florida houses? We're protecting our treasure.' Then Jed pulled down his glasses so he could look them in the eye. 'Saw your group down by the Burns land. You're smart young college students. You've already found the diamonds, right? With all this coal, there has to be a diamond column coming from the earth's mantle.' He then gave them a myth about diamonds forming from coal and they bought it hook, line, and sinker. The boys even salted the edge of Tweedy's stream with uncuttable diamonds one of them had gotten at Diamond Crater in Arkansas."

Cheryl Lynn snorted through her nose. "Now, Jed used to be a drinker and the boys thought he'd done such a good job they wanted to take him out on a bender, but he said coffee and a donut would suit fine." With that comment she wiped her eyes on a napkin, sat back, and finished her tea while we digested all she had said.

"That of course, is not all." Meemaw squinted at her youngest granddaughter. Cheryl Lynn sighed and held up her hands. "Okay, okay. It got a little bit more complicated. The corporation also salted the creek with some gold nuggets Joe McIver got in Alaska."

Lyle caught her eye. "Where does Jackman come in?"

"Ah, the latest macho man." The owner of the Coffee Maid sighed. "Our newest resident wasn't supposed to get the flimflam. He shows up and Jed strings him along too."

"Why?"

"Amusement."

Gold hunting explained why Jackman was stalking through the woods. Long before the Colorado man got to Horsetail Falls, the FBI were on the hunt for the drug traffickers. Kennedy must have been sent in to make the connection to Smothers, the cadaver in Lexington. Then the O'Neals made a few moves, and the Feds discovered the realtor had been hand and glove with the O'Neals and Clarisse.

I tapped a fingernail on the table top, thinking about all the cogs of the real estate machinations coming together. Who'd killed Smothers though? And why? And last question for the moment was, what was Clarisse's involvement.

Lyle took my grandmother's hand. "Meemaw, allow me to speak for you at Kennedy's office. I think I know a way for the O'Neals to tip their hand."

The sky was a dark gray and a frigid wind almost knocked us flat when we exited the Coffee Maid. The rain had turned sleety. We got Mom and Meemaw ready to roll then hustled through the shower to Lyle's car. The lowering skies meant there might be ice on the roads before sunset.

We watched the O'Neal cousins head into the hotel down the block. They were carrying a six-pack of beer and a grocery bag. I glanced up to see Jed McMurry watching them from the confines of his old pickup.

Sheltering out of the rain with his car heater blasting us in the knees and chin, I said, "What do you have in mind to do at Kennedy's?"

"I'll keep it as a surprise. That way everyone will act naturally." A lazy smile crossed Lyle's lips. "Sweetheart. One look at you and everyone would know it is a ruse. You can't hide a thing behind those big, blue eyes." His chin was set in a stubborn jut. Dislodging it would take conniving which I wasn't about to do.

Chapter Twenty-Seven

WE SETTLED MEEMAW AT DADDY'S, TOLD Daddy about the meeting at Kennedy's office, then headed back toward Suzanne's.

The tires on Lyle's car weren't meant for slick mountain roads. As ice formed faster on our windshield than the wipers could manage, we skidded on the short drive from my homeplace to Suzanne's. I bit my lip. We had drop offs on either side of the road. Not nice gentle slopes down to a pristine valley but one-hundred-foot plunges. As we took the last hairpin turn before the falls, Lyle hit the brakes so hard we fishtailed. The sheriff's car was cattywampus across the road. If Lyle hadn't braked, we would have hit it crossways and catapulted Derek's car over the cliff.

I shut my eyes tight. Holding my breath, I prayed a staccato prayer. We jerked sideways. The car spun, then slid. The plink, plink of gravel hitting the bottom of the car forced me to open my eyes to the gray of the day and the closeness of the edge. We stopped inches before the drop off. Tight jawed, Lyle backed up and parked.

The driver's side of Sullivan's vehicle was rumpled like corrugated iron. Derek lifted his head and stared at us from his side window. A blank stare, no light in his eyes. His fingers went to his head. He was bleeding by his temple. Derek studied us a minute then leaned over the passenger seat and focused on something beside him.

Lyle turned off the engine, then flung open the door and headed out. Ice swirled into the car and deposited its crystals on the dash and Lyle's empty seat. Lyle didn't stop but shot past me before I could open my door. A dog whimpered.

Sliding across the tarmac, Lyle skated toward Derek's car. I inched along, my feet not coordinating with my brains as icy rain pummeled us from the gray-black heavens. Beating me to the car by a few seconds, Lyle fought to open the crumpled door.

A primordial sound of pain issued from the police car. The wolf like howl had to be from the dog. No human could make that sound. I peeked through the backseat window and saw Derek bent over the passenger seat, face toward the floor. "It's all right, Browning. We'll get you help, boy." Browning's left front leg was canted at an odd angle as he whimpered. Foam frothed from his mouth. With a protesting groan, Derek's door creaked open. Derek glanced at Lyle then his face turned to his companion. "Send Delilah to get Suzanne's truck. We'll need the vet."

Lyle peered over Derek's shoulder. "Right. And I need to see about you. How'd this happen?"

"A car spun out and hit us. When I righted my cruiser, the other car slammed into my side. Might not be an accident. I've made enemies."

Lyle peered down the road. No car in sight, nor had we passed one.

Tying the strings of the hood on my jacket, I trudged up the ice-covered hill toward my sister's. As my feet slid out from under me, I grabbed the warped sign saying, 'Horsetail Falls 300'. With effort I heaved myself from tree to tree to get up the slope to the closed gas station. Beyond the station the ground was flatter. I managed without a problem all the way to the parking area near the falls, then the fun began on the descent to Suzanne's. From the second gas pump, I saw lights on in Suzanne's studio. I aimed for the house where her truck keys hung on a hook by the back door.

With the steep decline to Suzanne's house, I began sweating with tension. Made it without ending on my rump, which was a miracle.

I thrust open the door to the warmth of her kitchen. She stood by the stove sipping a cup of aromatic coffee.

"Hey," she said.

"Derek's had an accident. He's hurt and so is Browning."

Suzanne dropped her cup on the counter, grabbed her jacket from the back of a kitchen chair, her truck keys from the rack, and rushed toward the door. "Getting slidey?"

"Yes, and the wind's picking up. Derek is going to need medical help and the dog a vet. Watch yourself. Someone hit them and took off. Don't know where they went."

Suzanne whipped her head around. "I heard a car a little bit ago. Left the studio to see if I had visitors. The Petersons are out of town as are the McMillans, so isn't them. Everyone else is working at Missy Ferris's place." With that comment she dashed out the door.

I made phone calls. Vet would be waiting, nurse at the small clinic in town was armed and ready for Derek, so I decided gathering a search party for the car that had struck Derek was in order. It wasn't hard to track down Derek's two new deputies. According to my cousin, they were eyeing the hotel in the comfort of her establishment. They didn't hem or haw but said they'd take care of it before I disconnected. Not that Jed and Tweedy would find anything. It was growing dark and the weather was closing in. Would anyone want to come up and search when they might not make it home for a few days?

If a drunk had hit Derek, by the time he was found, they'd be sober, and no test could prove they'd been impaired. Would they come back to hit Derek again? That didn't make sense. A few nights in jail would be a drop in the bucket for some of the locals. An attempted murder rap wasn't in anyone's plan.

I slipped off my shoes and walked through the house. Boots were in order. Boots with grips. I unearthed them from my suitcase and wiggled them on. Stuffing a flashlight from the nightstand into my coat pocket I headed out. The footing was treacherous. I slid through icy rain toward the derelict gas station. With the lowering sky growing darker and the ice thickening, I set my jaw tight and managed to slip down the hillside to the cars. The police car, now surrounded by little red cones, was empty. A splattering of blood was on the ground beside the passenger door. Derek, the dog, and Suzanne had disappeared. When I drew near, Lyle's face was as dark and foreboding as the clouds closing in on us.

He lifted his head when he heard the crunch of my steps on the gravel. "Suzanne hustled Derek and his dog into her truck and headed to town. It's too cold to stay here. I'm going to attempt to drive up the hill. Don't know if I'll make it." I started to get into his car. "No, Di. I don't want you hurt. These tires aren't made for icy roads, too wide."

Lyle settled into the seat. The car rumbled to life, then the tires spun, sending mud and ice flying all the way up my pant legs and onto my coat. I jumped toward the police car as he backed the Porsche onto the road. Needing the width of the road as the car skidded over the asphalt, Lyle barely missed a red oak on the left as he neared the gas station. He made it to the top of the hill before he did a 180 and faced the crumpled car. With infinite care, Lyle teased the car around until it pointed toward the falls.

I trudged up the hill and only fell once. Rubbing my knee, I grabbed a pine branch coated with ice and pulled myself toward the next tree. My boots had waffled soles and traction. Lyle was still in his slick soled boots. I hoped he'd make it from his car to Suzanne's without landing on his derriere and causing damage to ego and body.

A flash of yellow behind the gas station made me turn. The movement was by the McMillans' vacant house. My feet headed that direction as if on automatic snoop mode. I stayed in the shelter of the trees and hoped Jackman wasn't nearby with his grab and release act. At the back of the station and opposite the now empty propane tank I saw another flash of color, this time navy blue. It was to the side of the McMillans' one-story brick house and heading toward the back. The McMillans' yard sloped toward the river. They had a wire fence surrounding the backyard. They'd installed it to keep their kids and dogs from floating toward the falls. It was a dangerous spot. I shivered.

With the McMillans' in Florida from October until May, whoever was creeping around was up to no good. I fished my phone from my pocket and dashed from the trees to the propane tank, hoping to get a picture.

The dratted ice spun me sideways. I hit the tank with a thud that echoed across the landscape like a gun shot. After ten minutes, when the yellow and blue flashes hadn't reappeared, I aimed my sleuthing skills toward Suzanne's. Had Kennedy rented out the property or were there thieves casing the place?

Chapter Twenty-Eight

From the scrunched-up nose on Lyle's face, I knew he wasn't a happy man. He lifted his eyebrows when he saw me trudging up the road. "And exactly where have you been?"

"I think someone is wandering around by the McMillans' old place."

When I reached Lyle's side, he patted the gun he'd looped into his belt and took my arm. His head turned to look backward and his eyes narrowed. "I can't hide my car, so whoever is out there will know we're here."

Pointing at Suzanne's barn with its lights blazing I said, "I'll turn off her lights and meet you back here."

"Not on your life, Mrs. Henderson. We'll stick together."

I was relieved. Somehow the day had turned from light to dark in seconds and walking to the barn alone wasn't appealing. If someone was out there looking for trouble, I didn't want to be on their radar. Pocketing the keys to the barn I put my hand in Lyle's. We hunched over like meteorologists in a hurricane, braving the wind and sleet together. Lyle stood on the windward side of me, taking the brunt of the assault.

A forlorn lilac bush Suzanne had unearthed from Meemaw's farm clung to the dirt beside the barn door. The weathered barn siding, the desiccated leaves skirling along the walk, the trees bending with the wind, all made the place seem lonely and tired. Suzanne had been the most outgoing one of us all. I'd worried about her over the years but she had brushed me off with a toss of her long hair and a smile. How did my sister bear it, being here alone?

A new painting was on her monster easel. Browning stared at me with eager brown eyes that matched his liver spots. Suzanne had captured the dog's intensity.

"Oh, Lord, heal that sweet dog," I breathed as I went in search of light switches.

Lyle pointed to a book near the easel. "Did you see this?"

This was a book about hiking the Appalachian Trail. Beside it was an open note. Lyle read it and handed it to me. 'I've covered parts of this trail by myself but would like to have your companionship on the Tennessee bit. Interested? Derek.'

"They seem good together."

"Do you sense that love is in the air, Mrs. H? Gives old codgers like us hope." Lyle swung me into his arms and we stood together letting our bodies warm. "I can tell by your pinched-up nose that you're worried about Derek and Browning. If I could dance your fears away I would." Before I could comment he bent me backwards and planted a kiss that would give a codger a heart attack.

Still thinking about his kiss as I locked the door, I began to wonder if time alone meant now. I grabbed Lyle's hand and started to march toward the house when Jed McMurry eased his truck to a halt and gingerly stepped out.

"Hey," he yelled.

Lyle waved. "Hey, yourself."

Jed stomped our way, keeping his feet firmly planted on the dirt not the ice crusted walk. "Got some news."

We shook hands. His gloves were as cold as a frozen mackerel. "There's coffee inside. We'll talk there."

"I could use a cup. Then I've got to scoot." When Jed had settled at Suzanne's minute table and slurped loud and long from his mug, he began. "A man and woman have been sighted that are unfamiliar to all of us. Kennedy said they wanted to rent the McMillan place, but he didn't like the looks of them so said no." Jed lifted his mug in salute. "First time that real estate feller showed any sense."

The locals were in for a shock when they found out

Kennedy was a federal agent. I didn't know if they'd like that bit of information.

Lyle strode to the coffee maker and poured himself a mug. "What type of car did they drive?"

"Little blue job. Foreign one."

I lifted an eyebrow. "A Mazda?"

Jed McMurry snapped his fingers. "That's right. Friend of yours?"

Lyle answered for me. "Not a friendly, Jed. And you say he wasn't alone?"

Jed took off his baseball cap and rubbed the back of his head. "Had a woman with him. Long legs in those tight pants that they call skinny and blonde curls so long they hit her mid back."

"Clarisse?" Lyle and I said together. I wouldn't put it past her to grab a country western singer type wig. She'd done the wig act when leaving Paducah after bumping off her lover and his other girlfriend. She might have a handful of passports from a dozen countries as well. My bet was Neely had Clarisse in tow or maybe the other way around.

Jed drew a finger over his upper lip. "Derek gave me the heads up about the attack on him."

I put my hand on Jed's beefy one. "It might have just been an accident."

"I'm certain it was intentional. Why didn't they stop? Could be a drunk or a vendetta. Either way they need to be stopped. I'm heading over to my cousin's place to check things out. Make certain they aren't hiding out there, seeing Frank and Ethel are in Florida. Care to join me?"

Lyle grabbed his gun and thrust it in his coat pocket.

Jed nodded. "Yep. Got my pea-shooter handy too." He patted a holster resting at his hip.

I hefted logs into the fireplace to keep the flames going and settled nearby. "I'll stay. Someone needs to be here when Suzanne returns."

Lyle closed the front door gently as my thoughts

flitted from the car accident to Neely and maybe Clarisse roaming around. Loose. They both should have been locked in behind steel doors. The justice system stank. Wrinkling my nose, I got up and paced.

Why did Neely and his cousins want the Burns land? How easy would it be for them to find Meemaw at my parents? Did they hear about the phony gold scheme or diamonds being made from coal? All they had to do was get on the internet to check things out. But only Neely seemed tech savvy judging from the residual mess in Patrick and Patrick's office. And the wild card was Clarisse. I shivered and looked at my phone. Almost time to head to Kennedy's and meet with the O'Neals.

Footsteps sounded on the gravel walk leading to Suzanne's front door. I hadn't heard a car drive up. Dashing to the kitchen I went in search of a weapon. Rolling pin. Frying pan. My focus pounced on the copper tea kettle on the stove. Grabbing it, I skulked to the door and slid the lock into place. Whoever it was hadn't come to the front. Drat! I hadn't locked the kitchen door nor the slider from the living room. I snuck back toward the kitchen. Too many windows. A man jogged past the kitchen windows overlooking the falls. The blur of red wasn't Lyle nor Jed. Doubling over, I crouched and moved to the back door. It opened as I was halfway across the kitchen. Raising my arm to fling the kettle I stopped before I concussed Bruce Tweedy.

He pushed back his hat and scratched his chin. "Good try, Delilah, but that wouldn't stop a squirrel. Best get yourself armed with something lethal." He cleared his throat. "Derek sent me to find Jed. He's got two more deputies sworn in to watch the men at the hotel, and I'm to find the car that hit his."

"Is Derek all right?"

"Concussed, the nurse said at the drop-in clinic. I stopped by to check on him. Our sheriff had a guide, since he was a little wobbly. Seems he and your sister are right friendly."

"They went to school together."

"He's years older as I recall. Now, where is Jed?"

"He and Lyle went to the McMillan place. Thought they'd check it out."

"And a good thing we did." Lyle's voice from the living room made me jump and raise my weapon again. "Someone's been at the McMillans'. They broke in the back door and apparently spent the night. Could be anyone, but vagrants and homeless don't usually wander the mountains in the fall."

Tweedy smirked. "Except for that bomb fellow a few years back. He managed to stay ahead of the law for quite some time."

"We also found tire tracks in the mud on the drive. Not a truck or SUV judging from the distance between the tires."

"Where's Jed?" Tweedy sounded alarmed.

"Securing the place. He'll meet us back here."

"No. I'll mosey over." Tweedy turned toward the door. "Keep the doors locked. I don't like the smell of things." Lyle locked up behind Tweedy.

When doors were secure Lyle reached for me and we cuddled on the couch like two teenagers waiting for their parents' footsteps. I glanced at the clock by the fireplace. "Jeepers. We have to be at Kennedy's in twenty minutes."

The sun faded to shadows and the night breeze stirred the pines as we took off toward town. Evening slowly creeping over the land was my favorite time of day. It meant that Harry would be coming up the walk, the children would dribble in from their activities, and conversation around the dinner table would be filled with laughter.

I glanced at Lyle as he drove through the dusk. We will have a quiet life, Lord. No children to traipse through the kitchen snatching a cookie as they passed, or students ambling up the walk to mooch dinner and time with Harry.

Quiet is good, I told myself. You deserve a tranquil life, one where Lyle kept criminals from roaming freely and you scribble stories that told tales of long ago. My nose wrinkled. With dead bodies, stabbed kids, and a boy in the ICU after being pummeled, peace was more elusive than Sasquatch.

My Dad's pickup was parked at Kennedy's. I took a deep breath. Daddy wouldn't put up with nonsense and what Lyle had in mind might make things awkward. "Er, Daddy's truck is here."

"I noticed."

"Perhaps you'd better let me in on your thinking so I can help."

"Actually, my dear, I love it when you're surprised. Let me handle this. Kennedy may not be the savviest federal agent, but I think he'll keep up with me."

Lyle opened the realty office door and ushered me inside. Like a group photo, everyone was already in place. Kennedy stood by his desk, Meemaw seated in his comfortable chair had a smile from her eyes to her lips. Next to Meemaw, Daddy hunched over papers on Kennedy's desk, while Mom stood with crossed arms, looking down at the O'Neals. The pair were seated in hard backed wooden chairs as if they were naughty students. Daniel and Liam appeared to be more interested in the pattern of their socks than making eye contact with anyone in the room.

"Lyle," said my dad when we entered.

"Evening, sir." Lyle's glance cut to the pair of cousins. "Gentlemen." Lyle gave them a curt nod. "Kennedy, so glad you could fit us in. Meemaw has a proposition to make about her property. I'm here to be certain her wishes are adhered to."

My father lifted his face from his perusal of the papers. "And I'm here to lend credence to the proceedings. The land was to be my inheritance. I'm in agreement with my mother that the land was taken illegally from one Samuel Burns Ferris. There is a question about the transition of the land to my ownership. Clarification is in order." Daddy locked eyes with Lyle.

I don't know what they were telegraphing to one another, but the corner of Lyle's lips twitched.

Lyle turned to Kennedy. "What is the offer on the table from the O'Neal company?"

Kennedy nodded. "Around twenty-thousand an acre."

Lyle smiled his thoughtful smile. "Well, that is not going to suit. Gentlemen. Mrs. Burns has a far better offer and is going to sign the papers at the courthouse as soon as she gets there." Lyle didn't stop but kept talking so they couldn't. "Thank you for your time. If the new owner is interested in selling, perhaps you can contact him." Lyle turned away from the pair and offered his arm to Meemaw. "I suggest we head to the courthouse to sign the papers and get them notarized."

Liam's bandage went up and down as a vein in his head pulsed.

Lyle missed the startled look on the O'Neals' faces or its replacement—which was palpating rage.

Daddy watched the pair like a hunting dog watched a treed coon. He eased the papers back into their folder then his hand slipped into his pocket as did Kennedy's.

Danny boy jumped to his feet. "We'll up the offer. Say thirty thousand an acre in cash."

Meemaw rose and accepted Lyle's arm. "Oh, I don't think so. Keeping it local, you see. Part time tourists coming to fish isn't what our town needs. Thank you for visiting, though. You can always stay at the hotel when you come to fish." She toddled past them, a beatific smile on her lips.

Liam reached out a hand to stop her. "What did they offer?" His voice was a harsh growl.

Meemaw looked him in the eye, which made him squirm. "Something money can't buy."

"Ain't nothin' money can't buy," said Danny.

"I think you're mistaken." Meemaw nodded her head as she resumed her slow progress. "Peace can't be purchased. And what I'm about to do will rectify a wrong and bring this old woman peace."

Judging from their pursed lips, they didn't have a comment. The cousins followed Lyle and Meemaw out. Right behind them, Daddy, with the real estate papers, Kennedy, then Mom. The O'Neals began to talk as Lyle helped Meemaw into his mud-splattered car. "Who's the new owner?" Danny shouted as Lyle began to close her door.

Lyle shrugged. "You'll have to see the paperwork at the courthouse, I suppose."

While Lyle drove Meemaw the rest of us trooped down the alley to the courthouse. The rain began in earnest. Daddy, Mom, and I pulled up our collars and trotted around the mud puddles. The O'Neals dashed in front of us like they were on a track team. Kennedy brought up the rear.

I skirted around a blue car with a crumpled bumper. It stopped me in my sprint. Peeking in the passenger window I caught sight of a stack of papers on the seat. Advertising circulars were mixed with mail. Smiling at the name I'd read I followed my parents to the cement stairs.

Our real estate parade invaded Doreen Pebbles' office. Her assistant looked up with eyes enlarged and made a fast trot to her boss's sanctuary. With coat on and her purse in her hand, the county clerk spun out of her office. She stared at us as we queued at the desk. When her eyes latched onto Liam O'Neal, she blanched and quickly looked at the clock on the wall. "We're closing in five minutes." Her voice trembled.

"Won't take long, Doreen," Daddy said. "My mother wants to transfer some property and needs the paperwork notarized. According to the sign," he pointed to one posted on the wall, "you're qualified."

Daddy handed Doreen the file while Kennedy wandered along the counter separating clients from the working office. Casually he loitered behind the O'Neals, as if merely waiting, but his eyes were focused on their hands.

Daddy's face softened as he stood beside his

mother. "Did you make that call, Lyle?"

"I did. They will be here…" before he could finish, Tyler Ferris Sr. and Jr. entered the office.

"What is this about a mystery solved, Lyle?" T.J. Ferris asked.

Lyle pointed to the file Daddy had given to Doreen. "I think I'll let Delilah's grandmother explain." He missed the sudden tightening of Doreen's jaw. I didn't. I'd had my eye on her after learning that Joseph was her nephew and dealing drugs. Her nostrils pinched together like Charlene Higgenbottom's did when she looked at me.

Meemaw slowly moved toward the Ferris men, her hands outstretched in welcome. She took both of T.J.'s hands in hers and smiled up at him. "Remember that old song, "This Land is Your Land, this Land is My Land?""

T. J. nodded his head.

"Well, if we reverse that, I'll die a contented woman. The Burns homestead, with its house and twenty acres, was taken from your family. Promises broken need to be set right. I'm going to see that it is." She turned to Lyle. "What's next?"

"Signing the papers."

"Well, T.J." Meemaw cleared her throat. "I mentioned the Ecclesiastes portion of scripture to you once, but here is the part I think is pertinent today. This is 'the time to keep and a time to cast away'. I'm handing you land that was never mine. It was always your family's." With that Meemaw moved toward the flat top of the counter. "Doreen, close your mouth afore you catch a fly. It's time to begin again with something that will also change lives." She smiled the smile I remember from my childhood. An all's right with the world smile.

T.J. Ferris hesitated. Daddy stepped to his side. "T.J. No use quibbling about this. Our minds are made up and Burnses have been known to be stubborn. Fact is, they've been set in their ways since the time the promise was given. I'm a bit ashamed of them all. If my daddy had known he would have set things right."

As the clock on the wall hit five o'clock, the deal was done.

The O'Neals were apoplectic.

Meemaw ecstatic.

Ferris Sr. and Jr., were mute from astonishment.

Chapter Twenty-Nine

After the stamp of approval from Doreen, we began to trickle out. Doreen seemed in such a hurry she merely waved at her assistant as she hustled out the door. But before Doreen had gone three steps toward the building's exit, Liam O'Neal grabbed her by the elbow. "Not so fast," he growled.

Doreen glared. "What do you think you're doing?"

Kennedy stopped to listen as did Lyle.

Liam accidentally bathed her face in loose saliva as he said, "Is that land transfer legal?"

"Of course. And who are you to question it?"

"We met a couple of days ago having a little look see at the land map of the county." His voice was stiff.

"Oh, of course. You deal in real estate, like our Mr. Kennedy." Doreen Peebles nodded toward the FBI's fake salesman.

"Yes. Mr. Kennedy and I go *way* back." Liam smiled insincerely at Kennedy. He turned to T.J. Ferris with the same phony smile plastered on. "I've got a proposition for you, Mr. Ferris, or may I call you T.J.?"

T.J. slid his gaze up one side of Liam and down the other. "Mr. Ferris will do."

"I'm certain we can come to an agreement about the property."

"Why don't you speak with my lawyer about it." T.J. pointed his thumb at Lyle. "My family's been waiting one hundred and sixty years for this to be settled. I'm not in a hurry to undo the apology."

Lyle caught Daddy's eye and nodded. "What makes you so interested in the land, Liam? Did you fall for the rumor about gold nuggets as big as your fist laying around waiting to be picked up?"

Danny O'Neal jerked his head around to face Lyle. O'Neal's eyes were narrowed to a slit and his forehead wrinkled because he seemed to be thinking hard.

Daddy walked up to the O'Neals with a smile across his face he only used for simpletons. "Those boys sure set tongues wagging with their tall tale. Next thing you know they'll start bragging about a Kimberlite cone just under the ground. Some folks actually believe where coal is found there are diamonds too."

"What!" Liam O'Neal's word exploded all over us. "But...but Smothers had the geologist's report. We saw it, didn't we, Danny." Danny's eyes widened as if he'd seen a ghost. He moved toward the exit as Liam charged on. "He said there was a deposit so large it'd make the one found from Iceland to Ontario, Canada look puny."

Lyle laughed. "That's what you're up to? Taking Meemaw's land for a pittance because you thought treasure was hidden in the limestone?" Lyle's voice was dry with amusement. "They put one over on you too. It was a set up by the locals to rag a bunch of college kids, Liam."

Danny edged closer to the door as Kennedy stepped away from us, his eyes on the retreating O'Neal.

Liam's face drooped like a sad Beagle. He shook his head as if to realign his thoughts. "Nothing in the ground?"

Meemaw shook her head. "Dirt's been amended with manure over the years but cain't do much with rocky soil. Cain't till it much unless you bring in dirt, which we did. Good soil is worth its weight in gold, 'cause you can feed people." That said she grabbed hold of Daddy's arm for steadying and looked toward the exit sign above the hall door. "Oh, T.J., can you give me a couple of weeks to clear things out? I've a need to get to McKeansville and help Miss Vickie with her granddaughter." Meemaw's face broadened into a wide smile. "About time I quit pulling up dandelions and start loving some hurting girls."

Danny O'Neal's hand was on the door when Kennedy said, "Going somewhere, O'Neal?"

"Yeah. Need to get back to the hotel. Not feeling too

well.”

“I'll go with you. I'm feeling ill myself. Missing out on a sales commission is putting a dent in my expectations.” They left together—Liam a few steps behind. Stringing them along was interesting, but Kennedy better watch himself. The O'Neals were involved with Smothers which put them at the head of the list of suspects for his murder.

Daddy smiled at T.J. “This calls for a celebration. How about a sticky bun from the Coffee Maid and a great cup of Joe?”

“I think my wife needs to be in on this,” Tyler said. “She's been praying down heaven ever since she heard about the land fraud.”

“Doreen, you lead the way,” my mother said. “We need to include you for it's your stamp of approval that set this right.”

With her mouth scrunched up tight, Doreen Peebles was not a happy woman. I began connecting the dots between Doreen, Liam O'Neal, and Joseph. “Doreen probably has to speak with the sheriff about her nephew.” My feet reluctantly moved toward her. I don't know why Doreen Peebles made me cautious, but there was something in her eyes. A sneakiness.

“What?” Doreen shook her head. “My sister has a few things to say about it that I can't repeat. It's really none of my business. Joseph got caught up in things he's not responsible for, poor boy. Never had a lick of sense. Too trusting.”

“Especially if the person is a relative. Happens around here, the family getting all tied up because of an indiscretion.” I sighed.

Lyle's blue eyes opened wide. He knew I was up to something.

“Did you know Derek has a head injury?”

Doreen's hands flew to her bosom.

“So sad. Bad car accident on the road to my sister's place. Must have slid on the ice.”

“Treacherous out here just now.” Doreen began to

hustle toward the exit, an O'Neal escape move.

Walking with her I said, "Looks like you might have had a fender bender. Saw your little car in the alley behind the courthouse."

"Had an accident." She shrugged but kept moving. "Nothing to speak of. A little icy this morning."

I stepped in front of her so I could see her eyes. "Funny that the paint embedded in your bumper is the same color as the sheriff's car. Care to explain?"

Doreen Peebles' chin trembled as her eyes darted toward the exit then she looked at Daddy who'd withdrawn his revolver from his pocket. "Well, I...er..." she licked her lips, eyelids blinking fast. "Loaned the car to a friend and it came back dented."

Daddy's laser like gaze stayed on her face. Doreen's chest deflated.

He took a step toward her. "I think we need to speak with Derek."

"I thought he was in the ICU in Lexington."

I tossed her my no-nonsense look. "He has a concussion but Derek's hard headed and back on the job."

"That's a relief." Her voice was tight as a guy wire.

Lyle dialed the sheriff while I stayed so close to Doreen that you'd have thought we were hooked together like paper dolls.

I think she would have taken off if her assistant hadn't left the office, locked the door, and almost stumbled when she saw us cluttering the hallway. "I thought y'all had left. Where is your friend, Doreen? The man you have on speed dial." She gave a conspiratorial smile. "I call him Doreen's beau. They are always talking."

Sally Carter had loose lips even in high school. Spilling the beans on her boss would get her fired in a city. In the mountains, everyone knew everyone's business. I asked, "Was it the plump man or the thin one?"

"The one with the bandage on his head." She

laughed. "He was here a couple of days ago and they had a rendezvous in her office." She winked. "Y'all have a good night."

I don't think Doreen's night was going to be a good one, because after Derek hustled over, he invited her to have a conversation in his office.

In a sleety rain we headed to the Coffee Maid. Cheryl Lynn had turned over the sign from open to closed but Meemaw stood by the window and tapped on the glass anyway. She waved at her granddaughter. Cheryl Lynn galloped to the door and flung it open. "Looks like a party! Come in, come in before you drown."

Amid hot drinks and our finishing off her cupcakes, scones, and muffins, Meemaw held court with her soft, smiling eyes.

An hour into our party, Derek Sullivan arrived. His pupils were pin dots. What did they say about concussion protocol? Shouldn't he be in the hospital?

Sullivan started talking before he eased into a seat. "I've called in a forensic team to check out some things here. The FBI have Joseph confessing to everything from drug running to driving a get-away car for the O'Neals when they whacked Smothers. Looks like we can bottle up two or three cases all at once." I smiled inwardly as Derek talked, sounding assured and focused. "Your friend Madison sends his regards, Delilah. Says you and your new husband should soon be cleared to leave his jurisdiction." Derek looked at us for more information.

We didn't offer any. All I offered was a question. "How is Browning?"

Derek's eyes softened from their usual intensity. "Broken leg and got banged on the head. Guess we're alike in some ways. Your sister has carted my dog home to be spoiled. Next thing I know I'll have a lap dog like some city fella that lets his dog lead him around."

I didn't even glance at Lyle, knowing Bartles was getting more spoiled by the day with Josephine, Savannah, and all the assorted females that doted on that dog.

Crossing his arms, Lyle said, "If Doreen Peebles is the local linchpin of a drug gang the Ferrises are cleared."

"Seems likely. We're checking for her finger prints on a vial in Joseph's car."

We celebrated with another round of coffee.

Chapter Thirty

A SOFT MORNING GREETED US. SUN slanted in the windows with golden fingers. When Lyle and I appeared for breakfast, we found Madison and Derek lounging at Suzanne's kitchen table. Derek had propped his head up with his hand and stared at his mug of coffee like a zombie. Madison seemed even less perky.

Derek glanced up at Lyle, nodded his head then groaned. "Thought you might need an update," he said in a voice tense with pain.

"I'll give it," Madison interrupted. "You've got a headache that belies description." Madison was firm but he wasn't one to offer advice since he'd gotten back to his job within two weeks of trying to die with blood loss. "Joseph Peebles is a fountain that is not only overflowing but drowning us in information. He claims his Aunt Doreen is the organizer of a drug transfer station. That she got him the job at Ferrises' so he could pack and deliver opiates in the sculptures. He named contacts and said the O'Neals are the next rung up the ladder in the gang. I believe Derek mentioned to you that Joseph also swears that he drove the O'Neal cousins to the resort hotel where you honeymooned. Says they whacked Smothers because he cheated them out of the Kimberlite discovery."

Lyle nailed him with a skinny-eyed stare.

Madison pursed his lips. "Okay. I get it. An abbreviated honeymoon." He waved off any more protests. "Here me out. Pebbles says he didn't go in with the O'Neals but when they came out, Danny was stuffing a jacket dripping in blood into a bag. Says he'll swear to it in court. Also has no love lost for his aunt. Told us where to find the drug money she'd hidden around her house. We found a lot of loot. Freezer in the garage had deer sausage, steaks, and one hundred thousand dollars in bills."

"You two sticking around for my fried eggs?" Lyle asked as he aimed toward the refrigerator.

"Wouldn't interrupt your honeymoon, Lyle." Madison laughed.

"I need to see my dog then head back to town." Looking worried, Derek glanced around.

I smiled. "Suzanne has him sleeping beside her bed. Carted him to the studio this morning in a wheelbarrow with a squeaky wheel."

Lyle didn't look up from his pursuit of a spatula. "Think Di and I will head back to McKeansville. We're involved in a renovation project that needs our input."

Madison lifted up his cup. "I'm interested in what you create as a healing place. Might be able to make a few suggestions."

"That would be helpful. Thank you, Robert."

They left as Lyle put butter in the frying pan. It wasn't a leisurely breakfast. Packing was on both of our minds.

Living in a rural area makes you attuned to unexpected sounds. I heard one when I placed my suitcase in the Porsche's small trunk. It wasn't the rush of autumn rain water over the falls or the lapping sound of the water on the small beach below the parking lot. But something thumped, hard. Like a door slammed against wood. Then I heard the dog bark. And Browning's bark grew in volume and intensity.

Suzanne suddenly yelled, "Let go of me." Her voice came from behind the house, in the direction of her studio.

Running toward her voice I rounded the corner of her house and saw Neely Patrick had a gun pointed at Suzanne's chest. Browning stood in the doorway barking, his leg in a blue cast, his head down and forward. I dropped behind a scrawny hydrangea. Then, waddling backwards I headed for the car.

I needed to warn Lyle before he stumbled upon the trio. Besides, I wanted his gun. When the Smith and Wesson was in my palm, I headed to the front door. Throwing the door open I shouted, "Lyle, Clarisse and Neely are holding Suzanne hostage."

Lyle dashed out of the bedroom with a toothbrush in his hand. "Where?"

"By the studio. They might think she's me."

Across the living room expanse, the large windows revealed the trio marching down the walk. Neely gave Suzanne a shove. She stumbled. Head down, Browning hobbled along the rocky path behind them.

"Go to the bedroom and lock the door. I'll..." before we could move, the kitchen door opened and we heard voices.

"I know you're in here, Lyle. We've got your new bride or her look-alike sister. Thought we'd have a parley." From the strident tone in her voice, Clarisse didn't sound like she wanted to negotiate.

Lyle held out his hand for the gun. Relieved, I handed it over. We would have tiptoed across the living room to the corner that had cell service but they'd have spotted us.

Lyle's left hand moved me firmly behind him.

"This isn't Delilah," Neely Patrick whined. "Her eyes are the wrong color blue. These are greenish."

I squeezed between the front door and the hallway, my shoulder blades flat against the wall.

"Shut up, Neely."

"Actually," Suzanne spoke in her smooth as silk voice, "I'm Suzanne, Delilah's sister. And *you* are trespassing."

There was a slapping sound of skin hitting skin then a muffled cry from Suzanne. Something rose up in me and I took a step. Lyle waved me back. My hands tightened into balls.

"No need for that!" Neely sounded alarmed.

"Just get the keys to your truck and we're out of here," Clarisse ordered.

My feet itched to move.

"Remember, Neely, we didn't come to have a polite conversation. If we don't get Lyle and Delilah taken care of, we're in the state pen for decades."

Lyle inched toward the kitchen. The dog scraping his paws on the rocks covered the sound of Lyle's stealthy creep. Browning began to bark.

There was a jingle of keys. "Here," Suzanne said. "Take the Ford and go. You'll have a half hour before the sheriff knows about you. That should give you plenty of time to get away."

"Not a bad solution, Clarisse. We escape." Neely paused as if thinking. "Plenty of places to hide until we can get to the Caribbean. We don't need a murder charge against us."

I counted five before I stepped away from the wall. Two of us made a more difficult target, and Lyle had a gun.

"Too late. We need to eliminate witnesses." Clarisse words were clipped as she spoke. "And then there are extradition agreements. The U.S. can claw us back like they can money hidden from the IRS." Browning began to scrape the door with his paws.

"Of course, but I've a few friends I can count on." Neely's voice sounded whiney. "With my overseas accounts we'll do fine."

"You know we planned to take them out, so don't play chicken. Now give me the gun, you're shaking like a leaf."

Lyle turned his head and gave me his stink eye. I stopped moving but when he turned back to ease into the doorway, I slid one foot in front of the other until I was an arm length from him.

Neely cleared his throat. "Think I'll just keep my weapon, Clarisse. If this *is* Suzanne Burns, and I think it's likely, it would be a shame to rob the world of her talent."

"Ridding the world of any Burns should get you the Nobel Prize. And shoot that noisy dog. Thought we'd have gotten rid of it when you hit the sheriff's car. If that hound keeps barking someone might come to find out why." Clarisse sniffed. "This party starts with taking care of Lyle. Then after we escape, we make Delilah disappear. Forever."

Lyle moved into the kitchen entrance. He held his weapon with both hands. It was at eye level and aimed into the room. "Well, that all depends, Clarisse."

"Really, Lyle, I don't think you can shoot Neely before he dispatches your bride."

"Neely, this isn't going to look good on your rap sheet. Slide the gun to me and let Suzanne go." Lyle's voice was firm.

"I knew it wasn't Delilah!"

I peeked around Lyle's shoulder and caught Neely lowering the gun from Suzanne's temple and bending to slide it toward Lyle. "I'll not be up on murder charges, Lyle."

"Thought you'd see reason."

My little sister had eyes slit with anger. If she got free, they were in for trouble.

Neely pushed the gun across the floor. It spun toward Lyle but whacked the side of a cupboard and stopped.

I grabbed a breath.

"Step to me, Suzanne." Lyle words were smooth as cream.

My sister took a step, then another. She was four steps away when Clarisse grabbed her long reddish-gold ponytail and swung Suzanne around until they were face to face. "Turn around and keep moving." In Clarisse's hand was an open pocket knife with the blade pressed against Suzanne's neck.

Suzanne turned.

Clarisse shoved my sister forward.

Toward the gun, laying three feet away from them.

Cowering behind her, Neely pocketed the ring of keys and slunk toward the back door. He turned the handle. Before he could exit, the dog catapulted into him. Neely hit the floor. The dog stepped over him and headed toward Suzanne.

Forcing Suzanne to squat, Clarisse's hand snaked to the floor and snatched the weapon before Lyle could safely fire. The gun's barrel slammed against Suzanne's head. A red line appeared on her forehead, then a trickle of blood ran down her cheek. With a jerk of her hand, Clarisse pulled Suzanne up until my sister became Clarisse's shield. Suzanne stood poker stiff, her fingers clenching and unclenching.

Eyes focused on Suzanne, Browning started a frenzy of barking. Clarisse scowled and looked behind her, as if reassessing her exit strategy. Neely stepped out the door.

"Let Suzanne go, Clarisse." Lyle spoke in a low, firm tone.

"I don't take orders from you."

"Take Neely and head out."

"Neely's got the truck keys. Delilah and I are now going for a drive." By a jerk to her pony tail, Clarisse swiveled Suzanne's head around. With Suzanne's elbow cocked and ready to attack, if Clarisse didn't have the gun planted by her ear, she'd have been knocked flat.

"Clarisse." I spoke from behind Lyle. "You'd be better off leaving without my sister as a hostage."

"Still hiding behind Lyle, Delilah? You never could stand on your own two feet. Always needed a man to protect you."

Her statement was ridiculous. "I'm from the mountains, Clarisse. No woman around here needs a man's protection."

The truck engine roared to life.

"Time for my exit. Looks like I'll have to find you later, Delilah. I'll borrow your sister for a while, if you don't mind."

"No. Leave Suzanne and take me." I took a step to

move away from Lyle, but he grabbed my arm and thrust me further behind him.

Browning growled then nipped at Clarisse's gun hand. Hampered by his bandages, the dog jostled Clarisse instead of disarming her. Their collision forced Clarisse's hand away from Suzanne's head and a bullet exited the chamber and hit the family bean pot that had survived moves, floods, and the Great Depression. Fragments of pottery cascaded over the kitchen. Suzanne hit the floor, giving Lyle a clean shot.

He didn't take it. "No, Clarisse. Your quarrel is with me, not my wife. Drop the gun." I shivered at the rock hardness in his tone. "If you so much as twitch, I'll shoot."

His voice said he would.

I held my breath.

The truck horn blared as if Neely was leaning on it. "Ah, that must be my exit music. I suppose I'll have to take you up on your offer, Lyle." Clarisse flicked out her tongue and licked her upper lip. She studied Lyle then let the gun dangle from her trigger finger. She released the weapon and it hit the floor with a metallic shiver.

"Back away from the gun." Clarisse took a step away from Suzanne, then another.

"Before you and Neely pull your Houdini act and vanish, I suggest you sit at the table and put your hands on top." Lyle's Smith and Wesson pointed at her heart. She took another step toward the table next to the open door, then sat.

"Suzanne, please phone the sheriff. Should take him ten minutes to get here from town." Lyle's voice was now as calm as it had been on the day Clarisse shot him. The day he'd nearly died. Love was a tangled mess. Years before he'd given Clarisse his heart. She'd thrown it away. Now, on our honeymoon, he was standing in her way again. What would she do?

Eyes glazed, Suzanne's steps were unsteady as she moved. To reach the phone on the counter, Suzanne stepped between Lyle and Clarisse. Blocking Lyle's shot was all Clarisse needed to move. She jumped up and was out the door before he could stop her.

Lyle didn't pursue his ex-wife. Clarisse was unarmed and Lyle wouldn't shoot anyone in the back.

Chapter Thirty-One

"SUZANNE YOU ALL RIGHT?" LYLE'S VOICE was tight. My sister nodded. "Make the call then take the dog into the living room. And Delilah, keep your head down. Knowing Clarisse, she's got something planned."

"Use your gun, Lyle, and shoot out their tires," I said as he exited.

Heart hammering, I ran toward the front. Easing the door open I peeked out. Clarisse slid into the front seat of Suzanne's truck. Light and shadow danced along the rock-strewn path as clouds scurried through the sky. I squinted in a shaft of sunlight that hit the front step like a lightning bolt. At the turn in the road where the falls became exposed to visitors, a figure aimed toward the house. He was armed with a shot gun.

The stranger drew closer. Eyes focused on the running vehicle Jed McMurry moved at a trot. When Neely revved his engine and put the truck in gear, McMurry ducked behind the ancient oak anchoring the parking area's western border.

Clarisse pointed toward the vacant gas station. McMurry's truck was near there, crosswise in the road blocking their getaway. Neely turned off the engine. Stepping out of the Ford, Neely put his palm along his forehead to shield his eyes from the dazzle of light blazing off of the limestone. He gazed around, spotted Lyle but seemed unaware of McMurry.

Neely walked to the passenger door and knocked on the window. When Clarisse rolled it down, he said, "That wasn't here when we came up the road."

"Neely," Lyle shouted from the side of the house, "step away from the truck and let's end this."

Neely's face puckered into a frown. "End what? We're heading back to McKeansville." He stepped around the bumper to the front.

Lyle laughed his easy laugh. The one that usually made me join him. This time I felt my tears rising. "I may like the idea of a blaze of gunfire and the bad guys dead in the dirt. But I'm the one with the gun and it's time you both stopped running."

"You always were a sucker for a happy ending, Lyle. Only this time "—Clarisse yelled as she slid over the truck seat to the driver's side—"you're not going to be given the opportunity."

Her words sounded as brittle as icicles. And as cold.

The truck rumbled to life.

Neely's head swiveled from Lyle to the truck and he sprinted to get around the front. Clarisse stomped on the gas. The Ford's bumper struck Neely and he flew backwards into the soupy mud. Clarisse kept going, the truck bouncing in the air as she drove over Neely's legs then his chest.

A breath of air moved behind me. Suzanne stood in the doorway with her .22. Neely moaned in a voice as pitiful as a lost calf. His fingers were clamped onto his blood-soaked shirt as if they could throttle the pain. I flew to the writhing figure of Neely Patrick. His brown eyes fixed on my face. Lips moving, he whispered, "I'm sorry. I never intended for things to...to..."

Movement down the road made me glance that way. Jed had stepped out from behind the oak. His gun was too high to be aiming for the tires. Clarisse drove directly at him. Jed let out a blast of buckshot before jumping away and seeking shelter.

Glass scattered among the rocks. Through a hole in the front windshield I spied Clarisse. She stepped on the gas, plowing down the rhododendron planted sixty years ago and a whiskey barrel planter that had seen better days.

From the amount of blood running onto the rocks, Neely Patrick didn't have long to live. I took his right hand in mine. "Neely. Breathe. Help is coming. First, thing is, do you know that God loves you? Right now, He loves you?"

Moisture grew in Neely's pain-squinted eyes. "Yes," he croaked.

Lyle squatted beside me. He touched Neely's shoulder and winced as he looked at Neely's legs angled sideways.

Leading Neely to the Lord was beyond me. Oh, help, Lord.

The Ford backed and halted, then aimed up the pavement to the service station. Taking a breath, I whispered to Neely. "Ask His forgiveness for all you've done, Neely."

On the road toward town Tweedy's truck came into view. He took the curve at the top of the hill, tires squealing as he braked to avoid ramming the truck blocking the road. He parked directly in the Ford's path, on the exit drive from the station.

My eyes went back to the injured man. "How can He..." Neely's voice was faint. I leaned so my ear nearly touched his mouth.

Neely being Catholic, I knew he was familiar with the Bible stories of the crucifixion. "Remember the thief on the cross, Neely? He asked Jesus to remember him when He was in paradise. The thief acknowledged that Jesus was the Christ, the Son of God."

Neely gave my hand a squeeze. "Tell Olive...I'm sorry." And on the muddy rocks with the falls drowning out his final breath, he died.

Chapter Thirty-Two

I LOOKED INTO MY HUSBAND'S EYES. There were tears. I wanted a blanket to cover Neely, to hide the pain still distorting his face. Swiping at a tear, I looked down the road. Behind Tweedy was the Marlboro man's jeep with him at the wheel. He jumped out as did Derek, his passenger. Lyle might get his shoot out after all as the three began to walk up the drive toward Clarisse.

Jed McMurry climbed from behind his protective tree and strode toward Clarisse's side of the Ford. She put the truck in reverse. Jed leaped sideways and hit the ground, rolled, and was back on his feet in a second. He swung his gun up, firing. Pellets blasted through the passenger window, but Clarisse was nowhere to be seen. She must have been hit by flying glass or the pellets.

The truck backed toward the drop off above the falls. Then it jerked forward and aimed toward the vehicle blocking the road. The men turned and headed toward her. She reversed again and the truck's tires hit the softer shoulder dirt, spun, and lost traction. It kept moving, toward the sharp cliff's edge. Lyle and I ran toward the truck, waving our arms to get her to stop. But Clarisse backed until the rear tires were over the edge. Her head drooped to the left as the engine revved.

We came to a halt at the end of the fall's parking area. Lyle grabbed my hand and squeezed it so tightly that I winced with pain.

The Ford's cab lifted from the ground, then slipped sideways, and rolling from the driver's side onto the passenger side, descended the limestone cliff. The truck bounced on the cliffside like a rubber ball. Hearing metal striking the shrubbery, boulders, and thick forest of trees that lined the bank caused Lyle to wrap me in his arms before my knees gave way. The splash of the

Ford hitting the water overcame the thunder of the falls. With horrified eyes we watched the truck buck in the rapids before the falls. Clarisse waved an arm as the Ford spun in the rush of water and tipped over the lip of the cataract. Lyle embraced me, hiding my view of Horsetail Falls. On tiptoe, I peered over his shoulder, watching Suzanne's truck come up from the pool's bottom below us and float down the river. I couldn't see any movement in the cab.

The sun, blotted out by a black cloud, made shadows grow until the whole earth was swallowed into a black and white movie. Browning butted his head against my leg and left it there.

The truck spun as it danced downstream. It was a slow waltz on the water's foam. The river's descent at the bottom of the falls was slight, and the water spread out and lapped the shore.

As if moving from pause to warp speed, the men caught up with us. Suzanne went into the house to get a blanket to cover Neely, while Lyle and I dashed for the deer path that wandered along the water.

Panting at the bottom of the path, I waited for any sign of life. Kicking off his boots, Lyle leapt into the water and with sure strokes swam to the floating truck.

A rope in his hand, determination on his face, Derek skidded down the trail. He tossed one end to Jackman and wrapped the other around the trunk of an ancient willow. Without a word, Marlboro man flung off his boots, tossed his billfold at my feet, and followed Lyle into the frigid water.

Lyle had reached the truck by the time Jackman dove in. Trying to climb up the door to see inside, Lyle bobbed high enough to put his hands on the door handle. As he hauled himself up, the truck tipped toward him and he went under. Hands to my mouth, I stared at the gray-green water, bucking Ford, and the spot where Lyle had vanished. With the rope in his mouth like a waterdog with his quarry, the mining engineer kept swimming toward the Ford. Twenty feet separated Lyle and Jackman when Lyle rose like a geyser at the back of the truck.

Fifty yards from where I stood on the bank, trees and broken branches formed a log jam at a bend in the river. Floating like a duck, the truck veered toward it. With undertows and branches snagging whatever came near, the jam was a deathtrap.

The Ford pivoted and struck the jam, passenger side first. A snaggle of roots tumbled from the pile and somersaulted to the Ford's side. The movement caused the truck to sidle up to the pile. As the truck went nose down in the water the root ball anchored itself to the hood and shoved the truck into the jam.

Intent on watching my husband risk his life to rescue a woman who wanted to kill him, I didn't turn when Suzanne called my name.

Lyle and Jackman reached the truck's rear, grasped the tailgate, and hung on, simply breathing. In less than a minute Jackman dove underwater, came up on the other side of the truck, then went under again. He returned to the surface minus the rope. Waving toward shore his movements were sluggish. My thoughts bounced from hypothermia to injury.

Derek gave Jackman a thumbs up and Lyle and Jackman abandoned the truck. Straining against the pull of the water forcing them into the tangle of wood, they swam toward shore.

I ran down the brambly trail toward the log pile and my husband. Behind me other footsteps pounded, but my eyes were on the slippery, rooted path and the swimmers. The wind picked up and waves formed on the water. Jackman slipped under first. Lyle looked to his side, dove under, and hauled him up. They reached the bend where the cliffs narrowed and the river dropped another ten feet into rapids. Pushed along by the speed of the water, they disappeared from view.

Stumbling, I grabbed a sourwood branch to stay upright. The fissured bark ripped into my hand. Sucking on the blood pulsing from my palm, I continued downward, hearing the river's song not as a lullaby from my youth but as a drumbeat of a funeral march. I stayed ahead of Jed, Derek, and Tweedy until I rounded the corner of the bend and saw Lyle amid the slimy limestone rocks, his feet in the water, his body on land. Face down, he had landed before hitting the rapids. No sign of Jackman.

Drawing closer I watched Lyle's back move up and down as he grabbed breath. Slowly he pushed himself up until he kneeled on the rocks. Looking up at me, he shivered. Wrapping him in my arms, I knelt on the wet shore and rocked him. His temperature was ice cold.

"Look for Jackman," Derek shouted above the boiling water. Jed and Tweedy tore down the incline.

"Blankets!" Suzanne huffed as she tossed a pile onto the ground. She bent over and tried to grab a breath from her race down the hillside.

Before I could grab one, we were wrapped in a dry, scratchy blanket by Derek. Then he turned to Suzanne.

"I shouldn't have commandeered that engineer's jeep." Derek looked down the trail at the thin skim of water racing over the rapids. "If Jackman doesn't make it..." His voice dropped and he didn't finish. Throwing his shoulders back, Derek followed his friends.

The sound of the water, a comfort in the hot summer months brought no joy, only a duet of bass and alto as the water slapped the rocks. The metal of the Ford whacking the logs hushed the birdsong. Lyle's skin was turning from gray-blue to pink when we heard a shout rise from the copse of trees below.

Lyle's body tensed. I braced for bad news.

Chapter Thirty-Three

THREE MEN WALKING ONE IN FRONT of the other appeared like a hunting party on the narrow, deer path. Between two of them, a fourth was hauled along like a dead animal. Although they held Jackman upright, his limp legs dragged behind him.

Lyle tossed off the blanket and took a step toward the men. "Jackman alive?"

"Barely," came Derek's response.

Suzanne put her hand on Lyle's chest. "I'll go. You're both a wreck. Get to the house and warm up in a shower." She sounded as bossy as Meemaw.

When we reached the spot near the log jam, I grabbed Jackman's wallet from a muddy rock and hiked with Lyle up the path.

Lyle dripped icy water on Suzanne's step while the rescue party lumbered up the hillside, encumbered by the weight of Jackman and the incline. Jackman's head was upright, as the group neared the back door.

Sitting like clay lumps in the kitchen chairs, Jackman and Lyle rained water in the kitchen as Suzanne started her kettle and coffee pot. When she'd finished, she said, "Get thee hence to the showers, gentlemen. There will be sustenance when you're dry and changed." She looked them both over and puckered her brow. "Delilah, find something of Lyle's that what's his name can wear. I'll take him to my shower."

While Suzanne eased Jackman into her suite, I spread the damp contents of Jackman's wallet on the counter to dry then followed Lyle to the guest room.

Lyle wept in the shower. His sobs penetrated into the bedroom as I searched for clothes in his suitcase. How would he tell his boys that their mother was gone? Or was she? Clarisse had pulled a disappearing act eighteen years ago, so maybe she'd done it again.

Returning to the kitchen I spotted Derek grabbing a mug of coffee. He raised it in salute. "We've tackled the truck and I've sent Jed and Bruce to look for other er...evidence."

What Derek meant was, to find Clarisse, dead or alive.

After the men had showered and I'd put on dry clothes, we gathered in the warm kitchen. Jackman looked as worn as I'd ever seen a man. He winced when he raised his head and bruises purpled his hands. Lyle sat with fingers wrapped around a mug of hot chocolate altered by a generous serving of brandy. To warm you up, Suzanne had said.

With all her kitchen chairs occupied by guests, my sister plopped onto the floor and called the dog to her. Browning laid his head on Suzanne's knees. My sister stroked the spotted body. With a contented sigh, Browning closed his eyes. "Think I need to contact my auto insurance company." Suzanne didn't look up as she spoke but continued loving the dog.

Derek nodded. "I'll make a few phone calls and get a salvage team here. Don't figure anyone could survive the drop and going into the pool. Her body is either floating down the river or trapped in the Ford. Jed and Bruce are searching downstream."

Lyle stared into my eyes with a steadiness that took my breath away. I grieved for Lyle and his boys. They'd lost someone they'd once loved and trusted. However, if Clarisse was alive, she would need help. I hoped that Jed and Bruce Tweedy could find her so she wouldn't die alone.

The sun hung over the trees like a jack-o-lantern moon. An hour or more and daylight would be gone. It had been a long day and my emotions were as fragile as a china cup. I pushed away the police report I'd filled out and turned toward the figures shuffling up the path along the river. Bruce Tweedy came first, his arms around part of black garbage bags made into a body bag. The slender figure only needed McMurry and Tweedy to carry it up the steep trail. They walked slowly, not because of the burden but they were unbearably tired. Maybe all people in these parts were dog tired. The weight of poverty and the pull of the load to keep one step ahead of death coiled through the mountains like the dismal autumn fog.

We made grilled ham and cheese sandwiches, heated cans of tomato/basil soup, and sat like deflated lumps in front of the fireplace. When Jackman eased off the couch saying he needed to head home, Derek pushed him back. "You'll stay until someone can drive you." Jackman finally fell asleep. Suzanne lifted his legs and covered him with a blanket. We tiptoed away. Derek sent his deputies home with the mortician and bodies and accepted a sleeping bag from Suzanne so he could sleep in the living room.

Lyle slipped off to sleep seconds after his head hit the down pillow. I didn't. My mind kept seeing Lyle in the water swimming to rescue his ex-wife, then lying like a dead trout on the shore. Tears leaked from my eyes. I swiped them away. Derek promised he wouldn't let the press know about the bodies till morning. When the new day had dawned, Lyle could phone his kids.

I punched the pillow with my fist and dropped my head into it. And I'd have Lyle call Olive. He was just the person to tell her about Neely. Logical, kind Lyle would choose his words with grace. Closing my eyes, I drifted. About one, I sat up and glared.

"Really, Lord."

Lyle murmured in his sleep.

"Telling Harry's high school sweetheart about her

estranged husband's death is for someone else." The pressure on my heart didn't relent. The thought, why not me? chased me down. I fell asleep knowing that caring for Olive's heart was my gift to her.

"Hey, you two," Suzanne yelled as she knocked on the door. "Up and at 'em. Breakfast is awaiting."

There were five of us for Suzanne's version of scrambled eggs. With herbed Boursin cheese, ham, and green onions thrown in it was a winning concoction.

"What can you tell me about your aunt the painter?" Jackman asked over his second cup of coffee.

Suzanne turned from feeding the dog a biscuit. "What aunt?"

"The one who created the art piece over the mantle."

Derek lifted his mug toward Suzanne. "You're looking at the lady. Had a gift since she was little."

Marlboro man shook his head. "Well, I admire your talent, little lady."

His western twang accent didn't fool me anymore. "Care to explain who you really are, Mr. Jackman? Your accent gives you away. As does your driver's license."

A crooked smile shot across his lips. He dipped his head. "Should have known not to try and fool you, Delilah. As I recall, when you were a little thing you stood up to your brother James and told him you weren't about to go hiking where there were bears and poison ivy."

"Luke?" I jumped from my chair and grabbed him by the arm. He winced. I'd chosen the spot where a laceration had a bandage on it. "I thought you were in the Air Force."

"Who?" Suzanne stared up at us.

"Meet Luke Burns McCallister. Second cousin once removed and hails from Breathitt County."

Cousin Luke scratched the back of his head. "Retired after twenty years and went into another line of government work."

Lyle held up a finger. "Let me guess. DEA, FBI, some initial group you can't tell us about."

"Something like that. When I was ten my mama got a divorce and left the mountains. We moved north. I took my step-father's name. Didn't come back much after that. When I did, I never visited with my father's side of the family."

Derek leaned close to him. "You here on vacation?"

"Not exactly."

Our local sheriff didn't look pleased. "That's what I thought. Let's head down to my office. I've a few questions for you."

If cousin Luke thought he could sneak out of town and never have to fess up, he'd have to rethink that and right fast. Luke's clandestine work came to light when we stopped to get coffee to go and say goodbye to Cheryl Lynn. Jed stood by the display case where Lyle wanted to take a peek at Cheryl Lynn's baking skills.

"All I did," we heard Jed McMurry say as we opened the door, "was come into the sheriff's office to turn in my badge." Jed fingered it on his shirt as he talked. "I overhead Derek yelling about our new neighbor, Jackman. So...putting two and two together, I figure Jackman is with the Feds and he was here on business. Jed rocked back on his heels. "Turns out Jackman is kin to a quarter of the people in our county." Everyone shook their heads while Cheryl Lynn fiddled with her teaspoons, wiping the same one clean three times.

"Even though he was sneaking around here like a pole cat looking for a few chickens, think we'd better make apologies to the man." Jed slapped his knee.

The bell above Cheryl Lynn's door jingled. All eyes turned to see Jackman er...my cousin Luke... saunter in. He had his Stetson pushed back and a traveling coffee container in his hand. He smiled at Cheryl Lynn and lifted his hat. "I'd like a cup of your fine coffee, ma'am."

She took one look at him and started to cry. Tears rolled down her cheeks and she sniffed loudly. "Sorry," she mumbled, wiping her eyes with her flowered apron. "I think we all are sorry to have treated you badly. I'll get your coffee, Mr. Jackman. Why don't you pick out a muffin. The coffee and it are on the house today."

Jackman/Luke leaned on the counter. "Ma'am?"

"It's just...er...Jed told us about you diving into the river by Horsetail Falls and I wanted to thank you."

Cousin Luke unearthed a handkerchief from his pocket and handed it to her. A good move, since Lyle's had won a place in my heart.

Jed cleared his throat. "I'd like to say that was some rescue attempt yesterday." Jed held out his hand. They shook hands firmly. "What Cheryl Lynn is trying to say is that we owe you an apology. And to admit that we played a little joke on you. Considering that you're now part of the community, maybe you should know that there isn't gold around here."

"Oh, really?" said Jackman. He drew a small leather pouch from his jacket pocket. "Thought I'd get Cheryl to weigh out my findings so I could pay for a few of her treats." He tossed the bag in his hand. "With the muffin on the house, guess I'll keep this for another time."

Cheryl refilled his thermos. They didn't speak as Luke chose three muffins for the road while Lyle took two cinnamon rolls and we headed out of the Coffee Maid together.

"You think Luke was having them on?"

"That's one guess, my love. That leather bag looked like it came from a jewelry store. Probably Colorado gold." He smirked. "Or...he filled it with gold he'd found at the bottom of your meemaw's garden."

Our return home was easy until we reached Berea

and Lyle aimed his car north toward Lexington instead of the shorter route. "I believe I promised you a trip to Paris."

He waited for my response but I didn't have one. Paris was a phantom invading my wishful thinking. What with one thing and another we had to get back to McKeansville. There was a house to rearrange, mine. Lyle's things still hung in the closet of his bedroom across the street. Meemaw was going to be entering our fair city after Christmas. That gave us six-weeks to get things settled at the Morgan place and ready for habitation. I needed a notebook to write all the things that needed doing.

Lyle shook his head. "I can see that you are miles away. We could always stop for lunch in Paris, Kentucky on the way home and tell everyone we'd been there."

I laughed and patted his arm. "A bit inconvenient. Another time, Lyle. You must speak with your boys and I need to find out how Josephine is doing and go see Olive."

Olive met me for coffee. We sat on my living room couch because shoulder to shoulder seemed the best way to speak with her. If she needed me to hold her hand, I was ready. So was the Kleenex box on the coffee table.

"Olive." My voice clogged. I cleared it. "I believe the sheriff spoke to you about Neely."

Olive paled and nodded. She put down her coffee cup and grabbed a Kleenex.

"I was with him when he died and want you to know what happened."

Her head bobbed up and down but still she didn't speak.

"Clarisse ran him over..." Olive gasped. I wrapped her cold hands in mine. "And we spoke before he died." She wriggled a hand free and blew her nose on the tissue. I swallowed, wanting my heart to quit hammering. "I asked Neely if he knew that God loved him and he said he did."

Again, Olive nodded.

"I think he confessed his sins to God and squeezed my hand to let me know." I kissed her cheek. "Olive, there is one thing more. He said he was sorry for what he did to you."

Olive's arms encased my neck and she sobbed on my freshly ironed pink shirt. I held her until she withdrew but kept her hand in mine while she talked out her grief.

I don't know what God had in mind for Olive and Will, but she'd need a few months to sort things out. That I knew from experience.

Lyle and I slid easily into domestic bliss. My house was ours, but we slept in the downstairs bedroom because Lyle had his construction crew dismantling walls when they were hampered by weather out at the farm. Josephine's house had been moved to a park along with a vacant one Lyle unearthed near the bypass. They sat a bit forlorn as they tilted on their moving trailer foundations.

Our second morning home, Josephine stormed into my kitchen, bringing a blustery wind with her. "What am I supposed to do with my mess of a life?" I stared at the frying pan in my kitchen sink, then looked her square in the eye, and shrugged.

"Getting married is the least of my worries. Settling in at the farm will be a piece of cake compared to dealing with teenagers and their emotions."

Light dawned. I kept my mouth shut. I'd been in her shoes, but since the Weldons had returned home to work the farm, she had Elise and Savannah to contend with. Josephine put her hands on her hips. "I now understand why the word caterwauling came to be. You should have heard the shouting last night when Savannah turned up her music and Elise wanted to read. They sounded like two felines hissing and spitting with anger. The door slamming woke Mama up and then I had a mess on my hands."

"Want me to speak with them?"

"That's why I'm here. That, and your dust balls are calling me."

When I entered Lyle's house, I heard the girls in the kitchen. Heading that direction, I stopped at the dining room door and listened to Elise Weldon. "I don't care what she's written. I'm not forgiving her. Look at the needle marks on my arm." Elise's voice choked with emotion. "She was my friend and look what she caused."

"My mom says Elizabeth was blackmailed into helping the traffickers. She's going to prison, you know." The soft voice of my goddaughter held empathy.

"And I'm glad."

"I'm not. She's as much a victim as we are."

"If it wasn't for her, I wouldn't have the shakes from drug withdrawal and I wouldn't have been..." Elise broke into sobs.

"The kids that hurt you and David are going to trial. It's not going to be pretty. The D.A. says that David will take a long time to recover and they are responsible. If it weren't for the police video, they might get away with it. Now they can't and the evil that they did has ruined their lives."

Having no right to interfere I turned back. A weak November sun leaked through the front windows onto the thick Persian rug surrounding the table. Clarisse had brought that rug from her upscale family. She had decorated the house with expensive antiques and silver that shone in the pale light. A loving husband, two energetic sons, wealth, and position hadn't satisfied her craving for more. And in the end, she tumbled into the abyss of her own choices.

"Holding bitterness isn't going to help us heal,

Elise." Savannah's voice made me look to the glass fronted china cabinet glowing with silver. "We might as well be angry about every man who held us down, used us, starved us, and now looks at us as if we're loathsome and discardable refuse. And that isn't the way I want to live." Sobs cascaded through the house and I prayed their tears would begin the journey toward healing.

Epilogue

THE MOON, IN ITS GOLDEN GLORY, hovered above the yard when Lyle glided into the kitchen. A grin as broad as the Kentucky river made his eyes crinkle at the corners. I smiled back at him as I peeled potatoes for dinner. He grabbed me about the waist and leading me to the other side of the work island, whirled me around in a circle. "I've two tickets for a flight to Paris," he whispered.

My head jerked up and I stared into his pleased-with-himself face. "When?"

"Tomorrow. I've two weeks before I must be presiding in court."

"I...er...we aren't prepared to just leave with all the demolition, Josephine planning her wedding, the girls so fragile and..."

His forefinger tapped my lips. "Every objection you could think up I've countered, Mrs. H. I've a list, in duplicate," he tapped his coat as if I could see his shirt pocket. "No clothes? We'll shop in Paris. No rooms? I've already booked. Thanksgiving on the horizon? Our kids are doing it at home, and I refuse to have my new bride slave over dinner for the two of us."

"Paris?" I said, a little breathless. I put the pot on the warmer and danced down the hall with my groom, heart soaring.

Wrapping my scarf tightly at my neck, we stood in a blustery wind as we exited the Charles de Gaulle airport and boarded a taxi. Winter in France sent chills up my legs. It was late afternoon and the light, fading to pinky-gray made me press my nose against the cab's window to see what we raced past.

Our hotel was a block and a half from the Arc d'

Triumph. We had a top floor suite with a balcony overlooking a small, enclosed garden. I pinched myself. The desk clerk spoke French, but of course, *mon ami.* I attempted *Bon Nuit,* even though the sun hadn't quite set. He smiled kindly and rattled off a few sentences that left me blinking. Lyle and the clerk had a jolly conversation while I studied the marble lobby and the chandeliers that sparkled like diamonds.

In search of dinner we walked to the Champs Elysees. Fairy lights twinkled on the plane trees lining the sidewalks of the broad boulevard. I flung my arms into the cool evening air and breathed out, "Paris." Then, as Parisians scurrying home to dinner skirted us, I kissed the man who brought me such joy.

Author's Note

Have you ever driven back roads that serpentine into the past? In 1999 I ventured into Appalachia with my mother and aunt. They were not young—82 and 78-- when our adventure began. Like their frontier foremothers and forefathers, they seized each day with child-like zest.

Kin remained in the Bluegrass when my great-grandparents sold their coal lands and headed to Oregon. Our visit was illuminating. The what ifs of life in land scarred by man's machines and desire for riches haunted me. A tale began to weave into my thoughts.

The quote I use in this book from the ranger at Fort Boonesboro was told to me when I mentioned I was driving into the mountains. And that trip to Owsley County? We met 'kin' who led us on a merry romp over a river and through the woods. Our journey searching for the reason my beloved grandmother wept recalling the mist swirling through her home place seemed as natural as breathing.

The memory of exploring the byways of the past led me to embrace the aging process of Miss Vickie and Meemaw. How can people in their declining years make a profound difference in the world around them?

In choosing a woman of frail mind and one with disintegrating body to illustrate love, I've echoed a life I observed. I was inspired by a godly Texas woman who decided that life was too short to sit on her duff. After widowhood and her own heart attack, she came to Casa Esperanza to rock the child victims of trafficking when their memories brought fear. Loving sacrifice often brings healing. And that was her prayer. In *You Promised Me Paris*, Meemaw walks away from her home to become the tender arms of Jesus to the wounded girls and to complement Miss Vickie.

If you enjoyed this book, I'd so appreciate if you'd consider posting a review anywhere online where books are sold or reviewed. Thank you!!